Champagne
for
Breakfast

Maggie Christensen

Dedication

To my wonderful husband and soulmate of over thirty years

Also by Maggie Christensen

Oregon Coast Series
The Sand Dollar
The Dreamcatcher
Madeline House

Sydney books
Band of Gold
Broken Threads

Sign up for the author's mailing list – keep up-to-date
with news and new releases and get a **FREE BOOK**

http://maggiechristensenauthor.com/

One

Rosa tipped up the bottle and poured the last drops into her glass. Sipping what remained of the bottle of champagne, she gazed across the river, then looked at the empty bottle in dismay. Anyone walking past would imagine she was some cheap drunk – well, since it was a bottle of *Veuve Cliquot*, maybe not so cheap – getting blotto here by the river, alone. In fact, the bottle had been only half full – maybe not even quite that.

It was a glorious spring morning on the Noosa River. The calm blue water rippling and glistening in the sun, stretched across to Noosa Northshore, the homes there barely visible through the trees. The jet skis in the distance were hardly audible as their ribbons of spray rose up like rooster tails. Closer to the shore a couple of kayaks moved smoothly along and a pair of stand-up paddle boarders glided elegantly past. Nearby, a pelican perched on the wooden stump of an abandoned pier, watching her hopefully. Rosa was conscious of the curious glances of passers-by, shrinking away as they passed her – a middle-aged woman drinking alone by the side of the river at nine o'clock on a Sunday morning.

The previous evening Ken had appeared bearing both the champagne, tied with pink and silver ribbons, and an enormous bouquet of red roses.

'I thought we'd do this early,' he said, hugging her and planting a kiss on her lips. 'We have all night. Carol's away, but she'll be back tomorrow,' he added, reminding her why they were to celebrate her fiftieth birthday a day early.

They'd consumed half the bottle before she found the courage to say what she'd planned, her stomach churning as she uttered the words. 'It's over, Ken. I can't keep on with this secret life. I've had enough.'

Ken's mouth dropped open and he froze, glass halfway to his lips. 'But why now? You know I'm going to leave Carol soon. I told you. We only have to wait till...'

Rosa's hands trembled as she held them up to silence him. 'I've heard it all before. Many times. I'm sick and tired of being second best. You promised this time would be different, that you'd leave her, that this would be the year we'd....' Rosa clenched her fists and raised them as if to punch him, then let them fall to her sides. Her feelings of guilt regarding their relationship had faded over the years to be replaced by frustration at the waste of her own life and the realisation that her future was slipping away from her. Ken had justified his reluctance to leave his wife in so many ways, none of which now rang true. As her birthday approached, Rosa had taken a good hard look at their relationship and come to the conclusion Ken was using her. Oh, sure, maybe his marriage was one in name only, maybe there were no longer any real feelings between him and Carol, but he sure as hell wasn't going to leave her. Rosa shook with a mixture of frustration and anger. She loved Ken and leaving him would leave an empty ache in her life, but she'd had enough.

'Here we are, celebrating my birthday in this hole-in-the-corner yet again. It's not fair,' she said, tears not far from the surface. 'I can't take any more, Ken.'

'Sweetie!' Ken carefully set his glass down and moved towards her. Rosa felt the familiar tug of desire and began to weaken even while part of her wondered how he was able to remain calm in the face of her distress.

'Why? Why does it always have to be like this? You promised... you said it would be this year, this birthday...' Rosa's voice died away. How she hated to be so dependent on him.

Ken had the grace to look shamefaced. He seemed to be having trouble meeting Rosa's eyes. 'You know I want us to be together as much as you do, Rosie, but...'

Here it comes, Rosa thought, yet another excuse. The anger she'd been suppressing boiled up and she held her hands over her ears to block out Ken's words.

'No. I've made up my mind.' Rosa managed to stem the emotion threatening to engulf her. Knowing this was the right decision – the only decision – didn't make it any easier.

Ken spent the next hour trying to persuade her, but Rosa remained adamant. He began by pleading and begging her to reconsider, then when she refused to change her mind, became angry, even going so far as to threaten her. By the time he finally left, Rosa felt a tinge of alarm. As her boss, he had the power to ruin her career, but she stood by her decision. She looked at the half bottle, but had no desire to finish it. Champagne was for celebration, and the end of a six-year affair was no cause for celebration. She tried to subdue the sinking feeling in her stomach. It had been her choice, so why did she feel so bereft, so empty? She coldly reviewed the facts. Six years of hiding away, lying, meeting in dark corners. No commitment. No, she'd been right to finish it, but it still didn't sit comfortably with her. Maybe half a loaf was better than no bread at all. She remembered the line from a favourite movie "Sometimes nothing is better than just anything". She felt vindicated. It'd all look better in the morning.

*

Rosa awoke just as dawn was breaking with a sense of lightness. It was her fiftieth birthday and she had a fresh start ahead of her. Today was going to be rough, but she'd done what she'd planned. And she'd start by celebrating her birthday. By the river. On her own.

Now the bottle was empty, the crumbs from the almond croissant the only reminder of her special birthday treat. Rosa sighed. The champagne had been flat, as flat as she felt this morning. She picked up the bottle and the champagne glass depositing both in the garbage bin, already overflowing with Saturday night's debris. A waste of a good champagne glass, but for her the action was symbolic of the end of her affair. She brushed her hands together to rid herself of every vestige of Ken and had begun to walk home, her dark curls bobbing in the breeze, when the mobile in her pocket vibrated, letting her know she had a text. She stopped to check.

Happy birthday, walnut. Sorry can't be there. How's Mum?

Rosa grimaced. Her younger sister Vi was the only one who kept up the old nickname – walnut. It brought back memories.

'I was a walnut.' The twelve-year-old girl's voice quivered as she described her first grown up party.

'A walnut?' Her mother queried.

'No one asked me to be his partner. I sat there all night and no one invited me to dance.'

'Oh,' her mother laughed. 'You mean a wallflower, darling.'

'No! A walnut. I felt like a walnut. One of those crinkly ugly nuts that nobody wants.' She burst into tears and her head of black curls dropped. She was the odd one out. All of the other girls at the party had smooth, straight, blonde hair and wore prettier dresses. She hated her wiry curls and vowed that, when she grew up, she'd be just like the others; she'd grow a smooth helmet and no one would know about the wiry curls underneath.

Rosa shook her still wiry curls. She'd grown to accept them and manage them over the years, but her sister's childhood nickname could still irritate her, reduce her to that quivering little girl who felt unloved. Damn Vi! There was no need to remind her about Mum either. Rosa visited her mother religiously. The older woman was still alert, but now confined to a wheelchair and ensconced in a nursing home. She'd go this afternoon. But before that she had something to do.

When she returned to her apartment, Rosa went straight to her bedroom and drew out a box from the bottom of the wardrobe. She looked at it with a sigh. It held all of her treasures, the memories of her years with Ken. She pulled out a sheaf of letters tied up in pink ribbon from the first flowers he'd given her, the cards he'd sent or surreptitiously left on her desk at work, all sorts of mementoes she'd carefully collected over the six years. As she sat, surrounded by the reminders of those wasted years, a cold anger took hold of her, and she began to systematically shred each piece of paper and card. By the time she'd finished, there was nothing left but a heap of scraps. They could have been anything, but Rosa knew what they were and knew she had to rid herself of them. Calm now, she looked around trying to decide what to do. Then she had an idea. Collecting the pieces, she made her way to the ensuite and, little by little, she flushed away her memories, enjoying seeing them swirl and disappear.

*

'And what about that man of yours? When is he going to do the right thing by you?' Rosa's mum asked, pushing her glasses up her nose.

A shaft of sunlight peeked into the dreary room emphasising the dust particles floating in its ray as Rosa leant forward to pick up the newspaper which had fallen to the floor. She regretted having let slip Ken's name earlier in the year when her mother had been quizzing her about her love life. Love life – at fifty! That was a laugh – or would be if it wasn't so pathetic.

'It's over, Mum.' Rosa busied herself tidying her mother's pile of books to hide the tears which were still near the surface. 'Over and done with. You'll just have to accept me as your spinster daughter, your walnut.' Repeating her old nickname surprised her, making her realise her sister's use of it had hurt more than she'd known.

'What's that?' Ivy Taylor looked at her daughter sharply. 'Where did that old thing come from?'

'From Vi. She sends her best, by the way.'

'You spoke to Vi?' The eyes, still sharp in her eighties, lit up as she peered at her daughter. Vi was still the favourite. The fact that she'd lived in England for the past twenty years and rarely called her mother made not a jot of difference. Vi, the pretty one, she could do no wrong.

Rosa sighed in exasperation. 'No, Mum. She sent me a text. Birthday wishes, you know. Today's my birthday. Did you forget?'

'I knew that!' But Ivy's tone belied her words. One day must be very much like any other in this place, Rosa realised, immediately regretting her outburst.

'Don't think I don't appreciate what you do for me,' her mother continued, managing to fuel Rosa's guilt even further. As if she didn't have enough to contend with today. Turning fifty; the end of a long-term relationship; her sister's reminder of her youthful inadequacies and now her mother playing on her guilt. They passed the next half hour in desultory conversation with Rosa promising to renew her mother's library books and return later in the week, before she could take her leave.

Driving out through the automatic gates, Rosa stifled the shiver of revulsion which swept over her on these visits. Nursing homes were not pleasant places. Maybe she should have tried harder with Mum. Could she have found room for her mother in her own apartment when the family home had to be broken up? But it was her mother's choice. Ivy had made her own arrangements citing the friends who had already made the move and were happily living there. Rosa shook her head to dispel the uneasiness which passed through her mind each time she left the older woman. No, Mum said she was happy here, even though her friends had since passed away. And Rosa visited when she could. She mustn't allow the text from Vi to stir up feelings of remorse. Rosa hadn't flitted off to the other side of the world, seeking fame and fortune. Her lips tightened as she thought of her sister. She'd stayed here and look where that had got her – she'd become an old maid. At least she didn't have a collection of cats. Rosa smiled at this ridiculous thought and decided to forget about her family for the rest of the day.

*

As darkness began to fall, Rosa finally closed her book and, rising from her chair, leant on the balcony rail to survey the river, which flowed silently across the way from her third-floor apartment. She'd bought this place soon after the affair with Ken began. This was her home, her sanctuary – a place she could come to when everything else in her life was going awry. It had proved a godsend so many times and now it provided the safe haven where she could heal her wounds, wounds which had been self-inflicted.

She'd spent the afternoon alone. By choice. She needed time to herself. Her emails and Facebook page had been filled with birthday greetings and invitations, but she'd chosen to ignore them. Instead, she'd settled on her front balcony with a copy of the latest book by her favourite author and spent the time immersed in the characters' lives.

The coming week was not going to be easy. She'd have to face Ken at work. When the new Finance Director had arrived at Beachhead Health Service, the last thing on Rosa's mind had been a relationship. Now, she wished it had remained that way. He was her boss, for God's sake. There was no way of avoiding him.

'Have you met your new boss? What's he like?' Jenny was juggling her

coffee and plate of salad, while the two found a table in the hospital cafeteria.

Rosa sat down and placed her own lunch on the table before replying. 'Seems okay,' she said cautiously. 'Of course, I've only met him briefly with the others. He's set up times for one-on-one meetings later in the week.'

'Rumour is he's very dishy.' Jenny raised her eyebrows and looked at Rosa over her coffee cup. 'It's about time you settled down.'

'Come off it. When was the last time you went out with a man yourself?'

'That's different. After John…'

Rosa bit her lip. She'd overstepped the mark with her friend. Jenny had been a widow for ages, but had eschewed the thought of any other man in her life, whereas Rosa was still single in her forties and had given up hope of finding Mr Right, if such a person even existed.

'Anyway. I don't want a work romance. Can you imagine what would happen when it ended? And they always end,' she stated ruefully, taking a bite from her sandwich. 'Ugh, what do they put into these?' She peeled back the bread to investigate the filling which purported to be roast beef with mustard pickle.

'Don't change the subject. They don't always have to end. You just choose the wrong men.' Jenny forked up some salad before continuing. 'You don't give yourself a chance, too fussy by half. And you underestimate yourself too. Have you looked in the mirror recently?'

'I try not to,' Rosa joked. 'I mean, with this hair and these freckles!' She pulled on a curl which had escaped the confines of her tidy workaday hairstyle as she spoke. Her hair had been the bane of her life for as long as she could remember.

'That's what I mean. You're still an attractive woman, one who could have any man she wanted. You have those curls most women would kill for and have managed to avoid the middle-age spread that beats the rest of us. Oh, I give up!' Her friend was silent for a time then the pair had gone on to talk about other matters and the new Finance Director had disappeared from the conversation.

But he hadn't disappeared from Rosa's mind. Despite her denials, Rosa had noticed him "in that way" as her friend would have said, and was looking forward to working closely with him. How closely she hadn't realised until a couple of weeks later when he'd asked her to work late on the monthly reconciliations for the Corporate Services Department. One thing had led to another, and they'd ended up in Rosa's apartment close to midnight and her bed not much later.

She should have considered he might be married, but there was no sign of a wedding ring, no family photos on the desk. Or maybe she'd been too infatuated to care. It had been many years since she'd been so attracted to a man, felt that indefinable spark that signalled he was someone special. Not since she was in her early twenties. But Alan had been tragically killed in a car accident only two months before their wedding. How different her life might have been if he'd lived. There had been others since then, of course. She hadn't reached this age without the odd lover, but that's all they'd been, someone to share her bed. None had touched her heart, not till Ken.

It had been some time before the grapevine revealed Ken was married, leading to an embarrassed Ken begging Rosa to continue the relationship and promising that the marriage was all but over. Like a fool, she'd believed him, kept on believing him for six long years. Six years of lonely birthdays and holidays interspersed with some glorious moments together and the hope that, maybe… one day…

Thinking of Jenny made Rosa want to unburden herself to her friend, but Jenny had enough troubles of her own at the moment, and was in far off Oregon trying to put her own life back together. The restructure in the organisation hadn't been kind to Jenny while Rosa's own job remained secure. She sighed at the thought of her position and her daily proximity to Ken. It would take more energy than she could muster to continue to be in daily contact with him. She might have broken off her relationship with him, but that didn't mean she was immune to his sex appeal. Sexual chemistry wasn't something she could turn on and off like a tap.

Rosa was eating dinner in front of the television, when she remembered she'd seen an internal secondment advertised recently. The CEO required someone with a finance background to analyse historical data with a view to archiving it, prior to the introduction of a new system. At first glance she'd dismissed it out of hand, but given her new single status, it seemed like a perfect opportunity. It would get Ken out of her hair and provide a new challenge. She'd check it out first thing Monday.

But despite her resolution, Rosa quailed at the thought of facing Ken with her decision.

Two

The noise of a garbage truck wakened Rosa next morning. She jumped out of bed to close the sliding window to the balcony that she'd inadvertently left open the night before, shivering a little in the early morning air. Although winter didn't really come to the Sunshine Coast of Queensland, there was often a nip in the air at this time of day.

Drawing her white towelling robe around her and folding her arms across her chest in an attempt to keep warm, Rosa looked across the river which was misting in the early light. Straight across the expanse of water lay Noosa North Shore where she and Ken had managed to spend a few stolen weekends. She'd never asked him how he'd explained these away. Rosa shook herself. That part of her life was over.

Looking downriver her gaze fell on a flotilla of early morning kayaks and, just past them, the white hull of a large boat. That hadn't been there yesterday. As she scanned the still water, the gentle ripples on its surface sparkling in the early morning sun, Rosa thought she caught a flash of light from a camera or binoculars. Some rich bloke perving on the locals, she thought in contempt, turning to walk inside again and pulling the doors closed behind her.

*

On board the white catamaran the tall blond man performed his morning exercise routine. Living at sea was no excuse for idleness

9

and Harry Kennedy was not known for his laziness. Finishing his daily schedule, he took time to survey his new location. It had been dark when he arrived last night, but this morning his gaze took in a boardwalk bounded by a line of shops, cafes and apartment buildings, quite different from the busy metropolitan surroundings and high-rise structures he'd left behind in Sydney. He raised his binoculars to take a closer look. The buildings were mostly white, with lots of glass sparkling in the sun, and even at this early hour residents or holidaymakers were out on their balconies enjoying the view. Catching a glimpse of white bathrobe on one of the balconies and realising he was part of their view too, he turned his sights towards the opposite shore, deserted at this time of the morning.

His limbs now warmed from the sun, he went below to fix breakfast. Feeding the inner man was an important part of the new regime he'd promised himself. After breakfast, he planned to head upriver to the marina where he'd booked a berth.

*

Once Harry had moored his boat he picked up a hire car and returned to Noosaville. He'd decided to take a few weeks to explore his new surroundings before starting work. Finding a house to buy was top of Harry's list today. If he were to become part of the community, staying on the boat wasn't a long-term option.

Having parked at one end of the main shopping strip, he walked along the road, checking the list of estate agents he'd downloaded to his phone the night before. He needed somewhere low maintenance and wasn't averse to doing some renovation work, though not too much. The job would keep him busy.

He noted the apartments rising above the street, those he'd seen from the water. They looked good, but not for him. He had a yearning for a pet – a dog, or even a cat. He grinned as he imagined how his former colleagues would rib him for becoming so domesticated. Life was certainly going to be different from now on. The morning passed in a blur, and soon Harry headed back to the marina, musing how different the traffic was here from the bustle he'd been used to in the city.

*

Harry sat down to lunch in a café from which he could watch the Yarran sitting on the water. She was a great boat and had served him well on the sail up here. His mates back in Sydney had been envious of the trip, and full of suggestions for how he could spend his time sailing up the coast. As it turned out, the foul weather he'd run into had meant he'd been kept busy all the way, with little time to read the stack of books he'd packed to while away his lonely hours.

Today's sunshine provided a pleasant break. Noosa seemed to have escaped the storms which had ravaged the ocean. The marina with its sheltered waterfront and line of shops and cafes was a pleasant mooring for the time being, and he could live on the Yarran until he was able to take possession of his own home. He savoured the words. It would be good to settle down here, where no one knew him. No history, no baggage. That's how he wanted it.

Waiting for his meal – a giant serving of fish and chips with salad, Harry took a gulp of beer and flipped through the brochures he'd picked up that morning. His head reeled with the homes he'd viewed, ranging from waterfront mansions to old beach shacks needing masses of work to make them habitable. He rubbed his stubbled chin. Nothing appealed. Maybe he'd have more success this afternoon. One of the agents had promised to meet him at two. After that he'd call it a day and start again tomorrow.

*

As soon as he walked into the house, Harry could see its potential. Set on a canal in Noosa Waters, it was smaller than some of the other places he'd viewed, but more comfortable than the beach shacks. The home had the cosy atmosphere he was looking for, with its wooden floors and well-worn back deck. The entrance opened up into a large living/dining area and the kitchen looked out through a jungle of tropical foliage to the glistening water beyond. Three reasonably sized bedrooms completed the place, an ensuite to the master which opened onto the wide deck with its southerly view across the canal, protected from the northern sun. The pool, set at the front of the house, was the only drawback but the high front wall would provide privacy. The price was good too. Although the house seemed a bit tired, it had a character that spoke to him. The kitchen and bathrooms needed updating before he'd be happy with them, and the whole place could do with a paint job. Nothing he couldn't handle with a bit of help from the odd handyman. He could almost feel excited about this one.

After arranging with the realtor to make the purchase, Harry sauntered down the street. He was glad he'd chosen to walk around a bit for the first few days to get his bearings. He enjoyed the feel of this place, the well-maintained homes with glimpses of water between them. He took a deep breath of the balmy air as a light-hearted mood washed over him. He'd made the right decision in coming here. He could put everything that had happened in Sydney behind him and make a fresh start.

*

Rosa locked her car and looked up at the Health Service buildings. Wishing she could run away and avoid the confrontation awaiting her in the office, she took a deep calming breath and marched inside.

'Morning!' She greeted the other staff members brightly as usual, hoping they wouldn't hear the tremor in her voice as she made her way to her office. She dropped her bag on the floor, sat at her desk and turned on the computer. Her stomach churned as she waited for it to boot up, then scrolled through the emails. Surely she hadn't deleted it? She could hear Ken moving around in the office next door and bit her lip, hoping he'd keep out of her way.

Gotcha! She'd almost given up hope when she found what she'd been looking for. There it was – the request for expressions of interest for the position with the CEO. The closing date was... today. Just in time!

Rosa quickly read through the outline of the position. She met all the criteria. She could do it standing on her head and that's probably why she'd ignored it at the time. That, and the fact she'd wanted to stay close to Ken. Well, that no longer applied. The sooner she could get out of this department, the better. She pressed *Print* and was in the act of picking up the copy of the position description still warm from the printer, when her phone rang.

'Hello?' she said tentatively, knowing who it would be.

'We need to talk.'

Ken's voice still had the power to raise her blood pressure and bring a flush to her cheeks, but her nervousness at what she was about to do overcame any lingering desire. She wasn't to be swayed in her decision. It was just like him to use the telephone when he was right there in the next office. If she stood on tiptoes she could see him over the frosted glass. Rosa tried to concentrate on what he was saying, holding the phone with one hand while the other still clutched the printout.

'Sorry, what did you say, Ken?' *Damn and blast, she needed time to process this. And the events of Saturday night were still too raw. She wasn't ready to face Ken yet.*

'I asked you to come to my office. Now!' The phone went dead. Rosa put it down. She quailed, a twist of apprehension in her chest. Surely he didn't intend to carry out the threats he'd made? Allow their personal life to interfere with the good of the organisation? Couldn't he see her position was untenable? She'd thought he was better than that. Well, she'd better get it over with.

A quick glance in the mirror she kept on top of the filing cabinet showed her usual workaday self – hair neatly strained back into a bun, perfect make-up, the collar of her white blouse lying flat on the lapel of the jacket of her black suit. She pulled a face. Gripping the copy of the position description, she took a deep breath and walking slowly, stepped out of her office and into the one next door.

'Close the door behind you.' Ken's voice had an unfamiliar edge to it, far from the gentle requests and sweet nothings she was used to. 'I can't believe you meant it,' he began, walking toward her with hands outstretched. 'Rosa…'

'Don't.' Rosa held the printout in front of her to ward off his next words. 'This is … I want …' She drew a deep breath. 'I'm going to apply for this position. Can I count on your recommendation? You're my boss. I need your approval,' she finished in a small voice.

'Why should I?' Ken's voice was bitter. 'After all we've had together, not only do you want to finish our relationship, you want me to lose my right hand here at work? No, I don't think so.'

Rosa's hand dropped and she only just stopped the paper fluttering to the floor. This was the last reaction she'd expected. She thought he'd be glad to see her go, glad he no longer had to see her every day, to be reminded... But it seemed he didn't share her view on that. Her nervousness quickly morphed into anger. After leading her on for all that time, this man, the man she thought loved her, who wanted her happiness, was now prepared to scupper what might be her only opportunity to change jobs. Couldn't he see that it would be impossible for them to work together after this? Was the man so dumb he thought they could carry on at work as if... as if they'd never had a relationship? And after all of his threats to make her suffer at work. Was this what he'd meant? Did he intend to keep her hanging around to be fodder for his wrath?

'How can you say that? How can we continue to work together? How can I come here every day, sit in the next office and...' Rosa ran out of words.

Ken smiled in a knowing way she had never seen before. 'You should have thought of that before...'

'What would your wife think if she knew?' The words were out before Rosa considered the consequences. Ken's neck became rigid and his face turned brick red.

'Give it here.' Ken snatched the sheet from her, reading it quickly before raising his eyes to meet hers. 'You're serious about this then. I mean...' He waved the sheet in the air. 'I didn't think this was quite your thing.'

He sounded bitter and Rosa realised he could easily refuse to sign her release. Not for the first time she regretted having become involved with her boss. She should have known it would end badly, but... Rosa fought to curb her strong sexual desire for this man, who still had the power to make her knees tremble. She spoke as firmly as she could. 'Maybe not, but I need to move from the department and this would make use of my skills. I may even enjoy it – working at the top of the organisation,' she tried to joke but it fell on deaf ears.

'I'll miss you.' Ken's voice was low.

Rosa knew he wasn't only talking about her office presence, but refused to take the bait. 'You'll soon fill my position – all those staff who're being redeployed. Someone will be grateful to move into finance, I'm sure. You'll support me then?'

'Reluctantly.' Ken pursed his lips. 'Since you appear so determined I won't hold you back. I'll have a recommendation on your desk by lunchtime.'

Three

'Damn!' Harry surveyed the room from his position on the floor. Now he'd done it. He'd been sure he could manage to paint the ceiling on his own. Everything would have been fine, but the ladder had developed a wobble and he'd ended up down here in a heap, one leg twisted under him.

'Hey mate!' he yelled.

There was no answer. He called again. The pain was beginning to move in now, and he yelled louder. Finally, after what seemed like an age, an answering cry came from the other end of the house.

'Did you call?' The voice was followed by the tall gangling figure of Jack, the handyman who'd seemed the answer to Harry's prayers. He'd found him under an advertisement for Jack of All Trades in the local paper, and Jack had certainly lived up to his name. But this called for more expertise than Jack could possibly offer.

'Hell, what have you done to yourself?'

'Fell off the ladder,' Harry stated, as if that wasn't perfectly obvious. 'Think I've twisted or broken something.' He stifled a gasp of pain as he tried to move into a more comfortable position.

Jack was by his side in a flash. 'Don't move. We'll have you out of here in no time.' Kneeling beside Harry, Jack tried to help him up and pulled his mobile out of his pocket. Harry felt Jack's arm go around him and heard him ask for an ambulance before an excruciating white pain flashed through him and he blacked out.

When he came to, he was lying in bed surrounded by curtains and Jack was sitting in a chair beside him.

'Hey, you're back with us.' The man had a grin on his face. 'For a while there thought I'd lost a job. Would be the first time I lost a client.'

'You waited? There was no need.'

'I followed the ambulance to Emergency, went back and finished for the day. Locked the place up, then came over to give you the keys.'

Harry noticed the keyring dangling from Jack's fingers.

'Right. Thanks.' His head felt as if it was stuffed with cotton wool. He couldn't find any more words.

'That's okay. I'll be off now. Guess I'll wait to hear from you?'

Harry must have dozed off because when he opened his eyes again, a white blur was bending over him and a voice was asking him a question.

'Wh... what? Could you repeat that?' His throat felt scratchy and the voice didn't sound like his own. He tried to prop himself up on his elbows, but found it difficult.

'Don't try to move, Harry. I was asking if there's anyone you want us to call. I don't have any details here.' The blur became a smiling face as the question sank in.

'No, no one.' Harry closed his eyes again. No one who'd care that is. No one he wanted to know where he was.

*

Rosa opened the email with some trepidation. It had been a couple of weeks since she'd sent in her application, or expression of interest as it was called. Same thing. And nearly four days since her interview. It had seemed straightforward at the time, but you never knew in the current environment. Things were changing daily. This had to be the reply. She'd spent the past weeks avoiding being alone with Ken, not an easy task when she was accustomed to being his sounding board. The others in the department must have wondered what was wrong. She'd hinted at a throat infection which she wanted to keep to herself and the door to her office had remained closed. But she could only operate this way for so long before questions were asked.

Ken had continued to be difficult on the few occasions he'd managed to corner her. Unable to catch her alone at work, he'd turned up at her apartment one night, banging on the door till she'd been forced to open it before the neighbours started to complain. That had been a fiasco, ending with them yelling at each other before he strode off in anger, and she collapsed in tears.

She scanned the email, thanks for the application etc., etc., then, at the bottom: *We would like you to take up the position on Monday week.* She leant back in her chair with a great sigh of relief. Phew, that was a load off her mind. She printed it out and walked through to Ken's office, making sure she left the door wide open.

'Look what I just received.' She handed the copy of the email across the desk, but Ken brushed it away.

'I have a copy. I assume it's about your secondment to the CEO's office. I suppose you'll be wanting a week off first?'

Rosa did a double take. She hadn't expected this. 'Ye…es. I can finish up here tomorrow. If that suits you.'

Ken stood up and moved round to the front of his desk. 'I'm sorry it had to end like this. Can't we …?'

'Me too.' Rosa felt the familiar flutter in the pit of her stomach as he moved nearer, but it was quickly overtaken by anger. How dare he try to rekindle her affections. She'd made her decision perfectly clear – twice. She wanted to scream at him and could feel it begin to build up, only to be squashed by the realisation of where she was. She was good at hiding her feelings where Ken was concerned. Over the years she'd become quite adept at presenting a different Rosa on the surface, keeping all hint of passion well hidden. Now it came as second nature to suppress her anger. She bit her tongue, clenched her fists and said, 'Thanks. I'll pass on any outstanding matters.' She spun on her heel and stormed out, unsure why she was so annoyed.

'That would be good. Gerry will be handling them.' His words followed her.

'Right.' Rosa walked back into her office, her eyes misting. Although it was her own decision, she couldn't help but feel sad it had to come to this. She looked around the small cubicle that had been her office for the past ten years and knew she wouldn't be sorry to leave. It was time to move on.

The day passed quickly with Rosa sifting through the paperwork which cluttered her desk. As she surveyed the untidy pile, she could see how this business with Ken had affected her. She was usually so tidy and a stickler for detail. She sighed. Hopefully the new job would see her back to normal. She quickly worked through all the folders prioritising them into those she could complete the next day and those she would hand over. With the latter, she wrote brief descriptions on post-it notes to be attached to the front of the folders. Making a to-do list for the following day, Rosa finally pushed her chair back. One more day to go.

The thought of the week ahead buoyed her. A whole week to herself. Driving home, she planned what she would do. She'd keep well away from work and anyone associated with it. A few breakfasts in favourite cafes were certainly on the agenda along with a visit to the Regional Art Gallery which had an exhibition by a local photographer whose work she liked. She'd be able to visit her mum more often, maybe even persuade her to venture out to lunch. These were all things she didn't have enough time for in her usual working life. She couldn't wait.

As the sun was setting, creating a red glow over the water, she sat on her balcony with a glass of Merlot, enjoying the changing colours in the sky. Letting her eyes drop to the surface of the river and watching the birds swoop down for their evening feeds, she noticed there was no sign of the catamaran she'd seen on her birthday. But that was ages ago. It could be anywhere by now.

*

A few days later, Rosa was pottering about on the balcony, deadheading some geraniums and picking the weeds out of her herb garden. Raising her face to the sun, grateful Noosa was living up to its reputation for sunshine, she removed her gardening gloves, surveyed her work of the past few days and smiled with pleasure. She'd transformed her bare balcony into a gardener's delight. The baskets hanging from the balcony rail were sprouting miniature lettuce and tomato plants to complement the large tub of herbs she'd cared for over the past six years. Her geraniums had been joined by a lemon tree in a glazed pot in the corner and, right beside her favourite chair, an azalea was beginning to show its winter red bloom. A new look for a new life.

Going back into the apartment, Rosa blinked as her eyes became accustomed to the change in light. It was so bright outside. It would be lovely to enjoy a coffee by the river in her favourite café.

After a quick shower, she pulled on a pair of jeans and a long-sleeved cream tee-shirt. How relaxing to be able to wear casual clothes after the corporate business suits she was used to. Sliding into the car and pressing the button to release the garage door, she made an instant decision. Rather than her favourite café on the river, she turned the car northwards towards the marina. She'd be less likely to meet anyone from work there and would enjoy the view just as much.

Rosa turned up the radio and began to sing along to an old Beatles song. She'd experienced a sense of frustration since leaving the Finance Department, and this morning, despite a lightness of mood, she felt an impatience with her life. She knew there might be a few bumpy roads ahead, but it would all work out in the end.

Four

The tall fair-haired man turned quickly, bumping against the table. 'Sorry!'

'It's all…' Rosa began when the shaking of the table made her coffee splash onto its surface. Her cup almost crashed to the floor. She looked up into the deepest blue eyes she'd ever seen.

'Let me buy you another. Cappuccino?'

'No, it's…' But he'd already moved towards the counter, balancing awkwardly on a pair of crutches. Now she could see he was injured, Rosa bit back the retort which threatened to fall from her lips. The poor man. No wonder he'd found it difficult to navigate the narrow gaps between the tables. She saw him order then turn around, his eyes sweeping the busy café as if seeking an empty spot. He began to move clumsily towards Rosa.

'You can share my table,' she offered, silently cursing her politeness. The last thing she wanted was to share a table. She'd come here to be alone.

'Thanks.' He lowered himself carefully into the seat opposite. 'A bit difficult these days. I'm not usually such a klutz.'

His red face mirrored his embarrassment. Not accustomed to needing help, Rosa surmised, taking in the lean figure, the wide shoulders and the thatch of thick blond hair with just a few grey flecks. He looked as if he'd be more at home on a football field than sitting at a small table in a café on the Noosa Marina. Rosa averted her eyes and hid herself in the paper she'd been reading. No need to make conversation. They were only sharing a table.

'I'm Harry.' Her companion's deep voice broke the silence.

Looking up, Rosa smiled at the waitress who was placing two coffees on the table.

'I'll take the spilt one for you,' the waitress offered.

Rosa continued her reading only muttering a brief 'Thanks' to her companion.

Harry cleared his throat. 'Anything interesting?'

Rosa lowered the paper, inwardly sighing at this interruption. This was her week off and she'd intended to make it a solitary one. 'Nothing special.' Then she relented and put on her best polite face, prepared to make as much conversation as might be expected in such a situation. 'Are you a visitor to the coast?'

'Just moved here.' Harry smiled across the table, clearly amused at her curt enquiry. 'Seems a relaxed community. A bit more laidback than I'm used to.'

'Mmm.' Rosa cursed her rudeness. She really should make more effort. Customer service was the new motto for the local tourism industry. She should be playing her part. She put down her paper, folded it and prepared to continue the conversation.

'I'm from Sydney.' He seemed to prefer short answers. This might not be easy. But two could play at that game.

'Been here long?'

'A few weeks. I bought myself a place on the water and was doing a bit of fixing up when...' He indicated his leg with a rueful grin. 'Laid up for a time now so the rest of the work'll have to wait. What about you? Do you live here or are you visiting?'

'I live here. Work here too.' Rosa winced. It was all very well to make conversation with this stranger, but she didn't want to give too much away about herself. Instead she began to ask him about his recent purchase and found no need to say much as he became almost lyrical about his new home.

Rosa listened with feigned interest until feeling her temperature rise and fearing her face would turn beetroot red – one of the many downsides of menopause – she checked her watch and picked up her bag. 'I'd better be going. Thanks again for the coffee.' Realising her cup was still half full, Rosa gulped down the remainder and rose to leave with an apologetic smile at her companion.

'Nice…' he began, but the remainder of what he had to say was lost as Rosa hurried out to the car park.

She winced as another hot flush wreaked havoc with her body. She'd been feeling irritable all morning and knew anyone who crossed her would get the rough side of her tongue. At times like this she couldn't be responsible for her actions – or words. It was as if some evil manifestation took hold of her. Nothing to do with the real Rosa at all. She groaned to herself. It was hell while it lasted, but everyone said it would pass. That didn't help now. She'd probably seemed extremely ill-mannered to the man who'd shared her table. She opened her car door, sat silently for a several minutes, and took a few deep breaths till it passed and she was back to normal. As normal as could be, given the circumstances.

*

Harry stared at the retreating back of the dainty woman with the pretty dark curls. *Didn't make much headway there. What was wrong with the woman?* Everyone else in this place had been so friendly. Was it something he'd said or was she annoyed at the coffee incident? He looked down at his leg. It did make him a tad uncoordinated. He grimaced, frustrated at the delay to his plans. Moving into a part-renovated house was out of the question. He pushed himself up, left the café and walked slowly to his boat. He wasn't in the best shape for it, but had worked out a strategy for moving about. He was proud of the way he was handling himself – his clumsiness in the café had been an exception.

Putting the dark-haired woman out of his mind, Harry set to preparing bread, olives and cheese for lunch. He wasn't much of a cook. He guessed that was something else he could learn, but for the time being it was easier to snack on the boat and eat out. Lunch finished, Harry gathered together the papers he'd been working on for the past two days. This job would be a breeze after what he'd been used to.

Checking himself in the mirror hanging above the sink and hoisting up the dratted crutches, Harry slid his attaché case under his right arm. When he felt ready, he manoeuvred off the boat and onto dry land again, leaning heavily on his crutches to lock the place up. The cab he'd called earlier was waiting in the car park and he was soon on his way.

Harry clambered out of the cab and gazed up at the redbrick building rising in front of him. This was the administration block of the Health Service, one of the buildings which sat across the road from the hospital proper. He'd only been here once before, when he'd come to present his proposal to the IT guys. Now he was to meet the CEO who, he supposed, would outline the parameters of his task. It had all seemed pretty straightforward in the brief they'd sent him and a good project to set up his new business.

Fortunately, there were no steps. Pushing open the tall glass door, Harry couldn't resist the glimmer of a smile. He must look more like a patient than an IT consultant today. Harry showed his card at the desk and a slight woman with faded blonde hair and half-moon spectacles showed him into an office as big as his lounge room.

'Welcome!' A grey-haired man rose to shake hands, smiling above his double chins. His girth indicated he'd spent more time at his desk than on the football field of recent years, though Harry knew from his research that Pete Robson had once represented Queensland in several Origin matches. 'You look as if you've been in the wars. Sure you don't want In-patients?' he joked.

'Sorry about this. The cast'll be off soon. Won't affect my ability to get started.'

'Hmm. Good. Well, sit you down. I'll have Brenda bring up some coffee, or would you prefer tea?' He reached for his phone as he raised an eyebrow in enquiry.

'Coffee will be fine.'

'Good. I find a cup at this time of day keeps me alert. Coffee for two, Bren,' he said into the phone. 'Now where were we?'

The two men fell into a discussion during which Harry surmised that while Robson knew what he wanted of his consultant, he had no idea how it was to be achieved. Harry's suggestion of using the cloud as a receptacle for the data, both archived and new, seemed to be beyond the CEO's comprehension. Although Brenda had brought in the requested coffee along with a plate of carefully arranged biscuits, Harry barely sipped his, so intent was he on the conversation.

Finally, looking up from the paperwork, Harry made a suggestion. 'Maybe we should involve your IT manager in this discussion. After all, his team will be responsible for the upkeep.'

'No, no.' The CEO seemed concerned. 'No need to involve them at this stage. They're flat out. Don't want to burden them with all of this, do we?' he blustered.

Harry refrained from responding to this odd point of view, pretending to accept it as quite normal. 'Right then. If that's all for today.' He rose and struggled with his crutches again. God, he'd be glad to be rid of them.

'I'll have Brenda see you out.' The CEO rose too, seemingly glad the meeting was at an end. 'So we'll see you again ... when?'

Balancing on the two pieces of metal, Harry stretched out his hand to shake the other man's. 'A couple of weeks? That should give me time to develop an outline of the architecture, then I'll need to involve your guys – get some input from them.'

'I'm putting one of our finance people onto the archiving. She can be a resource for you too.'

'Right.' Harry was eager to leave now the business was over and was glad when Brenda entered with a smile. 'Thanks. I'll be off now.' She showed him out after offering to call a cab.

While Harry sat in the foyer waiting for his ride, he gazed around the large atrium. A pretty penny had been spent here, he calculated. He'd read in the local paper about the restructure in an attempt to save money. He supposed that was what his role was all about. Data stored offsite would act to reduce the number of bodies on the ground. He sighed. All in the name of progress, but it meant some poor sods would lose their jobs and he'd be part of it.

Five

Rosa set down her coffee and the tuna sandwich, prepared to have a solitary meal. She missed her regular lunch dates with Jenny and, now she was working in the executive suite, her lunchtimes didn't seem to coincide with those of anyone else she knew well. She'd been in her new role for a few weeks now and was finding it more interesting than she'd expected. Searching through old invoices and data might seem boring to some, but to Rosa's analytical mind it was fun.

She was opening the book she always carried with her when she became aware of someone stopping by her table.

'Do you mind if I share? The others all seem to be occupied.'

Looking up, Rosa saw the red hair, high cheekbones and black suit which was almost a uniform for the executive coach. Alex Carter had become well-known around the organisation in the past couple of months as she met with those staff members whose positions had become redundant. Rosa's friend Jenny had been one of those and she'd had nothing but praise for the young coach. Until now, Rosa had only seen her from a distance, through a doorway in the building where they both worked.

'Sure. I'm Rosa.'

'Alex.' The red-haired woman deposited her tray on the table and, removing a healthy-looking bowl of salad and a raspberry-coloured smoothie, put the tray on the floor by her chair. She sat down. 'I've seen you in the executive suite these past few weeks. Are you new to the organisation?'

'No. Used to be in finance and I've been seconded to help with the archiving of financial data. We're moving to a new system,' explained Rosa, seeing the other's blank look. 'And I'm the bunny who offered to do the boring numbers stuff.'

'Mmm. And is it boring?' Alex smiled and forked up some salad.

'Not for me. I like analysing documents, checking they're accurate – that sort of thing.'

Alex shook her head. 'Would bore me witless. I need to work with people.'

'And you're good at that. You met with my friend, Jenny. She's in Oregon right now. She was singing your praises after your first meeting.'

'I remember her. Nice lady. So how long have you been working here?' Alex was quick to change the subject and Rosa, realising the other needed to maintain the confidentiality of her clients, went along with the change.

'Thirty years, would you believe? A lifetime. I started as a ward clerk and moved around a bit before ending up in finance about ten years ago.'

'What made you move from finance? I'd have thought there was more opportunity for promotion there.'

Rosa hesitated, then encouraged by Alex's friendly face, found herself telling her the whole story, well not quite the whole story – she'd skirted around her relationship with Ken – but more than she'd told anyone else. It was a relief to unload to someone else, someone who was a good listener and whose infrequent comments only helped the story along. By the time they'd finished lunch Rosa knew she'd found a new friend.

*

The week passed quickly for Alex as she worked on the reports for her coaching assignment in the Health Service. She'd been involved with some interviews with the HR Director who turned out to be only slightly friendlier than the CEO. It seemed there were massive issues with morale among both managers and staff. This much she'd gleaned already. Not surprising given the size of the changes management were undertaking and the apparent lack of communication. The hidden agenda seemed to be a proposal to outsource many of the HR functions, the problem being what to do with the existing staff and managers. Alex's role in all of this was still unclear, but now she'd worked through the list of the senior HR managers and was to set up initial meetings with some of the other senior staff as soon as she could. It was a far cry from her usual modus operandi and hinted at shades of Big Brother. Alex felt torn, but needed the job and she needed to do it well. She just hoped she could work her usual magic and leave the individuals with clear goals and action plans, without subverting the intention of her client. The income was important to her, after all was said and done.

Now it was the weekend and all she wanted to do was relax with the papers and a good book then take a run on the beach with her golden cocker spaniel, Tess. She'd risen late and hadn't seen much of the morning. The phone rang when she was on her second cup of coffee and had the *Weekend Courier Mail* spread over the table in the garden.

'Hi Red.' Alex groaned. Her brother had started calling her that when she was about three, and the name had stuck. It had irritated her then and it still did, though she tried not to show it these days.

'Nick. Aren't you golfing this morning? Thought it was the tournament.'

'That's just it. I'm about to leave, but Kim's organised one of her lunch things and needs some help. I don't suppose...'

Alex moved the phone to her other ear and took a sip of coffee. Her sister-in-law was the most organised person she knew, but tended to panic at the last minute in case things didn't turn out perfectly.

'Who is it this time? The ladies auxiliary, the African Violet Association, the church flower group, Aid to Refugees? Why can't Sandy help?' Even as she asked, Alex knew the answer. Her nineteen-year-old niece had perfected a disappearing act whenever her mother's luncheons were proposed.

'Oh, you know Sandy. She's off somewhere. And it's the hospital auxiliary ladies. There are some real highfliers coming – to quote Kim – and she needs some moral support.'

'I suppose so.' Alex suddenly saw her lazy Saturday disappearing. Still, family was family, and she'd often helped Kim in this way and knew her assistance would be reciprocated sometime, somehow. Her sister-in-law was nothing if not generous with her own time. Alex had sometimes even gained some business from these luncheon meetings too, so she couldn't complain.

'I'll be over. Give me about thirty minutes to make myself respectable.'

The afternoon proved to be as boring as Alex had expected, but Kim's heartfelt, 'Thank God you're here. I'd be lost without you,' made it all worthwhile, even though Alex knew Kim could have managed perfectly well without her.

Alex had been letting the conversation flow over her when she heard something that caught her attention.

'The CEO has a lot to answer for, letting the service go so far over budget. We're supposed to be raising additional funds, not propping up bad management.'

Alex looked around. The voice seemed to be coming from the large lady dressed in purple sitting on the other side of the room. She remembered she'd been introduced as the treasurer of the group and was the wife of some local dignitary or other. Alex decided to listen.

'It'll all be sorted out soon. Top heavy, my husband says. Get rid of some of the useless managers and things'll soon get back on track. The CEO may have to go too. It was a bad appointment. All the government's fault.'

Alex recognised this voice. The wife of the local Member of Parliament, whose husband was currently in the opposition, made no bones of her disapproval.

*

It was eight o'clock before Alex arrived home. She'd helped Kim clear up after the guests had left, then Nick had returned from golf and Sandy from her afternoon event. The place had been a madhouse with everyone talking at once, and Alex had been persuaded to stay to dinner. Sandy's, 'Please, please, Aunty A. We don't see you nearly often enough,' had been the final inducement.

So it wasn't until she reached home that Alex was able to consider what she'd heard. Of course, it was only women's gossip, and heaven knows there was plenty of that around. But the comments about the CEO had a ring of truth about them. She fed Tess, filled her water bowel, brewed herself a mug of camomile tea then sat down on one of her kitchen stools, hands cradling the mug, while she contemplated the situation.

So what if the CEO was on the take? Did it affect her position? Alex had always valued integrity and preferred to work with people who shared her values. She placed her mug on the bench top and rubbed her forehead. The problem with being a consultant was that you never knew who you were working for. She wasn't an employee, so she could leave at any time. But that didn't fit with her value system either. Once she made a commitment to a task, she preferred to see it through to the end. She remembered the staff members she'd spoken to and helped through their difficulties in the past few weeks. She hardly ever saw Pete Robson, except as a figure flying past to one meeting or another. Her main contact was with the HR manager. Surely he wasn't bent too? He certainly seemed to be an upright soul, but who could tell?

Rosa was the key, she decided. She worked in the executive suite. She must have an idea of what was going on and she'd been with the organisation for years. If only she'd be prepared to talk.

*

Rosa stared again at the entry she was checking. It looked familiar, as if she'd seen it before. She checked back to the previous week's work. Yes, there it was. An invoice for $10,500 made out to a firm in Sydney for office furniture. She printed them both out. They were identical. She wondered which department had been fortunate enough to be the recipient of what appeared to be a number of upholstered chairs. In these stringent times, she'd have thought chairs were the last thing to be purchased.

She put the invoices aside, planning to check again the next day, and was turning off her computer when she heard a cheery 'Hello' and saw Alex's face peering round her door.

'Fancy a glass of wine? You look like you could do with one. Only proviso. No shop talk. I can't be accused of breaching confidentiality.'

'Sure thing. No secret's safe with me.' Rosa joked, picking up her bag and following Alex out.

Once the pair were settled in a bistro by the river with a glass of red wine in front of each of them and a plate of tapas in the middle of the table, they both breathed a sigh of relief, then laughed.

'One of those days?' asked Alex. 'Me too, but let's not talk about that. I'm a great believer in leaving work behind me when I walk out the door.'

'Right.' Rosa smiled. Even though she'd have liked to share her frustration at the invoices she'd discovered, she knew it was best to keep it to herself. 'Well, I spilled my guts to you last time. What about you? What makes you tick when you're not coaching? Married? Single? Still looking?'

'Single and not sure if I'm still looking.' Alex leaned back in her chair, glass in hand. She took a sip and stroked the glass with her fingers.

'Bad experience?' Rosa didn't want to pry, but she sensed that the other woman needed someone to talk to. Alex spent her working days listening to other people, helping them sort out their lives. Maybe she needed someone to listen to *her*.

Alex hesitated. She probably wasn't used to baring her innermost feelings to a stranger, though Rosa was hardly that. Since their initial meeting, the pair had shared lunch and coffee breaks on several occasions and Rosa had told her the whole story of her relationship with Ken.

Still holding her glass in one hand, she tapped on the table with the fingers of the other as if working out what to say. Finally she sighed, put her glass down and leaned forward. 'I'm not like you,' she began. 'I knew I couldn't continue to have an affair with Connor once he was married.'

Rosa's eyes widened and Alex twisted her fingers together on the table. 'Not that I'm maligning you or anything,' she continued, 'It just wasn't for me.'

Rosa was stunned. 'You mean...'

'I mean that Connor and I were in a relationship, practically living together. When I was at a conference in Perth, seems he met up with – *bumped into* was his version – his ex. He'd broken up with her just before we met. Well, as he told it, he got pissed and they had a one-night stand – *for old time's sake* – if you can believe it.' Alex gave a bitter smile, laid down her glass again and gazed into it. 'It was a Friday evening, he was different, distracted. Then he told me. April – that's her name – was pregnant.'

Rosa gasped.

'Oh, he assured me he didn't love her, he loved me. But since she was younger and I was *more resilient*, he'd agreed to marry her. He tried to convince me we could still carry on our relationship, that nothing had changed. Can you imagine?'

Rosa certainly could imagine. 'So you finished it?'

'That's when I came up here. I couldn't bear to be in the same city as him. How could I possible carry on as if nothing had happened?'

'And that was?'

'A couple of years ago. But that's not all. It wasn't the end of it.' Alex started twirling the stem of her glass, her eyes focussed on the table as if she didn't want to see Rosa's expression. 'Connor's in veterinary sales now, so he gets around. He found out where I was and turned up in Noosa – around six months ago.'

'Wanting to continue…?'

'Right. He caught me at a weak moment.'

'Oh!' Rosa's voice spoke volumes. 'And you…'

'Fell right in. It was just one night. We went out to dinner at Berardo's – wagu steak with all the trimmings, luscious dessert, and tons of champagne. I was weak, what can I say?'

'And?'

'And nothing. I threw him out next morning, and he won't be back, not after the names I called him – and myself.' Alex lifted her eyes to meet Rosa's. 'So that's my story.'

Although Alex had made it clear she didn't think less of Rosa for her affair with a married man, Rosa couldn't dismiss the feeling that Alex didn't altogether approve. Well, Rosa didn't approve of her own behaviour either. She'd never intended to get involved with someone who was married. It went against all the values she'd grown up with. But when Ken appeared in her life, good sense seemed to fly out of the window. Rosa suppressed her own guilty feelings and turned to her companion.

'And there's been no one else?'

'Not unless you count the handyman who's helping with my renovation. Jack of All Trades.'

'Jack of all trades?' Rosa's lips turned up in a smile.

'And master of none.' Alex waved her hands in the air. 'I know, crazy isn't it? That's what he calls his business. His name *is* Jack,' Alex laughed, 'and he's actually pretty good at what he does.'

'So tell me about this renovation,' Rosa asked. 'I've gone the other route and live in a fairly new apartment. Don't think I could hack the bother of renovating.'

'Well,' Alex propped her elbows on the table, glass in both hands. 'I bought this rundown seventies place at Peregian when I came up here. I planned to do it up myself and made a great start, but my brother was right when he said I was a fool to try doing it all myself.' Putting down her glass, Alex rubbed her brow. 'It all became too much so I looked for a handyman and found this guy.'

'And?'

'And he's been doing some work for me. Nothing more.' Alex blushed, making Rosa think there was more, but that Alex didn't want to talk about it.

'So you'd recommend him?' Rosa couldn't see where this was going.

'Sure.' Alex seemed tired of the conversation. There was a long pause while both women sipped their wine and looked around. Then Alex appeared to make a decision.

'Look, I know we said we wouldn't talk about your workplace, but…' She paused, biting her lip, then seemed to take courage. 'Is there something going on? Something odd, I mean. I've talked to a lot of people now and I get this feeling…'

'Oh!' Rosa didn't know what to say. She was desperate to share her own concerns, but not ready to open up to Alex who was external to the organisation, even though – especially as – she was working closely with it.

'What sort of feeling?' she asked.

'That's it. I can't explain it.' Alex waved her hands in the air. 'It may all be in my imagination. Forget it.'

'No, I think you may be right. There are a few things I've discovered too, but I'm still trying to find the answers. It may be nothing.' Suddenly Rosa felt guilty talking about her suspicions. Alex wasn't on staff and she ought not to be sharing work confidences with her. She put her glass down with a thump. 'No, it's probably nothing, Forget I spoke.'

Six

The rain was pelting down as Rosa hurried back to her car, trying to avoid the puddles. The small *For Sale* sign in the shop window leapt out at her. She stopped, drops of water from the edge of her umbrella falling into her eyes. *Jenny*, she thought. Only a week ago her friend had emailed her about a new plan – to buy a bookshop on her return. This one was perfect. She and Jenny had spent many a Sunday afternoon browsing the books in this very shop. Taking a note of the contact details she continued on her way, shaking the rain off her brolly as she got into the car.

Rosa wished her own problems could be solved as quickly. Her thoughts returned to the anomalies she'd come across at work. There had to be something… She sighed. Nothing was ever easy. What she had expected to be boring and routine was turning into a veritable mine of intrigue.

*

Rosa stared at the computer screen again and shook her head. This couldn't be right. Here was this same contractor she'd come across twice already and the same items were listed. She needed to find the original invoices. Maybe there had been a triple entry, though the dates were different. Leaving her desk, she started searching in the filing cabinet. They should still be here. She'd been charged with archiving the data and told she could destroy the originals once that was done but not before.

It took her almost an hour, but she finally found five similar invoices from the same company. She examined them carefully. Yes, they were identical except for the dates and they'd been signed off by... Ken. She sat down with a thump. Ken might have lied to her. He might have lied to his wife. But she'd been sure he was impeccable in his dealings with Beachhead Health. Hell, she'd have to ask him about this.

Picking up the invoices she walked up the three flights of stairs to the Finance Department. It would have been quicker to have taken the lift, but she needed time to mentally prepare herself. She'd managed to keep out of Ken's way since moving to her new position, but this required an answer. She took a deep breath as she pushed open the door to the department.

'Long time no see.'

'What's it like in the big time?'

'Good to see you haven't forgotten us.'

'Catch up for coffee sometime?'

Acknowledging the flurry of comments, she approached the Finance Director's open door and walked straight in.

'And to what do we owe this pleasure?' Ken's sarcastic greeting grated on her. Rosa felt a small tingle of something, but today it wasn't attraction. She examined the feeling as she walked into the room, head high. It was relief, relief that she no longer needed to hide away, that there no longer needed to be any subtext to their conversations.

'I need to ask you about these.' Rosa was aware her voice had an edge to it. She waved the invoices at him.

'Take a seat.' Ken moved around her to close the door, and Rosa twisted in her seat to watch him. He still looked the same. The suave business suit, the immaculate hairstyle. Rosa caught a faint whiff of his cologne as he passed her on the way back to his desk. She drew herself up, invoices held tightly in her hand. When he returned to his seat behind the desk, she handed the papers to him.

'I found these. They appear to be identical. I thought...' Her voice faltered as she saw him peer at them then remove his glasses. 'I thought there must be some mistake. You signed them off, so...' Rosa's voice died away as Ken studied them in silence. This was more difficult than she'd anticipated.

'They look fine to me.' Ken threw the papers down on the desk and leant across the desk towards her. 'How about you? Did *you* make a mistake?'

'No!' Rosa rose, rapidly snatching up the offending invoices. 'No mistake. My work is always precise,' she assured him, deliberately misunderstanding the question. She had to get out of here before she said something she'd regret. The gall of the man, thinking he could move back to their former footing. Any feelings she'd had for him were dead. Her only regret was that it had taken her so long to see past the image he presented, lying bastard that he was.

Rosa wasn't conscious of leaving the office. She didn't draw breath again till she was in the stairwell. She looked at the papers grasped firmly in her hand. Well, that had been a pointless exercise. She'd have to find a different way to check them out.

She was almost back in her office when the penny dropped. Chairs. They'd surely be on the asset list. All she needed to do was check with Capital Works to find out where they'd been delivered, how many and on what dates. It should be straightforward. She cursed herself for fussing so much over such a small thing, but she liked to maintain accurate records. After all, that was what she was being paid to do. No sooner said than done, but a phone call to John in Capital Works proved no more fruitful than her earlier enquiries. His blunt suggestion she just forget it and get on with her job left her fuming and even more determined to get to the bottom of it. She was tired of being patronised, especially when she *was* only trying to do her job.

An hour later, Rosa dragged her fingers through her already unruly hair and looked at the computer screen. Domino Holdings didn't seem to exist. She'd been searching all morning for the company name at the top of those damned invoices, but couldn't find it anywhere. She checked the headings again. Yes, she'd spelled the name correctly. There was the name, address, phone number and email address. She sighed. She'd try to call or email. There must be a good explanation – an honest mistake. But – the thought niggled – Ken had signed them off.

Deciding to leave it till another day, Rosa was lost in listing documents and reconciling them with the pile of files on her desk, when she became aware of someone standing in front of her. Since she was in the habit of working with her door open and had become used to one or other of the office staff popping a head in to offer tea or coffee, she spoke without looking up. 'Coffee would be great, thanks. Be with you in a sec.'

She heard a male throat-clearing sound and glanced up with a start. 'Oh!' Rosa couldn't immediately place the tall figure standing in the doorway.

'I believe you like cappuccino.'

She'd heard that voice somewhere before. She moved her head so that the sun was out of her eyes. 'You! What are you doing here?'

'I might ask you the same question.' The voice was deep and smooth – like a tub of Greek yoghurt – much like the man it belonged to. 'I'm here in my capacity as consultant.'

'Shit!'

'Well, I don't usually attract such strong sentiments on first – or even second meetings. Women usually get to know me first before they start swearing at me.' Rosa detected a twinkle in his eye. 'No, it's not you. Damn! I forgot. The consultant – you – was, were arriving today. You must be…'

'Harry, Harry Kennedy.'

'Of course. Pete didn't give me your name. He passed on your card. It's here, somewhere.' Rosa searched around her desk for a moment, then held it up triumphantly. 'Here it is: Dr Harold Kennedy, HK Solutions, Managing Director.'

'That's me. And you're Rosa Taylor.'

Rosa's eyes travelled down the immaculate grey suit, white shirt and tie to the two undamaged legs, then back up to meet an amused pair of blue eyes.

Her cheeks reddened as she remembered her offhand manner when they'd met in the café.

'I'm whole again, and I promise not to upset anything.' Harry gestured to the unstable pile of files. 'Is this a good time?'

'As good as any.' Rosa sighed. Now she'd been interrupted, she'd lost her train of thought, so might as well meet with this guy. 'Pull up a chair.'

She lifted the pile of folders and repositioned them on the floor. 'I'm not usually this disorganised.' She drew her fingers through her wiry curls, making them even more dishevelled than before, and pushed her glasses up on top of her head. He'd had to appear on the one day she hadn't taken time to fix her hair into its usual tidy bun.

She looked across at Harry, who had taken a seat opposite and was looking very relaxed, legs crossed with one ankle on the other knee, hands loosely clasped. For the first time she took a good look at him. She remembered him from the café. He'd done his utmost to be friendly, and she'd brushed him off quite rudely. She supposed he deserved an apology, but that would put her at a disadvantage, and this was *her* territory so he wouldn't be getting one soon.

He smiled that amused smile again. Damn the man. He was a magnificent specimen of raw masculinity. At the first meeting she'd recognised his innate sexiness but now, with the grey business suit fitting him like a glove, he was seriously hot. Rosa suppressed the spark of attraction that flared up and dropped her eyes. She was done with men.

'Where would you like to begin? I understand you're to develop the system that's going to maintain all of this.' She indicated the files on the floor and the boxes along the walls of the office.

'Why don't you tell me what you've been doing, and we can go on from there?' Harry suggested, taking his iPad out of its case. 'Then we can figure out how we can work together on this.'

Work together?

'I don't think that's what Pete had in mind.' Rosa's mind flew over the brief meetings she'd had with the CEO. No, working together with the consultant hadn't been mooted.

'Mmm, maybe not. Not very knowledgeable about this stuff is he?' Harry Kennedy seemed determined to get her on-side, but Rosa wouldn't be drawn.

'He has an IT department for that. Maybe you'd be best speaking to them.' Rosa replaced her glasses and glanced at the computer, hoping he'd take the hint and leave, but the man opposite her showed no sign of moving. He was opening up something on his tablet.

'Look here.' He rose and came round to stand behind her, placing the tablet on her desk and leaning over her left shoulder to point out a diagram.

Rosa breathed in the scent of aftershave and manly sweat emanating from him, and realised she couldn't move. She was hemmed in between him and the shelves on her other side. She focussed on the diagram and his words as he explained how the new system would work.

When at last he picked up the tablet, turned it off, and stood upright again, Rosa felt a sense of relief. She stretched her head around to look up at him. 'Thanks, but I'm not sure how I can help.'

'You have a lot of history with this organisation. Anything you can tell me will help. How about we start with coffee and I can redeem myself by not tipping it over?'

Rosa considered the pile of untouched work on her desk and the call and email to Domino Holdings she still had to make. However, the thought of getting out of the office was attractive, the promise of coffee seductive, and the opportunity to get to know this intriguing man better too good to miss.

'I suppose I could spare a few minutes,' she said.

Once seated in the hospital cafeteria with a steaming cappuccino in front of her, Rosa became more relaxed and was soon chatting away. To begin with, the conversation was fairly neutral as Harry asked about the local area and its attractions. His relaxed manner put Rosa at her ease, so she was surprised when he suddenly asked, 'What about Beachhead Health? What's going on?'

'I beg your pardon?' Rosa put down the cup she'd been about to raise to her lips. 'What do you mean?'

'This new system I'm contracted to develop and install. What's the buzz? Your IT chaps no good?'

Rosa spluttered. This was something that hadn't occurred to her. She gave the question serious thought. 'No, they're okay. Just flat out, I think. Pete seemed to want an outsider.' Now she thought about it, the choice did seem a bit odd. 'I presume there was the usual tender process.'

'Sure.' Harry began to spoon up the last drops of coffee. Observing him, Rosa wondered why men seemed to do this. She'd never seen a woman spoon up the dregs, but men seemed to do it all the time. She watched his firm tanned hands manipulate the tiny spoon.

'What did you say?' She drew herself up. Harry had been talking while he spooned, and she'd been so focussed on those long fingers she'd missed what he'd said.

'I was asking what exactly your role is in all of this.'

'Oh that's easy. I'm the dogsbody who's digging through the old documents; ensuring the paperwork is consistent with the computer data so that we can ditch the hard copies and have everything online in your new system.'

'And is it?' He raised his eyebrows.

'Does that matter? It will be. You needn't worry. You'll receive accurate data for your baby.' As she uttered those words, Rosa was struck with the realisation that at this point she wasn't completely sure that would happen. She needed to get back to the anomaly she'd discovered, ring Domino, and sort it all out.

'I must get back.' Rosa rose to leave.

'Something I've said?' Harry rose and pushed back his chair which screeched on the polished concrete floor. 'You always seem to be running out on me.'

'No.' Rosa hesitated, still unsure of this man. He was appointed by the CEO, so she should be able to trust him, but just how far, she wasn't sure. 'I really do need to get back to work. I have a deadline to meet and…'

'Okay. I was teasing you a little. Am I forgiven?' Harry's lips twisted up into a smile bringing an answering one to Rosa's lips.

'Of course. Now if you'll excuse me?' Rosa walked off. She was confused. What was it about his man that could disconcert her? She shook her head, and hurried back to take care of her workload.

Rosa sat down behind her desk and surveyed the work to be done. First things first. She checked her watch. Eleven o'clock. Should be a good time to ring this Domino company. She picked up the phone and dialled the number, mentally preparing what she'd say. But it was in vain. The number wasn't connected.

She tried again, fearing she'd input the wrong numbers. Same result. Strange. Maybe they'd changed their number, but rather than try directory enquiries, Rosa sent an email. It was easier to explain what she wanted in print anyway, and she'd have a record of both her request and their response.

She pressed *Send* then busied herself with other matters, not checking her emails till some time later when she returned from lunch. Wondering if there would be a reply already, Rosa quickly scanned the received emails and, to her dismay, saw one from Mail Administrator – *returned email*. She checked the address. Yes, she'd got it right. It was beginning to look as if Domino Holdings didn't exist.

Worried, she picked up the Domino paperwork and carried it through to the CEO's office. 'Pete available?' she asked Brenda, seeing his door was closed.

'I'll check.' Brenda picked up her phone and called the internal line. 'Rosa would like to see you. Is it…?' She put her hand over the mouthpiece. 'Okay, you can go right in,' she said to Rosa. 'She's on her way,' she said into the phone before putting it down again and smiling. 'He's been working on some reports and didn't want to be disturbed, but he'll see you.'

Rosa pushed the door gently, and entered to find Pete at his desk surrounded by papers. As she walked in he looked up, moved his glasses to the top of his head, and shuffled the papers together.

'Now what is it you want?' he asked somewhat testily.

'Sorry to disturb you. It's just that…' Rosa looked around unsure whether to sit down or remain standing.

'Take a seat.' Pete seemed to relax all of a sudden. He moved the pile of papers aside and pointed to a chair against the wall. 'Pull that forward. Sorry, it's been one of those days.'

Rosa took a seat and held up her own papers. 'It's these. I've come across some anomalies and wanted to clear them up.'

'Let me see.' Pete replaced his glasses on the bridge of his nose and held out his hand with a smile. Rosa handed them over and waited.

The CEO studied the papers then handed them back. 'Don't see the problem here, Rosa. I expect you to work things out for yourself, you know. Not to be coming to me with every little detail.'

Rosa felt this was pretty unfair. She'd been working in the executive unit for several weeks now, and this was the first time she'd come to him with a question. She drew herself up and slid forward to perch on the edge of the seat.

'These invoices, they're all the same, and I can't seem to locate the chairs they refer to. And…' She took a deep breath. 'And I can't contact Domino Holdings. They don't seem to exist.' She stopped, shocked by the glare from across the desk.

'I didn't hire you to conduct an audit. Can you archive this data or not?'

'I can, but…,' Rosa stammered, unsure how to proceed. She'd come here in good faith to see if she could sort this out and was getting no help at all. Worse, she was being accused of making a fuss over nothing. 'So you want me to ignore this anomaly and go ahead?' she asked, trying to work out if she'd heard correctly.

'That's what I pay you for, isn't it?' Pete handed the invoices back. 'They're only invoices,' he said wearily. 'I'm sure the goods are somewhere in this huge place, and I guess the company has gone out of business. It happens. Is that all?'

The afternoon passed quickly for Rosa. She put aside the bothersome invoices and moved on to another box of paperwork, relegating the Domino fiasco to the back of her mind. It wasn't till she was driving home that the issue rose to the surface again.

Really, Pete's reaction had been over the top. She'd expected some interest, concern even. But to be summarily dismissed was a bit out of order. Rosa worried the matter over in her head all the way home, but by the time she drove into her garage, she was no clearer as to why Pete had reacted in the way he had.

Ken too, she realised. As she kicked off her shoes, and poured a glass of wine, it suddenly occurred to her. Pete and Ken were acting as if she, Rosa, was the one at fault. As if she was manufacturing problems. Well, she couldn't do anything about it.

Fixing a plate of cheese and biscuits for dinner, she vowed to do a proper shop soon and to develop more regular eating habits. She looked down at her still trim body and pulled a flap of skin at her waist between two fingers. No, this poor diet she'd let herself fall into wasn't doing her any favours. She resolutely took her dirty plate and glass into the kitchen and, yawning and stretching her arms above her head, prepared for bed.

Pulling the curtains on the balcony windows she peered out at the moon shining on the river and turning it into a ghostly mirror. No pesky sailors tonight, she thought, remembering the flash from the lonely catamaran a few weeks ago. The boat had quickly disappeared so it must have been a stray tourist as she'd thought at the time. She took herself off to bed, her head filled with thoughts of sailing off into the sunset and leaving all the mess behind her.

*

Harry placed the dog bowl on the kitchen floor and laughed as the black spaniel pup tried to chase his tail. 'No, mate. *This* is for eating.' Harry pushed the bowl towards the animal, pleased he'd made buying a pup a top priority when he'd moved into his new home. The little fellow was proving to be good company and a regular sounding board. Satisfied the dog was beginning to eat, Harry fixed his own meal and took it through to the living area. He settled into one of his new armchairs, stroked the beige leather and took a long swallow of beer. That certainly hit the spot.

Putting the can down on the coffee table, he picked up the thick sandwich of rare roast beef on rye, complete with his favourite dill pickle and took a bite. The pup – he'd need to find a name for him soon – loped in to nibble on Harry's big toe. Harry grinned as it tickled – the teeth were too small to do any damage right now, but it wouldn't be long... He supposed he shouldn't encourage it.

He looked around the room furnished, if sparsely, with the new gear he'd bought in the past few weeks. It was beginning to look like home, his home. He was satisfied with what he'd accomplished since arriving in Noosa, and with the people he'd met here too. There hadn't been many. Pete, the CEO, Jack, his handyman, a couple of neighbours to say g'day to across the fence or in the driveway. And Rosa.

An image of the dainty dark-haired lady he'd had coffee with flashed past his inner eye. She sure was a nervous one, friendly one minute, yet eager to leave his presence the next. But there was something about her, something that made him want to know her better. Harry took another gulp of his beer, reminding himself of the hassles women had caused him in the past, hassles that had led to his moving up here. Maybe he should leave well alone. Still, he was intrigued, feeling sure there was more to her than met the eye. Well, they'd be working together in order to store the data, so...

Finishing his sandwich, he crushed the now empty beer can in his hand and reached down to fondle the pup's ears. Enough thinking for one night. 'Come on, Tiger,' he said without thinking, leading the little dog into his bed in the laundry. *Hmm, Tiger, not a bad name for the little fellow.*

Seven

Rosa pulled open the drapes and let in the sunlight, the bright beams showing up the dust on the tiled floor. Almost blinded by the sun's glare she walked back to the kitchen to prepare breakfast. The brightness of the morning was at odds with her mood. She grimaced. She certainly didn't take after her mother in that respect. No, come to think of it, she wasn't her mother's daughter in any respect. That's why Vi was the favourite, she guessed.

Rosa decided to resign from work. It was no use. She couldn't be party to the scam that appeared to be going on. She couldn't seem to get to the bottom of it, and not only did no one seem to care, they were acting as if she was crazy. She'd lain awake all night trying to figure out what to do, torn between her loyalty to the organisation and frustration that she wasn't being allowed to do her job properly. That, on top of the possibility of running into Ken every day, was just too much.

She knew it was the coward's way out, but she'd seen what had happened to whistle-blowers in the past. Regardless of the legislation in place, they always got a raw deal. That wasn't for her. No, she'd keep her suspicions to herself and slip out quietly.

Jenny would be home soon. She could open her heart to her friend. It wouldn't be fair to burden Alex with it all. She still had a contract to fulfil. And Harry Kennedy... She stopped and smiled, thinking of the tall blond guy who'd appeared as if from nowhere, looking like God's gift to lonely women and who seemed to want to be friends.

She dropped two slices of bread into the toaster and pushed the lever down with more force than was necessary. He could be part of all the whole mess. He'd been appointed by Pete after all.

*

Rosa signed the letter with a flourish. Two weeks and she'd be out of here. It was odd. Thirty years of her career tied up in the place, and she could throw it away with a stroke of the pen. She folded the A4 sheet of paper and slid it into an envelope, printing the CEO's name carefully on the front of it.

When she read Jenny's email to say she'd be back on Monday, a vague idea occurred to her. But she'd keep it to herself for now. Play it by ear. With her long service leave, she'd be right financially for a few months anyway; enough to take time to work something out.

Rosa looked back up at the building as she made her way to her car. The end of an era. What a pity it had to finish like this.

She was about to leave for home when her mobile buzzed, and she saw the number of her mum's nursing home. Her heart sank. It had to be bad news. There was no other reason for the call, not when she was due to visit soon. She pressed to receive the call, her stomach fluttering with anxiety. 'Yes? This is Rosa.'

'Ms Taylor?'

'Yes, Rosa Taylor. Is my mother…?'

'Sorry to trouble you. We know you're planning to visit in a couple of days, but…'

Get on with it, Rosa thought, tapping her foot impatiently, while she began to imagine all the possible scenarios that would require the urgent call. She heard a gentle cough on the other end of the phone.

'I'm afraid Ivy has broken her glasses. She's become very distressed, and we wondered…'

'I have her spare pair at home. I'll bring them over as soon as I can.'

Rosa quickly drove home, then to the nursing home. When she entered her mum's room, she was upset to see the older woman almost in tears and gripping her broken spectacles in her lap.

'Mum, it's all right. I've brought your spare pair and I can get these

46

ones fixed.' She managed to pry the broken glasses from her mother's fingers and replaced them with the ones she'd brought.

'I feel so helpless,' Ivy sniffed, grasping them tightly. 'I'm an old woman, and no use to anyone. I'd be better off dead.'

'Mum! Don't say that!' Rosa wondered how she could cope with this, just as she'd made the decision to move on with her life. Although she found the atmosphere in the home depressing, until now she'd felt sure her mother was happy here. What could she do if that wasn't the case? Rosa was torn between feeling sorry for her mother's distress, and trying to imagine how they could both live in her tiny apartment. 'Has something happened to upset you?'

'I… I fell this morning,' she said. 'That's how they broke. And…' Her eyes, full of unshed tears, met Rosa's. 'It's the first time I've felt so helpless. I hate being old. I hate becoming a burden to everyone. I don't want to become one of those old people who can't take care of themselves. There are enough of them here, I see them every day.' Rosa thought Ivy was going to break down, but instead her voice was becoming stronger, and Rosa could see her mother's old self beginning to reassert itself. 'Thanks for my specs, Rosa. You're good to your old mum.'

Rosa relaxed. This was more like it. For a moment she'd panicked, her old doubts and insecurities coming to the fore. She felt guilty for even having such thoughts, for thinking of herself, her own life, when her mother might need her. But the experience had shaken her, made her realise her mother was feebler that she'd supposed. She made a mental note to call Vi. Her sister might be in far-off London, but she needed to be made aware their mother was failing.

Checking Ivy had everything she needed and was feeling more settled, Rosa left, promising to return for her usual visit on Sunday and to bring new library books along with some fresh magazines. Although the nursing home provided a daily newspaper, it was the lives and disasters of the British royal family and other celebrities that retained her mother's interest more than the goings-on in the daily life of everyday Australians or their politicians.

But, once home, Rosa couldn't put her mother's initial frailty out of her head. Yes, she 'd rallied and seemed more like herself, but Rosa's heart had plummeted at her first glimpse of Ivy today and at her talk of being better off dead. It suddenly occurred to her just how fragile a hold on life her mother had. She needed to let her sister know. Vi would never forgive her if anything happened and Rosa hadn't prepared her.

Rosa checked the time and did a calculation. It would be early morning in London. She might just be able to catch Vi before she left for work. Rosa pressed her speed dial before she changed her mind and was rewarded by her sister's voice.

'Rosa? What's wrong?' Rosa almost smiled at the shock in Vi's voice. She rarely rang her sister, the two preferring to maintain contact through texts or emails. 'Is Mum…?'

'No, but she's not good. She's failing faster than I expected. Could you…?' She heard a sharp indrawn breath and waited for Vi's response.

There was a long pause, during which Rosa imagined Vi in her spotless designer kitchen tapping her fingers impatiently on a marble benchtop while she tried to think up a plausible reason why she couldn't make the trip to Australia. Rosa had never been in Vi's house or kitchen, had never even seen photos of it, but she could imagine it in all its glory.

'I can't just drop everything and head off to the other side of the world,' Vi said finally. 'Is she… do you…?' she stammered.

'She's not dying, if that's what you mean. But if you want to see her while you can still have a conversation with her, before she fails any more…' Rosa's voice dropped as she remembered her mother's depressed state.

'Well, then. It's okay, isn't it? You're still seeing her and can let me know if she gets any worse, if… Look, I need to go. I was about to walk out the door when you rang. I'll be late if I don't leave now.'

The call cut off and Rosa was left looking at the silent mobile. Damn her sister. She should have known Vi would take this attitude, but there'd have been hell to pay if Rosa didn't keep her informed.

After the call, Rosa had trouble settling to anything, even Helene Young's latest novel failed to hold her interest. She really wanted to talk to Jenny. But although her friend was back in Australia, Rosa knew she was in Sydney with her family, and probably wouldn't welcome any interruptions. No, she'd have to wait till Monday before confiding in her friend. Maybe she should have told Jenny what was going on in her life before now. But Jenny had enough to contend with in far-off Oregon, so she'd decided to keep it all to herself.

Alex was the only person she'd confided in, the only person she felt she could trust. She checked her watch. Maybe…, but it was Friday night. Most people had somewhere to go, someone to be with on a Friday night.

The years with Ken had taken their toll. Rosa had no close friends. They'd all disappeared over the years, as she'd kept her time free for her lover she'd managed to alienate almost everyone she knew.

She sighed and going to the window gazed out at the groups of people enjoying the evening by the river. Suddenly her apartment, usually so warm and welcoming, felt claustrophobic. She had to get out of it, needed some fresh air. Shrugging on a warm jacket, she closed the door behind her and walked down the stairs to the street.

Rosa shoved her hands in her pockets and tried to avoid the eyes of passers-by. As she crossed the road, she saw a blond-haired man standing by the Big Pelican. He glanced up. It was Harry Kennedy. She'd thought she'd never see him again.

Now that she'd dropped off those documents to him, he had no need to come to the office over the next two weeks. Then she'd be gone. Not that she'd anything against him personally, but she just wasn't sure she could trust him. He could be mixed up in the discrepancies she'd uncovered, and she didn't want to risk it. What if there really was something criminal going on and he was part of it? And she was off men, though he had managed to leave her with a good impression – his politeness and friendliness were a balm to her troubled soul.

*

Harry's table was covered with papers, his laptop almost hidden. He dragged a hand through his hair. Who said computers would kill the paper war? They should be shot. Rosa had dropped this bundle off to him on her way home last night. Why the hell couldn't she have emailed them? She'd seemed remarkably pleased with herself too, not like the grave and often infuriating woman he'd been dealing with who'd piqued his curiosity. For a second he wondered what was up, then dismissed the thought.

He wandered into the kitchen and poured himself a glass of Merlot, then walked out onto the deck. He breathed in the clear evening air. Hearing a loud screeching, he looked up to see a huge flock of rosellas fly overhead, seeking their evening roosts. It was too nice an evening to stay inside. He skolled his wine, dumped his empty glass on the draining board, headed out and made for the boardwalk.

Once there, he walked the whole length of the river, enjoying the fresh air on his face, stopping from time to time, to watch the evening sailors and kayakers. He thought of his own boat, languishing up at the marina. He needed to make a decision about that soon. If he didn't intend to sail again, he should sell it, save the marina fees and the maintenance.

But he wasn't sure what he wanted. He'd left Sydney in a rush, hardly taking time to pack. His boat, the Yarran, belonged to that old life, the one he'd abandoned. There was no going back. He couldn't face that. It was amazing how the trip up the coast had changed his state of mind, removed most of the bitterness he'd felt for Hillie and Bernie. They were together now. Good luck to them. They probably deserved each other.

But could he stay here for the rest of his life? Why not? He looked up at the sky, now glowing red with the setting sun. It was as good a place as any. He owned a house here now, too. He'd snagged one job pretty smartly. There would be others. Working as a consultant gave him freedom – the freedom he'd lacked down south. He was making friends. Correction. Apart from the CEO in the Health Service, he'd really only spoken to Jack, his handyman, and Rosa.

Thinking of Rosa brought a smile to his lips. There was something about her, something that intrigued him. She was different from the women he and Hillie had mixed with in Sydney – the social butterflies. He sensed a sadness there, a… Just as he was trying to figure out what he felt, he saw her familiar figure cross the road in front of him. For a moment, he started towards her, then stopped in his tracks. Her body language told him his approach wouldn't be welcome. She was walking swiftly, head down, hands thrust into her pockets. As he watched, she moved quickly on, looking neither to right or left.

Ah well, Harry thought. He gazed up at the enormous painted pelican in front of him and grinned. Who on earth had the idea of sticking that thing here when there were so many real birds around?

There were three live ones perched on posts in the river right now. Watching them, Harry's eyes fell on a sign offering sunset drinks and he noticed a large floating restaurant with the sign: Noosa Boathouse. That sounded good. He stepped in, made his way up the stairs and walked through a narrow bar to the deck. Ordering a beer and a serving of calamari and chips, Harry found a seat facing the river and managed to catch the dying rays of the setting sun. If this wasn't paradise, it wasn't far from it.

He was on his second beer and feeling very relaxed when his phone rang. Checking the screen, before answering, he cursed. Hillary! What did she want now?

Eight

Rosa stood at the edge of the balcony watching Jenny drive off, then picked up the empty bottle and glasses and walked back into the apartment, sliding the door closed behind her with her foot. What had she got herself into? She'd toyed with the idea before her friend had returned, but now she'd committed herself. She was going to join Jenny in her bookshop. It would be a new beginning. What did she know about running a bookshop? More than Jenny probably. At least she could do the accounts.

Thinking of accounts reminded her of the mess at Beachhead Health. Maybe she *should* have reported it. No, she'd made the right decision. She'd let sleeping dogs lie, and the new system could wipe out all the nefarious goings on. Surely she could survive there for two more weeks?

Once in bed, Rosa couldn't sleep. She tossed and turned. Finally she rose and, pulling on her towelling robe, padded through to the kitchen to heat up some milk. Maybe a hot drink would do the trick?

Rather than take it back to bed, she curled up in her favourite chair, wrapped her hands around the mug and thought back over the last few weeks, the weeks since she'd given Ken the boot. He'd certainly changed, or maybe Rosa had been so besotted with the man she'd failed to notice his bullying manner. During the past week, she'd become convinced that there was some dirty business going on and that Ken, if not at the heart of it, was somehow involved.

Men! They were always trouble. Look at poor Jenny: after years of widowhood, she'd let this man get under her skin over there in Oregon, and that had ended badly too. Though reading between the lines and seeing Jenny's expression when she talked about this Oregon man, Rosa's friend may not have completely given up hope.

It was good to have Jenny back. There was only so much Rosa could share with Alex, but she'd been able to bare her soul to Jenny, who'd agreed Ken was a complete bastard and assured Rosa she was doing the right thing in leaving the Health Service. She also appeared delighted to have Rosa join forces in her new venture.

As Rosa rinsed out her mug and prepared for bed again, it occurred to her that the one thing she'd omitted to mention to Jenny was her dealings with Harry Kennedy. But there was no reason why she should have mentioned him. He was part of the whole Beachhead debacle and probably part of whatever intrigue Pete and Ken were involved in. She'd passed on all of her paperwork to him and there was no reason to believe she'd ever meet him again. Now why did that cause her a tinge of disappointment?

*

Harry shut down his laptop and stretched his arms above his head. Enough for today. He was making good progress on the material Rosa had left for him. She certainly knew her stuff. There were a few anomalies, but he was sure he'd be able to sort them out. At this rate he'd finish the job ahead of schedule. He took a sip of the red wine he'd poured earlier.

Now that work was over for the day, the phone call he'd received last week popped into his head. Damn Hillary! His soon-to-be-ex-wife, was making things difficult. It seemed it wasn't enough he'd left town, she still wanted her pound of flesh along with the divorce. And with all their friends and colleagues believing he was the guilty party, she looked like getting her way.

He could still hear her shrewish voice with its unreasonable demands. When had she changed? Or was it Harry who'd changed? They'd had some good years when Lucy was small, but somewhere along the line, they'd drifted in different directions. He sighed. Bernie was probably a better match for Hillie as she was now, the sharp vixen she'd become when the business had taken off.

It hadn't happened all at once. The change had been subtle, barely noticeable. Then one day, they'd had nothing to talk about. Lucy, becoming a teenager, had her own friends and didn't want to be bored by her parents' company; neither, it seemed, did Hillie want to be bored by his. But Bernie! That had been a shock. He'd trusted him, trusted Hillie too, despite the growing distance between them.

He looked down at the pup lying asleep at his feet and thought of the phrase *a dog's life*. Tiger's life did seem much happier and less complicated than his own right now. The divorce should have been simple – irreconcilable differences, a straight division of their assets. But Hillie wanted him to take the blame and was claiming most of their abundant assets including the house on the harbour in Hunter's Hill, their holiday home at Bateman's Bay and the boat. The last one was what really annoyed him. Hillie had never even liked his catamaran, refused to go on the boat with him and had complained bitterly about the time he spent sailing.

He remembered only too well the headlines in the *Sydney Morning Herald*. It had been a slow news day, so the item covering the messy divorce of one of Sydney's leading financiers had made the front page. Unfortunately for Harry, the journalist had failed to reveal the full name of the co-respondent and had only mentioned an H Kennedy. Naturally everyone had assumed it referred to Harry and that he was embroiled in an affair with his partner's exotic Italian born wife. Instead it was his wife, Hillary who had been having a clandestine affair with Harry's partner for over five years.

He'd been too much of a gentleman to correct them, but the whole matter had left a bad taste in his mouth. That the two people he trusted most had treated him this way left him stunned, and all he wanted to do was get away. That's what had brought him here. He'd planned to disappear without a fight. Now he wasn't so sure.

A loud knock on the door broke into his thoughts. A bit late for a visitor, and he didn't know anyone here. Putting down his glass he walked to the door, on the way waking Tiger, who gambolled at his feet.

'Hi mate. Called round on the off-chance.' The handyman was standing at the door, a sheepish look on his face.

'Yes?' Puzzled, Harry opened the door wider to admit Jack.

'Seem to be missing one of my saws. Wondered if I left it here.'

'Come on in. I'll have a look. You can help me finish this bottle. You a red man?'

Jack murmured an agreement and the pair settled down with their drinks, the saw momentarily forgotten.

'So, you're settling in?' Jack's eyes ranged across the room, taking in the furniture Harry had organised and the dog, now lying again at his master's feet.

'Seem to be.' Harry leant back, trying to see the room through a stranger's eyes. In the lamplight it appeared warm, welcoming. He grinned with pleasure. Maybe he'd left a mess behind him in Sydney, but at least he'd made a good start here.

'I...' Jack paused, seemingly having difficulty in getting the words out.

'Spit it out, man.' Harry reached for the wine bottle and filled both glasses.

'I was talking with a mate in Sydney. Happened to mention the job I did for you. Seems you're pretty well-known down there.'

Harry's glass tipped, sending red wine everywhere. 'Shit!' Harry tried to wipe down the spilt wine from the table. This was the last thing he needed – his ruined Sydney reputation following him up here.

Jack held up his hands. 'No worries. None of my business. Just thought I'd mention it. A lot of Sydney folk come up here for a holiday. Might not be so easy to live it down.'

'Let's look for that saw,' Harry said brusquely, leading the way into the garage. He looked around for a bit, before his eyes fell on a serrated edge peeking out from under one of the boxes 'This it?' he asked, lifting the box out of the way.

'Sure is. Thanks. I'll be off then.'

'No need to rush away.' Harry had had time to recover from the shock of Jack's comments and was beginning to regret his earlier reaction. 'Have another glass. Sorry, I got carried away. Not your fault. I know you were trying to be a friend.' He rubbed a hand over the top of his head. 'Thought I'd left all that behind me. It wasn't the way the papers said. It was just easier that way... to let everyone believe...'

'Want to talk about it?' Jack offered awkwardly.

'Thanks, Jack. Maybe another time.'

'We're all running away from something.' Jack rolled his glass in his hands.

'Hmmm.' Harry drained his glass, and Jack, as if sensing his host had had enough for the night, rose to leave.

'Thanks for this.' He motioned to the saw. 'Been lost without it. Have another...' But Harry had stopped listening. He was thinking that it had come to this – the only person he could talk to was his handyman. What a crock!

Nine

Rosa had a spring in her step as she entered her office. Humming to herself, she sorted through the remaining bundles of files, feeling pretty sure she'd manage to have most of the work completed before she left – all except these damned invoices. Lost in her own little world, she was startled when a phone call summoned her to the CEO's office.

'Close the door, Rosa.'

Rosa did as Pete instructed, astounded to see Ken sitting there with him. *What was going on?* Something began to shrivel in her gut. The resentment she'd managed to suppress started to simmer again. She should have known Pete would involve him.

'I have your letter of resignation.' Pete waved the sheet of paper in the air before dropping it on the desk.

Rosa looked at Ken in the faint hope of reassurance, but only a cold glare met her eyes. There was going to be no help from him. She took a deep breath. 'I should be finished most tasks by the end of my notice. It won't be hard for someone else to fill in.' She glanced from one man to the other. *Was this just about her resignation?*

Pete tapped the desk with his forefinger, then took his glasses off and laid them down. 'You've been a busy little lady,' he said. 'I… we…' He looked pointedly at Ken, Rosa's eyes following his. 'We wouldn't like to think you were going to do anything rash.'

Rosa felt anger build inside. *So they intended to treat her like a naughty child. She'd show…* Then Ken began to speak, his voice oily. Why had she never realised how smarmy the man was? Six years of her life, wasted on this mongrel.

'Rosa,' Ken began. 'I know you. I know we can count on you. You've always proved trustworthy in the past. But Pete…' He coughed. 'He doesn't know you like I do. He's worried your little mistake will have repercussions.'

'Mistake?' Rosa's voice rose. 'I haven't made any mistakes. I don't make mistakes. You've always complimented me on my accuracy, my attention to detail. Why…'

'So it seemed,' Ken interrupted. 'Maybe I was blinded by…' He winked. That wink was the last straw for Rosa. She rose.

'If that's all you have to say…'

'Sit down.' Pete's strident voice forced her back into her seat. This time she perched on the edge of the chair. His voice softened. 'All we want, my dear, is an assurance. An assurance you don't intend to spread your little rumours around. Maybe something in writing?' He looked across at Ken who was nodding in agreement. 'That way you can leave with a good reference, and no more need be said.'

Rosa cringed as his threat hit home. Did he really think she intended to report them? But even though she'd decided against this course of action… to put it in writing… that was too much to ask.

'You can stuff your reference.' She stood up again, this time making it as far as the door. Pete's words followed her.

'You'd better finish up today. Ken will see to your final pay. We're done here.'

Fuming, Rosa strode back to her office. *How dare they? But if that's the way they wanted to play it, so be it.* Leaving the files on the desk, she quickly packed her personal belongings. By the time she'd finished, anger had given way to sadness and her eyes were brimming with tears. She'd given the best years of her life to this organisation only to be tossed out like this, as if she were at fault. Damn them! Damn them all, and Ken most of all. After all they'd been to each other, he could at least have stood up for her. He was just as much of a shit as his boss.

'Rosa.'

She looked up to see Bill Holmes, one of the security staff, in the doorway.

He coughed. 'I'm to make sure you leave, that you don't remove any Health Service property. I'm sorry.'

Rosa blanched. This was the final humiliation. She'd known Bill for years. She'd hoped to slip away quietly. Now everyone would hear about her humiliating departure.

She hoisted the box of her belongings under her arm, pressed her lips together and allowed him to escort her out. Thankfully he left her at the door, permitting Rosa to make her way to the car park by herself.

'Can I help?'

Rosa glanced up. She was fumbling in her bag for her car key, the box balanced awkwardly on her thigh. 'Alex! Thanks, but...'

The presence of her new friend brought the tears back to her eyes, and this time she didn't have a free hand to wipe them away. 'Damn! Sorry.' She finally found what she was searching for and pressed the control. The boot swung open, allowing her to dump the box inside. 'What must you think of me?' She wiped her eyes and was able to see Alex's concern.

'What's wrong?' Alex moved closer.

Rosa wished she could disappear. She'd hoped to escape unseen. Now she'd have to explain herself to Alex.

'It...,' she began, not clear what she was going to say.

'You look as if you need a cup of tea – hot and sweet. I was just about to have one. Join me?'

'Not here.' Rosa just wanted to leave, the sooner the better, before she disgraced herself by breaking down right here in the car park. It was bad enough that Alex had chanced on her. She didn't want anyone else – people she'd worked with for thirty years – seeing her like this. The humiliation of this untimely end to what seemed to be a lifetime's work, was almost too much to bear.

She was happy to forego an elaborate farewell. She'd never been one for gestures, and that's all these things were. But she wasn't even being allowed to leave on her own terms. That's what rankled. That, and the smug expressions on Pete and Ken's faces. She winced, imagining their relief now she was gone.

Alex seemed to understand her reluctance to talk. 'I have to go into town. Why don't we meet up there? Sirocco?'

'Okay.' Rosa breathed a sigh of relief, slid into the car and started the engine. With one last lingering look at the building, she drove off.

*

'So there you have it,' Rosa finished, and broke off a piece of the triple chocolate muffin her friend had insisted on. Alex had proven to be a good sounding board. Rosa guessed it was a skill Alex had developed in her coaching, and she felt better having got everything off her chest.

'Mmm. I had a feeling something was wrong there, but since it wasn't really anything to do with me, I couldn't investigate. What will you do now?'

Rosa's face brightened. 'That's one good thing. Even before that scene today I'd had enough. Jenny's back. Remember her? Jenny Sullivan?'

'Of course I do. Didn't she go to Oregon?'

'That's right. She's back now and she's bought a bookshop. I plan to join her. We'll be partners,' Rosa said proudly.

'Really? How exciting. Tell me more.'

Encouraged by Alex's interest, Rosa was soon explaining how she'd found the shop for sale while Jenny was in Oregon. 'And she agreed I can join her,' she concluded, smiling at last. 'Of course, that was when I thought I would still have two more weeks of work. Now, I guess…' She thought for a moment. 'Now I can help her to set it all up,' she said. 'I should call her. She doesn't know.'

Rosa slumped back in her seat, the enormity of the day's events resurfacing and a curl of panic gripping her stomach. She'd been cast aside, just as Jenny had all those months earlier. 'I didn't fully understand how Jenny felt. Now…'

Alex's hand covered Rosa's on the table. 'It's rough. Happening to a lot of you these days. And I'm not proud of my part in it.'

'It's not your fault. You have a job to do, just like the rest of us.'

'But *my* job seems to be putting others out of *theirs*.' Rosa saw Alex bite her lip. 'At least there are a few successes – people who do come out the other side with a new start. People like Jenny, and you. Not everyone is as lucky. All I can do is try to steer them in the right direction, have them examine their options.'

'You do all right. I've heard good things about you.'

'Thanks.' Alex rose to leave. 'Sorry, I need to get back. I have appointments all afternoon.'

'Of course, you must. I'll ring Jenny when I get home. Thanks for your support. I feel a lot better now. I can see why there are good reports about you.'

'Hmm. We'll see if this afternoon's crew think the same once I've done with them.'

After Alex left, Rosa sat for a few minutes looking out at the river flowing silently on the other side of the road. It never changed and it was almost her own backyard, living as she did just a few blocks away. Pulling herself together, she drew out her mobile and pressed Jenny's number on the speed dial.

'Rosa! I didn't expect to hear from you today. Thought you'd be flat out getting everything finished, ready for your departure.'

'My departure has come earlier than I expected. As of today, I'm a free woman.' There was a shriek on the other end of the phone. Rosa held it away from her ear. When she moved it back, Jenny was talking rapidly.

'Say again? Your shriek almost deafened me. Was it surprise or delight?'

'Surprise mostly, but delight too. It means you can be in from the start. I picked up the keys this morning and I'm dying to get going. Why don't you come over for dinner tonight? My turn to cook and you can tell me everything. You probably feel dreadful right now.' Jenny's voice became solemn, then brightened. 'But just you wait. You're well rid of that place. It's toxic. See you around six? This calls for a celebration.'

Rosa ended the call with a grin. Trust Jenny to force her to look on the bright side – and there was a bright side. She didn't have to face Ken again. Or worry about the damned invoices. They weren't her problem anymore.

*

Taking Jenny at her word that they had something to celebrate, Rosa was carrying a bottle of *Yellow Glen* sparkling wine when she knocked on Jenny's door that evening. When the door opened, an enticing aroma wafted out.

'Mmm, smells good. Mexican?'

'Correct. I brought a few of Maddy's recipes back with me,' Jenny said, referring to the godmother she'd stayed with in the States. 'Wish she was here now.' Her voice was low, but she spoke so cheerfully Rosa wondered if she was imagining the sadness. 'She's a wise woman, full of good advice. She'd soon talk you out of any lingering doubts you might have,' Jenny added.

'Doubts? Me?'

'I know you.' Jenny was opening the wine as she spoke and a stream of froth threatened to flow onto the table, before she managed to catch it in a glass. 'Oops. Need to keep my mind on what I'm doing. Yes, doubts. It's only natural, after all you've been through. But that bastard, Ken. I bet he had something to do with what happened today.'

'Well, he was there, part of the Mafioso.'

'Here. Get that down you.' Jenny handed Rosa a glass, and tipped her own to clink it. 'Here's to the future. Here's to our bookshop. And if we can make it half as good as Ellen's in Florence, I'll be thrilled.'

'Ellen? You mentioned her on Friday. A cousin, you said?'

'Yes, part of my newfound family. She has this amazing bookshop. I felt at home there right away, the feel, the smell.' Jenny inhaled as if she was able to recreate the smell of Ellen's shop right there in her living room. 'That's what made me decide to open one of my own.'

Rosa studied her friend. She hadn't changed much since her trip to the States. She was still a tall elegant woman, her dark hair a little longer than it used to be, her violet eyes twinkling in her eagerness to begin.

'So, where do we start?' Rosa took a sip of wine, savouring its sweetness. She was beginning to feel more cheerful. Between them, Alex and Jenny were working their magic on her. The humiliating experience in Pete's office was beginning to fade.

'Right here.' Jenny put down her glass and turned to a folder lying open on the table. 'I've been looking at the accounts. Things don't seem as good as I anticipated. Maybe you can cast your eyes over them and let me know what you think.'

Rosa gulped. This wasn't what she'd expected. Surely the business was going to manage to support both of them? 'Now?'

'Not now. Take them home with you. We can meet up again tomorrow at the shop. I'm dying to actually get my hands on the place. As you said in your emails, it's looking a bit tired, but I'm sure we can revitalise the old girl. Let's have dinner and think about what we can do to freshen the place up.'

Ten

After going through the accounts, Rosa was regretting Jenny hadn't done this more thoroughly earlier, quite a bit earlier. The accountant had said it wasn't great but had potential, and Jenny had been so keen to buy, she'd taken his recommendation at face value. She'd honed in on "potential". "Rundown" was more like it. But would it really have made any difference to Jenny if she'd known? Being honest with Rosa, Jenny had admitted she'd jumped in with both feet. She'd wanted the bookshop so much she'd probably have bought it anyway. Jenny had a stubborn streak from way back and was determined to make a go of it. Now it was up to Rosa to help her do exactly that.

Having made her decision, Rosa felt better and was looking forward to inspecting the shop with Jenny. They'd come up with a few ideas last night. It would be good to find out how they looked in the light of day – and in the shop itself.

Rosa arrived first and was checking the outside of the building when Jenny drove up. Part of a row of other shops, it had been a bookshop for as long as she could remember. The brick walls were still in good shape, but the white paint was beginning to flake from the door and window and the shop sign had faded giving the whole place a tired appearance.

'Here we are.' Jenny held out the key and the pair entered together. The shop was full of morning sunlight and Rosa could see a stream of dust motes dancing in its beams as it hit the wooden floor. The familiar bookshop aroma was almost masked by a pervading trace of neglect.

'We'll need to do quite a bit of cleaning before we can open.' Rosa drew her hand across the counter and looked at the thick coating of dust on her fingers. 'Luckily the books were stored in crates. The shelves will need a good clean before we can fill them again.'

Jenny pulled one of the chairs up to a low table and signalled Rosa to do the same.

'I looked through the accounts after I got home last night,' Rosa began. 'It's not good, but you probably know that already.' She smiled at Jenny who nodded. 'However, it could be worse. We can do it. Those ideas we had last night. We need to work out how soon we can put them into place.'

'Let's look at what we can accomplish today. Why don't we set up a weekly routine here and note down what's outstanding?' Jenny said. 'We need to start somewhere and I'm sure that there are a lot of routine things that need doing – cleaning, cataloguing, shelving, things like that.'

By the end of the day it was as if Jenny and Rosa had been working together for years. There was a fresh energy about the place that both commented on as they closed the door.

'It's as if the shop has a new lease of life,' Rosa said. 'Will you keep the old name?'

Jenny looked up at the faded sign. It still held the name of the previous owner. 'I hadn't thought about that, but it would be nice to put our own mark on it.' She was silent for a full minute, then, 'The Book Nook. What do you think? Ellen calls hers The Reading Nook and it's full of nooks and crannies where people can relax with a book. It's a calm and peaceful place to be. I'd like to create that same mood here.'

'It'll be like a whole new shop,' Rosa said. 'I like it, but don't you want to have your name on it?'

'No, it's to belong to both of us.'

'So this is where you are?' The cheerful voice made both women turn around to see Alex's smiling face. 'Rosa said you were opening a bookshop,' Alex said to Jenny. 'So this is it? I was walking Tess and we saw the pair of you.'

Rosa realised Alex had a gold-coloured dog on a lead. It looked like a well-behaved creature as it sat at its mistress's feet. Rosa had never had much to do with dogs, but Jenny bent to pat it and ruffle its ears.

'It's looking a bit tired right now. But just wait a couple of weeks. You won't recognise the place. A touch of paint, some new shelving, and we were just deciding on a new name,' she said.

'Wow! You'll be busy. Doing it all yourselves?'

Rosa and Jenny looked at each other.

'Well, most of it, but I guess we'll need some help with the big things…' Jenny said.

'Like the new sign,' Rosa added. 'That's probably a bit beyond us.'

'I know someone…,' Alex began, then stopped as if embarrassed. 'I mean, if you're looking for a handyman.'

Rosa and Jenny's eyes met again. 'We are,' said Rosa firmly, daring Jenny to contradict her. 'That handyman you mentioned. What was his name again?'

'It's Jack. Jack of All Trades. Literally.' The three women laughed. 'But he's good. He's done a bit of work for me.' Alex's face turned red. 'I'm renovating my place at Peregian. Thought I could manage it all by myself, but…' She grimaced. 'Anyway, I'm happy to recommend him.'

'Can you send us his details?' Rosa asked.

'I have them here.' Alex took out her mobile and read out a number.

'Got it, thanks.' Jenny entered the number into her phone. 'You must come to our opening. We'll make sure you get an invite, and we're hoping to have a piece in the local paper.'

'Great. I look forward to it, and good luck with everything.' Alex smiled again and walked off.

Jenny and Rosa talked for a few more minutes, deciding who would contact the handyman. Then, satisfied with the day's work, they finally parted, promising to meet again at the shop next morning. Rosa sighed. She was feeling more confident about her decision. It was going to work out.

*

'What happened to that consultant you were working with?' Jenny asked. 'He sounded interesting.'

Rosa looked up from the floor where she was attempting to scrub away several years of ingrained dirt. 'Think we should stain this?' she asked.

'Probably. But you're avoiding my question. Maybe time for a break? I'll make us a cuppa.'

The pair had been working steadily in the shop for a few days now and it was beginning to show results. While Rosa went into the tiny kitchen at the rear of the shop to boil the jug for the herbal tea they both enjoyed, she turned over Jenny's question in her head. She'd forgotten mentioning Harry Kennedy to Jenny in a weak moment. She'd wondered a bit about him herself – what had brought him to Noosa and why he'd taken the job with Beachhead Health. He'd given the impression of being accustomed to a more high-powered position. But now she'd left the Health Service, she was unlikely to bump into him again. Rosa poured the hot water into two mugs and carefully carried them back through.

'About your question,' Rosa began, having decided to pre-empt her friend's repeating it. 'I've no idea what Harry Kennedy is up to – completing his project, I expect. No reason why I should know, or ever see him again.' She took a gulp of the lemon and ginger tea to signify that, for her at least, the topic was at an end. Talking about Harry made her feel uncomfortable, as if she had an itch she couldn't reach.

But Jenny wasn't going to let it go so easily. 'When you spoke of him, you sounded…'

'What? How did I sound? Exasperated? Annoyed? Irritated?' Rosa raised her eyebrows. The very thought of him set her on edge. Why couldn't she have left it alone?

'Interested, I'd say.' Jenny tilted her head to one side and grinned wickedly.

'No.' Rosa shook her head, her untethered curls flying wildly. 'Damn, I knew I should have put it into a bun today.'

She put down her mug and grasped her hair, trying ineffectually to tie it in a knot at the back of her neck. 'Since you got back from Oregon, you've been obsessed with trying to put my life in order. What about you? What about that guy you met over there – Mike wasn't it?'

'I messed up.' Jenny's lips tightened. 'That's why I don't want to see you making the same mistake. When things got difficult I ran away – put the Pacific Ocean between us.'

'And now you're regretting it?'

'Don't have time for regrets. Too much to do here. Finished?' Jenny held up her empty mug and collected Rosa's before disappearing into the kitchen, leaving Rosa looking after her in surprise.

She'd been teasing Jenny who had only mentioned her godmother's neighbour briefly, stating that the friendship was over. Maybe there was more to it. Maybe it wasn't over. Maybe... Perhaps she should listen to Jenny's advice. Should she have given Harry a chance? A chance for what? Anyway she was unlikely to meet him again. And she still wasn't convinced he wasn't part of the conspiracy – or part of the cover-up.

*

Harry hoisted the folders under his arm, locked the car and made his way into the redbrick building. He pushed the office door and opened his mouth to greet Rosa, but instead of seeing a familiar head of wiry black hair bent over the computer, he was faced with an empty desk. What the....?

'Can I help you?'

Harry turned quickly, only to see the CEO's dowdy secretary peering at him over her half-moon glasses.

'No... yes... maybe.' Harry was confused. 'I'm looking for the lady who sits here – Rosa Taylor?'

'She's gone.' The woman sniffed. 'You can give those to me.'

She reached out a hand to take the folders Harry was holding.

He tightened his grip. 'Gone? But...'

'Gone. She left last week. Suddenly.' She sniffed again.

'Left?' Harry realised he must sound like an idiot. He hadn't been aware how much he was looking forward to seeing Rosa again. 'Do you know...?' But the woman was already walking away. *Damn!*

He stood indecisively for a moment, then followed her to her desk. 'Can I see Mr Robson?' he asked. Although Harry could see the CEO sitting at his desk through the open door, he thought it imprudent to barge straight in.

'I'll check if he's available.' She had a brief conversation on the phone, then, 'You can go in.'

Pete Robson looked up as Harry entered, removed his glasses and placed them on the desk. 'Harry. What can I do for you? Everything going well?'

'Fine,' Harry wondered if he should take a seat, but since he hadn't been invited to sit, remained standing, awkwardly shifting from one foot to the other. He decided to get straight to the point. 'Rosa Taylor. You asked me to work with her. She's left?'

'Yes, sadly.' Pete replaced his glasses and leant back in his chair. 'We had to let her go. A pity, but you never really know someone, do you? You can deal directly with me now, or our Finance Director, Ken Steele. I don't believe you've met. Brenda,' he called out into the neighbouring office. 'Can you get Ken down here? Take a seat while you're waiting, Harry.'

Harry sat down opposite the CEO, crossed his legs, placed his briefcase on the floor beside him and held the folders on his lap. While they waited, Pete returned to perusing a document on his desk, discouraging further conversation. Harry wondered why Rosa had left. Judging from Pete's comments it hadn't been voluntarily. *What the hell had he got into? Surely she hadn't been behaving corruptly?*

He sat there, his mind going round in circles, till a tall man wearing dark-rimmed spectacles hurried in and took a seat beside him.

'Sorry to take so long, Pete. Is…?'

'Harry Kennedy. The consultant who's migrating our data. I had him working with Rosa till…'

'Yes, sorry state of affairs. Ken Steele.' Ken held out a hand and Harry shook it, perplexed. Whatever was going on, this guy was privy to it.

'Rosa worked for me in finance, before coming over here.' He shook his head. 'I never… Well, least said, soonest mended.'

Harry looked from one man to the other, but nothing more was said.

'So, if I'm busy, you can check with Ken. How far ahead are you?'

Harry cleared his throat and provided an update on his progress, which seemed to please the two men.

'So, no glitches, Good, good.' Pete rose and Ken joined him, leaving Harry no option but to do the same. 'Maybe you can pop in again next week?'

Harry agreed, handed over the folders and left, still puzzling over the uncomfortable feeling that something wasn't quite right. The two men had been too… glib. That was the word. He'd seen enough of that sort of behaviour in Sydney. Over the years he'd developed a nose for it. They were up to something and Rosa Taylor was implicated in some way.

He drove home quickly, then decided he needed some fresh air. After that strange episode in Pete's office, he had a strong desire to wash away the feeling of something dirty going on. As he walked down toward the river, he passed the bookshop he'd noticed a few weeks ago. It had been all closed up, had a tired and abandoned air about it, but today it looked as if there were people inside working. Maybe there were new owners. He made a mental note to check it out later. He loved wandering around bookshops and this one looked interesting.

Eleven

The library was set among a grove of shade-giving trees well back from the main road in a precinct that had once been a family estate, and Rosa always enjoyed visiting it, whether to select books for her mum or herself. It had a peaceful atmosphere, not unlike the one they were trying to create in the bookshop. She was on her weekly visit and lost in her own little world when she heard a familiar voice.

'Hello there!'

Startled, Rosa turned quickly, almost dropping the bundle of books she was carrying. She looked up and met a pair of quizzical blue eyes. Harry Kennedy was standing gazing down at her. 'Oh!' She tightened her grasp on the books, but one managed to fall to the ground.

Harry picked it up and handed it to her, but not before she saw him peruse the cover which featured a gory corpse. He grinned, 'I wouldn't have thought this was to your taste.'

'They're for my mother,' Rosa said, omitting to mention he didn't know her well enough to be aware of her taste in literature and it was none of his business anyway.

'I hear you've left the Health Service. Moved on?'

'Yes. And I need to move on now, too. Mum will be expecting me with this lot. She relies on her reading to pass the time now she's in a nursing home.' Rosa walked across to check out the books, wondering what it was about the man that got under her skin. He'd always been perfectly pleasant to her, but there was something about him – something she couldn't quite put her finger on – that made her want to lash out. It could be his seemingly implicit involvement with Ken and Pete. But, she reminded herself, she hadn't been aware of that the first time they'd met.

All of this was going through her mind as she placed one book after another under the scanner. When all were done, she picked them up again, only to find Harry waiting patiently behind her.

'Sorry, I didn't mean to hold you up,' she said, moving out of the way before realising his hands were empty. 'You didn't find any that appealed to you?' she asked.

'I found a lot that appealed to me,' he said with another grin. 'Do you have time for coffee? I believe there's a café across the way.'

By this time, Harry had followed her outside and was pointing to the café in the Leisure Centre, where she often took the opportunity to take a break at just this time. She hesitated, only for a moment, but it was long enough for this infuriating man to pick the bundle of books out of her hands and stride along the path, leaving her with no alternative but to follow.

'So,' Harry began, when they were both seated on green plastic chairs, the books carefully piled to form a barrier on the metal table between them. 'You've left me to the tender mercies of Robson and his finance guy?'

'Ken?' Rosa looked around wildly, wishing there was some escape, but at that moment, two cappuccinos appeared in front of them. She gulped hers eagerly, to avoid saying the first thing that came into her mind. Then feeling calmer, spoke again. 'You've met the Finance Director then?'

'He joined Robson when I dropped in to see *you*. It seemed a bit odd to me, but I guess you must have passed everything to him before you left.'

Ken, Rosa thought. *So I was right. They were in it together all along, whatever "it" is.* 'I gave you all the documentation I had before I left. I guess Ken and Pete will fill you in on anything else they need.'

Gazing across at Harry, she saw him scratch his head. 'What I don't understand,' he said, 'is why you had to leave. We still have a way to go, and Robson seems determined to keep me away from his IT guys. It's…'

'I really must go.' Rosa finished her drink quickly and stood up.

'Thanks for the coffee.' She gave a nervous smile and hesitated, unsure whether she should shake his hand or make some other friendly gesture. Still undecided, she scooped up her books and walked off.

She still wasn't sure of Harry's role in all this and didn't want to give him an opportunity to ask any more questions. If he *was* involved with these two rogues, she didn't want to provide them with any information about her new project. While if he wasn't, then… Confused, Rosa felt her face redden. *What must Harry think of her? Did she care what he thought?*

Reaching her car, she sat staring through the windscreen at the trees which lined the car park, and decided sadly that she did. For some unfathomable reason, Harry Kennedy's opinion did matter to her.

*

For what seemed to him the umpteenth time, Harry gazed at Rosa's stiff back as she walked briskly away from him. He shook his head in disbelief. *What was it with the woman? Was it just him, or did she behave this way with everyone – or with all men?*

He leaned back and drained his cup, enjoying the ambiance, the twittering of the birds in the distance and even the peeping of the fruit bats. They lived in the surrounding trees, and he'd read they were considered a menace to the neighbourhood. He could understand why. Besides their endless peeping they exuded a distinctly unpleasant odour.

Each time he'd met Rosa, he had the impression she harboured suspicions about him. Could she somehow have heard rumours about the scandal he'd left behind in Sydney? That didn't seem possible. Then there were the oblique comments about her made by Robson and his sidekick. If he wasn't mistaken that pair were up to no good. Could Rosa be implicated in something at the Health Service, something illegal? Was that why she'd left? But that hadn't been his impression of her. If anything, he'd have been prepared to swear she was squeaky clean. Which led him to wonder about the two men and what they might be up to.

As he strolled to his own car, Harry decided to put his suspicions on hold, for the time being at least. He needed this job if he was to establish his consultancy here on the Sunshine Coast. The Health Service was the largest employer and it would look good on his website to list them as a client.

One part of him regretted such a mercenary point of view, while another knew how important a good reference would be to any future clients.

And why was he so concerned about Rosa anyway? He was in the process of being done over by one woman. It made more sense to keep all members of the female sex at arm's length. Having settled that to his own satisfaction, Harry hopped into his Prius and drove home.

Once there his mind started going round in circles. In an attempt to relax, he poured himself a beer and settled at his computer, Tiger at his feet. He stacked the remaining Health Service files on the desk, and got stuck into the sort of task he was familiar with. But today, even his beloved computer was not sufficient to engage him totally. The job itself was pretty routine, the sort of thing he'd done many times before. It was really a simple task, one which could be done by any computer techie with a bit of experience in cloud technology. Something he could do with one hand tied behind his back, something he'd have expected the IT guys in Health to have managed themselves.

He sat back and pushed his fingers through his hair, realising that's what bothered him, had from the beginning. Although he was grateful for the work, he still didn't understand why he'd been employed. Pete's explanation that his own IT staff were too busy didn't wash. He'd heard the place was short of cash, so why employ an outside consultant? And Harry didn't come cheap. He stood up and wandered out onto the deck, Tiger following loyally at his heels.

'What d'you think, mate?' he asked the dog. 'Something rotten in the state of Denmark, or in this case the Health Service?'

Tiger barked and tried to jump up.

'How about a walk? Heard there's a good dog beach. Maybe we should try it out?'

Tiger seemed to understand and bounded inside with Harry, his feet scrabbling on the tiled floor in his excitement.

Harry laughed at his antics, thinking how Hillie would have hated the dog. He smiled. At least she was almost out of his hair. Hopefully the divorce would go through soon and he'd be completely shot of her – a free man again, though free for what, he wasn't sure.

Once in the car, with Tiger firmly secured behind him, Harry avoided the closest beach, instead driving down the coast road. Opening the sunroof to enjoy the wind in his hair, he marvelled at the beauty of this part of the world. How lucky he was to have landed here – to have chosen here, he corrected himself. As the car coasted a rise in the road, a magnificent panorama of beach and ocean appeared on his left, the white crested waves begging him to stop for a swim or surf. But he managed to ignore them, continuing till he reached the beach he'd heard someone mention.

Here it was – Peregian Beach. He turned left at the roundabout, drove past what looked like a village green on the right with several little boutiques and cafes on the left, and found a parking spot at the foot of the road, opposite a few more shops and cafes.

'Here we are, boy.' Man and dog hopped out of the car and made their way over a sand-covered path to the beach. Reaching the top of the dunes, Harry unleashed Tiger, who immediately made a beeline for the edge of the water while Harry gazed around him with delight at what seemed like miles of pristine sand stretching in both directions. Raising his eyes, Harry focussed on the blue, turquoise and green layers of colour extending out towards the horizon. The beach was practically deserted. The only other people he could see were a couple in the distance with two dogs cavorting around them.

Whistling to Tiger, who bounded back at his master's signal, Harry joined the dog down on the hard sand by the edge of the ocean and started to walk along, keeping a wide distance between himself and the two figures. In his present frame of mind, the only company he wanted was his pet. He was in no mood for conversation.

The long walk along the beach helped clear Harry's head. Out here, with only Tiger for company, it was easy to dismiss the worries fogging his brain and concentrate instead on the pleasure of living in this glorious part of the world.

The stuff for the Health Service was only a job, after all. There would be others, once he began marketing himself. That was something he still needed to do. He'd start today, put his work aside and build the website he'd intended before becoming side-tracked by his current project. Maybe even try to set up an interview with the local paper. He'd noticed it often seemed to feature local businesses. Once more work started to come in, he could put this one to bed without another thought.

By the time he'd reached this decision, he and Tiger were on their way back, the dog energetically fetching the stick Harry threw into the ocean, much to the animal's enjoyment. He was so engrossed both in the task and his thoughts that it was a surprise to hear his name being called. He stopped in his tracks and looked up.

'Thought it was you, mate.'

As a shadow fell over him Harry recognised Jack, the handyman. Harry wasn't sure whether to grin or grimace. The guy seemed to have the habit of appearing in Harry's life when least expected. This time he was accompanied by a woman whose long auburn hair was blowing over her face. As she raised a hand to push it aside, Harry smiled and said hello.

'This is Alex,' Jack said, 'and these two area Tess and Steed.' He pointed to a spaniel and German shepherd sniffing around Tiger.

'Here,' called the woman, slipping a lead onto each dog, while Harry did the same with Tiger. 'No sense asking for trouble, though they're both pretty friendly.' When she'd finished restraining the dogs, she looked up.

'Harry,' he said by way of introduction, realising this was the couple he'd been at pains to ignore earlier. Then he gave her a closer look. She looked familiar. 'Have we met?'

'I don't think so.'

'Alex is doing some work at the Health Service,' Jack said. 'Maybe you've seen each other there?'

'You work there?' Alex asked.

Harry shifted uncomfortably, his feet sinking into the soft sand. 'On a consultancy basis. I'm working on some data – IT stuff.'

'Oh, so you're...'

Harry was puzzled, sure they'd never actually met. 'Maybe we've passed in a corridor or something. I don't think we've ever spoken. But sounds as if you know who I am.'

'I know Rosa Taylor.'

'Oh.' Harry wasn't quite sure what she meant by that, so remained silent, waiting for further clarification. But none was forthcoming.

'Alex is an executive coach,' Jack said. 'She's employed to help the bosses get rid of the staff they don't want.'

'Not exactly.' Alex reddened. 'But sometimes it seems like that.' She shrugged. 'So how do you two know each other?'

'Did some work for him. This is the dude I told you about – the one who fell off his ladder.'

'Mmm.'

The conversation stalled.

'Better be getting back,' Harry said, giving Tiger's lead a tug. 'Good to meet you.' He headed up the dunes towards the car park, Tiger following contentedly. The fresh air had had the intended effect on Harry. His mind was clear again and he was ready to get back to work.

*

'So that's Harry Kennedy,' Alex said. 'Good looking guy. I wonder…'

'What? He's okay. Got to know him a bit. Has had it tough, but seems to be making the best of it. Starting afresh.'

'I'm not sure.' Alex wrinkled her brow. 'There seems to be something going on and he could be involved in it.'

'What sort of something – something illegal? I can't believe that of him. Seems straight as a die to me. The guy's just a consultant like you are. Who's this Rosa?'

'Someone I met there. She's left now, thrown out. One of the women I told you about who are opening the bookshop.'

'Oh them? I'm stopping by tomorrow to see what they want done. I think the one I spoke with was called Jenny.'

'That's the other one. She used to work at the Health Service too. One of the lucky ones who got out early. Rosa's position looked secure, but some personal junk got in the way and then she came across some weird stuff, decided to leave and was chucked out before she could say "boo".'

'Maybe you should give it a miss too, if you're right about what's happening.' Jack grabbed Alex's hand and swung it. 'They're not the only employer in town.'

'But they're a big one.' Alex laughed. 'No. It doesn't really affect me. I rarely have to deal with the senior bods, not like Rosa did. And not like your friend, Harry. But you're right. I need to keep looking for other clients. This contract won't last forever.' She tightened her hand in his and they walked slowly back to the pathway up from the beach.

Twelve

Harry was in a quandary. He read the solicitor's letter again, but no matter how often he went over it, the message was the same. Hillie wanted to take him for as much as possible. As he'd suspected, she wasn't going to be satisfied with an equal split of assets. Damn! She'd already got what she wanted.

After some judicious snooping on the internet, he'd managed to piece together the details of Bernie's split from his wife. It wasn't pretty. He'd screwed her stupid, clearly hidden most of the company's assets from the court, along with his own adultery, and come out looking sweet. He and Hillie had kept their relationship under wraps till it was all over – unlike his own catastrophe. Now they were being hailed as two innocents who'd come together to comfort each other.

What a whitewash! But he wasn't sure what he could do about it.

He dragged one hand through his already tousled hair and reached down to stroke Tiger with the other. Maybe he needed a good solicitor too, one who could see through all the balderdash the pair were presenting to the world, to Sydney anyway. Maybe he needed to come clean, to abandon his gentlemanly stand and speak out. But who'd believe him? That was the trouble with lying – or allowing a lie to stand. It was going to be difficult to refute now. It could look as if he was simply trying to evade paying out.

He was still puzzling out what to do, when his mobile rang. He automatically checked the screen before answering. Lucy? What the hell! He hadn't heard from his daughter since well before he left Sydney, not since the shit hit the fan to be exact.

At university down in Melbourne, Lucy had heard her mother's side of the story, which concurred with the trash being touted in the media. It had been all too easy for Hillie to pick up on that and pretend to be the injured party with all the sympathy it engendered. It had been too hard to contradict it and easier to leave town, even if it meant his special relationship with Lucy went by the board too.

If he'd thought about it at all, it had been that he'd set the record straight one day, but hadn't been clear as to when that day might be.

He couldn't imagine why Lucy was calling him now. Frowning, he put the phone to his ear.

'Dad?'

'Lucy!' Harry couldn't disguise his pleasure at the sound of his daughter's voice. 'How're things?'

Lucy ignored his question and went straight into a long spiel. 'I'm back in Sydney, Dad, and...' Harry heard a sob in her voice. 'It's Mum. Did you know? Her and Bernie? It's horrible. She's preparing to sell the house and move in with him. Into that showy apartment on the harbour. Looks as if it's been going on for ages. They're being so smug about it. It makes me sick. I can't stand being here with the pair of them. They're all over each other. At their age. It's disgusting!' She stopped to draw breath.

Harry smiled to himself. This was a turn-up for the books. *So Hillie was showing her real self to their daughter, and Lucy didn't like what she saw?* Lucy was speaking again.

'Where are you, Dad? Can I come? I can't stay here, that's for sure. And I've nowhere else to go. Unless I go back to Melbourne, but it's uni break and...'

Without thinking Harry answered, 'Of course you can come here, but it might not be much fun for you. I'll be working. I'm in Noosa.'

'On the Sunshine Coast? Oh, wow! That sounds cool. How do I get there?'

After explaining there was an airport close by and frequent flights from Sydney, Harry hung up. He padded into the kitchen to make coffee and began a conversation with Tiger who wasn't in a position to answer back. 'How about that, Tiger? You'll get to meet my Lucy. Wonder what she'll make of you?' He remembered how, as a young girl, Lucy had begged for a puppy of her own, only to be refused time and time again by her mother who characterised all dogs as too smelly and hairy for her perfect home.

The pleasure of Lucy's imminent arrival – flights permitting she planned to fly up next day – temporarily put the problem with Hillie out of his mind. Checking the pantry and the fridge, he soon realised that the meagre rations of a man on his own, wouldn't meet his daughter's appetite or her taste. Slipping on his sandals, and shutting Tiger in the courtyard, Harry fetched the car and drove to the shopping centre for provisions. He was heading out of the supermarket with a full trolley when a familiar voice stopped him in his tracks.

'Expecting company?' Jack laughed indicating the trolley stacked with grey plastic bags. 'Or planning a party?'

'Hi! My daughter is coming to visit and I realised my paltry food supply won't go anywhere to satisfying her appetite.'

'Daughter?' Jack whistled. 'Hadn't you pegged for the family type. How old is she?'

It was Harry's turn to laugh. 'Old enough to know her own mind. She's just turned twenty. In second year of uni down in Melbourne. Arrived back in Sydney for the break and didn't like what she walked into, so she's coming to visit her old dad.'

'She...? Oh, you mean...?'

Harry remembered how he'd revealed his wife's duplicity to Jack over a few beers and sighed. 'She's arriving tomorrow, hence...' He indicated the trolley and shuffled his feet, eager to get back to the car and home. 'Not sure what I'm going to do with her.' He pushed back a lock of hair which threatened to fall into his eyes.

'Plenty for a young girl to do in Noosa,' Jack replied. 'For a start there's a bookshop opening on Friday night. I've been making the new sign for it, so got an invite. Why don't the pair of you come along with me?'

'Bookshop? Would that be the one on Hamilton Street? Saw some movement there a couple of weeks ago.'

'That's the one. They're planning a champagne do with these canapé things – finger food or some such. Probably be a bit in the paper about it. They want to make a bit of a splash. Everyone welcome.'

'Hmm. I'll have to see what Lucy fancies when she gets here, but she's always loved to read so it may be right up her alley.'

'Do that. Six-thirty on Friday.' Jack moved off, humming under his breath. Harry reflected that the man seemed to have no worries. Jack was always in a positive frame of mind. Harry wondered what his story was. His accent indicated he wasn't from around here, and his conversation pegged him as too well-educated to be satisfied with the menial handyman work he was engaged in. But he appeared content with his lot. Maybe Harry could learn something from him.

*

Harry paced up and down the airport lounge as he waited for Lucy's flight to disembark. He had a couple of near misses as children ran in and out among the seats and bundles of hand luggage lying on the floor. School holidays! He guessed that was one of the downsides of living in a spot others chose as a holiday destination. But gazing out at the clear blue sky and remembering yesterday's long beach walk – the clear air, the splash of the waves, the joy of the pup beside him – he knew he wouldn't trade it for the city.

It would be odd to see Lucy again, up here. He could still picture her angry, tearstained face before she left for Melbourne at the beginning of the year. 'I hope you're satisfied,' she'd yelled at him as, at her mother's urging, she dived into the car that was to take her to the airport. 'It'll all your fault if I fail this semester. How can I possibly concentrate when you and Mum...? How could you do this to me, and with your partner's wife? Gee, Dad. Have some sense. Aren't Mum and I good enough for you? How can I face my friends from school? They *do* read the papers, you know. Thank God I chose Melbourne University. I can't imagine being at Sydney with everyone talking about the scandal.' She shook with anger and disappeared into the car without a proper goodbye.

He left Sydney the next day. Now Lucy was on her way to him, having discovered the truth in all its sordidness. How would...?

Suddenly he was conscious of a figure behind him and a pair of long arms wrapped themselves around his neck.

'Dreaming, Dad?'

'Lucy!' Harry turned and, grasping his daughter's hands, held her at arm's length, stunned by the recognition of this beautiful human being he and Hillie had created together. At least they'd got this right. And there didn't appear to be any of the embarrassment he'd feared. The young were indeed resilient. 'Looking good.'

Lucy tossed her blonde hair, so like his own thick mop, her eyes twinkling. 'You're not so bad yourself. Noosa clearly suits you. Now tell me what you've been up to.' She linked arms with him and they walked over to the baggage collection together. 'I travel light,' she said, without waiting for his response. 'Just my old red Country Road bag.'

In no time they were back in the car and driving up along the coast road.

'Wow, look at this!' Lucy's head twisted from side to side as each turn in the road revealed yet another stretch of unspoiled beach. Along the way, parked cars topped with surfboards, their owners either unloading their boards or standing chatting, nether regions wrapped in towels, or wetsuits hanging from their waists. 'Can't wait to get out there. It's years since…' Her voice broke and they were both silent remembering how the annual family beach holidays had gradually dwindled into the odd weekend down the south coast, weekends which became more and more difficult for everyone as Hillie managed to find fault with Harry most of the time.

'I think she's happy. Mum,' Lucy said, as if reading Harry's mind. 'I mean, she doesn't… She doesn't get angry with Bernie. Not like she did… She's all over him. It's gross.' Lucy grimaced, then turned to face her father. 'How are you really, Dad? You shouldn't have had to leave. It was all her fault – her and that guy who pretended to be your friend. They let you take the blame. I can't believe…'

'It's okay, honey. Your mum's always been good at getting her own way. The papers made a perfectly natural mistake and it was easier to let it stand.'

'Easier for them you mean? Everyone thinks… Even *I* thought you were to blame. I should have known that slimy Bernie had something to do with it. Bloody Uncle Bernie.'

'We were all friends, socialised together a lot. It was an easy mistake to make. The papers picked up on the H Kennedy. The fact your mum and I had the same initial failed to register. But it's over now.' Harry covered Lucy's hand with his. 'I'm glad you worked it out. And you're here now. Let's focus on that and on making this a good holiday for you. There's lots to do here.'

'I know. I checked out Noosa on the way up. I plan on going to the beach every day and take Stand up Paddle Board lessons. They look so cool. And the National Park looks pretty awesome, too. Will you be working all the time or can we do some stuff together?'

'Oh, I think I can allocate some time to you.' Harry smiled at her enthusiasm. 'I've set up a consultancy. Just have one client at the moment and work from home most of the time. But are you sure you want to be seen with your old dad? I wouldn't want to cramp your style.'

Lucy punched Harry gently on the arm. 'You're not bad for an old guy. You can pretend to be my sugar daddy. Do your cred good. Met any nice ladies up here?'

Harry almost choked. This was the last thing he expected to hear from his daughter. 'Give me a break, Lulu. I'm still trying to disentangle myself from your mum. Do you really think I'd rush headlong into another relationship?'

'I wouldn't mind,' Lucy said, surprising him. 'Mum's been pretty horrible to you. You deserve better. And you may be no George Clooney, but you're still pretty okay looking. I'd think there might be someone willing it give you a shot. Hey,' she said, as they approached a roundabout with a sign to Sunshine Beach on the right hand side of the road. 'Can we stop for coffee? The stuff on the plane was yuck and I'm dying for a macchiato, I suppose they do them up here?'

'Sure.' Harry turned the steering wheel just in time and drove in towards the beachside village. He recalled seeing the line of cafes here when he and Tiger took a walk on the beach. 'I saw a few places when Tige and I came down here.'

'Tige?' Lucy twisted right around in her seat, eyes widening. 'Don't tell me...'

'I have a dog!'

'Dad!'

'I know, I know. We never let you have one when you were younger, but...'

'It was Mum who put the kybosh on it, wasn't it? I always suspected that, but you toed the party line and pretended it was a joint decision

– not a good idea in the city, no one home during the day, blah, blah. What sort is he? It is a he, I presume.'

'Yep. A male cocker spaniel. You'll meet him when we get home. He's a friendly little critter. Here we are.' Harry turned into a parking spot. 'Where do you fancy?'

Lucy gazed around and pointed to a café with a multitude of tables and a number of black market-umbrellas providing shade. 'Let's try that one. It looks popular.'

They found an empty table and with Lucy's, 'Macchiato for me – a large one,' ringing in his ears, Harry entered to place his order.

In no time they were served their drinks – Harry opting for a long black – and a couple of slices of some delicious looking strawberry flan.

'Now!' Lucy leant her elbows on the table, propping up her chin with her hands. 'Tell me what you've been up to. Why here? Why not Melbourne, Canberra, even Brisbane? Surely it'd have been easier to have found work if you'd stayed in a city?'

'Maybe,' Harry took a long swig of coffee before continuing, while Lucy impatiently tapped on the table with one hand, cutting off a large corner of her flan with the other.

'Mmm. This is yum,' she said, wiping the crumbs from her lips. 'So, Dad?'

'Well, Lulu. When I packed up the Yarran, I just wanted to get away. I didn't have any clear idea of where I was headed. I stopped off on the New South Wales Central Coast – nice spot – and caught up with an old sailing mate. He put me onto this project with the Health Service up here, and it seemed like a good place to settle. It's far enough away from Sydney – and the Sydney papers and rumour mill – and there are beaches and bushland. It's idyllic. Even you must see that.'

'Idyllic, yes. For a holiday. But to bury yourself here?'

Harry chuckled. 'Listen to yourself. Most city folk only *dream* of retiring to a spot like this. I've been fortunate enough to put down roots here while I'm still young enough to enjoy it.'

Suddenly something Harry had said seemed to strike Lucy. 'The Yarran? You sailed up in her? Is she still here?' She gazed around as if expecting the vessel to suddenly appear.

'Not right here. No. She's at the Noosa Marina.' Harry rubbed his chin. 'I need to decide what to do with her, but I can't do anything till your mum and I settle things. She…'

'She's not trying to get her hands on the catamaran is she? She hated it, and Bernie doesn't sail.'

'Liking or hating something doesn't come into it in a divorce settlement, but it's not your worry. Mum and I will sort it out.' *And I hope to God we do,* he thought, *and soon.* 'How about you? How's uni?'

'Okay.' Lucy picked up her teaspoon and started to draw circles in some spilt sugar on the table. 'But, I'm not sure...'

'What's wrong?' All of his own worries disappeared in a flash at the thought that Lucy might be having problems. Always in the top section of her school classes, it had never occurred to him that she might have problems with university studies. 'Are you finding it difficult to keep up?'

'No, it's not that.' Lucy stared down at the cup as if it held the answer to the meaning of life. Then she raised her eyes to meet Harry's. 'I don't think it's for me. All this study, Dad. I've had enough. I want to do something worthwhile. I've been thinking...'

'Well, that makes a change.' Harry tried to inject a touch of humour into the situation, but Lucy wasn't in the mood for levity.

'Seriously, Dad. I want to make a difference. I've been reading about a program in Africa. I can go there, be part of it, help the children. It's a school.' She leant forward, her eyes full of excitement, and proceeded to give Harry a complete run down on the project.

Harry put down his coffee cup and regarded his daughter with new eyes. She'd grown up, this daughter who, until now, he'd still considered a child. Although he was sorry she wanted to drop out of uni – for that was clearly her intention – he was proud she wanted to take this step.

'Well,' he said. 'I can't pretend I won't be sorry if you drop out of your course, but you do know I did a year overseas after my degree, so I can't fault your humane goals.'

'Really?' Lucy beamed. 'I thought you'd go off on me. I know Mum...'

'Have you mentioned this to her?'

'No. Wouldn't dare. She'd really hit the roof, tell me I'd wasted all the money you've spent on me, etcetera, etcetera.'

Harry frowned. He'd been against paying all Lucy's fees up front, saying she should take out a student loan, get a part-time job, but Hillie had argued against that, saying they only had one child and should give her everything they hadn't had themselves.

'Maybe you don't need to drop out completely,' he suggested. 'How about finishing this year, then taking leave. That would give you more options. You could go back if you feel like it afterwards. And it might get Mum onside too.'

'Hmm.'

Harry could see the thoughts flitting behind Lucy's eyes. 'Think about it, honey. You don't need to decide right away. It's a great thing you want to do. But if you finish the year, you'll have a bit more experience behind you. Maybe you can find some voluntary work in Melbourne, which would help prepare you for it?'

'You think I could? That would certainly help.'

Thirteen

'I think that's everything.' Rosa stood, hands on hips, and gazed around the shop, pleased with what she saw. The counter near the door was covered with bottles and glasses, while several small tables had been strategically placed among the shelves. These held platters of nibbles ranging from delicate canapés, cheese and biscuits and morsels of cut fruit to more substantial tiny bagels and wraps for those with larger appetites or who'd come straight from work.

'Let's have a drink before everyone arrives.' Jenny appeared from the rear of the shop brandishing a bottle of champagne and two glasses. 'I think we deserve it after the past weeks. It was a lot of work, but we did it.'

Her eyes met Rosa's with a gleam of pleasure. 'After tonight's grand opening, The Book Nook will be ready for business. Cheers!' She filled two glasses and, handing one to Rosa, raised her own.

'To us,' Rosa said, joining in the toast.

Any further conversation was stymied by a flurry at the door as the first guests arrived, and from then on she and Jenny barely saw each other as they were congratulated on their enterprise by a succession of friends and locals.

It wasn't till well into the evening that Rosa noticed a familiar tall figure at the other end of the room. She blinked. It couldn't be, but it was. Harry Kennedy! What was he doing here and – she looked again – who was that young woman with him? She felt a wrench in her gut, which she immediately stifled, taking another gulp from her glass to calm the unwelcome sensation. At this rate, she'd be drunk before the end of the evening.

Even though she had no inclination in that direction herself, Rosa hadn't pegged him for the type of man to latch onto someone young enough to be his daughter. But, she reminded herself, she barely knew the man. Rosa stiffened her back and turned in the other direction, only to be greeted by Alex, accompanied by the gangly dark-haired fellow who'd made their shop sign.

'Great evening. You've done wonders with this place.' Alex gesticulated with her glass, letting some of the liquid spill over. 'Oops.' She laughed. 'You know Jack, of course. And…' Her eyes searched the room, as if looking for someone.

'I hope you don't mind,' Jack said. 'I invited a mate and…'

'I think you know each other,' Alex began, when another familiar voice spoke from behind Rosa.

'We do.'

Rosa swivelled around to find herself looking up into a pair of amused blue eyes. 'So this is where you got to? When Jack told me about the two women who were opening a bookshop, I didn't make the connection. Nice place.' He gestured to the interior of the shop. 'I'll have to come back when you're open for business.'

'That'll be Monday,' Jenny said, coming up behind Rosa and smiling. 'I don't believe we've met.'

'Harry Kennedy.' His face creased into a smile and he held out his hand to grasp Jenny's. 'So you're the other half of this initiative?'

'It was Jenny's idea. She's recently returned from Florence – Florence, Oregon, that is – and we've based this on a bookshop she saw there. We…' Rosa's voice died away as she realised she was babbling on to hide her sudden embarrassment.

'And this is Lucy.' Harry threw an arm around the shoulder of the young blonde woman who joined them, beaming with what appeared to be pride.

Rosa saw Jenny's raised eyebrows, recognising the message that they should discuss this later. In the meantime, both women smiled their acknowledgement of the introduction before moving off into the crowd.

*

'What gives?'

'I don't know, mate.' Harry rubbed his chin and met Jack's eyes. 'I seem to be *persona non grata* with the lady. Can't think why.'

'Didn't you say you were working together?' Alex asked.

'Sort of. There was something a bit off about it all, then she left suddenly – and now she's here. Do you know anything?'

Alex seemed about to say something, then her lips tightened. 'You'll have to ask Rosa. I'm not at liberty to divulge that sort of thing. I *do* think you should ask her, but tonight's probably not the best time.'

'No.' Harry's arm dropped from Lucy's shoulder as he gazed in the direction Rosa had taken, almost losing sight of her in the crush. He was confused. He hadn't expected to see Rosa here, to find her in partnership in a bookshop when she'd just left...

Maybe there *was* something odd about her leaving? But he couldn't believe the insinuations of those two guys. He mentally reaffirmed his decision to finish the Health Service job as quickly as he could and move on. His new website was bringing in enquiries, and he had a meeting set up with the local paper on Tuesday.

But there *was* something, something he couldn't quite put his finger on. He frowned, trying to remember. It concerned Rosa and... No, it was just out of reach. Maybe if he concentrated hard, he'd...

'So you've made some friends here already, Dad?' Lucy's voice in his ear drew him back to the present.

'What? No. Oh, you mean...?' Harry could see Lucy observing him with the expression she reserved for her aging parents – part amusement, part exasperation. 'Jack helped me with some renovation work on the house, and Alex... I only met her recently with Jack.'

'And that woman? The one who looked at me as if she'd like to stick a knife in my back?'

'Rosa?' Harry's eyes crinkled at the idea of Rosa and Lucy in armed combat. 'We worked together for a bit, then she left and now...'

'She's part owner of this.' Lucy finished for him.

Harry realised it *was* quite a shift and wondered how it had come about. One day Rosa had been collating data to hand over to him, part of the power structure in the Health Service, the next, it seemed, she was here, owning a bookshop and appearing distinctly uncomfortable at seeing him again.

'You should ask her.' Lucy picked up a cracker and balanced a piece of camembert on it before swallowing it in one bite. 'Mmm. These are good. Want one?'

'No.' Harry was beginning to wish they hadn't come. Now that Rosa had left the Health Service, he hadn't expected to see her again so soon. There had been that time at the library, but in what seemed to be her usual fashion she'd rushed off before they could have any real conversation. If he was honest with himself, he'd harboured the hope that in such a small town, they'd bump into each other again sooner or later, but he hadn't expected to meet her tonight, here, like this.

He'd promised himself if he did meet her again, he'd invite her for a drink, or even dinner. Tonight might have provided just such an opportunity, but given her reaction he wasn't sure what her response might be.

Harry sighed. Why did life have to be so complicated? When he arrived in Noosa, he'd had no intention of becoming involved with anyone or anything. A new life, one free of any commitment, stretched out ahead of him. Now, here he was, seemingly involved in something weird with the Health Service and wondering how to mend his fences with the mysterious Rosa Taylor.

'Dad?' Harry felt Lucy tugging on his arm. 'You're doing it again. I asked if you wanted one of these.' She held up another biscuit topped with cheese before popping it into her mouth.

'No thanks. I think we've about done here, don't you?'

'What's the matter? You're acting a bit weird. You *did* want to come here, didn't you?'

'Yes, I…' Harry drew a hand through his hair, and gazed around the room, trying without success to identify Rosa's dark curls. He wanted to say something to her before they left, even though in this crowd it would be difficult to say much. He wanted to find out why she'd been so distant, why…

'You're lost in la-la land. I'm going to check out those shelves in the corner. Will you be okay if I leave you for a bit?'

'Sure.' Harry drained his glass and picked up another from the nearby counter. Good job they'd walked here, he thought as he downed it quickly.

'So that's your daughter. Good-looking girl,' Jack said, moving back to Harry's side. 'She looks a bit like you.'

'Only in colouring. Her features are all from her mother's side.'

'Your daughter?' Alex said, joining them. 'Why…' Then she stopped as if struck by a sudden thought. 'So that's…'

Harry was puzzled, but Alex didn't say any more.

*

'Well!' Rosa surveyed the debris as the last guests finally took their leave, many promising to return when the shop was open for business. 'It seemed to go well.'

'I think we can say it was a success,' Jenny replied. 'And Alex and Jack have promised to come around early tomorrow to help with the clean-up.'

'That's good of them. They didn't need to do that.'

'They offered, and it would've been churlish to refuse. And a couple more pairs of hands will help. Let's just leave all this till then.'

'Good idea.' Rosa put down the empty glasses she'd started to collect. 'Gosh, I'm tired.' She yawned. 'We both need a good night's sleep. What time…?'

'I told them not to front up till at least nine. Hey, there's still a bit left in this one.' Jenny held up a half-full bottle of sparkling wine. 'How about we finish it before we go? I don't know about you, but I didn't get much chance to have any once people started arriving.'

'Too busy schmoozing our guests,' Rosa laughed. 'But you're right. Pity all the food has gone. Let's go through to the back.'

Once there, glass filled to the brim, Rosa relaxed into a chair and propped her feet up on the coffee table.

'So that was Harry Kennedy.' Jenny began the conversation Rosa had expected, given her friend's raised eyebrows earlier in the evening. 'A bit of a spunk. You didn't say. And the girl…'

'That was a surprise. But you never can tell. These middle-aged guys. Some of them manage to attract young women like flies. I…' To Rosa's astonishment, she experienced a twist in her gut at the memory of Harry with his arm around the young woman's shoulders. A coil of… surely it wasn't jealousy?

'I thought from what you'd said about him…,' Jenny began as if picking her words carefully, 'that maybe… you and he… in time…'

'Don't be stupid! Harry Kennedy? And me? Not in a month of Sundays. Anyway, I'm not entirely sure he's completely innocent of whatever cover-up Pete and Ken are into. Seeing him with that bimbo just confirms I'd have been mad to think there could be anything…'

'So you did consider him?' Jenny grinned.

'No!'

'Methinks the lady doth protest too much. I've been there, remember. And not too long ago, either. And just because it didn't work out for me, doesn't mean…'

'Sorry. I forgot,' Rosa said, remembering Jenny's account of the man she'd met and left in Oregon. 'We're a right pair, aren't we?' She let her legs drop to the floor. 'Maybe we should call it a night.'

'You're right. Let's close up here and come back in the morning. It'll all look different then. Around eight-thirty?'

'Sounds good.'

But as the two parted, Rosa wondered exactly what her friend had meant. What would all look different in the morning – the bookshop, or the two men, one on the other side of the world in Oregon and the other only a few streets away? One thing was for sure, Harry Kennedy wasn't going to change overnight.

*

When Rosa awoke next morning, there was something niggling at the back of her mind. It wasn't until she was standing under the shower that she identified it as the image of Harry Kennedy smiling down at that young girl with such pride. Damn the man! He was no different from all the rest, swayed by a pretty face and… Just like Ken. No, that wasn't quite fair, since *she'd* been the one who'd swayed Ken, or at least helped him swerve from his marriage. But she'd fixed that and she wasn't about to make the same mistake again. Ever.

She and Jenny were alike in that respect. Though, Rosa considered, as she poured herself a coffee and waited for the bread to pop out of the toaster, she wasn't too sure about Jenny. She had the feeling her friend hadn't been completely honest about her indifference to the person Rosa jokingly referred to as "Oregon Man".

By the time Rosa arrived at the bookshop she was feeling a lot brighter and was able to greet Jenny cheerfully. The place looked a mess in the light of day and Rosa was standing in the middle of the floor wondering where to begin when Jenny spoke.

'I think we need a coffee before we make a start on this.'

'But I've just had one,' Rosa objected, beginning to pick up some glasses. 'You go ahead.'

'Sure?'

'Yep. I'll make a start here. Alex and Jack should arrive soon. We'll be done in no time.'

Alone in the shop, Rosa hummed to herself as she found a box into which she could load the dirty glasses. They'd hired them for the evening and she wasn't sure if they needed to wash them before they were returned. Sighing, she guessed they did and was preparing to fill the tiny sink with hot water when she heard a loud knocking.

But before she could reach the door, it opened and Jenny walked in followed by a laughing Alex and Jack.

'Look who I found at the coffee shop,' Jenny said. 'And I picked up a herbal tea for you, in case you changed your mind.'

Despite her earlier refusal, the hot drink did look attractive and Rosa gratefully accepted the cardboard cup while the others milled around discussing the previous evening.

'So you know Harry Kennedy too?' Jenny asked Jack to Rosa's embarrassment.

'Good guy. His daughter's a lot like him.'

His...? Rosa gazed down into her tea to hide her awkwardness. She'd been too quick to jump to conclusions. But who'd have thought he'd have a daughter – and one who looked so...? Rosa realised she knew nothing about the man or how he had landed up here in Noosa. Everyone had a story, and he hadn't shared his with her. *Nor did you share yours with him,* she reminded herself. They hadn't ever touched on personal matters.

'That was his daughter?' Jenny spoke for her. 'I – we – thought...'

'I did too, for a few moments,' Alex said, smiling. 'Then Jack enlightened me. She did look a bit young for anything else, but...'

'One never knows,' Jenny said.

Rosa was conscious of her friend glancing in her direction.

'So, let's get to it.' Jack crushed his takeaway cup. 'Looks like you've already made a good start.'

'I began on the glasses,' Rosa said, finishing her own drink. 'I'm happy to keep washing.'

'Right.' Jack took charge and soon all four were engaged in the clean-up, Jack whistling as he worked, while the others chatted from time to time.

It seemed no time before the shop was looking spotless with only the boxes of glasses sitting in the middle of the floor waiting to be returned.

'Thanks, guys. It would've taken us all day on our own,' Jenny said, Rosa nodding her agreement. 'How about we shout you lunch as a thank-you?'

Rosa saw Jack and Alex exchange glances. 'Or do you have other plans?' she asked.

'Sort of,' Alex said. 'Jack's been helping me renovate and we've almost done, so...'

'I said I'd have it completed today and invited her to a special dinner at my place afterwards,' Jack finished for her.

Alex turned a pretty shade of red. 'Sorry.'

'Another time then? We'll be in touch,' Rosa said.

'So,' Jenny began when the door had closed behind the pair. 'His daughter? Hmm.' She grinned.

'Don't!' Rosa lifted her hand to partially cover her face. 'What must he think of me? I was unbearably rude. I practically snubbed the man.'

'No practically about it. You did. But you've changed your tune. Last night there was no way you'd be interested in him.'

'I didn't say I was interested in him. Only that I regret my behaviour. It was uncalled for. He was our guest.'

'You might have thought of that last night,' Jenny said, then appeared to relent and put her hand on Rosa's shoulder. 'Don't worry. It was a natural mistake to make. I'm only curious as to why you jumped to that conclusion, though I wasn't far behind you. Probably says something about our experiences with men. You'd think at our age we'd have learnt some sense.'

'Hell, if he thought I was odd before this, he'll be sure of it now. Every time I've met him, I seem to have dashed off for one reason or another. Anyway, I still haven't worked out his role in this health fiasco, so it's best I keep out of his way.'

'Mmm. Maybe. On the other hand…,' Jenny paused, 'if he *is* involved you might be able to suss out what's really going on. If you want to, that is.'

Rosa pursed her lips while she considered this option. *Did she want to uncover the truth about Pete and Ken's odd behaviour and what was behind it, or did she want to put it all behind her and concentrate on her new life?*

Fourteen

Lucy's university break passed too swiftly for Harry, and soon they were back at the airport, this time saying goodbye.

'I promise to buckle down, Dad,' Lucy murmured as they hugged. 'And I'll do what you suggested. I'm sure I can find some worthy volunteer work right there in town.'

Suspecting her comments were offered tongue-in-cheek to placate him, Harry hid a smile and agreed. 'It'll be the end of the year before you know it and we can tackle Mum together.' He grimaced inwardly as he spoke, hoping against hope the divorce would be settled by then and Hillie and he might even be on speaking terms again – for Lucy's sake at least.

The announcement to board the plane came before either could say any more, and with another quick hug, a smile and a wave Lucy walked through the departure gate. Harry stood watching as the plane taxied down the runway and lifted off. He watched till it became a speck in the sky, before returning to his car and driving home.

Once there, he sat down at his computer. His new website was now functional and he'd managed to set up an interview with the local paper which, fortuitously, was planning a section on new local businesses. That had gone to press the previous week and when he opened his emails, he found several enquiries and requests for quotes. The jobs looked to be smaller than the one he was currently engaged in, but that was no bad thing. It meant he would be in and out of the organisations before he knew it, and before he could become part of their problems.

That was it, he realised. He had the strangest feeling that, somehow, without any intention or action on his part, he'd become party to… what? He stood up and headed to the kitchen, Tiger padding along in his wake, as he tried to work out exactly how he'd arrived at this conclusion.

He made coffee and was on his way back to the office when it occurred to him. It was those two guys – Pete Robson and the other one, the finance guy. What was his name? Ken Steele. That was it. There had been something going on at that meeting. He'd been distracted by learning about Rosa's departure, and had failed notice the subtext, but it had been there. It was only now he identified it. *What was it about? What were they afraid of? And where did Rosa come in? Was she involved, or had she discovered something, something illegal?*

He shook his head. Rosa's behaviour at the opening of the bookshop had been distinctly odd, even odder than usual. It was as if… as if he'd done something to offend her. She'd never been really friendly, but he'd thought there was some potential there to become closer, to become friends – maybe even more than friends.

Harry turned back to his computer, but couldn't settle. He replayed Rosa's reaction in his mind. *What was wrong with the woman?* He sighed and drained his coffee. He got up, took the cup back to the kitchen and was about to refill it, when it occurred to him. The bookshop. It would be open for business now. He'd pay it a visit. It would be interesting to see how the two women were doing, and to meet Rosa again.

Telling Tiger to stay and mind the house, while reminding himself that talking to a dog in this way was a sure sign he was either going slowly mad, or missing Lucy's company, he locked the house and set off. It was only a five minute walk to the river and the side street where The Book Nook was located. Harry admired the window display before walking in through the open door.

He looked around. The shop seemed much larger than it had on his previous visit, when a jostling crowd of well-wishers had thronged the aisles and filled the space with their chattering. Now it had more of the feel of a library with shelves of books stretching higgledy-piggledy towards the back corner, soft chairs and bean bags seemingly tossed haphazardly in odd spots. At first, the only people Harry could see were a pair of young girls whispering and giggling over a book in one corner and an older couple seriously examining a display of books by local authors. Then a figure whirled out from the rear of the shop.

'Can I help you? Oh!' Rosa stopped short and, for a moment, Harry had the impression she was going to spin on one foot and retreat to where she'd come from. He saw her take a deep breath. 'It's you,' she said.

'I thought I'd come to see how you were getting on. And I wanted to check if you had Tony Cavanagh's books. I believe he's set some of them locally.' This last request had come to him like a bolt out of the blue. *Inspired*, he thought, remembering a recent article he'd read about the author.

'We certainly do. The first one, *Promise*, is set around Noosa. I can show you where to find it.'

Feeling foolish, Harry followed Rosa to the shelf which was clearly labelled as *Crime* and took the book she offered him.

'Let me know if I can help you with anything else,' she said, before withdrawing to help the couple who had finally decided to make a purchase.

Harry turned to the back of the book and began to read the blurb while keeping one eye on Rosa's actions at the counter. When he saw her customers leave, he moved towards her. 'I'll take it,' he said.

As Rosa processed his transaction, he saw her bite her lip. She raised her eyes to meet his. 'I think I owe you an apology,' she said in a small voice. 'I think..., no, I know I was a bit rude to you at the opening. I...'

Harry fished in his pocket for some notes and dropped them on the counter before replying, 'Not at all. I guess it was a stressful evening for you. A big night. But it seemed to go well. The place looks good now.' He gazed around. 'It's pretty impressive what you two have done. In a short time too, it seems.'

'Yes, we're happy with it.' She seemed about to say more, but merely handed Harry his change along with the book in a paper bag emblazoned with the name of the shop.

'Thanks. I don't suppose...' Harry hesitated, wondering if he should risk being rebuffed again. 'Would you like to come for a drink sometime? I mean, now that we're no longer working together, maybe...' Hell, he was making a dog's breakfast of this. Come to think of it, where had that expression come from? His dog's breakfast was far from a mess – a neat bowl of dry food suited Tiger very well. He munched it up and looked for more.

Harry tried his best to smile encouragingly as Rosa seemed to be considering his invitation.

'Well…,' she began.

'Maybe sunset drinks at the Boathouse? No strings,' he said, holding his hands up, palms outstretched. He saw Rosa's lips twitch into a smile, almost as if against her will.

'Okay. That sounds nice. I haven't been there for ages.'

Harry relaxed. He hadn't been aware of holding his breath while he waited for her response, but noted a sense of something like relief in her voice. Could it really be relief? And if so, why? *What was she afraid of? Surely she couldn't be afraid of him?*

'Friday? I can pick you up…'

'No.' Rosa shook her head, her dark curls flying in all directions, making her look like the kewpie doll Lucy had as a child. 'I can walk there. I'll meet you at the entrance. What time?'

'Well, if we're to make sunset, we should get there around five, and I notice it gets pretty busy up top. How about quarter to?'

'Done. Now, was there anything else?'

Surprised by Rosa's swift return to a business-like tone, Harry shook his head and, picking up his package, left, still uncertain of why she'd accepted, though pleased she had. He had a twofold purpose for the invite. On the one hand, he wanted to get to know Rosa better. She intrigued him. On the other, it would give him an opportunity to find out more about those two fellows. Not that he intended to interrogate Rosa, just ask a few well-placed questions and watch her face closely as she answered. Over the years, he'd developed quite a sense for judging people's honesty. He'd soon be able to tell if her answers were truthful or if she was spinning him a line.

*

Damn! Now what had she done? Rosa placed both hands on the counter and gave a deep sigh. She'd just agreed to have drinks with Harry

Kennedy, the man who could well be in league with Pete and Ken, be part of the conspiracy, whatever it might be. How dumb was that? But he'd been so... so friendly. That was it. He acted friendly. Always had, she realised. She'd been the one to hold suspicions, to be defensive – right from the start.

Though, at that time, she'd been suspicious of every man. That's what Ken had done to her. And Harry's invite... drinks at the Boathouse... one of her favourite spots in the old days, before Ken took over her life.

But back then, she'd gone on her own. Sat there enjoying the sunset with her lonely glass of wine, watching the golden orb of the sun drop down over the river to the horizon, and wishing for a loving companion.

Maybe that's why she'd agreed. Though Harry wouldn't be the loving companion she'd yearned for. He'd be...? He'd be another human being, a friendly acquaintance, that's all.

'What are you daydreaming about?' Jenny's arrival shook Rosa out of her reverie.

'Guess who was just here?' Rosa asked, before immediately answering her own question. 'Harry Kennedy!'

Jenny raised her eyebrows. 'And?'

'He invited me for sunset drinks on Friday.'

'You're going, of course?' Jenny couldn't hide her delight.

'I said "yes", but...'

'But nothing. You get asked out by a hunk of a guy and you want to second-guess his intentions?'

'How did you know?'

'I know you. That bastard, Ken, tried to ruin you for all men. Don't let him succeed. You won't, will you?'

'No, but... what if... what if he's part of it... part of all the stuff at the Health Service. I thought I'd left all that behind me. Him too,' she added, not sure whether she meant Harry or Ken – or even Pete.

'Maybe you should look on this as an opportunity.'

'To do what? Start again? You must be kidding. I've just got one man out of my hair. I don't...'

'No, not that, though that might not be such a bad idea, either. The best way to forget one man is to find another.'

'Huh, look who's talking.'

'But that's not what I meant,' said Jenny, ignoring Rosa's barbed comment. 'No, it might be an opportunity to find out a bit more about what's going on there. Find out if he *is* involved, what he knows or suspects. He could be a mine of information.'

Rosa's eyes gleamed. 'Hey, you could be right. But do I really want to know?'

Rosa tried to put Harry's visit and the proposed date out of her mind as the shop filled and she became busy serving customers. It wasn't till she was back home that evening, sitting on her balcony with her usual glass of red wine, that the full import of what Jenny had suggested hit home.

Could she do it? Could she pretend to be charming and friendly while trying to extract as much information as she could from Harry? What if...? But she was tired of "what ifs". She gulped down the remaining drops of wine and took her glass inside. As she rinsed it out and set it upside down on the draining board, Rosa felt a tinge of excitement. This date with Harry could prove interesting.

Fifteen

The doorbell rang just as Rosa was stepping out of the shower. Drat! She checked the bedside clock. Who could it be at this time of night? It had been a busy day and she'd promised herself an early night with a good book. Jenn J McLeod's latest release was sitting on her bedside table along with a glass of Merlot. She really must cut down on the wine, but not just yet. Dragging on her white, knee-length towelling robe she pressed the intercom.

'Rosa. It's me. Can I come up?' Ken's familiar voice echoed from the speaker, leaving Rosa lost for words. She automatically drew the neckline of her robe closer, remembering all those other times – times when she'd been filled with excitement at the sound of that same voice, agonised when its owner didn't appear at her door. Now her feeling was one of revulsion and surprise tinged with a question. *What the hell did he want?*

Rosa hadn't seen or heard from either Ken or Pete since that awful scene in the CEO's office, when she'd been given her marching orders. She hadn't expected to see or hear from either of them again. That part of her life was over. Finished.

'Rosa? Are you there?'

The words, loud in her ear, made her realise she hadn't responded, and the line was still open.

'What do you want? It's late.' Nine o'clock wasn't really late for Rosa as Ken would be well aware. He'd often dropped in at this time after one of his meetings, no doubt pretending to his long-suffering

102

wife that the meeting had gone on till much later. She heard him chuckle, the formerly welcome sound now unnerving.

'I want to talk to you. Will you open the blasted door?'

Ken's voice was becoming louder. Was he drunk? Surely that could be the only explanation for his behaviour. Disinclined to let him in, but conscious of the risk of his causing a disturbance to the neighbours, Rosa reluctantly pressed the button to release the outside door. Before she had time to consider her state of undress or to change into something less revealing, there was a knock on the apartment door.

Rosa looked around wildly, but her living area was tidy, almost too tidy. It looked unlived in. Since opening the bookshop, she'd spent as much time there and at Jenny's as she had here, often coming home late to a hot shower and to fall into bed – as she'd planned to tonight. Hitching her robe even closer to her neck and tightening the belt, Rosa opened the door.

'Well?' Rosa wrapped her arms around her body and stood just inside the door, hoping whatever Ken wanted wouldn't take long.

She felt at a distinct disadvantage standing there half-dressed while Ken was in his usual immaculate business attire. Clearly he'd come directly from work or some other business meeting. Where did his wife imagine he was tonight?

Rosa thought longingly of her comfy bed, the glass of wine and the new book, all waiting for her in the next room. Her eyes must have drifted in that direction because Ken's next words came as a shock.

'I… I miss you. I miss us, Rosa. Can't we…?' He glanced towards the bedroom door, thankfully closed.

Her glare said more than any words she could have mustered.

Ken sighed. 'Can we at least talk, now I'm here? Let's sit down.' He proceeded to cross the room and settled himself on the sofa, patting the spot beside him where Rosa used to sit and cuddle up to him. There would be no cuddling tonight. Instead she took a seat on one of the upright dining chairs to leave him in no doubt of her position.

'Why are you here, Ken? We've said all we have to say to each other. I thought I'd made that clear. And after you and Pete… in his office. Well, I wonder how you dare show your face anywhere near me.'

Rosa's arms were still wrapped around her body and she could feel herself trembling. She wasn't sure why. Ken was no stranger. She wasn't afraid of him. But she didn't want him here. This was her territory and now they were no longer an item, he had no place here.

'Don't be like that, Rosie. You didn't used to be so cold. Why...' He began to smile, the smile that used to make her knees turn to jelly, to make her want to curl up inside him.

Rosa tested her feelings the way she'd use her tongue to test a sore tooth. Nothing! She couldn't resist the surge of delight she experienced to know for sure that Ken no longer had the power to move her. Her only desire now was for him to leave.

'Why are you here?' she repeated, pulling her robe down over her knees and folding her arms more tightly.

'Well,' Ken said, huffing a bit.

Why had she never noticed how arrogant and pretentious he was?

'It's like this.' He paused, as if wondering how to put it. 'Pete's worried.'

'Pete?' Rosa was puzzled. If Ken had come here to rekindle their affair, what had Pete got to do with it? Ken's next words answered her question.

'He wants to be sure you won't say anything... about that matter... the stuff you were asking about.' The words seemed to tumble out. It was unlike Ken's usual measured speech. 'You won't, will you?'

Rosa was too stunned to speak. Her tongue stuck to the roof of her mouth. So this is what Ken's visit was about. She almost burst out laughing. Far from wanting to rekindle their relationship, he was here to... to do what exactly?

'It would be best if you kept quiet about it. You wouldn't want...'

Was he threatening her?

'I think you'd better leave. You've said what you came here to say. Now, you should go.' Rosa stood up and, as gracefully as she could in the circumstances, moved towards the door.

'So, what can I tell Pete?' Ken asked as he stood in the open doorway.

'Tell him whatever you like. But I don't want to see you here ever again. Do you understand?'

Rosa closed the door behind him and stood with her back to it as if to prevent his return. Her whole body was shaking. She felt nothing but disgust for the man she'd once loved to distraction.

Sixteen

Rosa turned the key in the door and walked into The Book Nook, enjoying as always the unique aroma of the bookshop – a mixture of paper, dust and an elusive fragrance that was difficult to identify.

As she booted up the computer and sipped the cappuccino she'd picked up on the way, Rosa wondered if Jenny would make it in this morning. A smile reached her lips as she remembered her friend's surprise the previous evening. The man Jenny had left behind in Oregon – the one Rosa had jokingly called "Oregon man" – had appeared just as they were about to close up and Jenny had left with him.

Despite all of her friend's assertions to the contrary, Jenny had clearly been pleased to see her Mike, and his face had been full of delight at seeing Jenny again. It had been so wonderful to see them together, so in love, that Rosa had felt a tinge of envy which she quickly squashed.

She was setting up a new book display in preparation for an author talk planned for the coming weekend, when her phone pinged. Picking it up, she saw a text from Jenny.

May be late today, but will def be in. J x

Rosa's smile widened as she pictured Jenny in her lakeside home. Things must have gone well with Mike. Rosa hoped so, though she wasn't sure what it might mean for her own future and that of the bookshop. But there was no sense in worrying about that now.

The shop was busy all morning and it wasn't till lunchtime that Jenny walked in, followed by the man who'd appeared in the shop the previous evening.

'This is Mike,' Jenny said, blushing. 'He...'

'I think she knows who I am.'

Rosa saw him squeeze Jenny's hand. 'So this is Oregon Man?'

Jenny blushed again and Rosa saw her try to pull her hand from Mike's grasp as she turned towards him. 'I need to do some things here. Maybe...'

'I'll find something to keep me busy. That river looks like an interesting spot. And maybe that ferry trip you mentioned? When would you like me to pick you up?'

'Around five?' Jenny said. He gave her a quick peck on the cheek and left, the door clanging shut behind him.

'Well!' Rosa laid the books she was holding down on the display table and met Jenny's embarrassed gaze. 'Oregon Man? Hmm. So?'

Jenny glowed and twisted her hands together. 'He... he wants... he said... he asked... Oh, Rosa. He came all this way for me. I never thought... I...'

Rosa laughed to see her super-organised friend lost for words. 'So what happens now?'

'We haven't got that far. He only arrived here yesterday. It's a lot to take in. His life is there. Mine is here. We've just got this going.' She looked around the shop. 'But... maybe... Oh, I don't know, Rosa. It may all come to nothing.'

Rosa didn't believe that for a minute. She'd never seen Jenny so radiant. 'Maybe you can find a compromise, one that would work for both of you?'

'Perhaps... No, we have to work it out if we want to be together. It's still so new to me, I thought when I left Florence that it was all over, but Maddy...' Jenny grinned as she said her godmother's name. 'I think she was determined we make a match of it.'

'And will you...?' Rosa wasn't sure how to phrase the question. Jenny had been a widow for as long as she'd known her. Would she consider marrying again?

Jenny seemed to read her mind. 'We haven't discussed it, but I don't want to marry again. Once was enough and I suspect Mike feels the same. At our age we can settle down without the paperwork. Helen will have a fit at the thought of me having a relationship,' she said, referring to her daughter. 'She'd like to think I'm past all that sort of thing.' She smiled, as if remembering some delightful moments.

Again Rosa felt the twinge she'd noted last night, but this time it was accompanied by the image of Harry Kennedy. His thick blond hair and smiling face rose up behind her eyes with such intensity she had to stifle a gasp.

'Now we just need to get you fixed up!' Jenny laughed.

'No chance of that.' But Rosa was aware of the trace of envy in her voice. She decided to change the subject, 'Have you had lunch?'

'What am I thinking of? We ate before leaving home, but you must be starving. I can hold the fort here while you pop out for something.'

When Rosa returned, Jenny was standing in the middle of the shop looking bemused. 'I'm sorry,' she said. 'I'm not much good today. I still can't believe it. It's all been so...' She waved her hands around as if to express the monumental event that had happened to her. Then she stopped and gazed at Rosa as if suddenly remembering something. 'Isn't it tonight? Your date with the hunky Harry?'

Despite herself, Rosa had to laugh at Jenny's description of Harry Kennedy. Hunky Harry, indeed. But he was a bit of a hunk. No, she didn't intend to think of him that way. She'd jumped into the relationship with Ken and look where that had got her. 'It's tonight I agreed to meet him, yes. But...'

'You can't back out now. And you still want to find out what he knows about all the garbage Pete and Ken are involved in.'

'Mmm.' Rosa realised she hadn't told Jenny about Ken's visit. The previous day had been busy in the shop, then Jenny's Mike had arrived and she'd lost her opportunity. She moistened her suddenly dry lips. 'Ken. He came to see me again – the night before last.'

'He what? Why didn't you say? What did he want?'

'I'm not sure.' Rosa gazed into space, her eyes blurring, remembering the look in his eyes. Had he really wanted to rekindle their affair or...? She shivered at the idea she might have succumbed to his calculated advances. 'He threatened me,' she stammered at last. 'Lucky I was wise to him. It seems he and Pete are worried I'll say something about those invoices... or maybe there's more. More than I'm aware of.' She dragged a hand through her hair. 'Oh, Jenny. I thought I'd left all of this behind when I resigned. But...'

'I hope you showed him the door.'

'I did.' Rosa laughed nervously. 'He's toast.'

'All the more reason to keep this date with Harry. Maybe he can throw more light on it. Let you know why they're so concerned. It does sound as if they have more to hide.'

'You're right.' Rosa sighed, remembering her vow to use the date to quiz Harry, to find out what he knew and if he was involved in the whole fiasco.

*

At Jenny's prompting Rosa had left the shop early and as she dressed for the evening she spared a fleeting thought for her friend. She was delighted for Jenny's good fortune. No doubt she and Mike would be celebrating their renewed relationship this evening while she... Rosa shook her head to dispel the image of Ken's face as it had been the other night – red with anger, his lips tight with displeasure, his eyes slits of hatred. She shivered. She wouldn't think of it, wouldn't let it upset her.

She selected a smart pair of black pants teamed with a pale pink shirt. Throwing her favourite wrap striped in varied shades of purple around her shoulders to protect her from the evening chill, she checked herself in the full-length mirror. A quick glance satisfied her, although she wondered why she was taking such pains for an evening with Harry Kennedy, a man she wasn't the slightest bit interested in.

Walking along the riverbank, Rosa lifted her face to the sky, enjoying the light breeze on this mild winter evening. Living in a place to which many Australians only ventured for a holiday was one of her enduring pleasures. Although she'd grown up in nearby Tewantin, Rosa never took it for granted and gave thanks every day for her good fortune.

But this was far from her mind as she made her way to the Boathouse. She was trying to work out how to get the information she wanted without arousing Harry's suspicions, when her destination appeared by the river to her right. She blinked. There was Harry, standing at the edge of the deck, waiting for her.

He was looking in the other direction and, for a moment, she admired his broad shoulders, his erect figure, dressed this evening in a pair of pressed jeans teamed with a black leather jacket which set off his faded fair hair. *Hunky Harry*- the phrase came back to her. Her lips twitched. Jenny was right. To Rosa's embarrassment Harry turned at just that instant and, realising it was too late to look away, she smiled a greeting.

*

Harry returned Rosa's smile, thinking how delightful she looked. Having lived with two women for years, he could tell she'd made an effort for this evening. Gone was the tight bun of her office persona and the wild curls of her off-duty days. Tonight her hair had been tamed into soft curls. He recognised the work which both Hillie and Lucy put into achieving such an effect. He wasn't sure what Rosa was wearing as her garments were covered by a bright striped purple wrap of some sort. She looked right in that colour – a bit like a multi-coloured bird.

'Hi there,' he greeted her. 'Shall we go in?'

He held open the door, and followed Rosa up two flights of stairs to the top level where they managed to snare a table on the deck with a perfect view of the horizon. Leaving Rosa to enjoy the vista, Harry went to the bar and ordered two glasses of sparkling wine and a plate of bread and dips. He wasn't sure how the evening would pan out and knew he'd be hungry before long. He'd suggested drinks but had dinner in mind if things went well.

'Here we are.' Harry placed the glasses on the round table and joined Rosa on a high stool facing the water. 'Just in time,' he added.

The pair watched in silence as the sky turned golden, then red as the sun sank below the horizon.

'Cheers.' He held his glass towards Rosa.

'Cheers.' She clinked it with hers. 'Isn't it beautiful? I never tire of sunset over the river.'

'Beautiful,' Harry echoed. But he was looking at his companion rather than the sunset. The dying sun was casting a glow around her hair giving her an ethereal appearance. Enough. But that wasn't why he was here. Fortunately, his thoughts were interrupted by the waitress delivering the plate of dips.

'I thought... maybe you'd be hungry,' Harry said.

'What a nice idea,' Rosa said and there was silence as the pair helped themselves to the food. 'You're still working with the Health Service?' she asked, picking up an olive and popping it into her mouth.

Harry took a sip of wine before replying. 'Yeah, still there. Should have a few more weeks, then I'll be done.' He twirled his glass. 'You left pretty suddenly,' he said, wondering as he did so, whether he'd been too intrusive. 'Was there any particular reason?'

He could see from the way Rosa was twisting her hands together before taking a long drink of wine that he'd touched a sore spot. *What did the woman have to hide? Was she part of the conspiracy he was now sure was going on there? Had she finished her part or got out before the shit hit the fan?*

*

Rosa almost choked at Harry's question. She'd been hesitant to mention her former employers and now he'd put her on the spot. She sipped her wine while considering how to reply. An honest response was out of the question if she wanted to get any information out of him. But, if he was involved with that pair, why the question? Unless... Yes, that could be it. Maybe they'd asked him to find out if she'd spill the beans, reveal the discrepancies she'd discovered – blow the whistle on them. Ken's face, red with rage as she showed him the door, came to mind. Was this another of their ploys? Had Harry been sent to trap her?

She could feel a flash of anger rise and took a deep breath, reminding herself to remain calm.

Harry was looking at her. He was clearly waiting for an answer. She met his puzzled eyes and the perfect response came to her lips. 'My friend, Jenny. She returned from the States and asked me to join her in the bookshop. She used to work in the Health Service too, before she took a redundancy. It was too good an opportunity to miss.' She stopped talking. I'm babbling again, she thought, but Harry's more relaxed expression told her he'd bought it, hook, line and sinker.

'So it wasn't anything...'

'Nothing to do with the Health Service,' she said too quickly, feeling a blush work its way up her neck.

'Another?' Harry held up his empty glass and nodded towards hers. 'Yes, please.'

He headed off to the bar giving Rosa time to collect herself. She picked up a coaster and fanned her face in an attempt to cool down. *Had he believed her? He seemed to. He really did have an honest face and seemed so open. Could he be involved with those scoundrels? But he had appeared out of nowhere and did seem on good terms with Pete, so maybe… She had to try to find out.*

Harry returned and placed Rosa's glass on the table, taking a long draught from the beer he'd bought himself.

'So tell me about this cloud storage. Will it really save money – and jobs?' she asked.

'Yes, and yes. It seems most big companies are heading that way these days. My…' He coughed. 'Before I came up here, I was a partner in a management consultancy in Sydney. We had a large client base and kept everything in the cloud. It's the way of the future. What I don't understand…,' he hesitated, as if wondering if he could trust Rosa, then seemed to make a decision and continued, 'is why they brought me in. Surely the IT guys could have done all this in-house? Unless…' He paused again and met Rosa's eyes, as if seeking confirmation of his unspoken suspicions.

Feigning misunderstanding, Rosa rubbed a finger in a pool of condensation forming on the table under her glass, then moved the glass onto a coaster. 'You mean the IT department would be reduced? Some of them would lose their jobs?'

'That, too. But is there more to it? I met with Robson and this Steele guy – the Finance Director – and something stinks. You worked closely with both of them. I'm not asking you to be disloyal, but what's your honest opinion? I get the distinct feeling they're up to something. Am I wrong?'

Seeing him sitting there, his hair tousled by the slight breeze, his eyes gazing into hers, Rosa felt a tinge of something she had trouble identifying. But one thing she was suddenly sure of: Harry Kennedy was honest. He wasn't part of whatever crooked game those two were playing. She sighed with relief, and leaned forward. 'You may well be right,' she said in a low voice. 'I came across some things, some discrepancies. They didn't want to know. And Ken… he threatened me,' she said, her voice bitter. 'After all…' Her lips tightened. There was no need for Harry to know about her past with Ken, that was her shame, her own secret. Everyone had secrets. She was learning that to her cost. The man sitting opposite her probably had secrets too.

'Mmm.' His eyes softened. 'So you got out? Wise move. Good you had somewhere to go. Be glad to finish with them myself to tell the truth.'

Rosa shuddered. *Had she said too much?* But Harry was speaking again.

'Dinner?'

Rosa looked across at Harry. *Had she heard correctly? She'd assumed the invitation was only for a drink. It had stretched to two drinks and nibbles and now…*

'Dinner?' he repeated. 'We both have to eat and I hear they do a good meal downstairs. If you're not tired of my company,' he said, his eyes crinkling in a way she couldn't help finding attractive.

'No. I mean, yes.'

'Is that a "yes" to dinner?'

'Yes,' Rosa repeated, feeling slightly foolish. *What on earth must he think of her? Probably had her down as a weirdo, but then he wouldn't have asked her to dinner, would he? And he had a daughter. What if he was still married too?* All these thoughts were whirling around in her head as she followed him down the narrow stairs and allowed herself to be ushered to a table facing the river.

'Now,' Harry said when they were settled, had placed their orders and each had a glass of white wine. 'Tell me about yourself. Who is Rosa Taylor when she's not working in health or in her bookshop?' He sat back, a smile on his face.

Rosa winced. She wasn't used to talking about herself, liked to keep her personal life private. But Harry was looking directly at her. She had to say something.

Taking a gulp of wine and swallowing it quickly she moistened her lips. 'Not much to tell. Grew up here on the coast, worked in Health for thirty years, began as a clerk, got my degree in business, moved to finance, then left. Now I'm part owner of a bookshop. That's me in a nutshell.'

'That's your CV. But what about the woman? Never married?'

Rosa hesitated and had to take another drink to calm herself. At this rate she'd be drunk before their meals arrived. 'No,' she said, shortly, then daringly, 'but you are. That was your daughter with you at the opening.'

'Lucy, yes. She's gone back to Melbourne. She's studying there. My… her mother… lives in Sydney. We're divorcing.'

Rosa felt a clamp tighten her gut. She knew it! He *was* married. Another Ken. But as Harry continued to talk, she realised that wasn't quite fair. Harry had left his wife in Sydney. Unlike Ken who was still living with his. And she wasn't considering getting into a relationship with Harry Kennedy, was she? Suddenly Rosa noted his grim expression and realised she'd missed what he was saying.

'I'm sorry, I was daydreaming.'

'That's okay. My story is a pretty boring one. I was just saying how Lucy is thinking of giving up her studies. I was wondering how I can change her mind.'

At that moment they were interrupted by the waiter bringing them their meals – the three-tiered "seafood experience for two" Harry had insisted on. Rosa gasped as what appeared to be a large cake-stand, its three levels filled with a variety of seafood was placed in the centre of the table and a plate appeared in front of each of them.

'Help yourself,' Harry nodded towards the tower of seafood as the waiter returned with a platter of salad.

Rosa did as he instructed, then they both became so engrossed in their meals that little more was said.

'That was delicious. I've never dared to order one myself, though I've seen them served to others.'

'Same here. It was delicious.' Harry leant back and sipped his wine.

'You were talking about your daughter, before…' Rosa waved her hand to encompass the now empty stand and platter. 'Does she live with her mother?'

'That's part of the problem.' Harry dragged a hand through his hair, forcing it to almost stand on end and making Rosa want to smooth it into shape. 'Right now she's not living with either of us. She… her mother… Oh, you don't want to hear about my problems.'

'I don't mind if you don't.' *At least it would take her mind off her own.*

Harry leant his elbows on the table. 'When Hillie and I split, Lucy took her mother's side. No harm in that. But then… she found out the truth of the matter. That's what brought her up here. Now she won't even speak to her mother.'

Rosa's curiosity was aroused. So Harry did have a secret in his past, one he wasn't willing to divulge. Well, at least she could offer a suggestion about his daughter. 'Has she thought of transferring up here? There's a pretty good university in the hinterland. In fact I think Alex Carter – she's currently doing some coaching at the Health Service – worked there at one point.' She paused wondering if she'd said too much.

'Alex Carter? I know her. She and…'

'Oh, that's right. You were with her and Jack at our opening. Well, she can tell you more about the programs than I can, but there may be something to suit your daughter. If living with you is an option.'

Harry seemed to give this suggestion serious consideration before replying slowly, 'Hmm. I'd love to have Lucy with me, but I'm not sure how she'd feel about it. And Hillie would probably go spare,' he added ruefully, stroking his chin. 'I'm not her favourite person at the moment, anyway.'

'I could talk with Alex if you like,' Rosa offered, wondering if this was a wise move. When she'd agreed to this evening's outing, she'd intended it to be a one-off. This suggestion would mean further meetings. *Did she want that? Was she ready for a closer relationship with this man?* She drew back, removing her elbows which had been leaning on the table. *Why couldn't she keep her big mouth shut? She had no business interfering in his affairs.*

But it seemed Harry had no such qualms. 'Would you? I don't really know the woman. Lucy's currently enrolled in a business degree, but she's bored with it. She's interested in doing some overseas volunteer work.' He sighed and dragged a hand through his hair again. 'I don't have a problem with that, but I'd prefer her to get a degree behind her first. Not sure what sort of study would be of most use to her.'

'I'm not sure, either, but I can ask.'

The conversation stalled as Rosa tried to come to terms with the realisation she was pleased to have an excuse to see Harry again. He was good company and now she'd decided he was an innocent party, there was no reason to keep him at arm's length. *Except for the fact he's still married*, a little voice inside her head reminded her. She shook her head to dismiss it.

'Ready to go?'

'Yes.' Rosa picked up her bag and threw her wrap around her shoulders following Harry to the cash register and offering to pay her share of the meal. He waved her away.

'My treat. I *did* invite you.'

When they reached the boardwalk again, the pair stood awkwardly in the semi-darkness, the birds wheeling and cackling above them. Harry laughed. 'This is one of the things I love about Noosa.' He gestured to the squawking cockatoos roosting in the trees above them, the fleet of noisy lorikeets flying overhead and the dark cloud of bats squealing and heading across the river.

'Different from Sydney? Do you miss it?' Rosa asked, tipping her head back to look up at Harry, curious to discover how he was adapting to the relative peace and quiet of the coastal town after the buzz of the big city. Here the native life often proved noisier than the traffic.

'Not at all. It was a good move.' He exhaled loudly. 'What started as a way out has proved to be a godsend for me. When I finish this project, I have a few more lined up. The pace is slower; I'll never be a kingpin in the business community up here, not as I was when…'

For a moment Rosa thought he was going to say more, to explain why he'd left Sydney, but he only sighed and gazed into space.

'I'll be off then. Thanks for the drinks and dinner.' She turned, only to find his hand on her arm.

'I'd like to do this again. Would you…?'

Rosa placed her hand over his and gently disengaged it. 'Give me a call, or drop into the shop. I'll be in touch when I've talked with Alex.'

'Of course.' He let his hand fall, looked as if he was going to add something or move closer, then turned and walked off, his stride lengthening as the distance between them grew.

Rosa made her way home, her mind in a spin. *What had she expected? His hand on her arm had felt so… Had she wanted him to kiss her? Surely not. She'd removed his hand before it could…* She was confused. The evening which she'd intended as a fishing expedition had turned into something more, much more. She felt that, somehow, without either of them intending it, a barrier had been taken down.

From being work associates they'd become... friends? Was that what they were? Was that what she wanted? Or did she want more? Harry Kennedy was still an enigma. She'd learnt a bit about him, but she felt he was still holding back. There was something in his past he didn't want to reveal. Was it something he was ashamed of?

The innate curiosity in Rosa couldn't let it go. She was determined to find out one way or another. If she couldn't winkle it out of him, there must be another way. By the time she reached her door, she was working out the various means by which she could discover the secret in his past, forgetting she had a secret of her own which she was at pains to keep hidden from him.

Seventeen

Harry was humming under his breath as he brewed his morning coffee. Almost tripping over Tiger whose favourite spot was always at his master's feet, he tossed the toast onto a plate and topped it generously with slices of avocado and tomato. Balancing the plate and mug of coffee precariously, Harry slid open the glass door and settled himself on the deck, Tiger flopping down happily beside him.

As he sipped his coffee, Harry's mind roamed over the previous evening. A smile appeared on his lips at the memory of Rosa's sweetness and her confusion as they stood outside the restaurant in the dim evening light. He'd dearly like to have kissed her, almost had, but something had held him back. As if sensing his master's thoughts, Tiger whined and moved closer, his head now resting on Harry's instep, his floppy ears tickling Harry's toes.

'What do you think, mate?' he asked. 'Would she have kissed me back or pulled away?' He sighed, suspecting the latter. But there was something about the woman that intrigued him. With her wild hair and candid comments, Rosa was the complete opposite of Hillie and her friends back in Sydney. But despite that, or maybe because of it, there was something, an elusive quality that made him want to break through the barriers she was erecting between them. No, that wasn't quite accurate. Last night there'd been the beginning of... a chink in her armour. She gave the impression of someone who'd been hurt, and he'd love to know by whom and how.

But he had work to do. Draining his coffee and gently nudging

Tiger out of the way, Harry took his breakfast dishes into the kitchen, rinsed them and set them on the rack to dry. Heading into the room he'd designated as his office, he booted up his laptop and drew a folder of papers towards him.

Harry worked solidly all morning, but when he stopped for lunch, he realised something didn't quite gel. He pushed back a lock of hair which had fallen over his forehead and leant his head on his hand. Something wasn't right. He'd had his feeling before, but hadn't been able to put his finger on it. But there it was, he'd been staring at it for the past ten minutes.

Duplicate entries. His experienced eyes recognised fraud when they saw it. Someone was milking the organisation, and it had been going on for years.

He rubbed his hand across his eyes. Was this what Rosa had uncovered? Was this why she'd left? But why hadn't she said anything? She'd mentioned anomalies. That could mean anything. These weren't anomalies. It was downright crooked accounting.

Then he felt a rush of anger. *Did they think he wouldn't notice? Did they take him for an idiot? Or were they so blasé they thought they could get away with it?*

His burst of rage over, Harry tried to work out what to do. It was clear to him he couldn't continue with what he now regarded as data-laundering without further information, and Rosa might be the key to that. But he didn't want to jeopardise their new friendship by racing off to ask her about it. Neither did he want to face Robson and Steele with his findings, though he knew he'd have to do something.

*

'So, how did it go last night?' Jenny asked.

The shop had kept the two women busy all day and it wasn't till near closing time that Jenny and Rosa had time to chat.

'Good. Surprisingly good.' Rosa didn't meet Jenny's eyes. 'He... he's a nice guy.'

'Not part of the conspiracy, then?'

'No... no, definitely not. I suspect he's too honest to get involved in anything shady like that.'

'Well, you've changed your tune.' Jenny paused from tidying the shelves, a book in hand. 'What gives? Do I detect...'

'No,' Rosa denied quickly, feeling a blush rise up her neck and hating her body for giving her away. 'We had a couple of drinks, watched the sunset, then went downstairs for dinner. We talked. He... he talked about his daughter.'

'So, he's married too, isn't he? Another...'

'Married, yes. Another Ken, no. His wife's in Sydney, they're getting divorced and I'm not becoming involved with him.' Rosa was tempted to stamp her feet and add, 'So there!' But she remembered just in time that she was fifty not five, so refrained, instead raising her head to meet Jenny's unconvinced gaze.

'So, are you seeing him again?'

Rosa shuffled her feet awkwardly. 'Well, yes. I promised to get some information from Alex for him... for his daughter.'

When Jenny looked dubious, Rosa quickly explained the situation, finishing with, 'So I promised to let him know.'

Jenny laughed.

'What?'

'You said you'd have to ask Alex about a course at Beachhead Uni? The man could check it out himself on their website.'

This time Rosa really did blush, the redness and the heat leaving her feeling very uncomfortable. 'Oh, heck. Why didn't I think of that? Why didn't he? Do you think he...'

'You're overthinking this. Seems to me you both want to see each other again, but are too dumb to admit it.'

'Well, he did suggest...'

'And I suppose you fobbed him off?'

'How do you know?' Rosa glared at her friend.

'Because I was there not so long ago. Never mind.' Jenny moved forward to give Rosa a hug.

'How's Mike?' Rosa asked, realising Jenny hadn't mentioned him, nor had he appeared in the shop.

Jenny smiled, her face glowing with a happiness that made Rosa envious. 'Doing a bit of sightseeing and research. I think I told you about his interest in indigenous peoples. He's mainly written about Native Americans, but wants to make use of his time here to contact some people he met at a conference a few years ago.' She shook her head. 'When he gets into all that, he forgets the time. But we're going to dinner with Alex and her Jack tonight.' She hesitated, seemed to consider for a moment, then added, 'Why don't you join us?'

'Oh, I don't think…' Rosa began, envisaging herself as the odd one out, as she'd often been, sitting with two couples.

'Don't be daft.' Jenny seemed to understand her hesitation. 'It's casual, nothing fancy. We're going for pizza at Zachary's in Peregian Beach Village. Alex lives there and…'

'So, Jack and she are really a couple?'

'Seem to be. And you can ask her about that course for what's her name?'

'Lucy,' Rosa said automatically, bemused at how it suddenly seemed both her friends had paired up.

'So, you'll come? We're meeting there at seven. Do you want a ride?'

'What?' Rosa realised her mind had wandered again, visualising not two but three couples enjoying pizzas, herself sitting beside Harry Kennedy, his arm around… 'No, thanks, I'll make my own way and see you there.'

*

By the time Rosa arrived at the restaurant the others were already enjoying large glasses of beer and, as she stood across the road watching them talking and laughing, she was tempted to turn tail and flee home. She was poised on one foot, ready to leave, when Jenny caught sight of her and waved, forcing her to smile and wave back, before crossing the road to join them.

Soon Rosa was welcomed into the group, a glass in her hand and feeling pleased she'd come. While they waited for the pizzas the conversation roamed over the success of the bookshop, Alex's home renovation, and Mike's impression of Noosa. When they discovered that both Jack and Mike hailed from San Francisco, the two men spent a few minutes trying to work out if their paths had ever crossed.

It wasn't till the meal was over and the group was enjoying coffee, that Rosa had the opportunity she was waiting for. She turned to Alex. 'I wondered,' she said. 'Harry Kennedy, the…'

'I know who you mean,' Alex said, apparently puzzled.

'His daughter wants to do something relating to overseas aid. I know you have some connections with Beachhead Uni.' She paused, realising that, as Jenny said, anyone could look this up, but continued regardless. 'Is there anything she could study that would help her?'

'His daughter? The one who was with him at the opening? The one who...?'

'Yes, that one.' Rosa was able to laugh at herself now.

'There is, as a matter of fact. She could study a Bachelor in International Aid and Development. But he could have...'

'Don't we know it,' Jenny said, while Rosa turned red and the two men looked on in surprise.

'Thanks,' said Rosa softly.

'Now there's something *I* need to ask *you*,' Alex said, turning her back toward the others and leaning closer to Rosa. 'It's about the Health Service. I know I've mentioned it before and quite rightly you didn't feel you could talk about it. But now you've left, surely... I mean, I keep hearing things that worry me. Am I imagining it or is there something really bad going on there?'

Rosa sighed and moved awkwardly on her high stool, her legs barely reaching to the bar. She felt uncomfortable, but Alex was right. There *was* something going on, something which at the very least was fraud, but could be much more. And did she owe them any loyalty now? After all, Alex was working for them. She deserved to know if things weren't what they seemed.

Rosa pushed a hand through her already wild curls – she hadn't taken the same care with her hair as on the previous evening. She took a deep breath and began. 'You're right. It's a mess. I'm not sure exactly what's happening, or how big it is. I only know I found some duplicate invoices and neither Ken nor Pete wanted to know. But I'm sure they already did know, that they were behind it. That's why I left.' Rosa stopped, feeling better now that she'd got it out.

Alex's eyes widened. 'Ken and Pete? You mean... the CEO and the Finance Director? Anyone else?'

'I'm not really sure.' Rosa thought back to her conversations with Corporate Services and Capital Works. 'But it's a bit of a boy's club. They all belong to the same golf club and drink together on weekends.

It wouldn't surprise me if all of the senior managers were involved. But even if they're not, they'd back up Pete and Ken without question.'

'Mmm.' Alex bit her lip. 'Most of my communication is via the HR Manager. He's not an easy person to deal with – not a barrel of laughs – but I think he's honest. Do you…?'

'He's always been straight with me,' Rosa replied. 'But then, I would have said that about Ken and Pete a few months back.' She gazed moodily down into her coffee, realising how everything had gone downhill since her split with Ken. Then she gave herself a mental shake. That had nothing to do with it. Whatever those guys were involved in had been going on for some time. Maybe she did need to talk more with Harry. He was still in the firing line, as it were.

'Hello?'

Rosa looked up in surprise. She'd been lost in her thoughts and it seemed Alex had been asking her something.

'Sorry, I was miles away. Did you say something?'

'Isn't Ken the one…?'

'Yes. Seems you never really know anyone. Present company excepted,' she added seeing their three companions chatting and laughing happily together.

'Yeah. I think we're all pretty normal,' Alex agreed.

At that moment Jack called over, 'Are you two finished your confab? We're thinking of calling it a day.'

'Sure,' Alex replied and Rosa quickly finished her coffee and smiled at the others. 'Sorry if we seemed rude. There was something we needed to talk about and…'

'No worries,' Jenny said. 'But it's getting late and turning a bit chilly. We thought it might be time to head for home.'

Rosa realised that there was a bit of a cool breeze blowing up from the ocean across the way and drew her wrap closer around her as she stood up and prepared to leave.

'Thanks for inviting me along,' she said, hugging Jenny and Alex and receiving pecks on the cheek from Mike and Jack.

Driving home, Rosa reflected that she was glad she'd gone. For once, she hadn't felt awkward, but it did give her food for thought. For years she'd been involved in a hole-in-the-corner affair, afraid to be seen with her lover, afraid to leave her phone unattended lest he find a spare moment to spend with her. Seeing Alex and Jenny so happy, so open in their relationships, made her want that for herself. She thought of the famous line from Harry Meets Sally – "I'll have what she's having." She wanted what they had, but had she left it too late? No, Jenny was older than Rosa and she'd managed to find her Mike, even if she'd had to travel all the way to Oregon to do so.

But was there anyone out there for Rosa? She grimaced as she pressed the electronic control and turned into her underground garage. The only man on her horizon was Harry Kennedy and he... She shut down the thought that he'd do very nicely. No. She had enough going on in her life without that complication, thank you very much. But she *had* promised to contact him again with the information regarding his daughter and she *did* want to discuss the Pete and Ken business with him. Damn! It seemed there was no avoiding him.

Eighteen

The shop door opened bringing in a trace of cool air, and Rosa looked up from the pile of new books she was entering into the system. It was him! For the past two days, she'd been trying to put the image of Harry Kennedy out of her head while mindful of her promise to get in touch. Now here he was, standing in front of her, large as life, with that lopsided grin and his windblown hair falling down over his forehead, making her want to run her fingers through it.

'Blast!' she said as she realised she'd doubled up the last title.

'Did I disturb you?'

'No. Sorry, I...' Rosa stammered and blushed. It was as if she'd conjured him up. He'd been at the back of her mind since the pizza night, and Jenny had been encouraging her to contact him. She put both hands flat on the counter and met his eyes. 'How can I help you?'

Harry's grin widened. 'You look busy, but I wondered if you could take some time out for coffee. I seem to recall your mentioning you liked the coffee at Sirocco...' His voice tailed off, clearly conscious of her confusion.

'I don't...' Rosa began only to see Jenny suddenly appear from among the shelves.

'Of course you can,' she said. 'I can cope here and you...'

'Harry, Harry Kennedy.'

'Of course.' Jenny smiled approvingly. 'We've met. At the opening. What do you think?' She waved her arms to encompass the whole shop.

'You've done well.'

Both women smiled.

'If you're sure…,' Rosa said to Jenny, a flutter of excitement replacing her earlier confusion. She'd delayed this meeting for long enough. No wonder the poor man had taken matters into his own hands. 'I'll just fetch my bag.' She disappeared into the back office where she took the opportunity to try taming her hair, refreshed her lipstick and made a face at herself in the mirror, before re-appearing with a smile.

'Ready to go?' asked Harry, reaching out to take her by the elbow, a move which she neatly evaded.

'I'm sorry I haven't been in touch,' Rosa apologised as they walked along, skirting the groups of tourists who seemed intent on blocking their path.

'No worries. You're a busy lady.'

Rosa glanced up to check he wasn't being facetious, but Harry's face was impassive. She swallowed and replied, 'Yes, but I *have* been meaning to contact you.' She moistened her lips as the white lie fell into the silence. Well, she had, she reassured herself, just not yet. 'I do have some information for you and…'

'Here we are.' Harry allowed Rosa to climb the few steps up to the cafe ahead of him and pointed to a table facing the river. 'This suit you?'

Rosa sank into the seat with relief. This was a place she felt comfortable, one where she was known as she often breakfasted here on weekends. She smiled at the waitress who came to take their orders.

'Cappuccino?' Harry raised an eyebrow.

Rosa nodded.

'And a short black for me,' he said.

'Well, then.' Harry leaned back in his chair and observed Rosa with a grin. 'So, you spoke with Alex?'

'Yes, though…' Rosa paused wondering how to suggest there had been no need for all of this, then just blurted it out. 'You could have looked it up yourself.'

Harry's grin widened. 'So I could. But then there'd be no reason for us to be sitting here, would there?'

Rosa dropped her eyes and drew her finger across the edge of the table, not knowing how to reply. Then she looked up to see her companion was now looking distinctly gleeful. 'Well,' she said, 'Alex mentioned a course which might suit your daughter – Lucy. It's a degree in International Aid and Development. She... she should be able to get some credit for what's she's been studying in Melbourne. Have you spoken with her about it?'

'Not yet. It's tricky. I need to choose my moment. Then there's her mother...' He ran his fingers through his hair, then threw his head back. 'But that's not your worry. I'll handle it.'

But his sigh as he spoke told Rosa it wasn't a conversation he was looking forward to. She wondered what his story was. Maybe she'd never find out, but she was curious. *What had brought this obvious high-flier to sleepy old Noosa and why was he content to take those jobs which were clearly way below his capabilities?*

As if reading her mind, his next question floored her. 'And what's your story, Miss Rosa? I wasn't put off by your cleverly sanitised version last time. There's more to you than that. For a start, I can't believe you threw away your career in Health to run a bookshop.'

Rosa felt herself redden, but was saved from an immediate reply by the arrival of their coffees.

She bought herself some time as she carefully lifted Sirocco's signature spoonful of chocolate and deposited it on top of her coffee, marvelling for what must be the thousandth time at such a unique method of serving it. But she couldn't delay forever and when she looked up again, she found Harry's eyes still on her, his own coffee untouched.

'I...,' she began, then her voice cracked. She picked up her spoon again and scooped up some chocolate from the top of her cup only to feel a large hand on hers stilling it.

'Let me help you. I think I know what happened, or I guessed. It was about those invoices, wasn't it?'

Rosa gulped and, freeing her hand from his light grasp, picked up her coffee and took a long swallow. How did he know? Of course, he had the files. He wasn't stupid. 'You found them too?'

'They were only the start, the tip of the iceberg.' Harry drained his cup in one gulp, then set it down. 'They're crooks. At least someone is, and it has to come from the top. Which means Robson and his finance guy – what's his name?'

'Ken,' Rosa almost whispered. 'Ken Steele.'

'That's the one. I can't believe they took me for a mug. Any fool with half a brain could see what they've been up to. No wonder they wanted to keep it away from their IT guys until it was all safely in the cloud. What I can't understand is how *you* got involved. Weren't you safely ensconced in finance? How did they manage to entice you down to the CEO's office to get involved in all this? Yes, please,' Harry nodded to the waitress who had appeared asking if he wanted another coffee.

Rosa put her hand over her cup indicating she didn't. She was stunned by Harry's summing up of the situation and unsure how to respond to his questions.

'I... there were reasons, personal reasons. I had to leave finance, and the job came up. It seemed like a good move at the time. I enjoy working with data. I'm a details person, and...'

'Too much of a details person for them.'

'Yes.' Rosa buried her nose in her cup, hoping he wouldn't ask any more.

'Hmm.'

She could see he was itching to know what her personal reasons were, but was too polite to ask. She heaved a sigh of relief. Then his second coffee arrived and the conversation took a different turn. It was as if Harry had decided he'd interrogated her enough for the moment, though she got the distinct feeling she wasn't completely off the hook.

To Rosa's surprise, she discovered they shared an interest in reading and discovering new Australian authors and they spent the remainder of the time swopping titles of favourite books.

It wasn't till she checked her watch and suggested it might be time for her to get back to the bookshop that Harry returned to the Health situation. 'So you didn't think to report it?' he asked.

'No,' she replied shortly. 'Whistle-blowers get short shrift, despite the legislation. And who would I report it to anyway?' She blanched remembering the threats and bitterness she'd already suffered at the hands of Pete and Ken. 'I'm out of it now. Put it behind me. And you?' she asked, curious as to Harry's reaction.

He rubbed his chin. 'I'm not sure. They shouldn't get away with it. It's public money – taxpayers' money. But...'

'You're working for them too.'

Harry grimaced, drained his cup and rose. 'Let's get you back.'

'You don't need to leave. I can manage…'

'I'm going that way anyway. I'll just settle up. Won't be long.'

Rosa watched Harry thread his way through the café, thinking what a strange conversation they'd had. She rose when he returned and this time, didn't edge away from the touch of his hand on her elbow as they descended the few steps to the street. When he removed his hand, she felt its absence as if a cool breeze had blown over her. Angrily, she dismissed the thought which had no business being there.

As they walked back, Harry talked about his house and his renovations, waxing lyrical about the work Jack had done. So it came as no surprise when, as they both paused outside the bookshop, he thrust a hand through his windblown hair and said, 'I'd love to show it off and introduce you to Tiger – you do like dogs, don't you? How about you come to dinner one night? I'm not much of a cook, but can grill a steak or roast a leg of lamb.'

'Mmm.' Rosa didn't know what to say. He was a nice guy – a bit of a hunk, just as Jenny had said – and he was good company, but did she want to spend another whole evening with him? At his place? Was she ready for that? She caught sight of Jenny through the window and immediately knew what her friend would say. She'd tell Rosa not to be silly. It was a kind invitation. The man probably didn't know many people in Noosa. It would be churlish to refuse and who knew where it might lead? While all this was spinning around in her head, Rosa found herself agreeing and was rewarded by Harry's infections grin.

'Great. How about Friday – around seven? I promise to behave myself.'

Where had that come from? It hadn't occurred to her he wouldn't – or had it? Was that what was at the bottom of her hesitation? Well, too late now.

'You know the address.'

Rosa nodded. She'd been there before, but hadn't ventured beyond the front door when they were still work colleagues. Somehow, their relationship had shifted from colleagues to… friends? As she said goodbye and pushed open the door, she realised the awkwardness she'd felt in Harry's presence had all but disappeared.

Jenny was busy serving a couple of customers, so Rosa slipped past to put her bag in the back office before returning to unpack a case of books which had arrived during her absence. She was still thinking of her conversation with Harry when she heard Jenny farewell her customers and the door close behind them.

'How was it?'

Rosa looked up to see Jenny's expectant face close by. She hesitated, but knew she wasn't going to escape without some sort of explanation. Sighing, she put down the bundle of books she was holding. 'He called them crooks,' she said. 'Said what I found was the tip of the iceberg.' Rosa rubbed her eyes. 'I'm not sure what he's going to do about it.'

Jenny's eyes widened. 'So they really *are* corrupt. Well, I'm glad you left when you did. Imagine. What if you'd become involved in it? I never liked Pete Robson, but didn't imagine he was actually dishonest, only a bully and a bit... She waved her hands around as if she couldn't think of the word. 'And Ken too? You're well out of that.'

'Seems so.' Rosa's voice was bitter. 'But it's all past history, and now I've talked with Harry, I intend to put it out of my mind and concentrate on my future.'

'And how *about* Harry?'

'I didn't really find out much about him, apart from the fact he enjoys reading and has renovated his house.' Rosa suddenly realised that was true. Harry had remained silent about anything more personal. But so did you, she reminded herself.

'And?'

'Does there have to be an "and"?'

Jenny didn't reply, but her face spoke volumes.

'Well, he did invite me to dinner.'

Jenny's eyes lit up.

'To see his renovation... and meet his dog.'

'The modern equivalent of "Come up and see my etchings"?' Jenny laughed, forcing Rosa to join her. 'So when is this happening?'

'Friday.'

'In two days. He doesn't waste any time.'

Rosa's feet shifted uncomfortably. *Was it too soon? Should she have refused? Suggested a later day? Maybe a week hence?* She was so out of practice with current dating etiquette. But he'd been married for years.

Maybe he was out of practice too. Heck, she could go crazy trying to work this out.

'Don't worry.' Jenny seemed to understand Rosa's discomfort. 'When you get to our age, all the rules of engagement go out the window. Do what seems right to you – and him, of course.'

'Mmm.' Rosa wasn't so sure, and it wasn't really a date, was it? Just an invitation to dinner.

'So, a dinner date?' Jenny's words put paid to that thought. 'Wonder if he can cook.'

'He said he can grill a steak or roast a leg of lamb,' Rosa repeated with a smile.

'Can't be all bad then. Hunky *and* a good cook. And a dog, you said. Says a lot about a man. Mike has a dog. Said it was the only thing that kept him sane when his wife was so sick with Alzheimer's. Ben's been a good friend to him – and now to me.' She grinned and gazed into space as if remembering her time in Oregon.

'Where's his dog now?' Rosa seized the opportunity to change the subject.

'He's with Maddy,' she said, referring to her godmother who was also Mike's nearest neighbour. 'She loves Ben too. He'll be waiting for us when...'

'So you *will* be going back?' Rosa had been trying to forget Jenny's possible return to Oregon and what it might mean for their fledgling business.

'I guess. Sometime. But nothing's been decided. And I love our little shop.' Her eyes roved around the shelves filled with books and the table of new releases set out by the door. Rosa could see Jenny's nostrils quiver as she inhaled the scent of the books. 'I adore this, this aroma. It reminds me of Ellen's shop. That's what gave me the idea to set up one of my own.'

'Yes. You said.' Rosa felt her worry evaporate at her friend's words, but it didn't disappear entirely. 'But, if – when – you do go back, how will we manage?'

Jenny moved closer to give Rosa a warm hug. 'You'll manage. Remember that I originally intended to run this by myself. And we can always find an assistant. Might be an idea anyway. Give us a chance to take a day off. Now, I'll let you get back to what you were doing. I need to deal with some paperwork in the back room.'

Rosa, feeling buoyed by this response, picked up another bundle of books and allowed her mind to wander. It didn't wander far. Harry Kennedy was right there in the forefront. She went over their conversation, wondering yet again what his story was. Each time they spoke, she became more aware that this was no common or garden IT guy. He'd run a large company down in Sydney, dealt with huge organisations, been someone to be reckoned with. She wouldn't be surprised if he and his wife had been part of the social scene, featured in the press as they swanned about in their finery. They'd moved in very different circles. Whatever had happened, it was huge, must have been to have him hide himself away up here. How could she ever imagine he'd be interested in her?

She almost dropped the books she was lifting out of the box. What was she thinking? He was a former work colleague, maybe becoming a friend. But interested in her? Did she want that? She stood, her eyes blurring as she pictured him, his thick floppy blond hair, with just a touch of grey at the sides, his deep blue eyes, so blue a person could drown in them, his quirky smile, the way his mouth curled up, his... It seemed she'd taken more note of him than she'd realised. Jenny's insinuations weren't too far from the truth. And, if she was honest with herself, she was looking forward to her "date" with him, looking forward to getting to know him better, to finding out more about him.

She tried to subdue the flicker of anticipation that began to surge at the thought of it. For the first time since she'd shown Ken the door, she admitted she was interested in a man.

Nineteen

Harry took the leg of lamb out of the fridge and looked at it sitting on the kitchen bench. He'd told Rosa he could cook a roast, but he'd never really done it. He'd been around when his mother had cooked one, and later when Hillie had cooked a roast for the family. He had watched the odd episode of Jamie Oliver and MasterChef with Lucy. Surely it couldn't be too difficult?

Looping a newly purchased apron over his head and setting up his iPad on a stand, Harry opened the YouTube video of Jamie making what was called an Italian Roast Leg of Lamb. *Thank God for the Internet!* To be on the safe side, he'd looked at it earlier and set up the kitchen surface to look exactly like the one in Jamie's kitchen.

Before pressing *play*, Harry checked he had all the ingredients ready. Yes, alongside the lamb, there was garlic, rosemary and anchovies. He wasn't sure about those. Not everyone liked their saltiness. Maybe Rosa didn't, and he so wanted to make a good impression. Perhaps he should leave them out. But would that spoil the recipe? Hell, this cooking lark wasn't his forte. But maybe he could learn?

Harry watched the beginning of the video, then hit *pause* while he chopped the garlic, filling the kitchen with its pungent odour. Then he made the requisite cuts in the meat, filling each with garlic, rosemary and the dubious anchovies as Jamie demonstrated. So far so good. This was going to be easier than he'd thought.

He poured himself a glass of wine and began to think about the evening ahead. His invitation to Rosa had been made on the spur of the moment. He'd had a few doubts since then about the wisdom of getting involved with another woman – one who was so clearly vulnerable – while he was still married to Hillie. But now the evening had arrived, Harry discovered he was looking forward to getting to know Rosa better. He pictured her dainty figure and the mop of curly hair which, since she'd left the Health Service, she rarely seemed to tame. She couldn't be more different from Hillie if she tried.

He considered her suggestion regarding Lucy. *Would his daughter agree to coming to live with him here in Noosa? What would she think of Rosa?* But he was getting ahead of himself. He'd had no indication that Rosa was interested in getting to know him better, never mind meeting Lucy as his… what? Friend? Companion? Partner?

Woah! He stopped himself right there. And if Lucy did join him, how would that affect any possible relationship with Rosa? Lucy had had enough of her mum and Bernie billing and cooing. "Gross", she'd called it – at their age. Though, he remembered, she *had* asked about *his* love life, suggesting he still had a lot to offer a woman.

Harry returned his attention to Jamie and pressed *play*. For the remainder of the video, he concentrated on the job at hand, breathing a sigh of relief when he finally slid his masterpiece into the pre-heated oven. Now for the table.

He fossicked around and managed to unearth a couple of tablemats he remembered Lucy buying when they visited the Eumundi Markets. They were a bit bizarre, the flamboyant rock star images being more Lucy's taste than his, but they'd have to do. Once he'd set out the cutlery and plates, he studied the table with a critical eye. A candle, that's what he needed. Lucy had… He stopped in his tracks. Maybe a candle was going overboard. He didn't want Rosa to think… What did he want her to think? He scratched his head. No, he'd leave the candle. The table looked fine as it was.

After a quick shower, Harry slipped into his best jeans and teamed them with a blue chambray shirt. Rolling the sleeves up, he patted down his hair and examined himself in the mirror. Lucy was right, he decided. Not bad for a man in his mid-fifties. His sailing and habit of jogging each morning had ensured his body remained trim, though, he thought, pulling in his slightly flabby stomach, he'd never again have the slim figure he'd been proud of in his early twenties. Who was he kidding? He was a middle-aged man about to have dinner with a woman who interested him. That was all. These days, his conversation was probably more important than his looks, though, heaven knows, that wasn't so scintillating either.

Harry strapped on his watch, noting that it was getting close to seven. Rosa would be here any minute. He looked down to see Tiger running in circles around his feet. Damn! In his flurry to get everything ready, he'd overlooked his faithful companion. 'Sorry, mate,' he said, heading for the dogfood and pouring an extra-large serving into Tiger's bowl to make up for his forgetfulness. He'd just finished when the doorbell rang. Taking a deep breath, Harry walked over to open it.

*

Rosa took a minute to gather her thoughts before ringing the bell. She glanced down at her neat jeans and white Eliot Kennedy top, smiling ruefully at the fact she was wearing a garment with the same name as the man she was about to have dinner with. She pressed her finger on the bell and waited, a twist of excitement in the base of her stomach at the thought of the evening ahead and what it might bring.

Her phone beeped. She drew it out of her pocket quickly, intending to turn it off. When she saw Ken's name, she cursed silently. What did he want now? She opened the message. *Remember – don't talk.* Rosa began to shake. She clutched the phone tightly as if she could squeeze away the message and the threat it contained. She could feel the blood drain from her face as she gazed at the three menacing words, unaware the door had opened.

'Is something wrong?'

Rosa looked up and thrust the phone back into her pocket. 'No – yes.' She was still shaking and her eyes began to fill. *Hell and damnation!* This wasn't how she wanted Harry to see her – this quivering mess.

'You'd better come in. You look as if you've had a shock. You need a drink.' Harry led her in, through the house and out onto the back deck, where she glimpsed a platter of nibbles sitting in the middle of a round glass-topped table, before closing her eyes to prevent the tears that were threatening to fall. 'Wait here. I'll be back in a tick.'

Left alone, Rosa dared to open her eyes again, then felt the soft touch of a little tongue on her ankles. Looking down she saw a small black dog with long ears and soulful eyes trying to lick them. She dropped her hand to stroke his head, the feel of the creature's soft coat beneath her fingers offering comfort. Her mind was darting back and forth. *That message! How dared he! Was she never to be free of Ken and Pete? And what could they do to her, now she was no longer an employee?*

'Here you are.' Harry placed a large glass of red wine into Rosa's hand and settled down beside her, their knees almost touching. 'Now, you've clearly had a shock. Want to tell me about it?'

Rosa hesitated. *Did she want to reveal all, as they say? Should she tell Harry all about Ken, their relationship, her real reason for moving to the job in Pete's office and their subsequent threats? Did she know Harry well enough? What would he think of her? Would he consider her a scarlet woman, or just a misguided fool?* She looked into his reassuring eyes, took a deep breath and began.

'So that's me,' she finished, raising the eyes she had kept lowered as she spoke. She was fearful to meet Harry's lest he change his opinion of her. Though she had no idea what that might be, she had hoped he liked her. More than liked, a small voice prompted her. But instead of the disgust she expected, there was only compassion in the eyes that met Rosa's, as his hands reached out to grasp hers.

'You've been through a lot,' he said. 'I can't imagine...' He shook his head, and tightened his fingers, giving her a warm feeling of wellbeing.

Rosa stifled a tear and tried to smile. He really was a good man. Kind too. This wasn't what she'd expected when she stood outside his door what seemed like hours earlier. She certainly hadn't intended to bare her soul, but now she had, she felt a burden had been lifted.

'Now that you've...,' he said slowly. 'I should share my story. It's not quite as colourful, but you deserve to know why I came up here, left my business, my home, my wife...' He grimaced, his mouth forming a taut line, etching a set of creases around his lips. 'It's a long story, and not a pretty one. I guess I could be seen as the victim, but I regard myself more as the unperceptive fool. It was like this.'

Keeping a firm hold of Rosa's hands and not allowing his eyes wander from hers, he proceeded to tell his story.

'So,' he said finishing, 'there's no fool like an old fool, and my wife and partner played me for one for sure.'

'But surely…,' Rosa began, only to feel a finger press on her mouth, preventing her from saying any more. She couldn't move. She didn't want to move. She felt she could sit like this forever with Harry's strong forefinger pressing against her lips.

'No need to say anything. I know I could have stayed and told the truth, but what would I have gained? A bitter wife and partner – more bitter than she is right now? A work situation which was untenable? And the ridicule of Sydney society? No, better I let it stand and left. So I stocked up my catamaran, the Yarran, headed north and here I am.' Harry removed his finger and Rosa tentatively put hers in its place, feeling the spot he'd touched. She blushed.

'But don't you miss it?' she wondered, forgetting she'd asked him that once before. 'The buzz of the city, big business, the bright lights and glitter? Most people come here to retire or for a holiday.'

'Surprisingly, no.' Harry dragged his hand through his hair. 'I'm finding it restful. I've slowed down. I don't need to make a lot of money anymore. I've been there, done that. I have enough for my needs. I can pick and choose jobs.' He frowned. 'May not have made the wisest choice first up.'

'What are you going to do about that?'

Harry paused, as if wondering what to say, then, 'I haven't quite decided. I'm still completing the job, but it won't take much longer, then…' He stopped mid-sentence and they both sniffed. There was a distinct smell of burning.

They both spoke at once.

'Is that…?'

'The lamb.'

Harry hurried to the kitchen closely followed by Rosa. When he opened the oven, they were greeted by a waft of smoke and the acrid smell of burnt meat. Rosa put her hand over her mouth and began to laugh, the relief at a respite from the intensity of their earlier conversation proving almost too much for her.

'What?'

'Jamie Oliver's Italian Roast Leg of Lamb,' Harry said, ruefully. 'Doesn't look much like the video. Must have left it in too long.' He checked the oven timer. 'No. That's odd.' His eyes moved from the oven to the roast which was now sitting in a charred heap on the kitchen bench.

'I wonder...' Rosa bent to check the oven setting. '400? Did the recipe really call for the oven to be that hot? 200 is more usual for roasting.' Then it dawned on her, and she began to laugh more hysterically. 'I know what's happened. You've set it for Fahrenheit instead of Centigrade. No wonder you've ended up with a burnt offering.'

Harry frowned, then began to see the funny side and joined her laughter. 'Okay, maybe I exaggerated when I said I could cook a roast, but I thought I'd be fine with Jamie's YouTube video to instruct me.'

'You probably would have been if...' Rosa began laughing again. 'Sorry. It's not that funny, but...' She realised Harry had been trying to impress her and began to calm down. 'Guess we won't be having lamb for dinner.'

'I guess not.' Harry glanced around the kitchen as if seeking inspiration, the carefully set table now appearing to mock him. 'How about I order pizza?' he said at last with a sheepish smile.

'Fine by me. Maybe you should let me cook the lamb next time.' As soon as the words were out of her mouth, Rosa realised what they implied. She'd made the assumption there would be a next time, that this wasn't a one-off date. Well, she rationalised, now they'd shared their secrets, they'd moved a step closer and... She couldn't help but recall the closeness of his knees against hers, his hands holding hers and his finger on her lips. Yes, they'd moved quite a step closer.

By the time the pizzas arrived, the atmosphere in the room had become relaxed and Rosa felt like they were old friends. Well, not friends exactly, because she was aware of a blaze of attraction, a flash of chemistry when Harry moved close which he seemed to do rather more often than was necessary. They worked companionably together to clean up the kitchen and reset the table outside on the deck, both agreeing that the formality of the dining area didn't lend itself to pizza.

While Harry answered the door to the delivery boy, Rosa examined a couple of books lying on the coffee table. There was the Tony Cavanaugh Harry had purchased from their shop alongside several library books and a pictorial volume featuring Noosa and the surrounding region.

'Been boning up on the local area?' she asked when he returned balancing two large pizza boxes.

'What? Oh, yes,' he replied, as Rosa held up the volume produced by a popular Noosa writer and photographer. 'It's fascinating and the photographs are amazing. I have some catching up to do if I'm to become familiar with all of the beauty spots. Maybe we can...' He seemed to collect himself. 'But let's eat these before they get cold. Don't want to spoil another meal.'

While they dug into the pizzas and washed them down with more red wine, Harry quizzed Rosa on her favourite tourist attractions, their earlier confidences seemingly forgotten, or at least put aside for the moment.

'Coffee?' he asked, when they finally decided they could eat no more, and Harry had begun to pack up the remaining slices prior to putting them in the fridge.

'Yes, please.' Rosa leaned back, feeling replete and comfortable. The evening certainly hadn't turned out to be what she'd expected. It had been... She considered. It had been fun. She'd found someone she could talk to, someone with whom there was no need for subterfuge, for any sort of false modesty or pretending. Someone with whom she could be herself. For Rosa that was rare, especially where men were concerned. Even – maybe especially – for the six years of her relationship with Ken, she'd often felt she was playing a part, being the sort of woman he wanted her to be.

Coffee over, Rosa rose to leave with regret. She'd developed a new respect for this man who, while willing to show his folly, had a refreshing honesty. At the door she turned to say farewell only to find Harry's face so close to hers she could feel his breath on her cheek. She experienced a familiar flutter of desire as the moment lengthened, then his lips touched hers. For just a second she allowed herself to enjoy the sensation of their firm pressure, inhaled the clean aroma of soap and shave foam, so different from Ken's familiar spicy cologne, before drawing back.

'I... thanks for a lovely evening,' she stammered. 'I meant what I said about cooking a leg of lamb for you.' She saw the expression of surprise in Harry's eyes, and hurriedly added, 'What about next Friday?'

'Same time?'

Rosa nodded, gave a fleeting smile, then turned and pressed the control for her car. She stepped in quickly and started the engine, giving a brief wave to the figure still standing in the doorway outlined by the light from the house, his lovely little dog by his side.

As she drove away she chastised herself for being such a fool. *Why had she drawn back so fast?* It was because of the rush of desire she'd felt at the touch of his lips, a desire so strong it took her breath away. Probing her reaction, Rosa realised it was stronger than the yearning she'd felt for Ken, even in their early years. She needed time to process this. *What if he didn't feel the same way? If it was just a goodbye-thanks-for-the-evening kiss?* She'd already wasted six years of her life on a relationship with no future. She was too old to start that again, and he was still married, regardless of his talk of divorce.

*

Harry scratched his head as he gazed after the departing car. She'd done it again. Dashed off just as… Just as what? Her lips had been soft and yielding. He'd felt – thought – his feelings were reciprocated. Surely he couldn't be so far off the mark? It had been a good evening. They'd got along well, had shared confidences. He thought he'd made some headway, but perhaps not. Rosa had been through the mill. He'd never have guessed about her and that Ken guy. But it explained a lot. There was bad feeling there, not entirely related to Rosa's discovery of the fake invoices.

He could understand if she felt cautious about getting involved in another relationship so soon. But it was only a kiss. Though if she'd been more responsive, hadn't drawn away, Harry would have liked to have taken it further. How much further he wasn't sure, but he'd felt a stirring he hadn't experienced with a woman for some time, for years. It was a long time since he'd felt that way about Hillie.

For the first time he acknowledged that his relationship with her had been on the skids for a long time. They'd only been going through the motions, staying together for Lucy, for appearances. It had only been a matter of time before it ended or blew up after Lucy left home.

Bernie hadn't taken anything Harry valued. The surprise was that it hadn't happened sooner. It was only the fact it had been Bernie, his friend and partner, that had made it so difficult to accept.

'So here we are, Tiger,' Harry said, closing the door at last and bending down to ruffle his pet's ears. 'Well, roll on next Friday.'

Who knew what that might bring? He determined to put all thought of women to the back of his mind till then and concentrate on finishing this damned contract. Tiger gave a sharp yelp as if he understood and trotted off to curl up in his basket in the laundry.

Harry slid shut the door to the deck and turned off the lights before heading to bed. But, despite his resolution and try as he might, he couldn't shift Rosa's face, her trusting grey eyes and the touch of her lips, from his thoughts as his own eyes closed and he drifted into slumber.

Twenty

By next morning, Rosa had gone over the entire evening at Harry's again and again, trying to work out her feelings, her mind reeling from one part of the night to another without resolution. The bottom line was that she lusted after the man and, if that wasn't enough, she actually liked and respected him.

She was dreading going to the shop, knowing Jenny would be eager for details. Rosa wondered how much she could avoid telling, very much aware her friend would quickly see through any attempt to dodge the truth.

She was right. No sooner had the door clanged shut behind her, than Jenny raised her eyebrows.

'Well?'

'It was good.' Rosa managed to avoid Jenny's eyes and pushed past into the back shop to deposit her bag and hang up the jacket she'd needed this sharp morning. She delayed as long as she could, but was aware of Jenny moving around. The shop didn't open for another thirty minutes. This was the time the two friends usually spent setting up for the day and getting caught up on each other's news. Though, since Mike's arrival, Jenny had been pretty close-mouthed about her own life.

When Rosa knew she couldn't delay any longer, she stepped out to be greeted by Jenny's searching scrutiny. She was familiar with that look. It meant her friend wouldn't rest till she had a blow-by-blow account of Rosa's dinner date.

'Well,' Rosa began, 'turns out he can't cook after all. At least not as well as he claimed. We ended up with pizza.'

'But what did you talk about?' Jenny asked. 'I presume you *did* talk?'

'Yes,' Rosa fiddled with her hair, twisting a strand into a tighter curl than usual. 'I... I got a text from Ken,' she blurted out. 'Another threat. Just as I rang Harry's doorbell and... He was very kind.' Rosa saw Harry in her mind's eye, felt his nearness, could almost smell him.

'Did you...?'

'I told him all about Ken, and he... he told me his story.'

'Oh?'

'Not mine to tell.'

'Right.' But Rosa could see Jenny was still curious. 'So, did you discuss those crooks and what he's going to do about them?'

'We started to, then there was this smell of burning and we had more to think about, so we didn't.'

'Burning?'

Rosa chuckled. 'He burnt the lamb, mistook Fahrenheit for Centigrade.'

'Easy mistake for a rookie.' Jenny laughed too. 'When are you going to see him again? You are going to, aren't you?'

Rosa felt herself redden. 'Next Friday,' she said in a low voice. 'I promised to cook him a proper leg of lamb.'

The two women smiled.

'And that's it?' Jenny wanted to know. 'No leg-trembling? No restrained kisses?'

Rosa was conscious of a flush rising up from the base of her neck to her cheeks and wished her emotions weren't so obvious.

'He did?'

'As I left.' She was spared from further interrogation by a customer knocking on the door and, checking her watch, said, 'Time to open up.'

Saturday was often their busiest day, and today was no exception. Rosa was glad as it gave Jenny no opportunity to quiz her further. It was only when they had placed the *Closed* sign on the door, and Jenny was checking the day's takings that she returned to the topic Rosa dreaded.

'He kissed you, then?'

'Mmm.'

'So there's some interest – not just a friendly former work associate? I told you he was a hunk and I bet you have more in common than a few dud invoices.'

'Maybe.' Rosa knew she sounded guarded, but since she was still trying to work out her feelings for herself, she was in no position to provide the sort of answer Jenny wanted. 'What are you and Mike doing this weekend?' she asked in an attempt to change the subject. It worked.

'A lazy night in, I think. Mike promised to cook dinner – and he *can* cook,' she laughed. 'Been doing it for years. Maybe he can give your Harry a few lessons.'

'He's not *my* Harry.' Rosa couldn't keep the irritation out of her voice. 'One date and you're reading I-don't-know-what into it.'

Jenny ignored Rosa's response, instead adding to her earlier statement. 'Then tomorrow we're going on the Everglades cruise. Now, that's something Harry might enjoy. It goes all the way up the Noosa River. An all-day thing, takes six hours and includes morning tea and lunch etcetera.'

'Yes, we talked about that.' Rosa wished she could take back the words as soon as they left her lips.

'So you did talk about other things?'

'He had a few books about Noosa and surrounds, so yes, we talked about local sightseeing, but we didn't make any plans or anything…' Rosa's voice tapered away, remembering how enthusiastic Harry had been and that there had been the assumption she might accompany him on some of the trips he mentioned. 'I'm sure you and Mike'll have a great time. I've heard good reports about the cruise.'

'I expect I'll feel a bit like a tourist, but Mike wants to see as much as he can while he's here and get a good handle on the whole Noosa River Catchment Area.'

'So how long is he here for?' Rosa dared to ask.

It was Jenny's turn to redden. She completed the work she'd been doing before replying. 'At least another couple of months, then… then we need to make some decisions,' she said after a long pause.

'You mean…?'

'I mean we won't be deciding anything in a hurry. But now we've found each other again. And at our age... It'd be foolish to let it all go.' She gazed into space for a moment, then her voice became brisker, the old Jenny reasserting herself. 'That's what I mean about you and Harry. When you find a good thing you should hang onto it. There aren't too many worthy men out there. And you're not getting any younger.' She stopped as if worried she might have overstepped the mark.

'Thanks for reminding me!' But Rosa couldn't take offence. Her friend had always said it like it was, a bit like Rosa herself. She guessed that was why they'd remained such good friends. 'Point taken. But Harry and I aren't like you and Mike. For a start he's still married, and there's his daughter to consider too. Until she mentioned Lucy, Rosa hadn't been aware that the girl's existence had been in the back of her mind, a reminder of Harry's other life.

'I have children too,' Jenny reminded her. 'Hugh will be fine with Mike, but heaven knows what Helen's reaction will be. She was pretty disgusted at the idea I'd met someone in Oregon, but now...' She shook her head.

'You haven't told them?'

'Not yet. We may take a trip down to Sydney to see the family. Probably best done face-to-face.'

'Rather you than me.' Rosa knew Jenny's spoilt daughter had harboured the idea her mum would be free to babysit when she left her Health Service position. Instead of which Jenny had traipsed off to visit her godmother in Oregon and the rest was now history.

'Well, that's in the future. Mike and I need some time together first and that's what we have here in Noosa. Speaking of which...'

The pair looked up as the subject of their conversation peered in the door.

'Hello, ladies. Not finished yet?'

Rosa noticed how Mike's arrival caused Jenny to sparkle. The chemistry between them was obvious. Rosa felt a familiar twinge of envy. Maybe there *was* someone out there for her too. If not Harry, then... She dismissed the image of Harry which appeared behind her eyes. Fat chance! No, she'd sworn off men after the Ken disaster, but she had to admit it would be nice to have someone to look at her the way Mike was looking at Jenny, to glow with happiness the way Jenny was and...

'We're off for a drink before dinner. Why don't you join us?' Mike's voice broke through Rosa's musings.

Rosa looked at the pair, now standing arm-in-arm, so clearly blissful in each other's company. She didn't want to be the third wheel. 'Thanks, but I'll pass this time. I have a few things to do,' she lied, contemplating her apartment and the evening which now stretched ahead in a seemingly endless emptiness.

'Well if you're sure,' Jenny said with a worried glance, before tightening her arm in Mike's.

Rosa farewelled the pair and walked slowly back home. Tonight she was blind to the beauty of the riverbank, the glory of the setting sun, and the strolling couples. She didn't know why, but she was dreading her own company. By the time she put the key into her door, she was feeling very sorry for herself and decided a warm shower would buck her up.

Holding her face up to the stream of water cascading over her body, Rosa tried to work out where this blue mood had come from. She thought back and realised it had started with Jenny's questions about her night with Harry and been exacerbated by Mike's arrival and the pair's obvious happiness. Yes, she did want that for herself, too. She remembered again, the touch of Harry's lips on hers. Why had she drawn away? She knew now it was fear, fear of being hurt again, fear that Harry could – did – mean more to her than Ken ever had.

The water began to run cold, dowsing Rosa's carnal thoughts. She stepped out of the shower and towelled herself dry, before slipping into her robe – an unwelcome reminder of the night Ken had arrived unannounced.

Feeling better now she'd worked out her motivation, Rosa pushed her fingers through her wet hair and made her way to the kitchen to fossick for something for dinner. She didn't feel like cooking so drew a packet of frozen spinach and ricotta cannelloni out of the freezer and placed it in the microwave, pouring herself a glass of Merlot while it heated.

Rosa carried her dinner to the sofa, switched on the television and curled up, prepared to watch whatever movie was available before having an early night. But the movie on offer was a romance, one of those in which the heroine first despised, then came to love the handsome hero who was in the midst of a difficult divorce.

She snapped it off before the final scene. She knew how it would end. In books and movies there was always a happy ending. Life wasn't like that. At least not in her experience. Then she pictured Jenny and her Mike. Life did seem to be working out for them. Maybe there could be a silver lining. Maybe…

She sat up in annoyance. This wasn't the evening she'd planned. Now she was wide awake, so the early night wasn't an option. Rosa thought back to Harry's story. The poor man, to be treated so badly by his wife and partner. Her curiosity aroused, she carried her half-empty glass to the computer, fired it up and opened Google, searching for any mention of Harry, his wife or his business partner.

She scrolled through a seemingly endless list of useless information till she came across an article in an old copy of *The Sydney Morning Herald*: Local businessman's divorce scandal. This might be it. It was.

Sipping the last dregs of wine, Rosa read the article which, though short, itemised the divorce as a result of an affair between an H. Kennedy, assumed to be Harry and an unnamed co-respondent. She could see how easily it would have been for anyone to read between the lines and make two and two add up to five.

Rosa tried to imagine how Harry must have felt, how he had become the unwitting accomplice in their deception and, instead of trying to clear his name had chosen to leave town. She stared at the article as if she could extract further information, but it didn't tell her any more than Harry had. Finally her eyes started to close and she knew it was time for bed.

To Rosa's surprise, she slept soundly, awakening to bright sunlight streaming through the vertical drapes. Feeling energised, she prepared for her planned visit to her mother. She had a selection of new library books for Ivy and wanted to ensure all was well with her.

Rosa quickly fixed breakfast and set off. She knew if she left it too late, it would be Ivy's lunchtime and her mother would become upset at the interruption to her routine.

As she drove towards the nursing home, Rosa's own problems took second place to her concerns about her mother. On her last visit she'd noticed Ivy wasn't as lively as usual, but when she'd asked the staff about this apparent deterioration, they'd shrugged it off as being "to be expected". It wasn't what Rosa expected at all. Ivy had always been sharp – to the point of cutting, some would say. Rosa frowned as she considered what the change might mean.

Parking close to the main building, Rosa walked briskly to her mother's room, tapped on the door, and pushed it open. Her mother was seated in her usual chair and looked up at Rosa's entrance, peering through her glasses. A smile lit up her face.

'It's you, Rosa.'

'I said I'd drop by today. Don't you remember? I have some new books for you.'

'You did? I forgot.' Ivy sounded puzzled, as if she couldn't believe she'd have forgotten. 'One day is very much like another. I get so tired.'

Rosa felt a jolt of alarm and looked more closely at the older woman. 'Are you okay, Mum? Feeling all right? Do you need anything?'

Ivy seemed to regain some energy and drew herself up. 'I'm fine, dear. I was just surprised to see you, but it's nice of you to come. Now tell me all your news.'

Rosa started to tell her mother about the bookshop, including some amusing anecdotes about their customers and how happy Jenny seemed with Mike.

'That Jenny always had her head screwed on the right way. A hard worker, that one. But I don't know why the pair of you needed to open a bookshop. I manage perfectly well with the library.'

Rosa hid a smile. The mother she knew so well was back. The frail woman who had greeted Rosa seemed to have vanished to be replaced by Ivy with her usual acerbic comments. 'Have you heard from Vi?' Rosa asked, curious to know if her sister was keeping her promise to make regular contact with their mother.

'She rang me… when was it? I think… She said… she said she's coming to visit me.' Ivy smiled smugly.

'No, Mum. You must have got it wrong. Vi's in England. Remember?'

'I know that!'

Rosa sighed. 'So Vi rang? How is she?' Thinking quickly, Rosa realised she hadn't heard from her sister since that disastrous phone call. Neither were very good at keeping in touch.

Her mind wandered as her mother rattled off a list of Vi's activities. She'd made a success of life in England, marrying, having two children in quick succession and managing her own career so well that she now held a senior position in a local real estate firm.

'And she said she was coming home,' Ivy finished. 'She did,' she added, as if daring Rosa to contradict her. 'It's been so long.' Ivy's eyes misted over and she reached for a tissue.

'Too long.' Rosa could barely remember her sister's last visit. It must have been at least ten years. She'd come over to show off her two precocious children, to gloat over her successful life and make Rosa feel she'd somehow missed out. Despite her own flourishing career, Rosa had received the distinct impression that, because she hadn't managed to snare a husband, Vi regarded her as a failure. Maybe that's why she'd been so quick to connect with Ken? She'd snared a husband all right, he just belonged to someone else. Rosa was brought back to the present by her mother's voice.

'She hasn't called you? She said she would.'

'No, Mum. When did you speak with her?'

Ivy looked puzzled again, so Rosa decided not to pursue it and soon rose to leave. As she hugged her mother and kissed her goodbye, the older woman felt fragile to her touch, almost like a little bird, just skin and bone. Rosa couldn't help thinking how, only a few years ago, her mother had been a lively eighty year-old whose appearance and vitality belied her age. How she'd changed. Perhaps it *was* time for Vi to come home for a visit – before it was too late.

Before she left the building, Rosa sought out one of the carers to find out more about the phone call.

'Yes, there was a call,' the dark-haired woman said. 'I think it was a couple of days ago. And it was international, I remember that. But I wouldn't know what was said.' She shrugged as if to indicate she didn't have the time or interest to monitor residents' phone calls.

'Of course not.'

That didn't help, but Rosa didn't know what she'd expected. She'd probably have been more worried if the staff did listen in to calls.

'Your mum did seem chirpier afterwards,' the woman added with a faint smile.

'Thanks. I'll be back next week, as usual.'

Rosa determined to contact Vi herself. It was the wrong time to ring and an email wouldn't cut it. She needed to find out if her sister really had called and what she'd said to have Ivy imagine she was coming home.

*

Rosa tapped her fingers impatiently on the kitchen benchtop as she waited for her sister to answer. She checked the time again. Had she left it too late? Had Vi already left for work?

'Hello?' Despite the distance the line was clear, though a little faint. It was a relief to hear her sister's voice. Rosa perched on a high stool and leant her elbow on the bench, holding the phone closer to her ear. Not one for wasting time on preliminaries she jumped straight in. 'Vi, it's me. Mum said you were going to call.'

'Well, hello to you, too.' But there was a smile in Vi's voice. 'I did mean to. I told Mum I would, but it's so difficult. I can never work out the time difference.'

'So you *did* call her?' *And managed the time difference for that call.*

'Why the questions? Yes, I called. She's *my* mum, too. After your call, I wanted to make sure she was okay. Why are you being so agro?'

You waited long enough, Rosa thought and bit the inside of her cheek in an attempt to rein in her anger. 'Sorry.' She drew her fingers through her hair 'I've just seen her and… she says you're planning a visit.'

'Oh, that?'

'That!' *So Vi had said something of the sort?* But Rosa knew her sister, and what she said and what she meant were often two different things. 'Did you mean it or…'

Before Rosa could finish, Vi interrupted, 'I guess I said it on the spur of the moment. Mum sounded so… so unlike herself, so down. And it did seem to cheer her up.'

'Of course it did. She's failing, Vi.' Rosa sighed and looked down at her feet which barely reached the bar on the stool. 'You haven't been here, haven't seen what…' She could feel her eyes begin to fill and angrily rubbed them with her knuckles. 'It might be good if you could come, even for a short visit.' She held her breath waiting for her sister's reply. It would mean so much to Ivy if she could see Vi.

'Oh, Rosa. I can't. Not right now. There's so much...' Rosa could almost hear Vi's brain working. 'You've no idea how busy I am. Things are difficult. You don't understand... You know I would if I could. But she has you. You do visit regularly, don't you?' she asked, as if it had only just occurred to her that Rosa might have other commitments too. 'And you'd let me know if... if anything happened?'

Rosa sighed again. Some things never changed, and her sister was one of those. In her mind, no one else, especially Rosa, could possibly be as busy as she was. Rosa made one more attempt. 'Wouldn't you rather come before...' She couldn't put her fears into words, remembering how different Ivy had been that day, but Vi had had enough of the conversation.

'Was that all? It's after nine here and I need to get to work. The others have already left. You were lucky to catch me, but now I need to dash.'

'Sure. Love to Rod and the girls.' But Rosa was speaking to empty air. She held the phone away from her ear, looked at it as if she could actually see Vi in it and hung up with yet another sigh. Vi was no help. Even when they'd been children Vi had managed to escape most of the routine chores by smiling prettily and pleading homework, a headache, or, in their teenage years, a hot date. It had always been left to Rosa to do the washing up, feed the pets or run down to the corner store for milk. And now she had to try to explain to her mother that Vi wouldn't be coming after all.

Rosa poured herself a glass of Merlot and took it out to the balcony. She should cut down on the wine, but surely one glass each evening didn't do any harm? Sitting there, glass in hand, looking out over the river front helped her calm down. She knew she shouldn't let Vi rile her, but she always had, ever since they were little. And now, Vi regarded her life as being far more important than Rosa's. Well, in Vi's eyes it was. But their mother was important too, and Rosa intended to make her last years ones of comfort and contentment if she possibly could.

She sat watching the passing parade of diners strolling along Gympie Terrace, no doubt in search of a restaurant in which to spend a pleasurable evening. She envied them. Most were couples wandering hand-in-hand or arm-in-arm. Others were taking their dogs for an evening walk. Everyone seemed to have someone whether partner or pet, someone to love and to love them. Everyone but her.

Rosa got up with a start, taking her glass to the sink to rinse it. There was no point in self-pity. She had a good life, owned her own home, was part-owner of a bookshop and, she admitted, had met a man who attracted her, more than attracted – and he was coming to dinner on Friday.

For the first time since inviting Harry, Rosa allowed herself to look forward to the evening without any misgivings.

Twenty-one

The week flew by and Friday proved to be a glorious day. Rosa was singing
under her breath when she entered the bookshop.

'Someone's happy,' Jenny greeted her. 'It's tonight, isn't it?'

'Yes. Do you think…?'

'I think you're having a gorgeous man to dinner, one who clearly finds you attractive and whose charms you're not immune to. Correct?'

Rosa beamed, her heart beating faster at the thought of the evening ahead. She'd prepared the lamb last night and it was marinating in the mix of herbs she'd blended in the food processor. It should be delicious served with couscous, yoghurt and beans. Then she'd made an apple cake for dessert. Surely Harry would like that?

'What are you cooking?'

'Moroccan roast lamb. I did promise him a leg of lamb and wanted to try something a bit different. His was Italian, Jamie Oliver, no less. But I don't think Jamie would have been impressed by his efforts.'

The pair laughed.

'And you will relax, won't you? Give the guy a chance?'

'Mmm.' Rosa's thoughts were jumbled. She'd admitted she liked the man, was attracted to him, but… And it was a big "but". While anticipating the evening with something akin to excitement, she was afraid of being hurt again.

Jenny seemed to understand her friend's dilemma. 'Sometimes we need to take a risk in life, to risk being hurt in order to find out if…'

She appeared to be searching for the right words. 'If something's right for us,' she finished. 'I know that sounds a bit weird and unlike me, but Maddy counselled me – or tried to. I was pretty pigheaded about Mike to begin with. But it worked out for us – eventually. And I'd like to see you happy too.'

'And you don't think I can be happy without a man?'

Jenny pursed her lips. 'I'm not saying it's impossible. I managed for years and, yes I was happy, but… it's different when you have someone, someone you care about, who cares about you too. I guess it's a sense of contentment, fulfilment, of belonging. Rosa, I want you to experience what Mike and I have and Harry may be your opportunity.'

Rosa hesitated. She heard what her friend was saying and recognised her sincerity, but it was a big step to acknowledge that Harry Kennedy might be what the romance novels called "the one". 'We'll see,' was all she said, before they were interrupted by the first customer of the day.

*

Rosa was aware of a fluttering, churning excitement as she put the final touches to the table. She stood back and examined the square white plates, the gleaming cutlery, the sparkling wine glasses, the low bowl of sweet-smelling blossoms and the musk-perfumed candle. All were set off by a pair of dark green damask placemats and matching napkins. Yes, she was satisfied. And the enticing aroma of the Moroccan roast lamb was beginning to fill the room with its unique fragrance.

As the doorbell rang, she glanced down at the soft blue dress she'd worn at Jenny's insistence. 'Time you looked more feminine,' she'd said, encouraging Rosa to shun her usual pants and shirt, despite the fact that Jenny herself rarely wore a dress, both women preferring a more tailored look.

'You need to make an effort. Show him your softer side,' she'd insisted before shooing Rosa out at lunchtime and warning her not to return till she'd purchased something suitable. To Rosa's surprise she'd found this softly-draped dress in periwinkle-blue in the first shop she'd entered and, as Jenny had assured her, it did make her feel different.

The dress, combined with the sleek hairstyle made her believe she was ready for anything the evening might bring.

Pressing the intercom, she heard Harry's voice and released the button to allow him to enter. A few seconds later he was standing at her open door, a liquor store bag in one hand and a bunch of flowers in the other.

Rosa had wondered if Harry would try to greet her with a kiss, but since both his hands were occupied, she was saved from the decision as to how to react if he did. Why did she feel disappointed?

Harry handed over the flowers and Rosa buried her face in the pink roses, inhaling their fragrance in an attempt to hide her pang of regret.

'Where would you like this?' He held up the bag which clinked with the sound of more than one bottle.

'In the kitchen.'

Rosa led the way and pointed to the benchtop, before finding an appropriate vase and arranging the flowers.

'This one should go in the fridge, unless you want to start on it now.' Harry held up a bottle of champagne, fortunately not the same vintage as the one Ken had produced on her birthday. Rosa blanched at the memory. It wasn't that she hadn't drunk champagne since then. She'd had a glass with Jenny, and another – more than one – with Harry at the Boathouse, and there'd been sparkling wine at the opening of the bookshop. But seeing the bottle, there in her kitchen, was too poignant.

'Not just yet,' she said, opening the fridge door for him.

'Mmm. Something smells good. No burnt offerings here. It's good of you…' They looked at each other and Rosa felt a bubble of laughter rise up. She started to giggle and Harry joined her.

'Why don't you open the red while I fetch some nibbles. There are glasses on the table.'

The ice was broken. Rosa knew it was going to be all right. She took a deep breath as she filled a couple of bowls with nuts and olives and carried them out to the balcony.

'Dinner's almost ready,' she said joining Harry at the round glass table high above the bustle of people strolling along Gympie Terrace.

'Great view.' Harry stood, glass in hand, surveying the street below and the river, dark and mysterious in the fading light, the few boats' masts sticking up like spears. 'It's almost as good as the view from the

Boathouse.' Rosa saw his eyes move over the river. 'I think I must have moored around there when I arrived,' he said, pointing outwards with his glass.

His words evoked a vague memory for Rosa. 'A white catamaran?'

Harry turned towards her. 'You saw the Yarran?'

'Maybe.' She blushed as she recalled the morning when she'd spied the flash from her balcony and made a hasty retreat.

They sat quietly, sipping wine and enjoying the view. Rosa was surprised yet again how comfortable she felt in Harry's company. There was no real need for conversation. It was as if they'd known each other for years. The beep-beep from the oven broke the silence.

'Dinner,' Rosa said, rising with regret and making her way to the kitchen. Harry followed more slowly.

The meal was all Rosa had intended and Harry was full of praise. The mention of Harry's yacht sparked a host of amusing anecdotes about his trip up the coast along with the offer that Rosa might like to take a trip on the yacht herself sometime. 'And maybe you can give me a few cooking lessons in return,' he suggested as he finished the last spoonful of his dessert, the decadent apple cake made from an old recipe of her mother's.

Rosa smiled and shook her head. 'You'll be right. You just need to read the instructions carefully. Remember to set the correct temperature, then there's nothing to it.'

Harry rubbed his chin. 'Maybe I tried to be too clever. I really can grill a mean steak. But I guess most men would say that. Anyway, that was delicious, Rosa. I…' He reached across the table to cover her hand with his. 'One good thing about Robson and Steele – they brought us together.'

Rosa's heart started thumping. *She'd thought she was prepared for this, but was she?* She barely heard Harry's next words, so intent was she on remaining calm. When she did start to listen again Harry was talking about the Everglades cruise Jenny and Mike had taken. 'Sorry?'

Harry gave her a lopsided grin. 'I thought you weren't listening. I was suggesting we take the cruise tomorrow… or Sunday,' he added as Rosa's mouth fell open in surprise.

'No. Tomorrow would be good,' she found herself saying, 'It's supposed to be wonderful. A whole day cruise up the river. There's morning tea and a barbecue lunch, swimming or nature walks, lots of birdlife. It's called the river of mirrors and…' Rosa stopped talking at the sight of Harry's amused expression and realised she'd been prattling. 'I mean… you'd enjoy it.'

'You too, I hope.' Harry's hand held hers more firmly. 'I *would* like to get to know you better, Rosa. How do you feel about that?'

All Rosa could think was *what a gentleman*. 'I… yes, I'd like that too,' she stammered, feeling foolish and trying to subdue the rush of excitement that threatened to overwhelm her. *Where had that come from? Had Jenny been right? Could there be a future with this man? Was she willing to give it a try, take a risk? Yes*, she decided, *a thousand times yes*.

This time, when they parted, Rosa didn't retreat from the gentle pressure of Harry's lips on hers. She allowed him to wrap his arms around her, enjoying the warmth and comfort they gave her while his lips and tongue continued to explore her willing mouth. She was surprised at the strong urge for something more which exploded sending her whole body into a frenzy as she pressed closer and closer to him.

When they finally drew apart, it was to gaze at each other in stunned silence.

'Wow!' Harry finally said, holding Rosa at arm's length. 'I think I'd better go. I…'

Rosa drew a deep breath and tried to voice a calm she was far from feeling. 'So, tomorrow?'

'I'll pick you up at nine-thirty.'

'But don't you need to book? These tours are very popular.'

'Already done.' Harry looked a tad shamefaced. 'I took a chance on your agreeing.'

'But…'

'And you did.'

After Harry had left, Rosa took the last of her wine out to the balcony and watched his jaunty figure striding down the street. There was a spring in his step, giving her a stab of pleasure. She turned back into her apartment, closed the sliding doors and drew the curtains, a little spring in her own step. She was going to see him again tomorrow.

Saturday proved to be another glorious day, the sun beaming down from a clear blue sky. Rosa had agreed to Harry's invitation without thinking of her work commitment, but a quick call to Jenny had fixed that, her friend assuring her that Mike would step into the breach and instructing her to enjoy herself.

Rosa dressed casually in a pair of faded jeans and pink tee-shirt, throwing a sweater around her shoulders in case it was cooler on the water. Harry arrived on time looking very cool in jeans and a striped pale blue and navy tee and smiling broadly. Rosa didn't object as he took hold of her hand, and they made their way to the pick-up point.

The boat was full of tourists and Rosa found it fun to pretend to be one of them, instead of a long-time resident. As she slid into the seat beside Harry, hearing various foreign accents in the crowd, she whispered, 'I bet no one thinks I grew up here.' They smiled like a pair of conspirators and settled back to enjoy the trip.

It seemed no time before they stopped for morning tea, then on again to the stop at Harry's Hut for a barbecue lunch. This caused a few chuckles as Harry revealed his name and asked if the guide had known he'd be on the trip that day and if the name changed each day to suit the travellers.

After a typical barbecue lunch of salads, steak and sausages, with a seafood option which suited Rosa, some of the group chose to take a swim, while Harry and Rosa elected for the nature walk, their pace soon leaving the others far behind. As they pushed through the bush, Harry grabbed Rosa's hand again, and this time her fingers curled trustingly in his as he led the way, stopping occasionally to enjoy the deep pool of silence interrupted only by the birdcalls.

Rosa was surprised when Harry proved knowledgeable not only about the more common egrets and herons, but also the birds he identified as the Noisy Pitta and the Black-tailed Nightjar.

'Did a lot of birdwatching in my younger days,' Harry told her. 'My parents took us camping every summer and, in between times, I read up on the different species. I became a bit of an expert, I suppose. Haven't had much of an opportunity to use the knowledge for a long time, but it never leaves you.'

One more side of this extraordinary man. Rosa tucked the knowledge away for future consideration. For the present she decided just to enjoy the moments with him. The more she learned about Harry, the more she liked him and the more she became aware how little she'd really known about Ken. She'd been part of his work life, slipped in between meetings, moments when he could sneak away from what had always been his real life; something she'd refused to accept.

The few times she'd spent with Harry already had shown her a different sort of relationship – one where there were no secrets, no need for subterfuge. It was a pleasant relief to be able to be open with her companion, not to worry about being seen or found out. This was what Jenny had meant.

Tripping over an exposed tree-root, Rosa almost fell. Only Harry's firm grip on her hand kept her upright. His other hand immediately went around her waist so that, instead of falling, she found her face so close to Harry's she could feel his breath on her cheek and smell the fresh tang of soap which seemed to be so much a part of him.

'Oh!' The word exploded from her lips. Rosa wasn't sure whether it was because of her close call or Harry's nearness. Still feeling slightly unstable, she gripped his shoulder with her free hand. Harry's grip tightened on her waist as she raised her face to his and their lips met. There was no sound except for a slight breeze in the treetops, the call of a distant bird and the faint rustle of something in the bush behind them – perhaps the frill-necked lizard they'd seen earlier. Their lips met and clung. She opened her mouth to allow his tongue to explore and, as it did, she felt a moistening between her legs and pushed closer.

'Rosa,' Harry breathed moving away slightly, but still holding her tightly. 'I want... Hell, this is neither the time nor place, but...'

Their eyes met and they embraced again, straining against each other and only breaking apart at the distant sound of a boat's horn. Smiling ruefully, Harry released his hold. 'I think that's our signal to return. Maybe we can continue this later?'

When they re-joined the rest of the group, Rosa felt somehow dislocated, as if she'd been somewhere far away and was only now beginning to return to earth. She couldn't remember ever feeling that way before. She wanted to sit quietly and enjoy it, while trying to work out whether the feeling was pleasurable or not. Definitely pleasurable, she decided as Harry's body fitted close to hers on the return journey, their thighs rubbing against each other, their hands tightly clasped, fingers laced.

They didn't speak. There was no need. But what would happen next? She shivered in anticipation at the thought of Harry's naked body next to hers. Was she being too brazen? Was this what Jenny had meant by taking a risk? She decided she was thinking too much and closed her eyes, but couldn't turn off her thoughts which were all of the man sitting right next to her, his strong arm around her shoulders and his warm hand holding hers as if he'd never let her go.

When they finally disembarked at the wharf on Gympie Terrace, it was late afternoon – a glorious sunny afternoon – and Rosa was unsure what Harry's plans were. Daringly she said, 'There's still that bottle of champagne you brought last night.'

Harry grinned. 'I think it's a champagne afternoon, don't you?' He drew Rosa's arm through his, and kept a firm hold on it as the pair meandered along the boardwalk, oblivious to the passers-by, savouring an acute anticipation of the moments and hours ahead.

As they walked along, Rosa changed her mind what seemed to be a thousand times about what would happen when they reached her apartment – they'd merely drink champagne; they'd drink champagne then make love; they'd tear off their clothes and make love on the living room floor; he'd carry her into the bedroom and ravish her on her white *broderie anglais* doona. It was almost a relief when they reached the building and Rosa finally put her key in the door.

As it turned out, none of her imaginings were close to reality. By the time they'd walked all the way along the river, Rosa was feeling hot and sticky, so disappeared to take a shower while Harry brewed some coffee and organised a platter of biscuits and cheese. As she stood in the shower under the stream of tepid water, it not only cooled her body, but brought her back to her senses. *What had she been thinking? How could she even have imagined the scenarios which had pulsated through her feverish mind?*

Refreshed and dressed comfortably in a pair of white capri pants and blue short-sleeved top, Rosa could smell the delicious aroma of freshly-brewed coffee as she stepped into the living area where Harry had already laid everything out on a low coffee table.

'You can't say I'm not house-trained,' he said, indicating the setting, 'I thought we could start with coffee and move on to the champagne later.'

'Right,' Rosa flushed, feeling awkward and a little embarrassed as she remembered her earlier thoughts. But Harry didn't appear to notice her discomfort and began to help himself to a cracker, topping it with a piece of brie.

'Come, sit down,' Harry said, before sliding the entire biscuit into his mouth and washing it down with a swig of coffee.

Rosa joined him on the sofa, sitting gingerly on the edge and picking up her mug. But as she took a first sip, she felt herself being pulled back, Harry's arm around her shoulders.

'That's better,' he murmured.

It was. Suddenly, it didn't matter what she had been thinking. It didn't matter what would happen. She only knew she was happy to be here. On this day. In this place. With this man. Drinking coffee and eating biscuits and cheese. The rest of the world could disappear and she wouldn't notice. Her world had shrunk to Harry and her and the sofa.

Twenty-two

Harry awoke with a start. He carefully disentangled himself from Rosa's sleeping figure. She looked so helpless, lying there, hair awry, arm thrown out above her head, a slight frown between her eyes. He dropped a kiss on her forehead and began to pull on his clothes which were strewn across the floor, his eyes falling on the two half-full glasses of champagne sitting on the bedside table.

He smiled, remembering. When they'd finally opened the bottle and poured the sparkling liquid, they'd barely sipped the wine before making their way to the bedroom where... *Wow!* Harry's smile widened at the memory of their love-making. They'd been in such a rush to embrace each other that the wine had been forgotten. The scattered clothing and the bedding were testament to their great need.

He sighed. He felt guilty at leaving, but he had to go home. His poor dog had been left alone since early morning and needed to be fed. He didn't want to go, wanted to wake up with Rosa's arms around him, her breath on his lips, to... Another time. There *would* be another time, many more if he had any say in it. Finding a piece of paper, he thought carefully before writing, *You are wonderful Sorry to go but Tiger needs seeing to. Be in touch.*

Harry let himself out quietly so as not to disturb Rosa and walked home, whistling to himself, through streets deserted apart from a few late-night revellers. He couldn't believe what had just happened. He and Rosa!

He'd hoped. Of course he had, but the reality of their coming together had been so much more than he could ever have imagined. For years he and Hillie had just gone through the motions, bored with each other, but accustomed to the routine of sex which became less frequent as time went by. He'd forgotten the joy in making love with a willing partner, with someone whose desire equalled his own, whose…

Harry reached home to see a figure on his doorstep which straightened up as he approached.

'Where've you been? I've been here for ages.' Lucy picked up the backpack he'd failed to notice and gazed at him accusingly.

'What are you doing here?'

The last thing he wanted or needed at this point was his daughter, but Lucy was there waiting for his return, yawning with tiredness, rubbing her already red eyes, her hair unkempt. His heart sank. Where was the smart, lively girl he'd farewelled not so long ago?

Lucy didn't answer, merely waited for Harry to unlock the door before asking, 'Same room as before?' and heading off to the spare room, the backpack bumping along behind her.

Harry was still standing dumbfounded when he heard Tiger give a sharp yelp and remembered the reason for his return. Pouring food and water into the little creature's bowls, he wondered what Lucy would have done if he'd given in to the urge to stay overnight with Rosa. Sat on the doorstep till morning, he guessed, becoming more and more tired and anxious. He scratched his head.

It wasn't like Lucy to arrive without warning, or to do anything impulsively. Since she'd been a small child, she'd always been a planner. He and Hillie had often laughed at how their daughter liked to organise every little event in her life and had joked that she'd make a wonderful manager one day. Something must have happened to really upset her. A sudden notion made him check his phone which he'd turned off at Rosa's. Yes, there it was, a text from Hillie, *Is Lucy with you? She left in a rush and she's not answering her phone.*

So Hillie had something to do with this. Quickly typing, *Yes, more later*, Harry turned the phone off again and prepared for bed. But once there, he tossed and turned, finally rising to make a hot chocolate, his old grandmother's cure-all, which usually worked for him. His head was buzzing with thoughts. Rosa was uppermost and how he could arrange to see her again – soon.

When he left, his intention had been to meet her for breakfast, to ring or text her early and arrange a rendezvous at Sirocco on Gympie Terrace, or perhaps Season on Noosa Main Beach, both restaurants he'd come to enjoy.

But Lucy's arrival had put a spanner in the works. Which took him to Lucy. Why had the girl chosen to leave Melbourne and uni mid-semester, and why had she been with her mother in Sydney? No doubt it would all become clear in the morning. Maybe… he took a sip of the hot drink which reminded him so much of his grandmother's warm kitchen, of sitting curled up in an old armchair, his legs under him, the grey Manx cat on his lap. He could almost feel Daisy's soft coat under his fingers.

His thoughts returned to the present and to Lucy's last visit, when it had been her custom to arise late, to wander into the kitchen around ten or even later, her eyes blurry with sleep, in search of her first coffee of the day.

That decided him. He would arrange to meet Rosa for breakfast. He could do that and still be back before Lucy made her appearance, he was sure. He took out his phone and, smiling, composed a text inviting Rosa to meet him at Sirocco at eight. She'd told him she was an early riser, waking when the sun began to peep through her windows. How Harry wished he could be there with her to see her eyes open, to seal her lips with that first kiss, to… His body ached at the very thought of her, naked, in the bed they'd shared.

To take his mind off it, he forced his thoughts to his work quandary. What was he going to do? He intended to complete his contract as best he could. He owed Robson that. But afterwards? He knew he must report their actions to the relevant authorities. But who were they? Having worked in Sydney for years, he was familiar with the New South Wales system where he would report them to ICAC, but here in Queensland? He'd need to research the appropriate body. He thought he'd read something about a Crime and Corruption Commission. He'd have to check. Then, he supposed he'd be required to make a statutory declaration or some such thing.

Harry felt his eyes begin to close. The hot chocolate was doing its work, or maybe it was the thought of taking legal action. Whatever, he was ready to return to bed. He rinsed his mug, placed it upside down on the draining board and turned out the light.

*

Rosa awoke with a smile on her face and stretched a hand over to the other side of the bed to encounter – nothing. She opened her eyes quickly and sat up. Where had he gone? Then she slithered back down the bed, luxuriating in the memory of the previous afternoon and evening. Harry was probably in the kitchen making coffee. But there was no delicious aroma of coffee beans, no sounds coming from the other part of the apartment which had a distinctly empty feel. Sitting up again, she looked around the room which, the night before, had resembled nothing less than a tip with clothes strewn everywhere in their urgency to become naked and feel flesh against flesh. She blushed at the memory. They weren't teenagers anymore, and she'd never behaved that way as a teenager. She'd been much more restrained and circumspect.

But it had been so long for her – and for Harry too, it seemed. Was that all it had been? The need to satisfy a physical hunger? She hadn't thought so at the time. Harry had been a gentle, considerate lover, had taken her to heights she'd only dreamt of before now. She'd begun to think, to imagine, to hope there was more to it, that they could form a proper relationship, one that would last. But now…?

She rose slowly, pulled on her robe and thrust a hand through her dishevelled mop of hair, grimacing at the sight of herself in the mirror as she passed. Vi was right. Who'd want someone like her? Thinking of Vi reminded Rosa that she still had to tell her mother that Vi wasn't going to be coming to visit. She dreaded that conversation, but should go to the nursing home today.

As she was fixing coffee and about to drop a slice of bread into the toaster,

she idly examined her phone, surprised to see a text from Harry. What…? Reading his words brought a smile to her face and galvanised her into action. She'd been wrong to rush to assumptions about the reason for his departure in the night. She'd forgotten about poor little Tiger, left alone all day, though Rosa wasn't sure how she felt about taking second place to a dog. Maybe he had altogether too many dependents to form another relationship. Still, breakfast at her favourite café sounded good.

Rosa dressed carefully in a pair of tailored white pants teamed with a short-sleeved top in hot pink, and spent extra time taming her wild hair into some semblance of a sleek cap, before heading out. As she walked briskly along the side of the river toward Sirocco, she smiled a greeting at everyone she met, many of whom were walking dogs on their leashes.

Maybe she'd been too harsh in her judgement. Rosa had never owned a dog herself, her mother refusing to countenance any animal larger than a budgerigar or goldfish for the two girls. Dog owners did have a responsibility to their pets. Her opinion of Harry's behaviour was beginning to undergo a change. Instead of an uncaring lover, she was beginning to view him as a caring pet owner, trying to juggle his competing priorities. By the time she reached the café, she was ready to forgive anything.

*

Harry leapt out of bed as soon as the sun began to peek through the window. Another glorious day in paradise, as he had begun to think of this place. He showered, humming to himself at the prospect of seeing Rosa again in a couple of hours. He intended to be abjectly apologetic for his untimely departure and leave her in no doubt of his feelings, which were stronger than he'd anticipated.

Once Tiger had been fed and allowed out into the courtyard, Harry brewed himself a coffee and stood, mug in hand, surveying the lush hedge of orange hibiscus bordering the yard and the pots of white impatiens he'd planted only a few weeks ago which were now flourishing.

'Dad.'

Harry turned sharply to see a sleepy Lucy wander into the kitchen, pushing back her long hair and blinking up at him.

'Is there coffee for me?'

Harry swore under his breath. *This wasn't happening. He was due to meet Rosa in less than an hour. Lucy should have been sound asleep for at least another two. How could she be standing in front of him demanding coffee as if it were the most normal thing in the world? He couldn't let Rosa down.*

'Sure, honey.' Harry poured out a cup for Lucy. 'You're up early.'

'Couldn't sleep. Thanks, Dad.' She took the coffee and plopped down on a chair, tucking her legs up under her.

Harry pulled out a seat and joined her, inwardly fuming at the delay, but knowing he had to spend some time with his daughter. 'Do you want breakfast?' he asked, forcing himself to sound calm.

'Nothing for me, but aren't you?' Lucy's eyes wandered around the kitchen as if seeking the makings or remains of her father's breakfast.

'No, I... I have a d... a breakfast engagement.' He hesitated, unwilling to provide more information, but his engagements, romantic or otherwise were of no interest to his daughter.

'Oh.' Lucy wrapped both hands around her cup and sipped the coffee, her hair falling across her face.

Harry watched her tenderly for a few minutes. Although now twenty, she was still his little girl. 'What's the matter, Lulu? Why are you here? Why didn't you let me know? What has your mother to do with it?'

'Shit! Has Mum been on to you? I might've known.' She slammed her cup down on the table with such force Harry thought it was going to smash into pieces.

'Steady on!'

'Sorry, Dad. She does it all the time. Every time I want to do something, she ruins it. I dropped in home to pick up some stuff on the way to a music festival and she started to read me the riot act – no drugs, no alcohol, no sex. As if... Then I mentioned your suggestion of volunteer work and she hit the roof.'

Harry tried to hide a smile. Is this what it was all about? Hillie deciding to lay down the law to her grown-up daughter? That was a joke, given her own recent behaviour. 'So what's new? You know your mum.'

Lucy's eyes met his, but her usual gleam of humour was absent. 'It's too much. I ditched the festival and came on up here... and you weren't home!' she added as if accusing her father of abandoning her.

'I was out late. Yes. But I did come home and you were able to sleep in a bed. Probably more that you'd have had at a music festival. I seem to recall they're pretty basic when it comes to accommodation.'

At his words, Harry saw the trace of a smile begin to etch itself around Lucy's mouth.

'Mmm.' She sipped her coffee, and reached down to scratch the head of the little dog, which had padded back into the room at the sound of their voices.

'What about uni?' Harry asked, feeling there was more to this visit than a dispute with Hillie. Lucy and her mother had always been at odds, so this was nothing new and certainly didn't explain a trip from Melbourne mid-semester. He surreptitiously checked his watch. *Still time.*

'If you're in a hurry, I won't hold you up.' Lucy's voice sounded petulant. *So he hadn't been as careful as he'd thought.*

'No.' Harry leant his elbows on the table as if he'd all the time in the world. 'What else is up, honey?'

Lucy sighed as if world-weary. 'It's everything. Uni isn't getting any more interesting. I haven't managed to find any volunteer stuff that appeals and…' Her head dropped and tears began to trickle down her cheeks. 'A guy I was seeing has…' She choked.

She's been dumped! My poor baby! Harry's heart went out to her. He wanted to hug her and reassure her, tell her he wasn't worth it – no one was worthy of her, his special girl. But her folded arms and obstinate expression were a clear indication a hug from her dad wouldn't fix things on this occasion.

'Was he someone special?' he asked gently.

'I thought so.' She lifted her tearstained face and Harry could see from her bloodshot eyes that she hadn't slept much, if at all.

'It's not what you want to hear, but there's someone better out there for you. Before your mum and I…'

'Well, that didn't last either, did it?'

'It lasted for twenty-one years and gave us you, so it wasn't all bad. We had lots of good years before… before we grew apart; realised we wanted different things out of life. It seems Bernie can give her those things I couldn't.'

It wasn't till he actually said these words that Harry realised the truth they held. He and Hillie had been so much in love when they first married and for many years after that. They'd delighted in the arrival of Lucy, saddened that her birth wasn't followed by the son they'd both hoped for. It had been a good life. When had it started to go wrong? When had Harry ceased to be enough for Hillie and she'd turned to his friend and business partner for the excitement and buzz she'd begun to crave?

'And what about you Dad? What do you want?' Lucy sniffed and picked up her cup again cradling it in both hands as before and running her finger around the rim.

'I want my Lulu to be happy. I want to see your smiling face again. I…'

'No, that's not what I mean.' She seemed to consider something for a moment, then surprised Harry. 'What were you doing out so late? Is there a woman involved? Have you met someone? Oh, that would really piss Mum off.' The thought seemed to cheer her up.

'What would you say if I have?'

'I'd say "Good on you." You deserve someone after Mum was so rotten to you.'

'You wouldn't mind? You were so down on your mum and Uncle Bernie.'

'That was different. They were all over each other. It was gross. And they let you take the blame too. I didn't like that. So you have?'

Harry checked his watch. 'I have and if I don't leave soon, I'm going to be late for breakfast with her. But first I need to know you haven't dropped out of uni. You made me a promise you'd finish the year.'

'Don't get your knickers in a twist. I know what I promised. When Greg told me…' Her eyes began to mist again, then she seemed to pull herself together. 'I couldn't think straight. There was this music festival. We were supposed to be going together – a group of us. He drew out. So I decided to go anyway. But when Mum started to do her thing, I knew I didn't want to join the others on my own, so…'

'But uni?' Harry prompted.

'This week's a break and it's almost study vac, I have a stack of assignments and I brought all my notes with me. They don't check attendance and I can submit online. I had intended sounding you out about coming here after the festival anyway, when… I can stay, can't I?'

'Of course you can.' Harry began to rise, unsure how he should react to Lucy's revelations.

'On you go,' she said. 'I'll have a hot bath, take your mutt for a walk or maybe have a swim, then try to get some sleep.'

'You should have something to eat,' Harry said, wondering if he should stay with her, text Rosa to cancel, but was loath to take such a step.

'Yeah, yeah. I'll be fine, Dad. Better not keep her waiting. I'll wash these.' She indicated the now empty cup and mug.

Harry bent to place a kiss on Lucy's forehead before saying, 'I won't be long. It's only breakfast,' and leaving. As he strode hurriedly along, his mind was full of the recent conversation with Lucy.

Until now she'd led a pretty sheltered life. To be disillusioned with her first choice of study, dumped by her boyfriend on the eve of a special weekend, then subjected to her mother's ravings wasn't the end of the world, but must seem like it. He wasn't sure what he could do to help, but had a warm glow that he'd been Lucy's port of call, her preferred harbour in her time of need.

As he drew closer to Sirocco, Harry's steps slowed. Rosa had already arrived and was seated at a table close to the top of the steps. She was studying the menu oblivious to his approach and he savoured the pleasure of watching her, unobserved. He noted that she looked especially smart this morning, dressed casually as most of the other women customers were, but in something bright pink that set off her hair. He could tell she'd taken trouble to tame her wild tresses, but was delighted to see a few stray curls escaping, the fingers on one hand unconsciously winding them into tighter spirals.

Just as he reached the foot of the steps, she looked up and Harry was rewarded by a wide smile as she noticed him.

'Good morning!' Harry bounded the steps, pecked Rosa on the cheek and drew out a chair. 'How are you this morning? I hope you slept well. I'm sorry...' He opened his hands, palms uppermost to demonstrate his regret.

'You're forgiven – this time,' Rosa said, her smile contradicting the inherent criticism. in her words. 'And you're here now.'

Harry rubbed his chin. 'I almost didn't make it. Lucy arrived.'

'Lucy? Your daughter? When?'

Harry picked up, then put down a menu, nodding to the waitress who had arrived to fill their water glasses. 'Coffee?' he asked, then, taking Rosa's silence for assent, said, 'A skinny cap and a short black. We'll order breakfast later. Okay with you?' he asked, realising he'd made an assumption regarding Rosa's choice of coffee. 'You've always...'

'That's fine.' She smiled again. 'Now, your daughter?'

'She was waiting when I arrived home. Guess it's just as well I got there when I did, or...' He thrust his fingers through his hair and began to relate his conversation with Lucy that morning. 'So,' he said at last, 'looks as if she's here to stay – for a bit anyway.'

'Well, that's what you had in mind, isn't it?'

'Just not yet. I thought... I wanted... Heck, we're only just getting to know each other. I thought we'd have more time to...' Harry dragged a hand through his already dishevelled hair. 'I'm putting this badly. What I want to say is...'

'Shh,' Rosa reached over to place a finger on his lips, stopping the flow of words. As he relished her gentle touch and resisted the urge to take the finger into his mouth, an unexpected tightness in his pants caused him to shift uneasily.

'It doesn't matter,' she reassured him. 'Your daughter is important. Right now, she needs you, needs to be the focus of your attention. We have time. It's enough to know that we want...'

She paused, and Harry detected a glimpse of uncertainty in the grey eyes meeting his. 'I mean... I thought... Last night... I felt...'

Harry covered Rosa's hand with his. 'You're right. We *do* have time. I felt it too. It's more than physical, it's...' He broke off, not quite sure what he was trying to say. He only knew that this woman made him feel as if he was ten feet tall, as if he could move mountains. This was a woman he would slay dragons for, as the saying went. He hadn't expected ever to feel this way again. It was as unsettling as it was exhilarating.

'Are you ready to order?'

The pair looked up, surprised to see the waitress had returned with their coffees. 'Not quite. Give us a few more minutes,' Harry muttered.

They both studied the menu avidly before deciding on their meals, Harry choosing the Baked Eggs Chachouka, while Rosa opted for the Huon Smoked Salmon on scrambled free-range eggs with watercress and sour dough bread. Their knees touched under the table while they drank their coffees and chatted inconsequentially about their Everglades trip and the drama of young love, recounting tales of their own early misadventures.

'At the time it seems like the end of the world,' Rosa admitted as they laughed over one particular disastrous relationship. 'But life goes on, and there are better people out there.'

'There certainly are,' Harry agreed, tightening his grip on her hands which had somehow found their way into his. 'Look at us.'

Their meals arrived at that point and conversation was postponed while they enjoyed breakfast.

'I expect you want to get back,' Rosa said when they'd finished eating and demolished a second cup of coffee.

Harry knew he should, but was loath to leave. It had been a pleasant interlude, but he was very aware that Lucy was waiting for him at home and he needed to check on her. He also knew he had to call Hillie and he wasn't looking forward to that. He could imagine her reaction, her demanding Lucy return to uni forthwith or her allowance would be cut. Sometimes Harry wondered if his soon-to-be-ex-wife had forgotten what it was like to be young.

'You're right,' he said, half-heartedly. 'I told Lucy I wouldn't be long, and that must have been...'

'We've been here at least two hours,' Rosa reminded him. 'Now go.'

'I'll be seeing you. I mean...' he added quickly, seeing a shadow fall across Rosa's face. 'I want to see you again soon, really soon, but I don't know... Damn Lucy. Why did she have to arrive right now? Just as we...'

'Why don't you drop into the shop when you know what's what,' Rosa suggested, clearly understanding his unspoken dilemma.

'Right.' Harry planted a kiss on her cheek, revelling the softness of her skin and breathing in her unique fragrance, before he turned and walked off. *What had he done to deserve such a woman, and how on earth was he going to retain her interest?*

Twenty-three

Contradictory thoughts were tumbling through Rosa's mind as she walked home. Had she been too forward suggesting Harry drop into the bookshop? He had indicated he had some feelings for her, hadn't he? She tried to remember his actual words, but they'd gone, gone in the mess that her brain was these days. Hadn't he said something about it being more than physical? Well, they'd certainly got the physical part right, but more? There hadn't been enough time to determine that.

Look how wrong she'd been about Ken. Damn! She'd meant to ask Harry what he intended to do about those two. Did he intend to do anything? Or was he going to let them get away with it? She doubted it. From what she knew of the man –granted, not much – he hadn't given the impression of someone who let sleeping dogs lie.

Then Rosa's thoughts darted to Harry's daughter and her brow furrowed. She'd never dated anyone with children, albeit a grown-up daughter. Or had much to do with children of any age. Childless herself, from circumstance rather than choice, Rosa had tended to avoid friends' children, managing to circumvent the usual fussing over babies that took place at their gatherings. Sure, she'd met Vi's girls on that one occasion they'd visited, but it was a fleeting visit and she could barely recall them or her interaction with them. Rosa didn't think she'd ever been in a room alone with them, so protective had Vi been.

On reflection, Rosa wasn't sure if the reason was an actual dislike of children, a wariness that they wouldn't like her – would somehow sense her ignorance – or that she actually wanted a child of her own and was afraid of tempting fate. Did that make her a bad person? Would she have made a bad mother? Whatever the reason, it was now too late in life to have second thoughts and the notion of meeting and trying to make friends with this Lucy was a daunting prospect.

Did one actually make friends with a young woman of Lucy's age, she wondered, remembering her initial impression of the girl at the bookshop opening. She'd appeared elegant, chic and sophisticated beyond her years. Would Harry expect Rosa to meet her? What if they did form a relationship – a proper one? Would that mean Lucy would become part of her life – her stepdaughter? Would she become the wicked stepmother of the fairy tale?

Rosa's musings took her all the way home and she entered her familiar apartment with a sense of relief, remembering the planned visit to the nursing home. Damn Vi and her so-called attempt to comfort to their mother. Now, as usual, it was Rosa's job to break the bad news.

By the time Rosa entered the nursing home carpark, she was in a calmer frame of mind and was able to greet her mother with a smile. She made the switch of library books and listened to Ivy's tales of her week which sounded much more hectic than Rosa's own with its busy schedule of social engagements. Listening to her mum's shrewd description of a recent trivia night and an amusing account of the antics of several residents, Rosa realised the vagueness her mum had shown on her previous visit had disappeared, making her wonder if she'd imagined it.

'Mum, about Vi,' she began, finally approaching the topic which hadn't been far from the forefront of her mind.

'You've spoken to her?' Ivy asked eagerly. 'She *is* coming? She said she was.' Her whole face lit up, forcing Rosa to silently curse her sister yet again.

'I'm afraid not, Mum. She... Something's come up and she can't get away right now.'

'Oh.' Ivy's voice sank, her eyes drooped and her fingers began to work on the edge of her sweater. 'She's so busy, such an important job. Rod too.' She sighed. 'But it would be nice to see her and the girls before I...'

'Mum!' Rosa leant down to give her mother a warm hug. 'You're not going anywhere. And she *will* come to see you. I promise,' she added crossing her fingers. She had no idea how she could keep that promise, but vowed that somehow she'd make her selfish sister see sense.

'Now, I need to go. I'll see you next week as usual,' Rosa gave her mother another hug, kissed her on the forehead and stroked back a strand of Ivy's thinning white hair, hair that had once been as golden and luxurious as Vi's.

Rosa felt her eyes mist over as she made her way back to the car and sat there for a few minutes before starting the engine. She hated it when Ivy talked that way. It was bad enough that she was stuck here in a nursing home. Most of the time she seemed to enjoy her days, as evidenced by her cheerful recounting of the week's activities, but there was no getting away from the fact that it was the last frontier. No one was going to leave that place alive.

It was late afternoon when Rosa arrived home and she found it difficult to settle to anything, so it was a relief when her mobile rang and she saw Jenny's smiling face on the screen. 'How did you know I needed to talk with someone?' she asked.

'I remember this time on a Sunday,' Jenny said. 'It's a lonely time and Mike and I wondered if you'd to come to dinner – if you're not otherwise engaged,' she added with a meaningful chuckle.

'No, quite alone and free,' Rosa replied, perfectly aware to whom Jenny was referring. 'I was feeling a bit lonesome. I'd love to join you, if you're sure you want company.' She paused, knowing how private Jenny and Mike had been, seeking company very rarely, and apparently preferring to keep to themselves. Not that she blamed them. She'd probably do the same if... She was so lost in thought, she almost missed Jenny's reply.

'I'm sure. We've kept pretty much to ourselves, I know. Getting accustomed to each other again, I expect. And to being part of a couple. It's a bit strange for us both, but we're getting used to it – and to each other. However it's time we became more sociable.' She chuckled and Rosa could hear Mike's voice in the background, but couldn't make out the words. 'So, dinner? Come around six and we can have a drink by the river first.'

Rosa closed her phone thinking how perfectly Jenny understood her. She knew Rosa had seen Harry on Friday and Saturday and no doubt wanted the low-down. But she must also be aware that Rosa might be feeling a bit low by now and would need some company.

Deciding a shower would make her feel better, Rosa headed for the ensuite. As soon as the stream of hot water began flowing over her body, she experienced a sense of wellbeing. What had she to be sad about? Her mother was in reasonably good health, albeit a tad fatalistic, she'd had amazing sex with Harry with the prospect of more when he could tear himself away from his daughter, and she had good friends who'd invited her to dinner.

Rosa deliberately relegated all thoughts of her sister and the Pete and Ken business to the back of her mind. She'd consider them later – or not as the case might be. Vi, yes; she'd have to deal with her. But maybe she could forget about Ken and company and let Harry or someone else handle them and do what needed to be done. It wasn't her business anymore.

Feeling much more cheerful, Rosa drew on a pair of jeans and a shirt, tying a sweater around her shoulders and selecting a bottle of wine from the wine rack – red, she decided. Mike was probably a red man, and she and Jenny would drink whatever was on offer.

As she drove to Jenny's cottage, Rosa reflected how peaceful this part of Noosa was. Accustomed to the continual flow of people and traffic outside her Gympie Terrace apartment, she enjoyed the buzz of the tourists. But here, only a few streets away, she could be in a different place altogether. Weyba Creek flowed slowly to her left, while on the right older homes on large blocks were interspersed with modern mansions which took up most of the available land.

Jenny's was one of the older ones, sitting low opposite the river. It faced a wide expanse of grass and a jetty to which was tied a tired-looking tinny. Mike appeared at the door as soon as she drove up. He was carrying a couple of folding chairs in one hand and a platter of something in the other. Jenny followed close behind with a third chair.

'Perfect timing,' she said. 'Though we'd hoped to have set up before you arrived. I'll just fetch the wine.'

'No need.' Rosa hopped out of her car flourishing the bottle of Shiraz. 'I came prepared.'

'Good stuff,' Mike said, beaming. 'Dinner's in the slow cooker, so we have plenty of time.'

As they settled in the canvas chairs facing the river, Mike sighed. 'It's beautiful here.'

'But it's not Oregon.' Jenny laughed at what was clearly a familiar topic of discussion or bone of contention between them.

'So you *do* intend to go back?' Rosa's fears for her future emerged again as she had known they would at any hint of the pair returning to the United States.

'It *is* Mike's home,' Jenny replied. 'And Maddy's there too – and Ben,' she added referring to Mike's Labrador. 'So, yes, we *will* be going back, but not for good. We've been talking about it and maybe we can come to some arrangement, six months in each place or something.'

Rosa saw the pair exchange a look, which spoke eloquently of many discussions and some sort of agreement.

'I couldn't leave here completely, or the shop, when it was my dream. I'm sure you could manage it for a time, and maybe get some part-time help. But don't worry, we're not dashing off just yet. We'll give you plenty of notice.' She smiled at Mike and patted his hand. 'Won't we, honey?'

Rosa felt the apprehension in her gut uncoil and began to relax. She should have known. Of course, Jenny and Mike would be going back to Oregon, and of course she could manage the shop on her own, as long as she knew Jenny would be returning.

'And what about you?' Jenny asked. 'How did the date go?'

Before Rosa could reply, Mike rose. 'I'll let you two ladies discuss your private details while I check on dinner.' He picked up his wine and disappeared in the direction of the house.

'Always tactful,' Jenny said, smiling after him fondly. 'Now, Harry. How did it go? Did…?'

Rosa blushed and stared down into her wine. 'I took your advice to take a risk and…' She could feel herself redden even more and took a gulp of wine in an effort to calm herself, almost choking.

'I knew it! And was it as good as…?'

'Better.' But Rosa decided she'd said enough about whatever was happening between Harry and her. She intended to keep some matters private. 'His daughter has arrived back,' she blurted out.

'And that means?'

'He has her on his mind. He's worried she's dropped out of uni, and now she's there, sharing his house so he can't…' Usually renowned for her plain speaking, Rosa couldn't bring herself to say it.

Jenny said it for her. 'He can't indulge in wild sex when his daughter's in town?' She raised her eyebrows.

'No. I mean… Well, yes, I suppose that is what I mean.'

The pair giggled.

'What's the joke? Have you two finished your girly confidences?' Mike returned with another bottle of wine. 'Dinner's almost ready, but we can fit in another glass.'

'Not for me. I have to drive home.' Rosa placed a hand over her glass.

'Go on. You can always stay here. There's a spare room.'

'And I'm sure Jenny hasn't finished grilling you yet. You'll need this.' Mike ignored Rosa's protestations and refilled her glass.

When they were finally seated inside and enjoying the slow-cooked pork casserole Mike had prepared, Jenny had another surprise for Rosa. 'We thought – Mike and I.' She threw a glance at him as she spoke. 'We'd like to arrange a bit of a gathering, not a party, but a get-together to celebrate *our* coming together. We don't intend marriage – we've both done that, and at our age, we don't feel the need. But…' She took a deep breath. 'We'd like to celebrate in some way, so…'

'What a lovely idea,' Rosa broke in. 'When did you envisage this not-party happening?' She looked from one to the other.

'Maybe in a week or so. We haven't quite decided. But of course you must come… and Harry?'

'Harry? I can't speak for him. He…'

'And his daughter too, of course. Though…' Then it seemed Jenny had an idea. 'Hang on. I think I've heard Alex talk about a niece who might be close to the daughter's age. What's her name, by the way? I can't keep calling her "the daughter".'

'Lucy, but…'

'No. It's decided. She probably needs to meet a few young people to hang out with.'

'I guess so. I can ask him.' Rosa wondered what Harry's reaction would be. It was one thing to see him, date him, sleep with him – a shudder ran through her body as she remembered their night together – but to bring him along to a social event as her partner, and to invite his daughter too? That might be a step too far.

'Do that. We'll work out a date in the next day or two and let you know. When are you going to see him again?'

'I... I don't know. He'll drop into the shop.' To Rosa's own ears this sounded remarkably vague, not any sort of arrangement, but it didn't seem to faze Jenny.

'Perfect. We can invite him then.'

Feeling she'd been completely thwarted, Rosa was glad when Mike rose to fetch coffee.

'It'll be fine. You'll see.' Jenny patted Rosa's arm.

Rosa wasn't so sure. It was all very well for Jenny to recount how Maddy had helped her and Mike get together. Harry wasn't Mike. And Jenny wasn't her godmother. She sighed as she drank her coffee then rose to go.

'Sure you won't stay?' Jenny asked.

'No, I'm fine now. The coffee did the trick.' Along with her refusal to drink any more wine with dinner, she thought. It was strange how she'd felt such a great desire for company, and she'd enjoyed being with Jenny and Mike, but now all she wanted was to be home alone. Home, where she could take time to process the past couple of days, where she could remember how she'd felt with Harry and figure out what she was going to do about it.

*

Lucy was nowhere to be seen when Harry returned from his breakfast with Rosa. Tiger was asleep in his basket and there was a trail of wet footprints leading through the hall, from which Harry guessed that Lucy had taken Tiger for a walk, gone for a swim and was now asleep herself. A quick glance into her room proved him correct. He closed the door quietly and settled down with his computer, determined to make a dent in the Health project, even while he was working on a couple of smaller jobs.

It wasn't till much later that a brighter Lucy made her appearance, brushing her hair out of her eyes and asking, 'What's for dinner?'

'Sleep well?'

'Mmm. Have you been working? It's Sunday.'

'No rest for the wicked, Lulu. I'm my own boss, so I work when I can and take time off when I want to. It's not like Sydney when I had to show up in the office every day. Want to go out for a meal?'

'Sure. I just need to do something with my hair first and put on something more...' She looked down at her ripped jeans and faded tee-shirt with something like disgust, and headed back to her bedroom.

Harry closed the computer and poured a beer while he waited, glad the long sleep had worked its magic. This was more like the Lucy he knew. When she reappeared, he whistled his appreciation. She was wearing something strappy with a short white jacket and a pair of heels which brought her almost up to his chin.

'Not too much?' she asked pouting a little. 'Last time I was here, I noticed the girls dressed with a lot of style.'

'You look just fine. Maybe we should try the surf club. I haven't been there yet, but it gets a good rap.'

'Suits me. Anywhere.'

Harry could see through Lucy's apparent disinterest. He knew his daughter well and recognised her reluctance to appear enthusiastic.

'Okay, the surf club it is. Let's go.'

The evening passed without incident, but Harry was aware Lucy was putting on a front. While she showed interest in their surroundings, he could tell she wasn't into it and when he mentioned the possibility of her transfer to the local university and a degree in International Aid, all she said was, 'Leave it out, Dad. I didn't come up here to be lectured at. I got enough from Mum,' then clammed up.

They drove home in silence, Lucy heading straight to bed and leaving Harry scratching his head and wondering how he could break through her defences enough for her to at least give his new idea a chance. It wasn't till he was on his way to bed himself and stopped outside her door, that he heard her sobbing and realised just how much she was hurting. The combination of the disappointment with her chosen course of study, her breakup and – the final straw – her mother's patent disapproval had taken more of a toll on her than Harry had supposed. Harry stood listening, then shook his head and continued to bed. He felt so helpless. His daughter was grieving and there wasn't a damn thing he could do to help.

Twenty-four

Wednesday arrived with no sign of Harry, and Rosa was beginning to have doubts. Maybe he'd decided a relationship with her was all too hard and it would be easier to keep away. Maybe something had happened to him – an accident – or to Lucy. Maybe… She had turned all the possible scenarios over and over without coming to a plausible conclusion other than that he didn't want to see her again.

Clearly tired of the nervous energy she was emitting, Jenny had told her to 'Get a grip. It's only been two days,' but to Rosa the two days seemed like forever. In her heart of hearts she knew Jenny was right, but she couldn't convince herself, instead expending energy in setting up the children's corner they'd planned and contacting some local children's authors to arrange storytelling sessions. This, at least, seemed to please Jenny who muttered something like, 'Thank goodness you've found something to do, but I swear if that man doesn't drop in soon, I'll go and drag him in by the hair.'

Fortunately, Jenny wasn't forced to make good her threat as, just before closing, the man in question walked in followed by a tall blonde girl in jeans and a tee-shirt which proudly proclaimed her to be a Friend of the Earth.

'Hi,' he said with his usual lopsided smile, and drew his daughter towards Rosa. 'This is Rosa, Lucy. D'you remember meeting her at the opening of this place?'

'Maybe,' Lucy kept her hands in her pockets, ignoring Rosa's outstretched one, but did meet her eyes, sizing Rosa up as if gauging her suitability. But, if she did reach a decision, she gave no hint.

'Lucy and I are planning to try that tapas place on the river and thought you might like to join us,' Harry said.

Rosa looked at Lucy who was taking no part in the interchange, but had walked off and was now mooching around the shelves. Clearly this wasn't *her* idea of a fun evening, but Rosa was so relieved to see Harry, she decided to ignore the sullen girl and returned his smile. 'Love to. We'll be through here in a bit. Do you want to wait or will I meet you there?'

'Lucy?' Harry turned to his daughter. 'Want to stay here for a bit or go ahead?'

'Whatever.'

Harry shrugged. 'We'll go then and see you there.'

'Before you go…' Jenny appeared as if from nowhere. 'Mike and I are planning a little celebration and would love you to come – both of you,' she emphasised, including Lucy in her gaze. Before Lucy had a chance to refuse, she added. 'There'll be other young people there too. It won't be all oldies like us and your dad.'

Lucy didn't give any indication she'd heard, but picked a book from the shelf. 'I'll take this one.'

'Good choice,' Jenny said as she wrapped it and took Lucy's money. 'She's a local author. So we'll see you both Friday week?'

Harry nodded while Lucy muttered, 'S'pose so.'

Recognising the girl didn't look sullen as much as unhappy, Rosa's heart went out to her, remembering what Harry had told her. The poor girl. She probably didn't know what she wanted, and here they were trying to manufacture a social life for her in a town where the only person she knew was her dad. And he'd just introduced her to his new squeeze. Rosa chuckled inwardly at the old-fashioned word which had come unbidden to mind. Was that really how she viewed herself?

When the pair left, Rosa managed to evade Jenny's "I told you so" expression while they closed up the shop, but by the time she walked out the door she'd been subjected to an unwelcome batch of advice on how to handle the situation.

'It'll be okay,' Jenny assured her as they parted, Rosa to walk to the tapas bar, and Jenny to her car.

Rosa wasn't so sure. What if Lucy resented her? Saw her as a potential threat to her relationship with her dad? And what about her mother? Rosa had no idea how young people thought and it seemed so long since she had been that age. She heaved a sigh as she hoisted her bag further up her shoulder. Well, she was about to find out.

*

'She's very different from Mum.' Lucy rolled the straw between her fingers, then took a sip of the lemon, lime and bitters she'd ordered while they awaited Rosa's arrival.

Glad she hadn't insisted on one of the beers he'd ordered for himself, Harry repositioned the beer mat under his glass and considered. It was true. Rosa who barely came up to his shoulder even in high heels and who, with her wild dark hair and spirited manner, was the antithesis of his tall, elegant, blonde wife. 'You're right,' he said at last. 'You'll like her when you get to know her.' He mentally crossed his fingers. It was important to him that those two – the most important women in his life – became friends. Was that even possible?

'She's not what I expected. When you said you'd met someone, I thought... There are so many women in Noosa who look...' Lucy waved her hands about as if to signify something Harry couldn't imagine. Clearly seeing his puzzlement, she added, 'You know, Dad. Women more like Mum. Women who dress well, who have a sense of style, who...'

'Here she comes.' Harry rose to greet Rosa with a peck on the cheek, while Lucy looked on, seemingly amused.

Rosa perched on one of the high stools facing the bench and the river. Her feet didn't touch the ground. Harry smiled. Lucy was so right when she said Rosa was different. She was nothing like Hillie, nothing like any of the women Harry knew in Sydney – mostly Hillie's friends. Maybe that was the attraction.

'What'll you have to drink?'

'That beer looks good.'

'And one for me too this time please, Dad,' Lucy piped in, grabbing a menu from a nearby table and beginning to study it fervently.

*

While Harry was fetching the drinks, Rosa looked across at Lucy, whose head was still bent over the menu. What could she say to the girl? She couldn't sit here in silence. 'You're at uni in Melbourne?' she asked, aware how inane she sounded but unable to think of a more appropriate conversation starter.

'Was.' Lucy looked up and appeared to study Rosa intently, making her wonder if she had a smut on her nose or her hair was falling down. Rosa forced a smile and resisted the temptation to check.

'You've left?'

'Maybe.' Lucy returned her attention to the menu.

'What looks good?' Rosa asked, looking around for another menu.

'They have pizza, but the tapas sound interesting, too.' Lucy finally looked up and pushed back the thick strands of hair falling over her face. 'Yours is naturally curly, isn't it?'

Surprised and without thinking, Rosa answered, 'Yes, for my sins. I'd have killed for straight hair like that at your age.'

'Really?' For the first time, Rosa thought she caught a glimmer of interest in Lucy's eyes. Was talking about hair all it took? She was really out of practice.

'Really. My sister has hair like yours, my mum too, though hers is thinner now, and white. You take after you dad I suppose?'

'Mum, too. We're all blonde. That's why...' Rosa saw the girl bite her lower lip. 'That's why I was surprised when I met you. When Dad said he'd met someone, I was pleased. He needs someone, now that Mum..., but,' she pushed her thick hair back again and took a long sip from her glass, 'you're not what I expected. I thought you'd be more like Mum, like all their friends in Sydney, not...'

'Not a short, dark bookshop owner with frizzy hair?' asked Rosa, smiling when she saw Lucy flush and drop her eyes again.

'How did you and Dad meet?'

'We were working together.' That seemed to spark Lucy's attention.

'Oh, yeah. Dad said. You're not in IT though.'

'Not quite. Until recently I was working in the Finance Department of the Health Service where your dad has a contract. It was my job to prepare the data for the off-site storage he's working on.'

'So why aren't you still there?' Once Lucy got started she could rival Jenny for her interrogation skills.

'My friend Jenny – you met her – came back from an overseas trip and asked me to join her in the bookshop.' Not completely accurate, but a good enough approximation, and more or less what she'd initially told Harry. Rosa could see Lucy processing this information.

'So you studied business or finance. Did you enjoy it?'

'I studied both and loved it. I enjoy figures and details. I guess I'm a bit odd that way.'

'Definitely not like Mum. No wonder Dad and you get on. I'm studying business and I hate it. That's one of the reasons I'm here,' she confided, returning to slurp up the remains of her drink in a way that would have put a ten year-old to shame.

'Sorry to take so long. The barman was an interesting guy.' Harry returned carrying three glasses of beer with another couple of menus under one arm.

Rosa threw him a sideways glance. Was he for real, or had he delayed to give her and Lucy time to get to know each other? It hadn't worked.

He dropped the menus on the benchtop. 'We should decide. The evening crowd will be arriving soon, and if we don't want to wait for ages, it would be a good idea to get our orders in first.'

All three gave serious attention to the large menu boards. Rosa wasn't accustomed to tapas so was unsure how it would all work, but Harry took charge. 'If we each choose a couple of tapas, we can share – or would you prefer pizza, Lucy?'

'No, tapas are fine. Maybe a pizza later if we're still hungry.'

Lucy seemed to have cheered up with Harry's return and started reading out items from the menu with comments as to their appeal. Rosa refrained from commenting, allowing father and daughter to choose, only nodding agreement when Harry turned to ask her opinion.

When their food arrived, the narrow bench-top which served as a table was filled with share plates of prawns piri piri, crumbed Spanish jumbo green olives stuffed with fetta, shredded duck with sticky black currants and chilli, chorizo meatballs and arancini.

'Yum.' Lucy picked up her plate and filled it with a selection of delicious looking morsels, while Harry encouraged Rosa to do the same, surreptitiously stroking her knee beneath the bench.

Rosa experienced an unexpected jolt of lust, which she disguised by shifting in her seat, taking a gulp of beer and picking up her plate to do as Harry had suggested. His fingers tightened on her thigh, causing her to almost choke. She moved away slightly, as best she could without falling from the stool.

'You two getting to know each other?'

Harry's unexpected and typically male comment made both women laugh. It was Lucy who answered. 'Give us a chance, Dad. Rosa was telling me how you worked together?'

Harry's eyes swivelled towards Rosa who shook her head slightly. 'That we did,' he said, perhaps a little too heartily. 'But... we're only getting to know each other better now she's left the organisation.' He popped an olive into his mouth and washed it down with a swig of beer.

Rosa opened her mouth to add something but, seeing Lucy appeared satisfied, she closed it again without speaking.

The evening progressed in an awkward mix of silences interspersed with innocuous conversation between Harry and Rosa. Lucy seemed intent on eating and rarely contributed to any part of the discussion. Rosa was surprised, therefore, when they rose to leave and the girl addressed her directly.

'I'm glad we met. I'm glad Dad has found someone. You seem like a nice person. But don't hurt him. I won't forgive you if you do.'

'I... I won't,' Rosa replied, while Harry appeared amused at Lucy's defence of him.

The three stood on the pathway for a few moments, then Harry seemed to make a decision. 'Can you make your own way back, Lulu? I'm going to see Rosa home. You have your key?'

Lucy nodded, said goodbye, turned and walked off.

Pleased, but with a churning in her gut, Rosa asked, 'Are you sure? Won't Lucy...?'

'I've never been more sure of anything. Lucy's not a child. She's had a relationship of her own. She knows – or has to learn – that I have my own life to live, just as she has hers. If she plans to live with me, it has to be on that basis. Now we've...' He took a deep breath and tightened his arm around Rosa's shoulders. 'I think what we have is something special. I'm hoping you see it that way too.'

Overcome with emotion, all Rosa could do was nod. The warmth of Harry's arm and hand was sending ripples of excitement through her body. She couldn't wait to get home, couldn't believe she felt this way and couldn't accept her feelings were reciprocated.

As the apartment door closed behind them, Rosa reached up to turn on the light, only to find herself pinned against the wall. 'I've been wanting to do this all day,' Harry said, his voice hoarse with desire.

Rosa felt her face being cupped in a warm pair of hands, then Harry's lips were on hers, his tongue forcing her mouth open. A wave of longing threatened to engulf her. She wanted this man, wanted him more than she'd wanted anyone or anything in her life, wanted him so much it scared her. She tried to draw back, but it was too late. Her body was moving of its own accord, moving with his in a fever of desire. 'Not here,' she managed to utter, her breath coming in gasps.

Harry picked her up and carried her to the bedroom, where he deposited her gently on the bed, before joining her to resume what they'd begun in the hallway, but with less urgency.

'This could become a habit,' Rosa murmured, undoing the buttons of Harry's shirt and kissing his chest, loving the sensation of the small hairs against her lips.

'A good one,' Harry's voice was muffled against her hair, then he moved away slightly to allow Rosa to slip the shirt off his shoulders. Their lips met again before he began to unfasten the white shirt Rosa had donned that morning, with no inkling that Harry would be the one to remove it.

The moonlight shining through the window lit up Harry's face. Rosa could see a flicker of something she couldn't identify in his eyes, then it was gone and the Harry she knew returned. She lay trembling as his lips sought out all her secret crevices, finishing by taking her nipples into his mouth one after the other and rolling his tongue around them. It wasn't till she was in an agony of yearning, that he finally entered her and slowly took her to the heights of fulfilment.

As they lay in each other's arms, spent, Harry pushed himself up to lean on one elbow and looked down into Rosa's eyes. 'I'm afraid I can't stay tonight either.' He stroked her eyelids with one finger, then kissed the spots his finger had touched.

'I know. It's okay. I understand. Lucy...'

'Shh. She'll come round and accept you. I know what she said, but she's only ever known me and Hillie. Then it was Hillie and Bernie which she found difficult to accept. Now it's me and you. It's a lot for her to cope with.' Harry dropped his arms and gazed into space as if he could see Hillie, Bernie and Lucy in the room with them.

A wave of pleasure flowed through Rosa at his words, at the idea that she was now part of something. Harry and Rosa; Rosa and Harry. It had a good sound, a good feel. What did it mean? Surely it was too soon for this sort of talk? They barely knew each other. Sure, they'd had good sex. Correction. They'd had superb sex. But there was more to a relationship than that, as she knew to her cost. And there was his daughter, not to mention his not-yet-ex-wife, and her mother, and the blasted business with Peter and Ken was still hanging over them; over her.

She slithered up to lean against the pillows, remembering she still hadn't found out what Harry intended to do about that pair. She knew it wasn't the time to bring it up, but the words popped out in spite of herself. 'What did you decide about Pete and Ken?' she asked, stroking Harry's hair back from his brow to soften her enquiry.

Harry took hold of her hand in both of his, rubbing it lightly. 'I've checked things out. I should be finished soon. I can't do anything till then, but as soon as I do, I plan to report them to the appropriate body. Seems you have something called the Crime and Corruption Commission here in Queensland.'

'That's right.' Although she now had her question answered, Rosa felt a tingle of fear. What if Pete thought she'd been the one to report them? Would the commission reveal the identity of the person who'd made the report? Would they then come after Harry? And what did their threats really mean? She shivered, although the bed and the room were both warm.

'It'll be okay,' Harry reassured her. 'They can't hurt me. And you're completely out of it.' Rosa shuddered again. She wasn't so sure.

Twenty-five

As Harry prepared breakfast next morning, he knew he couldn't delay calling Hillie any longer. He wasn't looking forward to the conversation, which he knew from past experience would be a difficult one. He and Hillie had rarely seen eye-to-eye about Lucy and now they'd parted, it seemed she'd become even more obdurate.

'Harry! At last!'

Harry knew he should have remembered Hillie's way of talking in exclamation marks. It had been an amusing trick she sometimes used when they were young, but the amusement had faded over the years as it turned into an annoying habit.

'So Lucy *did* go to you? I hope you don't condone what she's planning. She's too...'

'Hillie!' Harry almost lost his temper. No wonder their daughter had turned up on his doorstep. Sometimes her mother had no idea how to handle her. 'Yes. As I said in my text. She's here and will be till the end of semester. She assures me she can complete her assignments online. She hasn't dropped out yet, and...'

'But this crazy idea of volunteering, and the music festival. You know they're a hotbed of drugs and God knows what and...'

Harry sighed and moved the phone to his other hand as Tiger placed a paw on his knee. He'd taken the mobile out into the courtyard, hoping the ambiance of the peaceful spot would help the conversation – or at least his side if it. He stroked Tiger's silky coat and wondered how quickly he could finish the call.

'She didn't go to the festival. She was too upset, upset by your words. She came straight here and *I* was pleased to see her. As for the volunteering; it wouldn't be too bad, would it?' He had to hold the phone away from his ear as a wave of invective echoed across the line. 'She's safe with me right now. I think that's what you wanted to know. And let me remind you that our daughter *is* over eighteen and quite capable of making her own decisions.'

Hillie started to speak again, but Harry had had enough. 'I don't think we have anything left to say to each other.' He ended the call and sat staring into space, before rousing himself and returning to the house, Tiger padding behind him. He knew the discussion wasn't over. Hillie had the bit between her teeth on this one and wouldn't let go easily, but he hoped he'd stalled her for now.

He had to ensure what he said was true, and that Lucy *would* complete her uni commitments and finish the semester. Then, he hoped, she might reconsider the option he'd suggested. But there was no sense in pushing it. That was a sure-fire way for her to back off and take off to God knows where.

When Harry returned inside, Lucy was sitting at the table, head supported on one hand, hair hanging down over her face, the local newspaper spread out in front of her. Looking at her, Harry was reminded of her as a little girl. It seemed only yesterday she'd sat on his knee attempting to sound out the words as he read the morning paper. For a moment the image of the younger Lucy drifted before his eyes.

'Dad?' She was giving him an odd look. 'Are you okay?'

Harry dragged a hand through his hair. 'I was just talking to your mum.'

He could see Lucy immediately summon up her defences. Her face closed up and her lips tightened.

'What did Mum have to say? I suppose she did her usual diatribe about me? It's not fair. She doesn't understand.'

'You're right there, Lulu. I think she's forgotten what it was like to be your age. But she's not going to change. I told her you intended to finish your work here. You'd better not make me a liar.'

'Thanks, Dad.' Lucy leapt up, sending the paper flying, and hugged Harry, planting a kiss on his cheek. 'I promise.'

'Mmm. Now how about breakfast? I think I have some eggs...'

'Just toast, and maybe some fruit. And coffee if you're making it. I was reading about those Stand Up Paddle lessons. Think I may drift over to the river this morning and take in one. They look cool. I didn't get a chance last time.'

Harry shook his head. There wouldn't be much work done on her assignments today, but playing the heavy father wasn't going to work. 'Coffee coming up,' he said.

Once Lucy had left, Harry settled down to work again. He intended to get this Health job finished, then he could move on. He'd already drafted the necessary statutory declaration. All it needed was the signature of a justice of the peace.

He worked solidly till lunchtime, and had just formatted his final report when Lucy wafted in dripping water all over the floor.

'Have fun?'

'It was awesome. We went right down the river then along the other side, through the mangroves.'

'The lesson went all this time?' Checking his watch, Harry judged Lucy had been gone for several hours.

'No, Dad! After the lesson I got to spend more time practising. Should be able to go by myself next time.'

'Best have a shower before lunch.'

'None for me. I grabbed a burger on the way back. Might hit the books this afternoon.' Lucy scowled. 'I guess I can't have Mum call you a liar.' She grinned as she threw his words back at him, and waltzed off, towel around her shoulders.

With Lucy in her room, peace reigned again. Harry printed out the report, checking it carefully before placing it in a folder. He'd managed to avoid including the duplicate invoices, but had retained the paper copies of them as evidence, should they be required. He recalled Rosa telling him her instructions were to destroy the paperwork when she'd computerised the data, but she'd passed them on to him instead.

After a quick lunch of roast beef on rye with dill pickle, Harry called to Lucy that he was going out. Receiving only a vague murmur in reply, he assumed she was either hard at work or falling asleep. He hoped it was the former.

Harry parked in the Health Service car park for what he intended to be his last time. The appointment with Robson was at two. It was almost that now. He picked up the folder, took a deep breath and walked into the building.

Today, Robson was all smiles as he greeted Harry with outstretched hand.

'Take a seat. Brenda will be in with coffee in a tick.'

Harry took the seat indicated in front of a low coffee table and Pete Robson took one opposite. 'Well,' he said, slapping his hands on his knees. 'It's done? No problems?'

Harry thought he could detect a faint hint of concern underneath the man's bluff manner. He smiled and assured him that he hadn't encountered any. Robson's sigh of relief was almost palpable.

'Good, good. Here's Brenda with the coffee now.'

The faded blonde woman Harry had spoken with briefly on previous visits scuttled in with a tray which she placed on the table, before disappearing again.

'Help yourself.' Robson picked up a cup in one hand, grabbed a couple of chocolate biscuits in the other and nodded at Harry to do the same. Harry could see where the man's girth had come from if this was a daily routine. 'Now, your report?'

Harry took a sip of the instant coffee, tried to hide a grimace and placed the folder on the table. It sat between the two men like an elephant in the room.

Robson eyed it cautiously. 'So, no problems? Good,' he repeated.

'Were you expecting any?'

'No, no. But with such a massive project, you never know what'll turn up. We'd hoped...'

Harry raised his eyebrows.

'Ken Steele and I. My Finance Director. You met him last time.'

'Yes. I remember.' Harry could feel his hackles rise at the mention of Ken Steele. He was the man who had been Rosa's lover. The man who'd tried to besmirch her name. The man who'd threatened her. At least he wasn't here now or Harry didn't know if he'd be able to keep his hands to himself. He wasn't a violent man, but anyone who threatened Rosa... He came back to the present in time to hear Robson's apology.

'I'm sorry he couldn't join us. End of month reconciliation or some such thing, I believe.' His mouth twisted in an expression of derision. 'But I'm sure we can manage. Maybe you can just take me through it and he and I can read it later.' He pointed to the as yet unopened folder.

Robson leaned back and folded his arms while Harry explained what he'd done, how the data was set up in the cloud. Then he clarified that he'd set out clear instructions for the IT staff to follow. 'It's like a gigantic filing cabinet in the ether,' he concluded. 'Your data can be entered directly into it. Should do away with the need for paper copies and save time.'

'And staff, especially snooping, over-inquisitive ones,' Robson muttered.

Harry pretended he didn't hear. 'I'm happy to provide any staff training you require,' he added. 'You'll find I've included a costed outline in the report, should you wish to avail yourself of it.' Harry had felt obligated to make the offer which he was sure would be declined. It was.

'No. I think we can manage that part. So it's all ready to be handed over to our IT guys?'

'Yes, I...'

'Then I'll say thank you and good day.' Pete Robson rose, hand outstretched again. The meeting was at an end.

Harry was glad to be out in the fresh air once again. Something about the meeting had made him feel uneasy, unclean, as if he'd become part of a conspiracy, a conspiracy to defraud. He looked up to where a flock of white cockatoos were screeching their way across the deep blue sky and felt thankful this repugnant job was finally over.

Twenty-six

Rosa twirled in front of the mirror wondering if the blue dress was the right choice. Jenny had urged her to wear it, telling her once again that she needed to look more feminine. And Harry had seemed to like it last time. Her eyes half-closed and her mouth began to turn up at the memory of the last time she'd worn it; when Harry had come to dinner, when it had all started.

What was she thinking? When *what* had started? But she couldn't pretend anymore. Something had begun that night, something which was growing between them, something so special she wanted to grasp it with both hands lest it prove a mirage and disappear.

The intercom buzzed. They were here. Rosa grabbed her bag and a wrap, took a last glance in the mirror and patted her hair one more time, scowling as a few unruly curls threatened to escape the pins. She chastised herself for being so anxious, for paying so much attention to her appearance, but she couldn't deny the anticipation building up inside her, the shiver of excitement which flooded her.

'Wow!' Harry took her hands and held her at arm's length. 'I seem to remember the dress, and tonight you're positively radiant. Let's get you into the car. Lucy's waiting.'

'So she came?'

'Reluctantly. She said it could only be better than sitting home alone, though she does seem to have cheered up a bit since she discovered Stand Up Paddling.'

'And how are her assignments going?'

'I'm scared to ask.' Harry grinned.

As if he'd be scared of anything, Rosa thought, feeling the strength of his fingers laced in hers. He was the most confident person she'd ever met.

'Hi Lucy,' she greeted the girl as she slipped into the passenger seat of Harry's car. 'Looking forward to the evening?'

'Mmm.'

'I think Alex's niece is going to be there. She's around your age.'

'Dad said.'

'Just try to make an effort, will you?' Harry asked. 'Jenny and Mike are friends of Rosa's and this is *their* celebration.'

'She's the other owner of the bookshop, isn't she? And Dad says Mike is from Oregon. How did they meet?'

Hearing the flicker of interest in Lucy's voice, Rosa turned to face her. 'It's a lovely story. Jenny had been offered a redundancy here in Noosa – we worked together in the Health Service and her job was one of the first to go in the restructure. She went to visit her godmother in Oregon on the strength of finding an old sand dollar.'

'And she met Mike there?'

'He lived next door to Maddy, her godmother. Just proves you never know what's round the corner.' Rosa paused, thinking of her own situation. When the tall stranger had bumped into her table and spilled her coffee, she'd never expected to see him again, never mind that it would lead to... 'There'll be someone else out there for you too, probably a lot of someones,' she said daringly, hoping Lucy was ready to accept this advice.

'Mmm,' Lucy said again, but her faint smile told Rosa her advice wasn't unwelcome. 'And this Alex. Who's she?'

'She works as an executive coach. She helped Jenny plan her future, though a coach actually helps you make your own plans, at least that's how Jenny put it.'

'So she's a bit like a counsellor?'

'Not exactly. She doesn't try to fix things, more that she gets her clients to identify their own solutions.'

'Mum wanted me to see a counsellor.' Lucy scowled.

'What! First I've heard of it.' Rosa saw Harry's hands tighten on the steering wheel. 'When was this?'

'Before I came up that last time. When I tried to tell her a few home truths about her and Bernie.'

Rosa glanced across at Harry again in time to see his jaw constrict and a white line appear around his lips. She put her hand on his knee and patted it gently. 'I'm sure your mum meant well, but you seem pretty well-adjusted to me.'

'Maybe this *coach* could help me plan *my* future.' Lucy seemed to be thinking aloud. 'According to you and Mum, I'm not doing too good a job of it myself.'

'When have I ever said that?' Harry seemed to be having trouble driving and carrying on this conversation with his daughter at the same time, and Rosa was beginning to feel an awkward part of it.

'We're almost there. Turn right here.' Rosa was glad she was able to interrupt the conversation which was heading for a verbal impasse. To her relief, no more was said and they travelled in companionable silence until turning into Jenny's driveway.

'Hi there. You're the first to arrive. Come on in,' Jenny greeted them and led them through the house to a large courtyard in which a couple of tables were set out with drinks and platters of finger food.

While Mike poured the three drinks, others arrived and soon the area was filled with talk and laughter. It was a small gathering. There were some neighbours, a few women who'd been on Jenny's staff in the Health Service with their husbands – Rosa recognised the faces, but didn't know them well – and of course, Alex and Jack. They were accompanied by a tall girl with hair a lighter shade of red than Alex's who was dressed in a pair of cut-off jeans and a small white midriff top.

'This is Sandy,' Alex said, pulling the girl over to meet them. 'And you must be Lucy?' Alex said to Harry's daughter while the two young people sized each other up.

'You live here?' Lucy asked.

'All my life. You couldn't drag me away,' Sandy said with a wide smile. 'You just visiting?'

'I'm staying with my dad at the moment. No definite plans.' But Lucy seemed to brighten with the younger company.

'Drinks are over there, girls, and food at the other end. Help yourselves,' Mike said, joining the group.

Harry looked as if he'd like to follow Lucy, but Rosa grabbed his arm. 'Let her be. Maybe she needs some time with a younger set.'

'Set? It's one girl.'

'You know what I mean.'

As the evening progressed Rosa and Harry found lots to talk about, both with each other and the other guests, and lost sight of the two girls until they appeared behind them.

'Dad,' Lucy tugged his arm, which was encircling Rosa's waist. They both looked round. 'We're going to head down to the surf club. Sandy says there's always a good crowd there on a Friday night, and live music. Okay?'

Harry appeared dazed. 'But how will you...?'

'I'll find my own way home. I've got my key. Don't wait up.' She laughed and ran off.

Harry took two steps as if to follow her, but Rosa held him back again. 'It's what you wanted,' she reminded him. 'She won't come to any harm at the surf club. And that Sandy seems to have her head screwed on the right way.'

Harry pulled on his ear. 'You're right, of course. I just feel so responsible. After her mum...'

'She's twenty, remember? And this is Noosa. It's not Kings Cross in Sydney. She'll be right. Now forget about her. We're here to celebrate Jenny and Mike.'

At that moment, there was the sound of a spoon being knocked against a glass and Mike announced, 'Can I have your attention, please?' The chatter ceased as everyone quietened to hear what he had to say.

Looking a little embarrassed, he began to speak. 'I'm not one for flowery words, but I'd like to thank you all for coming here tonight to celebrate with Jenny and me.' He pulled Jenny towards him and for a moment they gazed into each other's eyes.

The courtyard had fallen silent. *You could hear a pin drop*, Rosa thought, her eyes misting over the sight of Jenny's obvious happiness.

Mike continued, 'We were lucky enough to find each other at a time in both our lives when a relationship was the last thing on our minds. But fate – with a bit of help from a wonderful old lady called Madeline de Ruis, Jenny's godmother and my neighbour – had other ideas, and now this wonderful woman has agreed to take me on and spend the rest of her life with me.'

There was a burst of cheering and applause. Mike held up his hand for silence again and looked at Jenny fondly. 'I just hope she doesn't live to regret it.'

Jenny took his hand and held their joined hands up in the air. 'Never,' she said. 'I want you all to know that life never ceases to surprise. I've always said that inside every cloud there's a silver lining, as one door closes another opens, but I've never quite believed it. When my job in Health disappeared,' she nodded in the direction of her former staff members, 'I travelled all the way to Oregon where another door did open and here is my silver lining.'

'That's the first time I've been called a silver lining,' Mike chuckled. 'Now, there's champagne going around. Fill your glasses, and I'll ask you to raise them in a toast.'

*

The evening finally wound up, and Rosa and Harry drove back to Rosa's apartment, but as they reached there and Rosa turned expectantly to Harry, he hesitated. 'I want to come up with you, but....' Her heart plummeted. What was wrong? They'd spent a lovely evening together. Harry had been as loving and solicitous as before. Why was he reluctant to finish the evening with more of the loving they'd already enjoyed together?

'I'm sorry,' he said, taking her hand and linking her fingers with his, before covering both with his other hand. 'You know I want to spend the rest of the evening with you, the entire night, but...'

There was that "but" again. Rosa shuddered. She tried to meet his eyes, to see what he meant, but it was futile. She couldn't figure out what he was thinking. Had Jenny and Mike's happiness been too much for him? Had he decided they needed to cool off? She forced herself to be calm and tried to listen to what he was telling her.

'It's Lucy. I know she said not to wait up and I know she's able to take care of herself – she's been living away from home for almost a year now, but I feel...' He dragged a hand through his hair. 'To me she's still my little girl and I want to be there when she gets home.'

'I see.' Rosa spoke slowly, but she really couldn't see, couldn't understand. Maybe because she'd never been a parent herself. 'So…'

'There'll be other times. I'm as disappointed as I hope you are.' He moved closer and their lips met, but it was far from the passionate kisses she'd become used to. Harry's mind was elsewhere.

'I'll call you tomorrow. Sleep well.'

Rosa stood on the sidewalk watching the white car disappear into the darkness, before heading up to her apartment. This wasn't the way the evening was supposed to end. Seeing Jenny and Mike's happiness, their joy in each other had ignited a spark of hope in Rosa, hope that she, too, could attract such happiness, and Harry's closeness throughout the evening, his attentiveness, his loving gestures had kindled that hope.

Now all she felt was an emptiness, a sense of loss, as if something which had been within her grasp had been stolen. She gave herself a shake. That sort of thinking was foolish. Harry had only gone home to be there for his daughter. It was what any caring father would do. But she couldn't stifle the suggestion of doubt that still lingered.

*

Harry hadn't been able to stay awake till Lucy arrived home. When he'd found himself dozing off in the chair and noticed it was almost midnight he'd reluctantly gone to bed, planning to read for a bit until he heard her return. Next thing he knew, the sun was shining on his face and the resident kookaburra was laughing from his perch on top of the back fence.

He picked up the book which had fallen to the floor, showered and made his way to the kitchen, resisting the impulse to check Lucy's room to ensure she'd reached home safely.

As he brewed his morning coffee and gazed out over the yard, he wondered how Rosa was this morning. It suddenly occurred to him that he had let her down dreadfully the previous evening, putting his concern over Lucy ahead of a night of passion with Rosa. And look where it had got him. He hadn't been awake when his daughter had returned home. He'd fallen asleep. He could just as well have been in Rosa's bed as his own. It would have made no difference to Lucy and would have cemented his relationship with Rosa. There was no doubt about it, he'd been a fool.

Deciding to drop into the bookshop that morning to make his profuse apologies to Rosa and hope to rectify the error of his ways, Harry was deciding between a hot and cold breakfast. He was standing holding the fridge door open when a sleepy looking Lucy, rubbing her eyes and pushing her hair off her face, still dressed in the clothes she'd been wearing the previous night, made an appearance. She was closely followed by a tall broad-shouldered guy whose blonde curls reached nearly to his shoulders. He pushed them back in a gesture almost identical to Lucy's.

What the?

'Dad, this is Jaz.'

'Good morning, Mr Kennedy.'

It spoke!

'We met at the surf club. He's a mate of Sandy's. Lives in Doonan. We were pretty late. There were no cabs and he was too pissed to walk there so he crashed on my floor.'

Harry's jaw dropped. This was a first. He'd wondered how he'd react when his little girl had a boy stay the night, and this was no boy. Jaz must be at least twenty-two, a man by anyone's standards. And he'd been sleeping in her room! He knew Lucy had boyfriends. He'd met a few when she lived at home, but they'd been boys her own age and still at school. He knew she'd met others at uni – including the one who'd dumped her. But this was all too much in his face.

'Breakfast?' he heard himself ask.

'That'd be great, Dad, but I can make it. I'll just have a shower first.' She disappeared, leaving an embarrassed Jaz standing in the middle of the kitchen, shuffling from one foot to the other.

'I should be going,' he said. 'Can you...' He looked expectantly in the direction Lucy had gone, but there was no help for him there.

'Not on an empty stomach. Sit down there. I'll pour you a coffee and have some breakfast ready in two ticks.' Harry decided to take pity on the guy. Jaz was around the same age he'd been when he met Lucy's mother and, if Lucy was to be believed, he hadn't slept with

Harry's daughter – not yet, anyway. But back then Harry'd no more have dreamt of sleeping in Hillie's room than… And if her parents had caught him, that'd have been the end of him, for sure.

'Thanks, Mr Kennedy. That'd be cool.'

'Harry,' Harry said without thinking. This Mr Kennedy stuff made him feel like Methuselah. But the guy had obviously been well-brought up, not quite the layabout he appeared.

'So you and Lucy got in late?' he asked, when there had been silence for a space of five or ten minutes, during which time, Harry had broken three eggs into the frypan and added several strips of bacon along with sliced tomatoes.

'Yeah,' Jaz stretched his arms above his head. 'Must have been around three.' He yawned.

No wonder Harry hadn't heard them come in. He'd have been dead to the world by then. He was itching to ask more questions, find out more about Jaz – what sort of a name was that? But any thought of a fatherly interrogation was put paid to by Lucy's return, smiling widely and looking fresh and pretty in a strappy summer dress covered in little flowers.

'Great,' she said, pouring herself a large glass of orange juice before taking a seat beside Jaz.

Harry silently continued making breakfast which he served up, before joining them.

'Thanks a lot Mr… Harry,' Jaz said, after breakfast, pushing back from the table, 'I'd better get home, now,' he said to Lucy. 'I need a shower too, and a change of clothes.'

'I'll see you out.'

The two went to the door while Harry poured himself another much-needed cup of coffee. When Lucy returned, he was full of questions. He began with, 'How will he – Jaz – get home?'

'He has a scooter. Left it at the surf club last night, he'll get a bus over there to pick it up.'

'Mmm.' Not completely stupid, then, but a motor scooter? Only slightly less dangerous than a motorbike, but Harry knew they were popular with the young crowd in Noosa. He saw so many of them on the roads on a daily basis.

'We're going surfing this afternoon. He's taking me to Little Bay,' she said, naming one of the popular surfing beaches in the Noosa National Park and sounding more enthusiastic than she had since she arrived.

So he was a surfer? That figured. Long sun-bleached hair, strong shoulders, dark tan and a devil-may-care attitude to life. Maybe Harry was being unfair about the latter assumption. He didn't really know the lad, and he did seem to have dragged Lucy out of her lethargy, but...

'I'll have time to get one of my assignments finished before he picks me up. Won't be home for lunch. Jaz said we'll pick up something on the way.' Lucy disappeared, presumably to complete the uni work she'd been procrastinating about.

Harry cleared the kitchen, then took Tiger for a walk, trying to come to terms with this overnight change in his daughter. On the one hand, he was glad she'd made friends here, well, one friend at least. But a surfer, who was in all probability also unemployed. Not what he wanted for his daughter. For once he found himself sympathising with Hillie. They hadn't spent big bucks on a private school education, then Melbourne University to have her throw it all away on a layabout.

Twenty-seven

'What a lovely evening,' Rosa greeted Jenny when she arrived at work. 'You and Mike make a striking couple.'

'Thanks. But what about you and Harry?' Jenny pointed at Rosa. 'You make a pretty stunning pair, too.'

'Stunning? I don't think so.' Rosa pulled a face.

'What's wrong?' Jenny asked, quick to detect Rosa wasn't her usual self. 'You seemed to be getting along like a house on fire, and his daughter went off with Alex's niece. So…?'

'We were. She did. And that was the problem. He felt he needed to be home for her, so…'

'You went home to a lonely bed?'

Rosa nodded.

'She *is* his daughter and he may feel responsible for her. A parent never loses that feeling of liability.' Jenny sighed. 'Even when they're quite grown up. It's not something you can slough off like an old skin. It stays with you. I remember staying awake till mine got home when they were a lot older than Lucy. I wouldn't let it worry you.'

Rosa groaned. 'Perhaps it's just me. I've never been a parent, so maybe I don't understand…'

'I didn't say that.'

'I know, but that's what you meant. It's just that, last night, when Harry rushed off to be there for Lucy, it reminded me so much of Ken rushing off to his wife. It brought it all back. I know I'm being silly. Harry isn't Ken. Lucy isn't his wife.'

'It's nothing like it.' Jenny's voice was brisk, pulling Rosa out of the melancholy that had descended on her the previous night, alone in her apartment.

'I know. It was only that, after seeing you and Mike so happy, so obviously a couple, Mike's words to you, I…'

'I know. He's a dear. I'm so lucky to have found him, to have him in my life. But it hasn't all been smooth sailing. Remember I *did* come back here on my own thinking it was all over, planning a life without him.'

'So you did. You think…?'

'If ever I saw a man in love it was Harry last night. Why, the man couldn't keep his hands off you. It was obvious to everyone.'

'Really?' Rosa flushed remembering the warmth of Harry's arms around her, the gentleness of his lips on hers.

'When are you seeing him again?'

'He said he'd call.'

'Call? My bet is he'll be here today.'

Rosa's heart lifted at her friend's words. Could Jenny be right? Would Harry appear as he'd done before? She decided to put the idea out of her mind and get on with the day.

It was a busy morning. Jenny had just taken a break and Rosa was serving a particularly difficult customer who refused to accept that Rosa couldn't identify the book she was looking for on the basis that 'the cover's green and I think it has a face on it.'

Her back was turned to the door as she stood in the middle of the shelves, but she became aware of a presence – of someone standing close by. Anticipating another customer, she turned and had started to say, 'I'll be with you shortly,' when she caught sight of a familiar pair of brown sandals. Her eyes rose up and there he was, hands clasped and with a penitent expression on his face.

Startled, Rosa almost dropped the book she was holding. 'Oh!'

'I can wait,' Harry said, moving away and beginning to browse in the thriller and crime section.

Rosa returned to her customer but her mind was elsewhere, and the woman soon left in disgust, annoyed Rosa hadn't been able to find what she was after.

'Can we talk?' Harry moved closer, and Rosa felt the now familiar flutter in her stomach. But at that moment, the door opened and another set of customers entered, with two small children jostling each other in their efforts to be first to reach the children's corner and claim a favourite cushion.

'Not now.'

Rosa smiled at the women and began to assist them in their selections, leaving Harry to continue browsing. Out of the corner of her eye she could see his broad shoulders between the shelves and hoped Jenny would return soon. What if he left before they had a chance to talk? What if…

'Sorry I took so long.' Jenny stepped in carrying a bag with the name of a neighbouring boutique emblazoned on it and coffee in a cardboard cup. 'I spent so much time talking with Julie,' she held up the bag, 'I had to get take-away. Have you been busy?' Her eyes moved to where Harry was lurking among the shelves rather than browsing. 'Oh! Let me put this through the back and I'll take over. Your break now, I think.'

She disappeared while Rosa managed to satisfy the customers, who then joined their children. Harry strolled back to the front of the shop.

'Now?'

'When Jenny comes back I can get out for a short break, but not for long.' She wasn't going to make it easy for him and didn't want him to think she could drop everything whenever he appeared on the scene. She'd been in that sort of relationship before and knew it wasn't healthy.

'Okay.' Harry rocked back on his heels and grinned, giving Rosa hope that Jenny had been right, and all of her misgivings had been a figment of her overactive imagination.

'Off you two go now.' Jenny returned to shoo the pair out the door.

Once outside they stood looking at each other, before Harry took Rosa by the arm and almost marched her along to a seat facing the river. 'I was going to suggest coffee, but I need to talk first and I don't want us to be surrounded by other people.'

Rosa looked down at her hands, clasped loosely in her lap and felt the sun beating down on her head. She raised her face to its warmth, trying to avoid Harry's gaze, but it was no good, she was intensely aware of his eyes on her. She turned towards him.

'Rosa. What can I say? I let you down. I know I shouldn't have left you last night. It was unforgiveable.' He dragged a hand through his hair, making Rosa want to still it, to take his hand in hers and smooth down the strands of hair which were sticking in all directions. But she didn't.

'How was Lucy?' she asked.

His hand rose again, and this time she *did* take hold of it, feeling his fingers curl around hers.

'That's the damnable thing. I fell asleep. They didn't get in till well after midnight and I slept right through. Some father I am.' His mouth turned up in that lopsided self-deprecating grin Rosa found so endearing.

'They?' she asked, her jaw dropping. 'Was Sandy with her?'

'Sandy?' Harry laughed. 'No, if only. Her companion was a young man called Jaz.'

'Jaz? What sort of name is that?'

They both laughed, then Harry became more serious. 'He's a surfer she picked up at the surf club and it seems he crashed on her floor.'

Rosa didn't know whether to laugh or cry. She'd been denied her night of passion in favour of Harry looking out for his daughter – a daughter who managed to bring a boy into her room right under her dad's nose. Laughter was winning and although she tried to stifle it, a giggle did break out.

For a moment Harry looked shocked then he appeared to see the funny side of it, too and joined her in loud guffaws of laughter.

'So it was all for nothing,' she said when they'd calmed down.

'So it seems. And I can't tell you how sorry I am. It won't happen again. I promise. In fact, why don't you come back to my place tonight?'

'Tonight? But Lucy…?'

'Hang Lucy,' he said, sounding more like the old Harry. 'Seems she's decided to get herself embroiled with this… this surfer. And he rides a scooter. They're going surfing this afternoon,' he finished, his voice dropping as if in disgust.

Rosa stretched up to give Harry a kiss on the cheek. 'But she's happy?'

'Seems to be. The brightest she's been since she arrived.'

'Well, it can't all be bad and if she met this Jaz when she was with Sandy, he's probably one of her friends. Don't kids usually hang out together these days? I'm sure Sandy wouldn't know anyone disreputable.' Rosa mentally crossed her fingers this was true. She really knew nothing about Sandy, but she was Alex's niece, and Alex was okay, hence... No, it didn't follow, but it might set Harry's mind at rest.

'You may be right,' he said, releasing her hands. 'So tonight? We can have a barbecue. I promise I can do that without burning anything. And you'll stay over? Maybe we can make up for what we missed last night.'

Rosa quivered in anticipation, her body remembering the heights of pleasure Harry had taken her to. 'All right.'

'Now, coffee?'

'Better not, I've been gone long enough. I'll grab a take-away on the way back.'

'Seven?' Harry pulled Rosa to him as they stood up.

'Seven,' she agreed, rising to her toes as he bent to touch her lips with his – a quick kiss, a taste of what was to come.

'See you tonight,' Rosa said with a smile, before hurrying back to work.

'Well,' Jenny greeted her. 'Was I right?'

'I'm going over for dinner tonight.'

'And the daughter – Lucy?'

'Seems she's found herself a boyfriend, a surfer by the sound of it, a friend of Alex's niece.'

'Should be all right then.'

'That's what I said. Harry's not so sure.'

'Overprotective dad?'

'I guess so. You'd have a better idea about that than I would, but he seems to have got over whatever was troubling him.'

'So you're going to risk his cooking again?'

'Barbecue this time, so he can't go wrong. I may take some dessert.'

'I can give you Maddy's pecan pie recipe, if you have time to make it.'

'Thanks, but probably not this time. Thought I'd pick up something from the bakery, if I can duck out again this afternoon?'

'Sure. Can't stand in the way of true love.'

'Don't tempt fate,' Rosa said smiling. Jenny could be right. This could be it. She spent the rest of the day in such a distracted haze it was a wonder to both her and Jenny that she managed to serve customers.

*

Rosa parked outside Harry's. As she stepped out, a red motor scooter drew up behind her, its engine revving. The door of the house opened and Lucy dashed past her in a cloud of perfume, hair flying and hopped onto the back of the scooter which roared off down the road.

'She's a different person,' Harry said as he led Rosa through to the kitchen. 'Wine?' he asked, picking up a bottle of Shiraz.

'Thanks.' Rosa perched on a high stool by the bench and leant her elbows on the surface. 'So that's the surfer. What did you say his name is?'

'Jaz. What did you make of him?'

'I didn't really see him, only a guy in a helmet on a scooter. Where are they off to?'

'Some party. I didn't get the details.' Harry frowned, then his face cleared. 'But let's not worry about them. We have the whole evening together. I've fired the barbecue and the steak's marinating. Bring your drink outside and we can talk while I cook.'

Rosa followed his directions and soon was comfortably ensconced in a cane chair close to the barbecue where Harry was deftly turning the steaks.

'I downloaded that form from the CCC website,' he said without turning round. 'Thought you'd want to know it was all underway. Seems I didn't need a letter or stat dec after all.'

'So you finished your contract?' Somehow this made Rosa feel better. She knew she'd always have worried when he was still working with those guys. 'Have you…?'

'All handed over. Though, Robson *did* seem a bit worried I might have come across the dodgy transactions. Seemed surprised – and relieved – when I didn't bring it up.'

'I'm glad you're shot of them.' The wave of relief that swept through

Rosa surprised her. Ken's threats had affected her more than she realised. 'So what happens now?'

'I fill it in and send it off. Then we wait. It'll probably take some time. They'll have to check it out, investigate, maybe talk to some people.'

Rosa felt a shiver of dread run through her. 'Talk to who? Me? I thought I was done with all that.'

Harry turned, spatula in hand, his eyes filled with concern. 'You may be able to stay out of it, but… you were working on the data, I'll have to name you as a witness, so it's likely…'

He didn't need to finish. Rosa knew exactly what he meant. Apart from Harry and the people involved in the swindle – Pete, Ken and their cronies, whoever they might be – she was the only one who'd been privy to the false data.

She took a deep breath. She could handle it. After all, despite Ken's threats, what could they do to her? 'Well, I'll face it when it happens.'

'You'll be right. Now, this steak looks ready. There are a couple of salads in the fridge. If you can get them out, I'll dish up here.'

For the remainder of the evening all thought of the Health Service and the nefarious goings-on there were put aside as the pair focused on getting to know each other better and sharing intimate details of their lives before they met.

As the evening wore on and there was no sign of Lucy, Rosa began to wonder if staying overnight here was really such a good idea. 'Your daughter,' she began, lifting her head which had been resting on Harry's lap, his fingers stroking her forehead and eyelids and twirling stray curls of her hair. 'Won't she…?'

'No.' Harry didn't allow her to finish. 'She'll be late if she gets home at all. She said she might crash at the party, or at Sandy's.'

Stunned at this apparently sudden change in Harry's attitude, Rosa sat up and stared at him. 'What's happened to change your mind? Yesterday you…'

'I know.' He looked embarrassed. 'But I listened to what you said, and remembered what I'd said to Hillie. I may not like it, but she *is* grown up and I have to accept she'll make her own decisions.' He sighed, then a devilish look came into his eyes and his mouth turned up. 'And we're grown up too, so how about I take you to bed?' And with that he picked her up and carried her into the bedroom.

*

When Rosa wakened, she lay still for a moment savouring the silence, then she remembered and opened her eyes. Yes, she hadn't dreamt it. Harry was lying beside her, his face burrowed into a pillow, hair mussed up. She reached out a finger to touch the faded blond mane, careful not to wake him. Her eyes roamed around the room which she'd been in too much of a hurry to notice the night before.

It was sparsely furnished with a bed and a couple of bedside tables, no soft touches to ameliorate the harsh white of the walls and the long, uncovered windows through which the morning sun was now blazing. It was a man's room, the only signs of habitation a novel open on one bedside table and the shoes and clothes they'd hurriedly shed before jumping into bed – and each other. She smiled as Harry's eyes opened and his arms wound around her.

Rosa could get used to this. They lay entwined for a few moments. 'What's the time?' she asked.

'Who cares? It's Sunday morning. We can stay here all day.'

While that was an attractive prospect, Rosa knew she would have to disappoint him. For one thing, she'd promised to visit her mother, for another… She couldn't; think of another. She was preparing to snuggle down again and enjoy Harry's embrace when a door banged and the dog began to bark.

'What the…?' Harry leapt out of bed and dragged on the pants he'd thrown across the room the night before. 'Lucy must be back. What the hell's Tiger making such a racket about?'

Rosa lay still, hearing voices and wondering whether to wait for Harry's return or get up. The voices continued with the dog barking, then there was silence. She waited, but nothing happened, so she rose and put her ear to the door. The only sound was from the birds outside and the buzz of a distant lawn mower. She was about to return to bed when the door opened.

'Sorry, Lucy's back and I'm going to make breakfast. Do you want to take a shower?' Without waiting for a reply, Harry drew on a tee-shirt and disappeared again.

Rosa headed to the shower and stood, relishing the sensation of the warm water gushing over her body. She tried to avoid wetting her hair but, without a shower cap it was impossible, so she gave up instead taking unexpected delight in the water soaking her curls, while knowing full well how they'd dry into a frizzy mess. Somehow she knew Harry wouldn't mind. It was refreshing to know that he liked her just the way she was, without artifice or pretence.

Sometimes she felt she'd been pretending all her life, ever since that dreadful "walnut" experience when she'd vowed to become "just like everyone else". That had entailed all the effort to maintain her hair as smooth as possible on every occasion and, even when she allowed her curls to show, they were carefully managed.

'Breakfast's ready.' Harry's face appeared round the bedroom door, just as Rosa emerged from the shower wrapped in a towel, her hair hanging damply around her shoulders. 'Wow! Maybe I should stay here instead.' He made an attempt to embrace her, but she managed to evade him, instead laughingly reaching for the jeans and shirt she'd worn to dinner. Next time –she was now sure there'd be a next time – she'd bring a change of clothes.

'Morning, Rosa.' Lucy looked up from the table where she was scoffing a bowl of cereal and fruit.

'How was the party?'

'Pretty good. I stayed with Sandy's aunt. The party was near her place at Peregian Beach, so a few of us stayed there. We got up early to go down to the beach to watch the sunrise. It was beautiful.'

'Nice spot.' Rosa hadn't known Alex lived at Peregian. It was one of her favourite beaches, such a beautiful stretch of pristine sand. If she'd been up at sunrise, Rosa guessed Lucy hadn't had much sleep, yet here she was as bright as a button and seemingly ready to meet the day.

'Eggs? Toast? Coffee?' Harry was juggling a pan of what looked like scrambled eggs while a couple of slices of toast popped up from the toaster and the coffee maker squealed in the background.

'Yes, please.' Rosa took a seat beside Lucy. 'And your friend?'

'Jaz has gone home to change and get his surfing gear. We're all meeting up at Little Cove again this morning. I'd better hurry.' She thrust a final spoonful of cereal into her mouth and rose. 'He'll be here soon and I still have to get ready.'

'And that's a major task,' Harry laughed, joining Rosa and setting down two plates of toast and scrambled eggs, along with two mugs of coffee.

'How shall we spend the day?' he asked when they'd finished eating.

'I'm sorry, but I can't... I have to visit Mum. She counts on me. Perhaps later,' she suggested, seeing his disappointment.

'Later it is. Drop round when you've seen her. Maybe we can go out to dinner?'

'That would be lovely.'

As she rose to leave, Rosa found herself wrapped in Harry's arms once more. 'Don't take too long,' he said. 'I'll miss you.'

Arm in arm they walked to the door to see the red scooter drawing up outside. This time, its driver had a large surfboard attached to his back. Rosa shook her head wondering how Lucy would manage to sit behind, then remembered the resilience and flexibility of youth and gave Harry one final kiss before getting into her car and driving off.

Twenty-eight

The next few weeks passed pleasantly for Rosa. Her weekends were spent with Harry at either her apartment or his house. They'd become an accepted couple often meeting with Jenny and Mike or Alex and Jack for drinks after work, and sometimes all six went to dinner.

Jenny and Mike were planning to return to Oregon after Christmas which they intended to spend with Jenny's family in Sydney to – as Jenny put it – get them used to the idea of Mike and to their relationship.

It was a Saturday which started out like any other, but when Harry picked Rosa up after work, he was scowling.

'What's up?' she asked stretching up to kiss his cheek. 'Lost a shilling and found a penny?' This had been a favourite expression of her grandma's and Rosa felt it described Harry's expression precisely.

'Let's get to your place first. We need to talk.'

'Sounds ominous.' Rosa tried to keep her voice light, but inwardly she began to quake. What could be wrong? Everything had been going so well. She said no more, but once at her apartment and after she'd made them both coffee, Harry pulled her down on the sofa.

'I need to go to Sydney for a bit.'

'To see…'

'Hillie. Yes.'

Rosa didn't know why that made her wince, but it did. Harry had left his wife. She'd been unfaithful, had betrayed him with his best friend and partner, was even now living with the man in his penthouse apartment. They were divorcing. Harry loved Rosa; he said so often enough. So why was her head reeling? Why did she feel as if her world was coming to an end?

'It's all right. I'm not leaving for good.' Seeming to sense her anguish, Harry drew Rosa to him and leant his chin on her head as he spoke. 'We're done, Hillie and I, but there are a few things I need to get straight before I can move on.'

Rosa could hear her heart thumping and Harry's was beating in time so close he was almost part of her. She tried to keep calm and listen to what he was telling her, to still the small voice which was trying to say it was never going to work, that she'd been foolish to believe it would.

'Hillie's still being so difficult about the divorce. It's dragging on and on. I want to get things settled and I can do that better if I'm there. I also need to talk to her about Lucy. She surprised me last night by saying she's decided on that course Alex told you about.'

'The one she rubbished when you first mentioned it?' Rosa managed to find her voice.

'That's the one. This crowd she's been going around with are mostly students. Seems this Jaz – it stands for Jason Alexander Zegers – is studying engineering there. Dutch name. His father is a professor.'

'Not the layabout you imagined, then?' Rosa lifted her head to meet his eyes.

'No.' Harry had the grace to look sheepish. 'Anyway, now she's made that decision, I need to persuade her mother it's a good plan. Hillie is still set on her completing her degree at Melbourne, she's accusing me of enticing her away.'

Rosa saw his lips grow taut. 'So when are you off?'

He hesitated. 'Tomorrow.'

'Right.' She tried to push herself upright, but found herself entangled in Harry's arms.

'We still have tonight.' His arms tightened and she relaxed into their embrace.

*

'I should go.' Harry mumbled into Rosa's hair, stroking it back from her forehead. His fingers moved over the face that had now become dear to him as if to imprint it on his memory. 'I want to make an early start. I really wish I didn't have to go. I plan to come back as soon as I can, but I don't know how long it'll take.'

Rosa burrowed her face into his shoulder. He felt her soft skin, her sweet body nestling against his, inhaled her unique fragrance and almost changed his mind about leaving. But it had to be done. He sat up. Rosa did the same, drawing the doona around her shoulders in unusual modesty as if to protect herself from his incipient absence.

'At least let me drive you to the airport,' Rosa said, referring to their conversation the previous evening when he told her he'd take a cab. 'Please!'

Seeing her gazing up at him with such soulful eyes, Harry relented. He'd initially refused to avoid a long drawn-out farewell at the airport, but now he agreed with Rosa and wanted to spend as much time with her as possible before he left. 'Okay, but…'

'No tears or histrionics. I know. I'm not like that.'

She was right. Rosa was more pragmatic. She'd probably cry, but she'd do it alone, after he'd left. Hillie was the one to throw a tantrum when things upset her or she didn't get her way. He fully expected one of major proportions when he reached Sydney. He wasn't sure how Bernie would react. He hadn't seen or spoken to his former partner and best friend since all this broke. Unless the guy had changed markedly, he'd keep well out of it and leave Harry and Hillie to sort matters out on their own, only appearing to comfort Hillie if she was thwarted, which Harry was determined she would be.

'You're exactly the way I like you and I'll miss you so much.'

'I'll miss you, too.' Rosa wrapped her arms around Harry's neck as if she'd never let him go, and Harry thought he detected a hint of moisture on the cheek touching his. Then she suddenly released him. 'Off you go then. Have your shower and I'll get breakfast going. Do you want to swing by home and check on Lucy before we take to the road?'

'Yes please.' He'd miss Lucy too, but he'd come to know her better over the past few weeks and knew she had her head screwed on properly. He and Hillie had done a good job there. He could trust her to look after the house and Tiger and not to have any wild parties. And Jaz was a good guy, too. Pretty thoughtful when you got talking with him – concerned about the environment and climate change like all the other young people around, but not fervent about it, not the type to be one of those protesters you read about – and he was serious about his studies, a good influence on Lucy. He had ideas of volunteering overseas too when his degree was completed, considering his engineering skills would stand him in good stead for helping underdeveloped communities. Hillie probably wouldn't like that either. He didn't know how much Lucy had told her mother about Jaz, but she was sure to be full of questions.

Harry watched Rosa shrug on a robe and disappear, then he went into the ensuite. The whole place was full of Rosa. The scent of her perfume and special bath oils and gels filled the air, and the surfaces and shelves were filled with her various lotions and potions. He drank it all in, storing it up for when he was no longer here, as if he could keep it packed away somewhere to be brought out when he needed it, as an antidote to Hillie and when he was missing Rosa.

This morning he didn't sing in the shower as usual. He let the water flow over him, choosing to use Rosa's favourite scented body gel instead of the more masculine one she'd purchased specially for him. That way, he could take her scent with him.

When he walked into the kitchen, the strong aroma of his favourite coffee blend met him and Rosa was breaking a couple of eggs into a pan.

'Can you keep an eye on these and pop some toast in while I take a quick shower?' she asked.

'Sure. Bacon too?'

'That'd be good.' She disappeared and Harry was left in the sun-drenched kitchen. He turned on the radio to check the day's news, and heard of several accidents blocking the main road to Brisbane. Lucky he'd chosen to fly directly from Sunshine Coast Airport. The rest of the news was the usual boring stuff – some politician had been caught out, the government might or might not be planning an election in the near future, and there was to be a flash new suburb developed which would reduce commuting, blah, blah, blah. He turned it off again and concentrated on the tasks at hand, managing to plate up the meal just as Rosa returned looking stunning in a soft pink dress. Despite his years of marriage and having a grown-up daughter Harry didn't pretend to know much about women's clothes, but this outfit brought a whistle to his lips.

'Going somewhere?'

'I'm taking this guy to the airport then...' She managed a wobbly smile.

'What'll you do for the rest of the day?'

'I'm not sure. I may call round to see Jenny and Mike if they're not too busy.'

'Good plan. I don't want to think of you sitting here on your own on a lovely day like this.'

'I'll be fine, I managed on my own for a long time before you came along,' she reminded him.

'Mmm. Can I ask you to do something for me?'

Rosa turned a surprised face towards him.

'Can you keep an eye on Lucy?' He took a sip of coffee, then added. 'I know she'll be right on her own, but I'd feel more comfortable if I knew that... Oh, maybe I'm being stupid. I know she can take care of herself, but it would make me feel better if...'

Rosa held up her hand. 'Enough said. Of course I'd be happy to drop in on her. As long as she doesn't think I'm checking up on her. Maybe I could offer to take Tiger for a walk from time to time?'

'That'd be perfect, then you can...'

'Take Tiger for a walk,' Rosa laughed. 'Nothing more. But it will give me a chance to check all is well with her, that Jaz hasn't moved in completely and the house isn't being trashed or used as a drug den.'

'Okay, so I'm being paranoid, but that would be good.' His eyes met hers and held for a moment. They were so in tune. What had he done to deserve this woman? He shook his head.

'What?'

'You, just you.' He took Rosa's hand in his and rubbed his thumb over the back of her fingers. 'I'm glad we met. That Health Service was good for something.' As soon as he'd spoken he wished he could take the words back as Rosa's face clouded over.

'You sent it off, didn't you?'

'Yes, I told you.'

'How long…'

'It'll probably be ages before we hear anything. I'll be back long before that.'

'Hope so.'

After breakfast, Harry led the way to Rosa's car and they drove the few streets to his home.

'Come on in,' he said. 'If Lucy's still asleep I'll waken her. I just have a bag and my briefcase to pick up. I'm travelling light.'

There was no sign of Lucy when they walked in, only Tiger who started running rings around them with his tongue hanging out, barking in delight.

'Can't take you for a walk now mate. Maybe…'

'I'll come round and take him later,' Rosa offered. 'I expect Lucy has better things to do on a Sunday.'

'Would you?' Harry looked up from where he'd been squatting to scratch the dog's head 'He has plenty of food and water, so Lucy must have topped it up before she went to bed.' He frowned. 'She knows he only gets fed twice a day.'

'Don't worry. He won't starve and he won't die from overeating either. You just need to concentrate on getting back here as soon as possible.' Rosa sounded almost fierce.

'Yes, ma'am.'

'Dad?' A sleepy Lucy appeared rubbing her eyes. 'I heard the dog. What's the time?'

'It's still pretty early, honey, but I have a plane to catch. Rosa's going to drive me to the airport and she's offered to take Tige for a walk later.'

'Mmm.'

His daughter was still half-asleep. He gave her a big hug and kiss. 'You can go back to bed now. Late night?'

'Mmm.'

'Do you have any message for your mum?'

Lucy scowled. 'Nothing you'd want to repeat. According to her, I can't do anything right.'

'Well, you're still my favourite daughter,' he said, giving her another hug. 'Now we really must go.' He picked up the two bags which were sitting just inside the door.

'Bye. See you later,' Rosa said as she followed him out.

'If I'm not here…,' Lucy began.

'I'll make sure Rosa has a key,' Harry said.

Lucy didn't reply. She pushed her hair back and turned towards her bedroom.

'Was that wise?' Rosa asked as they drove off.

'What? Giving you a key? It's high time you had one. You spend half your time here.'

'But when you're gone? I wouldn't like Lucy to think I'd be coming in when she wasn't there – snooping on her.'

'But you intend to walk Tiger. And she may not always be there when you drop round,' Harry said logically, as if it were the most natural thing in the world.

They reached the airport with little time to spare for Harry's flight, so he headed inside to check in, leaving Rosa to park her car. By the time she joined him, his flight had been called. Harry saw her eyes widen at the realisation there would be no more time to talk, barely time to say goodbye. He felt her distress as if it was a living thing.

'Remember, I'll be back, he said, his mind already working on what he had to do when he reached Sydney. It was something he'd learned to do early in his career – to compartmentalise his life. He loved Rosa and would miss her like the devil, but he had to take care of the Sydney side of things, be truly free of all that, before he could move on to a new life with her.

Harry kissed the top of Rosa's head and cradled her in one last hug, before giving her a squeeze. 'Need to go now. It's the last call.'

'I know.'

He could tell she was just holding back the tears and wanted to stay and wipe them away, tell her he'd changed his mind, that he'd deal with Hillie by phone and email, let the solicitors sort it out. But he'd tried that, and it hadn't worked.

Harry headed out the door towards the stairs leading up to the aircraft, taking one last backward glance, which showed him Rosa waving furiously.

*

Rosa watched Harry disappear up the steps and into the plane. She was proud she'd managed to stifle the tears, telling herself it wasn't over, he loved her, had even given her a key to his house and entrusted her with checking up on his daughter. But it was to no avail. She felt his absence so strongly, she wanted to scream, to shout out loud, to tell him to come back, that she didn't care if he never got a divorce, she just wanted to be with him. But she knew that was foolish.

Harry was someone who liked everything cut and dried. He needed to sort out his divorce settlement with Hillary before he could offer Rosa a future – he'd said as much. And there was more to Harry's trip to Sydney than that. He had to settle Lucy's plans to study at Beachhead Uni and live in Noosa. He needed her mother's agreement to prevent her from making Lucy's life a misery.

Rosa sighed and drove back into town. She'd take herself to Sirocco for coffee with a copy of the *Sunday Mail*, then drop back round to Harry's to take Tiger for his promised walk. It would be almost lunchtime by then. Surely Lucy would be awake. She fingered the key Harry had given her and hoped she wouldn't have to use it – not yet anyway. She didn't want the girl to think she'd let herself in as soon as Harry had left town.

*

Rosa rang the bell and dithered on the doorstep. She was wondering how long she should wait before using the key, when she was saved by the door being jerked open. Lucy's face fell when she saw Rosa standing there.

'Oh, it's you. I was expecting…' She looked over Rosa's shoulder as the sound of a motor scooter echoed behind them. 'I have to go. Will you…?'

'I can manage,' Rosa replied as, without waiting for a reply, Lucy jumped on the back of the scooter and rode off. So much for her worrying about my being here, Rosa thought as she went inside to collect a delighted Tiger, then set off towards the river.

She was walking along, enjoying the unfamiliar experience of walking a dog, amused by the way Tiger tended to keep his nose to the ground as if sniffing up as many scents as he could and completely ignoring any other dogs which passed.

'Rosa!'

Rosa turned around to see Alex with a spaniel who looked like Tiger's twin, only golden.

'That looks like Harry's dog. What have you done with him?'

'I'm… Oh, you mean Harry. He's gone to Sydney. Had a few things to sort out. You're not with Jack today?'

'He had a job to finish so I took the opportunity to take Tess for a walk. Shall we walk together and you can bring me up to date? Sandy tells me Lucy's hooked up with one of her uni friends. How's that going and is there any news about the business with the CEO?'

The pair meandered along the boardwalk skirting other dog walkers and dodging several young children careering along the path on scooters and skateboards. Rosa filled Alex in on Lucy's new plans and her apparent devotion to Jax who Alex described as 'the best-looking of Sandy's friends and a good bloke'. When Rosa began to tell her companion about Harry's report to the CCC, however, Alex stopped dead in her tracks, causing the two dog leads to become entangled.

When they'd finally managed to unravel them, Alex said, 'I knew it! There had to be something really wrong there. So many things just didn't add up.'

'Or added up too well.'

'So what happens now?'

'According to Harry, we wait. It could take ages for an investigation to get underway and he should be back by then.'

'You'll miss him.'

'I already do, but I'll manage.'

'We all manage, but it's never easy.' Alex looked as if she was about to say more, then seemed to think better of it. 'Fancy some lunch?' she asked.

'I was planning to take Tiger home first.'

'No need. If we go to the Lazy River we can tie the dogs to a post while we eat inside. They'll be happy sitting on the footpath below our feet and can have a bowl of water.'

'Sounds good.' Rosa marvelled at how much in her own town she'd been unaware of, never having owned or walked a dog before now.

While the two women ate lunch Alex quizzed Rosa on her relationship with Harry, making her feel uncomfortable. There were some things she preferred to keep private and how she and Harry felt about each other was one of them, so she deflected her friend's questions, instead asking her how she became involved in coaching and what her future plans were after the health job.

'I'll be looking for another organisation to work with,' Alex said. 'I started with individual coaching, but this job has given me a taste for what more can be achieved working with staff in an organisation. I think the HR Manager is pleased with me, so I should get a good reference.' She paused for a moment before continuing with the glimmer of a smile, 'I guess I'd better not count on a reference from the CEO. He might not be there.'

Rosa paused, her fork halfway to her mouth. She hadn't considered what might happen to Pete – and Ken too – as a result of Harry's report. 'Do you think he'll lose his job?' she asked, immediately realising how foolish the question was. If he was found guilty of corruption, losing his job would be the least that would happen to him. Hell, no wonder he and Ken were so worried about what she might do. Thank goodness it hadn't been her to file the report. She felt a shudder of apprehension.

Alex seemed to understand her uneasiness. She put a hand on Rosa's shoulder. 'Are you okay?'

'Yes. Sorry. I hadn't... Of course, they'll have to go, all of them.'

'All?' Alex raised her eyebrows. 'How many are involved?'

'There must be a few of them. Ken, for one and probably someone in Capital Works, maybe others. What a mess!'

'Well, it's out of your hands and quite outside my remit so we don't have to worry about it.'

'No,' Rosa agreed, but she wasn't convinced. Harry had named her as a witness and she had a dreadful feeling that, for her, it was far from over.

Twenty-nine

'How long's he been gone now?' Jenny asked as she set up a display ready for their author talk that evening.

'Three weeks.'

'Has it really been that long? Though I expect it feels longer to you. Any news of him coming back?'

'He says he's almost done,' Rosa replied to the second question first. 'And, yes, it seems like he's been gone forever. I know we speak every night, and there are the cute texts when he has time, but…'

'Calls and texts don't keep you warm in bed.'

'Jenny!' Rosa pretended to be shocked at her friend's blunt assessment, but it was true. She did miss Harry's warm body next to hers. She sighed, remembering their last night together.

'And you're seeing Lucy regularly?'

'Every couple of days. I drop round and take Tiger for a walk if she's too busy. I really enjoy it. Don't know why I always avoided having a dog of my own, though it's not possible where I'm living now. Lucy's a lovely girl. Despite the difference in our ages, I feel we've become friends.'

'She's still seeing that guy – what's his name? Baz?'

'Jaz, yes. They've become quite an item, planning all sorts of things together. And she seems to have settled down to her study too. Harry's pleased about that. How many do you think will be here tonight?' she asked, eager to change the subject.

'Difficult to say, but if we clear this area at the front and put out all the folding chairs, we should be right. Any extra bods can stand at the back.'

'Okay.' Rosa busied herself setting up the chairs, then went back to the office to fetch the box of glasses. Tonight wouldn't be anything like the gathering they'd had on opening night, but the launch of a new book by Ben Harris, the well-known local surfing guru, was sure to draw quite a crowd.

As Jenny had predicted, the seats were all filled with a few standing at the back. The evening was a success with lots of questions and book purchases. Towards the end, when the crowd was beginning to thin, Rosa found herself being backed into a corner by someone she'd hoped never to see again.

'What are you doing here?' Her eyes flickered from side to side, but there was no escape. Jenny was still busy with some last-minute sales, and the author was enjoying the admiration of a huddle of fans.

'You didn't expect to see me, did you?' Ken said, placing his hand on the wall above her head and putting paid to any opportunity of her making a break for it.

'So why are you here?'

'You didn't listen, did you?' Ken's voice held a threat.

'What do you mean?' Rosa drew herself up to her full height but even so, Ken towered over her.

'We're being audited, that's what.' He dropped his hand and thrust it in his pocket. 'Must have been you. Couldn't have been anyone else.'

So, it had started. Rosa felt a glow of triumph, which gave her the courage to speak out boldly. 'Serves you right, you and Pete and whoever else is in your foul band of crooks. What you're doing is criminal. It's public money you're messing with. You deserve to be caught.'

Rosa heard Ken draw in his breath.

He stood silent for what seemed like ages, his eyes full of animosity, before hissing, 'You'll be sorry.'

Ken strode off and Rosa closed her eyes. She was shaking. How could she have been so blind? To have slept with this man for all those years and not realised what a sleazebag he was? What did that make her?

'Are you all right? Was that…?' Jenny touched Rosa gently on her shoulder.

'Ken, yes, and I'm fine. Better than fine, actually. It's begun. The Health Service is being audited. They'll soon uncover what those villains have been up to and they'll get what they deserve.'

'Are you sure you're all right? You're as white as a sheet. Would you like a glass of something to calm you? I have some brandy in the filing cabinet. Mike swears by Jack Daniels, but brandy seems more appropriate here. It's for emergencies, and this sure seems like one.'

'No. Maybe a glass of water, or some tea. It was the shock of seeing him here, that's all.'

'Sweet tea coming up.'

Rosa sunk into a nearby chair. When Jenny returned with the tea, she clutched the cup gratefully in both hands.

'He didn't threaten you again, did he?' Jenny asked, taking a seat next to Rosa.

'He said I'd be sorry. But what can he do? He accused me of reporting them, even after I promised not to. That's how little he knew me,' she said sorrowfully.

'And how little you knew him. Through all those years, when you worked so closely with him, did you never suspect?'

'Not at all. I guess I was so caught up in my feelings I was blind to everything else.' Then a dreadful thought came to her. 'You don't think? No, he couldn't, not even Ken.'

'What?'

'You don't think he was using me all that time, keeping me amused in bed so that I wouldn't suspect what was really going on? No, that's too farfetched, isn't it?'

'You're right. I think you're letting your imagination run away with you. There's no reason to believe he was anything but sincere about your relationship – if it's possible for a married man having an affair in the workplace to be sincere, that is.'

Nothing more was said, but once home, Rosa couldn't help thinking about it. She was still dissecting the conversation when Harry called.

'Oh, God, I wish I wasn't still stuck in Sydney,' he said when she told him about Ken's visit. 'But it shouldn't take much longer here. My solicitor has managed to get Hillie's agreement to most of the areas of dispute, and I guess I can compromise on several more. There are just a few loose ends to tie up connected to the business. It's a bit complicated now that she and Bernie are together.'

Rosa listened with half an ear. She really didn't want or need to hear about his divorce arrangements, though part of her felt pleased he was comfortable sharing them with her. It was such a breath of fresh air after the secrecy of her previous relationship.

'You're sure you're all right?' he asked. 'They're bastards, but now the investigation seems to be in progress there's not much they can do. Anything they try will backfire on them. Can you hang in there till I get back?'

'Sure. I have Jenny and Mike to support me, and there's Alex and Jack too if it comes to that, though Alex must take care not to compromise herself. She's still under contract to the place.'

'I wish I was right there with you. I want to give you a big hug. You know that, don't you?'

Rosa smiled and experienced a warm fuzzy feeling right down to her toes as Harry proceeded to tell her what else he'd do if he was there with her. By the time the call ended, she was feeling much better. All thoughts of Ken and Pete had been banished and she was able to get a good night's sleep.

*

The following Tuesday after work, Rosa was in the library selecting books for her mum, when she noticed a familiar figure, seemingly agitated, at the self-checkout. Looking closer at the small woman with faded blonde hair, she recognised Brenda, Pete Robson's secretary. While she didn't know her well, and had never felt Brenda entirely approved of her presence in the executive suite, Rosa couldn't ignore the woman's distress.

'Can I help you?'

Brenda gave a start and turned round quickly. 'Oh, it's you. I can't seem to get this machine to work. I'm not sure what I'm doing wrong.'

Rosa looked around for a librarian. She couldn't see any within hailing distance, so did her best to assist. After several ineffectual attempts, she finally managed to check out the books.

'Here you are,' Rosa said, but as she handed Brenda her books she noticed the woman was looking very pale. 'Are you feeling all right?' she asked.

'Just a bit faint. Maybe if I sit down for a minute.'

Rosa helped her to a seat and fetched a drink of water. She dropped into a nearby chair, wondering if more professional help was going to be required.

'Thanks, Rosa. That's very kind of you. There was no need to... I wasn't always as nice to you as I might have been. Things have been a bit rough lately.'

Rosa wondered if she was going to say more, but Brenda only took a sip of the water and looked down at her feet, avoiding Rosa's eyes.

'I heard there's an audit going on,' Rosa said. 'That must be difficult for everyone.'

To Rosa's surprise, Brenda raised her eyes with something like relief. 'You heard? It's been dreadful. Queensland Health sent in those people. They've been through everything, turning out filing cabinets, computers. They started in the CEO's office, then mine. Now they've moved on to finance, capital works and I don't know where else. It's very upsetting. I've been in that office for years and I've never known anything like it.'

'And how's Pete coping?' Rosa asked, biting her lip.

'Terrible. He's so angry. I thought he was going to throw a punch at one of them.' She put her hand up to her mouth as if realising she may have said too much. 'Well, I'd better let you get on. I'll be all right now. Thanks for your help.'

She turned back into the tightly-wound woman Rosa was familiar with. There'd be no more confidences from that quarter. Rosa stood up and returned to searching for books to take to Ivy on her next visit.

Thirty

Rosa fingered the official looking envelope with the Queensland Health logo, her heart hammering. She slit it with her thumb and unfolded the sheet of paper. It was a request – more of a demand – that she present herself for an interview at Beachhead Health Service on Friday afternoon at two o'clock.

She flinched a little at the thought of going there, then realised that, of course she was being called as a witness. Harry had warned her this might happen but somehow she hadn't expected the interview to be held back there.

She checked the letter again. The interview was to take place in the meeting room in Human Resources. She breathed a sigh of relief. No need to go past the Executive Suite where Pete's office was, no need to go near the Finance Department and risk seeing or being seen by Ken. Human Resources was in a completely different wing of the building. It would be okay.

Somehow she managed to eat a slice of toast and honey, but it tasted like cardboard. Her head felt like cotton wool at the thought of fronting up at an interview, facing the suits from central office. That's what they'd always called them in jest when she worked in finance. But this was no jest. This was serious stuff. She might be the only person apart from Harry who knew what had been going on. What if they didn't believe her?

By the time Rosa reached The Book Nook, she was a mess. All the way along the road, she'd been imagining what they might ask her and how she might respond. Why hadn't *she* reported it? The answer was she'd been afraid. At the start she knew that, despite the legislation, there was no real protection for whistle-blowers.

After she left, she'd tried to put it behind her, told herself it wasn't her problem anymore. But that hadn't been true either. Was it an offence to ignore criminal activity? Could she be accused of being an accessory for refusing to report them?

'What's up with you?' Jenny greeted her. 'You look as if you have the cares of the world on your shoulders. I see we had a good day yesterday and you managed to fix up the delivery. Was it all too much for you?'

'It's not that.'

'That bastard Ken hasn't been bothering you again, has he? I'll get Mike to sort him out.'

'No, nothing like that. I received this letter. They want to interview me.' Rosa took the sheet of paper out of her bag and handed it to her friend.

'Who?' Jenny asked, taking the letter from Rosa. She stood reading it, then folded the sheet and returned it. 'So, the big guns are really here. What are you worried about? You've nothing to be ashamed of. You're not the criminal here. This is your opportunity to expose the truth. Isn't it?' she added, clearly seeing Rosa's dubious look.

'I suppose so, but it means going back there, back to…'

'But only to the HR office. No need to see the others.'

'I know. I've told myself that. And I've been trying to think what they might ask me.'

'All you have to do is tell the truth. What does Harry say?'

'I haven't told him yet. I haven't been able to think straight.'

'Bet you haven't had a coffee yet either. Why don't you handle the shop while I dash out for a couple of cappuccinos? I guarantee everything will look better after that.'

Rosa's mood improved as the day progressed. By the time Alex appeared in the shop at closing time, she'd become reconciled to the idea of the interview, though she was still not looking forward to it.

'Time for a drink?' Alex asked. 'Lots to tell you.'

Rosa hesitated, then made a snap decision. 'Just let me text Lucy to check on Tiger and I'll be with you. The message – *all done x* came back almost as soon as Rosa's fingers left the keyboard, making her wonder, not for the first time, how it was that the young could reply so quickly. 'Where will we go?'

'How does the tapas place sound? Then we don't need to worry about dinner.'

'Sounds good.'

Neither spoke much as they headed along the street, but once their wine had been served, Alex began, 'You won't believe the kerfuffle. The HR meeting room has been taken over by bods from Queensland Health and my unimportant sessions have been relegated to an empty office down the hall. It's all supposed to be very hush-hush, but my sources say...'

'It's the investigation,' Rosa interrupted. 'The one Harry instigated with his report to the triple C. Part of their process is that they hand it over to *the appropriate body* and they seem to have deemed the central office is exactly that. I heard there's been an audit – it may still be going on – and I've been summoned. I'm to go in on Friday at two.'

'And how do you feel about that?'

'Better than I did this morning.' Rosa smiled weakly. 'I was spitting chips when I read the letter, but Jenny managed to talk some sense into me. I'll be glad when it's over, though. Have you heard anything?'

'Everyone's keeping pretty mum, but I did hear they're turning finance upside down and that Ken Steele is in a panic. Isn't he the one...?'

'Yes.' Rosa felt her body tense at the sound of his name. 'And the CEO?'

'No one seems to have seen him for a few days. It's not clear whether he's holed up in his office or offsite. There are a whole lot of rumours going around, but no one I've spoken to really knows what it's all about. They're all waiting for the shit to hit the fan.'

'Mmm.' Rosa took a sip of wine. 'So, do you know who they've been interviewing?'

'I think it's only members of the executive at this stage. I did hear that the Director of Nursing stormed out with a face that would sink ships. They spent the first few days setting up computers and such like. I have a few sources in the HR department. Had coffee with the secretary from there the other day. She has her ear to the ground, but even *she* hasn't been able to get a handle on what's going on. I guess you're being called as a witness?'

'S'pose so.' Rosa stroked the damp glass with two fingers. 'I wish I wasn't. It's a dirty business and I can't help thinking something dreadful is going to happen.'

'You mean like those two getting what they deserve?'

'I don't know. I just have this feeling… Oh, ignore me, I'm probably imagining things. Harry'll be back soon, this'll all be over and we can get on with our lives.'

'When is he due to return?'

'He shouldn't be in Sydney too much longer, but there always seems to be just one more matter to take care of – his ex, the divorce, the business and I don't know what else.' Rosa placed her elbows on the table and stuck both hands in her hair. 'He's been gone too long, Alex. I need him here.'

Alex patted her arm in sympathy, then both women looked up as the mood was broken by the arrival of their food. As they nibbled on the cheese, olives and meatballs, Rosa began to feel better.

'What would you like the outcome of the interview to be?' Alex asked when their plates were almost empty.

Rosa reflected. She'd never thought about it from that angle. She'd been obsessing about what they might ask her, how she might answer. She considered Alex's question carefully before replying. 'I think,' she began, 'I'd like them to understand how I felt when I found the invoices and how Pete and Ken treated me when I tried to get to the bottom of it.'

Her eyes moved away from her companion, across the road to where the river was flowing as it did every day. It never changed, would never change, whereas her life was full of ups and downs. But she was in control of it. She pursed her lips as she considered Alex's question in more detail. 'What I'd like is to walk out of that interview having told them everything I know, without laying blame. That way I can still feel good about myself, can feel validated. I'd like them to have enough information to get the bastards.' She smiled. 'Thanks for helping.'

'All in a day's work.'

'So that's what you do? Get people to think for themselves? No wonder the staff are singing your praises. Jenny did say she worked it out for herself – the going to Oregon thing – but I didn't understand what she meant, not till now. I feel…,' she thought for a moment, 'empowered, I guess is the word I'm looking for, not a word I would normally use.'

*

Rosa parked close to her old parking spot. She was early, so had plenty of time. She sat taking the three deep breaths to a count of five as Jenny had recommended.

Harry's words came back to her. 'Just tell the truth. You can't do any better than that. By now, they'll have seen all the paperwork, the discrepancies you found. The forensic accountants will have been in and done their work. They'll have worked out exactly what's going on. All you'll be doing is confirming it.'

She stepped out of the car, drew herself up to her full height and walked into the building.

*

Half an hour later Rosa was sitting with sweaty palms, her head spinning. The interview wasn't going the way she'd expected. The two men on the other side of the table had started out being friendly and had asked the anticipated questions, but now it was all becoming distinctly odd.

'What exactly was your role in the Finance Department? Were you responsible for purchase orders?' asked the man on the right, the thin one with dark hair and horn-rimmed glasses who looked right through her as if she wasn't even there. At her faltering reply, his companion, a younger version of Pete Robson, took over and wanted to know exactly why she'd applied for the secondment to the CEO's office.

That was a difficult one. She had no intention off revealing her real reason, the end of her relationship with her boss. But other than that, there was no way of explaining why she'd chosen to leave the responsible position she'd held for so long to take a temporary secondment. Her answers sounded fabricated even to her own ears, so what must they sound like to those expert investigators?

'Well, that'll be all for now, Ms Taylor,' the thin one said at last. 'But we *will* need to talk with you again, so don't make any travel plans.' He gave a false-sounding laugh, more like a croak. 'Our investigation is far from over and you've failed to satisfy us today. We'll be calling you back as more evidence emerges. We may require access to your bank statements. And do remember, Ms Taylor, that the substance of our discussion today must remain confidential.'

But Rosa had stopped listening. She couldn't move. She was dazed, speechless. The phrases: 'investigation far from over', 'failed to satisfy', 'access to your bank statements' spun around in her head. Was *she* under investigation? She couldn't be. She found her voice. 'But…'

'You may go now.' The two men rose and, still confused, Rosa rose too and walked unsteadily to the door.

Once outside, she looked wildly around. Water, she needed a drink of water. There was a water dispenser in the far corner. If she could just make it that far without stumbling.

'Rosa, are you all right?'

Alex's familiar voice was music to Rosa's ears. She pointed to the water dispenser.

'Sit there, and I'll get you a drink.'

Alex took Rosa's arm and led her to a nearby chair as if she was sick, which is how she felt. She dropped into the chair and closed her eyes. This must be a dream – a nightmare. It couldn't be real. They couldn't think she was responsible.

'Thanks.' She took the paper cup from Alex and gulped greedily, then she pinched her hand.

'What are you doing?'

'Just making sure I'm not dreaming, that this really is happening. They think it was me, Alex. They think I'm the criminal.'

Thirty-one

Rosa tossed and turned. She couldn't stop thinking about what it would mean if she was right, if the investigative team really thought she was to blame. But how had they reached that conclusion? It was only as the first glimmer of dawn began to peep through the drapes that it occurred to her. She remembered Ken's words, 'You'll be sorry.' *Was this what he'd meant? Had he and Pete somehow managed to divert the blame to her? Were they going to get away guilt-free?* That thought energised her and, fuelled by anger, she leapt out of bed. She wasn't going to let them get away with it.

But once she'd showered and was sitting eating breakfast, a large mug of sustaining coffee at her elbow to provide the caffeine hit to compensate for the lack of sleep, her resolution shrivelled. Rosa propped her head up with her hands. What could she do? How could she fight those two maniacs? They were clearly stronger than she was – and not only physically.

She heard the dull ringing of her mobile and looked around. Where was it? That reminded her. She hadn't received her usual call from Harry last night. Or had she? Yesterday was a blur. She had no recollection of getting home. Rummaging in her bag, she finally unearthed the phone.

'Are you okay? I worried about leaving you yesterday, but you insisted you were fine. You didn't look it. You were in shock. Did you manage to get any sleep?'

'Alex?'

'You still sound weird. Would you like me to drop round?'

Rosa looked around her unusually tidy kitchen, trying to get her bearings. It was Saturday. She needed to… 'No, I need to get to work. How did…? Did you…?'

'I drove you home – in your car. You were in no fit state to drive yourself. Have you spoken to Harry?'

'Harry? No. I must've left my phone in my bag. Did I go straight to bed?'

'I've no idea what you did. You wouldn't let me come in with you. Are you sure you should be going to work today?'

'Yes, Jenny'll be expecting me. Thanks for calling, Alex, and for yesterday.'

As soon as she hung up, Rosa checked her phone. Yes, there they were – several missed calls from Harry, plus one from Jenny. She should call Harry back. She started to press speed dial, then stopped. What could she say to him? What if he thought they were right – that she *had* been at fault? No, better leave that for now.

When Rosa walked into the shop, Jenny took one look at her and said, 'Should you be here? You look awful.'

'Thanks. That's what every woman wants to hear first thing on a Saturday morning.'

'No seriously. What happened yesterday? Was it difficult?'

'Difficult doesn't begin to describe it.' Rosa sunk into a nearby seat. 'They grilled me for what seemed like hours, then suggested it was all my fault.'

'What?' Jenny's voice was outraged. 'How could they imagine you were to blame?'

'My guess is Pete and Ken have something to do with that, and I don't know how I'm going to prove otherwise. So you may be consorting with a criminal.' Rosa tried to raise a smile and failed, her mouth twisting into something more like a grimace.

'What does Harry say?'

'You too? That's what Alex wanted to know. I haven't spoken to him. I missed his calls. My phone…' She waved her hand in the air. 'I'm not ready to speak with him yet.'

'Why on earth not? Surely he's the first person to speak with. He's just as involved as you are. More so, as he reported it.'

'No. I can't involve him.'

'Rosa, he's already involved – with you *and* this damned business.'

'But no more,' Rosa said stubbornly. 'Now we have a shop to run.' She stood up and trudged to the back office to deposit her bag.

Rosa made it through a busy morning, but by lunchtime the lack of sleep was beginning to catch up with her.

'Why don't you go home and get some rest?' Jenny asked. 'I can manage here for the rest of the day.'

Rosa tried to resist, but finally acquiesced. After she'd left the shop however, instead of turning right towards her apartment, she took the opposite direction, ending up on a bench by the river. She leant back, feeling the spars of wood, hot from the midday sun, stabbing into her back. It would soon be Christmas, and instead of celebrating with her friends would she be locked up for a crime she hadn't committed?

Dismissing this as foolish musings, she couldn't decide what to do. She was exhausted, but knew she wouldn't be able to sleep and the thought of returning home to her empty apartment was abhorrent. Instead she found her feet taking her to Harry's. She'd take Tiger for a walk. The dog would be pleased to see her and wouldn't ask any awkward questions. But when she arrived, she found Lucy and Jaz sitting in the kitchen eating what appeared to be breakfast.

'Oh, hello. I didn't expect to see you today. Sandy's aunt said you weren't feeling well. Something about a shock?'

'It's none of Alex's business,' Rosa said shortly, annoyed to be the topic of conversation among her friends.

'She was concerned about you. She said…'

But Rosa didn't want to know what Alex had said. 'I thought I could take Tiger for a walk.'

'Sure. Dad…'

But Rosa didn't want to talk about Harry either, so she called the dog and grabbed his lead, before heading out, muttering, 'See you later,' over her shoulder without waiting to hear what Lucy had to say.

Walking along the river with the spaniel gave Rosa a sense of purpose and time to think more clearly than she had all day. She re-enacted the interview in her head, trying to figure out where she'd gone wrong. She'd hedged when they asked about her reasons for leaving finance, but that had been more a case of self-preservation than anything else, and surely her personal life was none of their business? It wasn't something she was proud of and preferred to keep it under wraps. They'd kept the relationship secret for six long years, surely now it was over it was irrelevant?

No, it couldn't have been anything she said. So that meant they'd suspected her before she even walked in, confirming her suspicion that Pete and Ken had somehow managed to shift the blame. The only other person they'd spoken to was Harry. Rosa remembered his telling her of the videoconference he'd participated in a few weeks earlier. It was either that or he'd have had to fly back as, according to the guidelines, a telephone interview was out of the question since it could lead to misunderstanding. But he hadn't said anything about mentioning her.

Well, there was nothing she could do about it other than wait, but she didn't expect she'd get much sleep until she heard more from them.

Rosa was walking back toward Noosa Waters when her phone pinged. She almost ignored it then, thinking it might be the nursing home, took it out of her pocket to read the message.

Where are you? Plane arrives 7pm Can U meet? H x

Rosa gazed at the message unable to believe her eyes. Harry was coming back. A wave of joy flooded her, drowning the fear and doubt which had plagued her all day, longer – ever since she walked out of the interview. She quickened her steps, pulling poor Tiger along, now regretting she'd missed Harry's calls, hadn't returned them, been too wrapped up in her own misery – and doubts about Harry too – to consider his feelings, his concern. Did he know? Was his business in Sydney completed? With her head full of questions, she walked through the open door of the house, releasing Tiger, who immediately ran to a favourite spot under the kitchen table.

Lucy and Jaz were sitting in front of the large television in the lounge room watching what looked to Rosa's uneducated eyes like a football game, thought she had no idea which code. Lucy looked up when Rosa walked in, but Jaz kept his eyes glued to the screen.

'Your dad's coming back tonight, on the seven o'clock plane.'

'I know.' Lucy stretched her legs out in front of her and pulled on her hair which was in a ponytail today. 'I tried to tell you before you left.'

Rosa thought back to Lucy's words. She had begun to say something about her dad, but Rosa had ignored her and left. 'So you did. I'm sorry. You knew he was arriving tonight?'

'Not exactly, but Sandy's aunt was so worried about you, she asked me for dad's number, so I thought he might come straight back.'

Rosa felt as if she'd been dealt a body blow. She couldn't decide whether she was annoyed with Alex for interfering in her life, or pleased someone had had the sense to contact Harry. She knew she should have called him herself, and wasn't sure why she hadn't. But the main thing was he was returning, coming to her aid like the knights in shining armour of her childhood storybooks. Though what Harry could do to help her in this instance, she couldn't imagine.

*

The road was unpredictably busy. According to the local radio, which she liked to listen to in the car, there had been an accident further down the highway which was delaying traffic. Rosa tried to stay calm, but patience wasn't her strong suit and she did so want to be there when Harry stepped off the plane.

Despite lingering doubts about how he'd react to this latest development, she couldn't wait to see him again. Deep down she knew his very presence would comfort her and she longed to feel his strong arms around her, to delight in his lips on hers and to enjoy the sense of security he evoked.

The cars moved slowly, but finally Rosa was able to take the turnoff to the Sunshine Coast Airport and easily found a parking spot. There was a buzz of excitement and anticipation in her gut as she walked into the building. Rosa loved this little airport, which had always reminded her of more tropical climes with its walls of glass and lush vegetation, but today she was oblivious to everything around her. She hurried through the entrance and reached the gate just as Harry's plane landed and the passengers were beginning to disembark.

For a moment, she couldn't see him in the crush. Then there he was, head and shoulders above the other passengers, his hair awry, his mouth turned up on one side, carrying his briefcase in one hand

and a carry bag in the other, his eyes darting from side to side as if in search of something or someone. For a moment, Rosa stood back, enjoying the sight of him while he still hadn't noticed her, seeing him as a stranger would, and a surge of pleasure engulfed her, dispelling any lingering doubts.

Smiling, Rosa ran toward him. Harry dropped his bags and she was in his arms, her face pressed hard against his chest, breathing in his clean manly smell, feeling the power of his embrace. She was safe again.

'Hey!' Harry loosened his grip. His lips met Rosa's and held as if they'd never let go, heedless of the crowds milling around them. Breathless, they moved apart.

'It's so good to see you,' Harry said. 'When Alex told me what you were going through, I caught the first flight I could. Why didn't *you* let me know?'

'Not here. Do you have any other luggage?'

'No, this is it.' Harry picked up his bags again and the pair made their way to Rosa's car.

Once inside, Harry turned to Rosa again, his brow furrowed, a question in his eyes. 'So?'

Rosa kept her eyes on the windscreen, unable to meet his. She wasn't sure why she hadn't been in touch with him. 'Last night, I... I was so upset, I don't know what happened. I wasn't thinking straight, wasn't thinking at all. My phone was in my bag. I found it this morning. That's why I missed your calls. I don't know why I didn't call back. I felt so ashamed. I couldn't...' She tightened her hands on the steering wheel and turned to face him, her eyes full of relief. 'I'm glad you're here.'

Thirty-two

During the drive home Rosa was conscious of the sexual tension building between them. With Harry's hand on her knee, the heat radiating from his body seemed to encapsulate them in a cocoon. By the time they reached her apartment, they could barely wait to get inside before they were reaching for each other.

'It's been so long,' Harry murmured, his hands reaching up under Rosa's tee-shirt to fondle her breasts.

'Too long,' Rosa breathed, lifting her arms to ease off the garment. She'd forgotten how his touch could arouse her. Her hands gripped his butt and she groaned as he caressed her breasts and teased her hardened nipples, then dipped his head to suck on them.

Without separating, they managed to make their way to the bedroom and onto the bed, where the rest of their clothes were soon scattered across the floor, a testament to their great need.

They made love with an urgency, as if their time together was limited, as if there was no tomorrow. Then they lay facing each other, smiling.

'I missed you so much,' Harry murmured tracing Rosa's lips with his forefinger. She took it into her mouth, sucking it gently before releasing it, cuddling into him and asking, 'Did you get it all done? In Sydney.'

'Not quite. But you needed me, so here I am.'

'Will you have to go back?'

'No. I can handle the rest by phone, email and mail. You need me here. Seems I can't let you out of my sight without you getting into trouble.' He smiled tenderly and stroked a strand of hair from Rosa's face.

Rosa frowned. Their lovemaking had sent her predicament out of her mind. Now it returned with a vengeance. She sighed and turned her face into Harry's shoulder, relishing the warmth and comfort it gave her. She drew her lips over his skin wondering how long she could delay the dread of what was to come.

As if reading her thoughts, Harry put a finger under Rosa's chin and tipped it up. 'I know you're innocent. Those guys are mad if they think otherwise. I'm sure we can clear it up.'

'We?'

'You don't think I'm going to let you face them alone again, do you? You have the right to a support person. Didn't you think of that last time?'

'I had no idea I'd need one. I thought I was only a witness. The interview started out that way, then it got a bit weird.'

'They recorded it?'

Rosa nodded.

Harry pursed his lips. 'There'll be other interviews on record too. Robson and your old mate for starters. There'll be a record of what they said about you.'

'But what good is that if we don't have access to the recordings?'

By this time both were sitting up in bed, arms and legs entwined. Harry squeezed Rosa tightly. 'Let me think on it for a bit. But I want you to stop worrying. Promise?'

'I promise,' Rosa said, but she knew that saying the words was the easy part.

'Good girl.'

They snuggled down together and the next thing Rosa knew it was morning. To her surprise she'd slept soundly all night. She could hear the sound of the shower running telling her Harry was already up and popped her head into the ensuite to receive an invitation to join him. Tempting though it was to have him soap her all over and then some, Rosa shook her head. They'd slept late. It was almost eleven. Instead, she slipped on a long shirt and went to the kitchen where she filled and turned on the coffee maker and began to mix up a pancake batter.

It was Sunday morning and Harry was back with her. She deserved to celebrate.

When they decided they couldn't eat another bite, and were relaxing, elbows on the table as they finished a last cup of coffee, Rosa ventured to ask, 'How was Sydney? Was it as difficult as you expected?'

Harry set down his cup before replying. 'To start with, Hillie was hell, exactly as I predicted. And poor old Bernie was faffing around trying to placate her. He has his work cut out there. I'm well out of it. But you don't need to hear all that.'

Rosa didn't, but she couldn't help but experience a small glow of complacency at his condemnation of his soon-to-be-ex-wife.

'I've a good lawyer in Bob Frazer. He's managed to work with her guy to negotiate a settlement which is pretty fair.' He rubbed his chin. 'At least she's not going to take me to the cleaners – and I get to keep my boat. She'll get the Hunters Hill house. I didn't want that anyway, and we'll split the money and the proceeds from the sale of the Batemans Bay house fifty-fifty. Seems reasonable. She wanted to hang out for sixty-forty in her favour. The main difficulty that arose was with the business. I wanted Bernie to buy me out, but Hillie stuck her oar in there too and got in his ear suggesting she have my share.' He shook his head. 'What she knows about business or management consulting could be written on the back of a postage stamp. Anyway Bob managed to iron that out too. Didn't get as much as I should have, but I'm satisfied. I don't want any more wrangling. So I'm done there and we can start afresh. There's really only the paperwork to finalise.' Harry dropped a kiss on Rosa's head as he finished speaking. 'So what shall we do today?' he asked, stretching out his legs under the table and tilting his chair back on two legs.

'I need to visit Mum this afternoon,' Rosa replied. 'But it would be good to catch up with Alex. I need to thank her for contacting you. And I should let Jenny know you're back. When she sent me home yesterday I think she believed I was heading for a nervous breakdown.'

'Why don't we aim to catch up with them all this evening? I want to check on Lucy. I need to break the bad news that Hillie wants her to go home to Sydney for Christmas. I can do that while you visit your mum, then maybe we can all go out to dinner. I'll book somewhere. My treat. Will you get in touch with Alex and Jenny?'

Rosa agreed and made the calls while Harry cleared the table and stacked the dishwasher. 'They'd be delighted,' she reported, 'but Jenny says Mike won't hear of your paying for everyone and Alex is sure Jack will say the same.'

'We'll handle that later. Now I'd better get off. I sent Lucy a text to let her know I'd be dropping round. Didn't want to surprise the couple.' He chuckled. 'She *is* my daughter, after all.'

Rosa gave him a punch on the arm. 'Some dad you are, but very tactful.'

After Harry had left, Rosa decided to check her emails before visit the nursing home. She hadn't been as punctilious as usual for the past week, with the interview at the Health Service hanging over her. She deleted several spam-type ads, saved a bank statement and phone bill to deal with later then saw one from her sister. She sighed. What did Vi want? She hadn't heard from her since that awful phone call where her sister had hung up on her. She clicked it open.

Hi Rosa,

I know you're probably still annoyed with me about your last call. It's not that I don't care about Mum. I do, but I know you're there to look after her and I do appreciate that, even if I don't always show it. I've been thinking what you said, about Mum, and Rod and the girls have been at me too. So the long and short of it is that we've booked a flight. We'll be there for Christmas. I don't suppose you can put us up, so I've booked us into a place called The Islander. It seems pretty central and close to you. I'll be I touch again closer to the time. Can you let Mum know?

Love

Vi x

Rosa stared at the screen, unable to believe her eyes. Vi was actually coming to Australia, to Noosa, for Christmas.

Thirty-three

The next few days were difficult for Rosa as she waited to hear more from the Queensland Health investigative team. Harry was doing what he could to help and his presence and support made it bearable. He'd contacted his Sydney lawyer, Bob Frazer, though Rosa couldn't imagine what a New South Wales solicitor could do in a Queensland corruption case. But it gave her some comfort to know she wasn't facing this alone.

So it was with some trepidation that she picked up the letter with the Queensland Health logo lying in her mailbox. Harry had collected her from work as usual that Friday night, planning to spend the weekend together. Her throat constricted as she looked at the envelope, turning it over and over in her shaking hands.

'Is that it?' Harry followed her into the apartment and holding out his hand.

'No. Yes. I can open it.' She slid her finger under the edge of the envelope and slit it open.

'What does it say?'

In a shaking voice, Rosa read the letter aloud,

Dear Ms Taylor,

Subsequent to our interview on Friday 5th and pursuant to our enquiries in the matter of Beachhead Health Service we request your presence at a further interview on Tuesday 16th at 11am to be held in the interview room in the Department of Human Resources at Beachhead Health Service. We would be grateful if on this occasion you could furnish us with copies of bank statements for the past three years. In accordance with the Guidelines for Dealing with Corruption in the Queensland Public Sector, you are permitted to have a support person of your choice present at the interview.

Rosa couldn't read any further. She dropped the letter, which fluttered to the floor, and covered her face with her hands.

'Come here.' Harry took Rosa's hands, pulled them away from her face and drew her into his arms. 'It's going to be all right. I'll go with you, be your support person.' He kissed the top of Rosa's head and tightened his arms around her shuddering body.

She stood still, his warmth infusing her with wellbeing, then drew away and bent to pick up the offending piece of paper. 'Are you sure? You were the one to report it. Won't there be a conflict of interest? Will they permit you to be my support person?'

'I'd like to see them try to stop me.' He pulled her into his arms again and hugged her with determination, his chin pressed firmly on her head. Rosa leaned confidently into him, but did still wonder if they'd allow him to accompany her.

'Now, I think we need to go out tonight,' he said, 'I know we'd planned to stay home but you need a change of surroundings. How about a movie? It'll take your mind off all this. Let's see what's on and we can have a pasta at that place next to the cinema either before or after.'

'Okay.' Rosa sighed. 'Let me shower and change first. Help yourself to a drink and I'll be with you in five.'

*

Harry poured himself a beer and sat down on the sofa, picking up the letter. Re-reading it as he sipped his drink, he shook his head. How had it come to this? What had those bastards told the investigative team? Harry had no doubt who had pointed the finger at Rosa.

He needed a plan. He leaned back, trying to work it out then, recalling what Rosa had said about a possible conflict of interest, a potential solution presented itself. Maybe he could use that, use the fact he'd been the one to report the matter, and insist on being interviewed again first – before Rosa.

He wouldn't mention it to Rosa, even if it meant he couldn't put her mind at ease, because it might not work. He'd keep it to himself for now.

'Ready?' He looked up as Rosa appeared in the doorway, looking stunning in a hot pink dress which skimmed her knees. 'Wow, honey, you look amazing!'

'Thanks.' She smiled.

'Let's go.'

'What's showing?'

'I didn't check. We can see when we get there. Bound to be something worth seeing.'

Once at the cinema, Harry scanned the list of movies. '*The Next Three Days* is starting soon. What do you think? It's an old one and stars Russell Crowe so it should be okay. At least it'll take our mind off things.'

'Okay. I don't really care what I see.'

They headed into the cinema prepared to be entertained for the next hour or so, but the movie wasn't quite what Harry had expected.

As they sat waiting for their order in the Italian restaurant afterwards, Harry apologised. 'Sorry. That didn't help much, did it?'

'A bit too close to home,' she said, referring to the plot of the movie in which a wife was falsely accused of murdering her boss and sentenced to life imprisonment. 'But at least I'm not being accused of murder.' Rosa gave a rueful smile. 'What *is* the penalty for fraud?'

'It's not going to come to that. I won't let it.' But even as he spoke, Harry wondered if he was right. Would his strategy work? Could he convince the team that Robson and Steele were the real criminals – that they'd lied about Rosa? Would his word be enough to exonerate her?

'He did save her in the end,' Rosa reminded him.

'Yeah. But I hope *I* don't need to break *you* out of jail,' Harry joked. 'Sorry,' he said, seeing Rosa's stunned expression. 'I'm not being much help either.'

'You're here,' Rosa said. 'Without you, I'd have been sitting at home worrying and feeling sorry for myself.'

'Instead of which I take you to a movie where a woman is wrongly accused of murder and ends up in jail. Fat lot of help I've been.'

Suddenly they both saw the funny side of it and burst out laughing. The waiter arrived at that moment to deliver their meals, and they tried to avoid each other's eyes as he placed two steaming bowls of pasta in front of them.

'Parmesan cheese, sir, madam?' the waiter asked holding a cheese shaker above their table.

'Yes, please,' Harry replied, while Rosa tried to stifle her laughter.

'He must think we're mad,' she said, picking up a glass of wine.

'There's nothing better to lift your spirits than a good laugh. Now, let's forget all about crime and its repercussions and enjoy our meal.'

*

Tuesday arrived all too soon and with it the dreaded interview. Rosa dressed carefully in one of her old black business suits, feeling as if she was dressing for her own funeral. Harry had stayed the night, but had gone home to change too, promising to pick her up in plenty of time.

Rosa checked over the bank statements she'd printed out, her hands trembling as she shuffled through them. They wouldn't find much there. Her careful savings over the years didn't amount to a lot, and the only lump sum was her severance pay most of which had quickly been transferred into the bookshop. Would they try to prove she'd salted away the supposed money somewhere else? In an offshore account or in a false name?

One part of her couldn't believe this was really happening. It was as if it was happening to someone else. As if she was outside her own body looking on. It didn't seem real. But it was. In less than an hour she would be grilled about a fraud *she'd* uncovered, a fraud perpetrated by her former boss and lover, and for which she was now being held responsible.

The pair didn't talk on the drive to the Health Service, and when they got out of the car, Rosa stared at the redbrick building looming up before her as if she'd never seen it before.

Harry, looking very smart in a grey pinstriped suit and carrying his briefcase, gripped her hand tightly. 'Chin up,' he said as they walked into the building.

He'd promised to help her but what could he do in the face of such blatant lies as Pete and Ken must have told? It was good of him to be there as her support person, but she didn't think a support person was permitted to speak. All he could do was listen. Rosa wondered what would happen next. Would she be allowed to return home or would the police be called and she be taken away there and then?

A cold shiver crawled up the back of her neck. This was it.

They reached the Human Resources Department with five minutes to spare and Harry fetched her a cup of water. Rosa tried to sip it, but her throat had closed up. She tried to moisten her parched lips and broke out in a cold sweat. She just wanted it to be over.

'Ms Taylor? They're ready for you now.' The receptionist gave her a sympathetic smile. Rosa began to rise, but Harry pushed her back.

'I need to speak with them first,' he said, moving toward the open door.

'I don't think...,' the woman began, but he'd already gone though and closed the door behind him, leaving Rosa wondering what was going on. She'd psyched herself up for this moment, and now felt somewhat flat, like a deflated balloon. What was Harry playing at?

Rosa couldn't sit still. She put the untouched water down on the floor and walked over to the window. Looking out, all she could see was the car park and the Emergency Department on the other side. As she watched, a few cars stopped to unload their passengers before driving off again. One parked hurriedly and carelessly, a woman carrying a small child running out and into the building. Another car pulled up disgorging a young man who was hobbling and holding a towel covered in blood to his head. Rosa turned away from the window. There was no relief to be had there, unless the fact she wasn't sick or injured could be taken as some sort of consolation. She supposed it could. What was worse, she conjectured, to be accused of a crime one didn't commit or to be in the thrall of some illness? At least most illnesses could be cured. There was no cure for what might befall her.

What on earth was Harry doing? Rosa checked her watch. He'd been gone for over half an hour. Surely quite long enough for whatever he intended. She sat down again, then got up and walked to the water dispenser and back. She felt the receptionist's eyes on her. Was she judging her? Did she know why Rosa had been summoned?

Rosa was about to sit down again when the door opened and Harry walked out. 'We can go now,' he said, taking her arm and leading her to the lift.

'But…,' Rosa protested, looking back toward the door which remained closed. 'Don't I… Don't they…?'

'It's over,' Harry said grimly. 'Let's get out of here. I'll fill you in when we get to the car.'

*

'What happened in there?' Rosa turned to Harry who was staring through the windscreen, a wicked smile on his face. Her head was reeling. One minute she'd been waiting for a summons, the next Harry was hustling her out of the building.

'I just told them the truth. I said we were in a relationship and you'd come to me with your suspicions, too scared by their threats to report them yourself.'

Rosa's stomach lurched. 'You said what? A relationship? Are we?'

Harry's grin said it all. 'Oh, I think so, don't you?'

Thirty-four

'So that's that. It's all over.' Rosa finished recounting her experience to her friends, who'd gathered for drinks at Harry's Noosa Waters home. It was only the day after her interview, and Rosa was still feeling fragile. Harry's arm around her shoulders gave her confidence, but the trauma was still too close. She couldn't quite believe it was all over.

'Just like that?' Jenny asked. 'No apology?'

'I'm just glad to be exonerated. It remains to be seen what'll happen next.'

'But it's no concern of ours now. We can get on with our lives.' Harry's arm tightened around Rosa as he spoke. 'Now, who's for more wine? And there's plenty to nibble on.' He gestured to the table which was laden with breads, cheeses, dips, crackers and a mixture of finger foods – enough to keep an army from starving.

'I think I know,' Alex interrupted, looking at her phone. 'I just got a text from Kim. My sister-in-law,' she explained. 'She belongs to several charity organisations.' She must have seen their blank looks, because she continued, 'One of those is the Hospital Auxiliary, a group of ladies who raise money for the hospital. It seems the gossip mill is going strong and Pete Robson has been suspended along with the Finance Director – isn't that your old buddy, Rosa?'

Rosa blushed and twisted her glass around, before taking a long gulp of the icy white liquid. She'd put Ken behind her. Never wanted to think of him again. But part of her was glad he'd got what he deserved. And maybe... maybe there'd be more to come.

Jack must have read her mind. 'It won't stop there,' he said. 'There'll be charges laid.'

He looked embarrassed as all eyes turned on him.

'I was speaking to an old mate today. He's with the Police Service. They'll be prosecuted. Could get up to fourteen years with a possible non-parole period of three.'

Rosa felt her mouth fall open. She was flooded with a torrent of contradictory emotions. She wanted the pair to be punished. She did. But... so many years in prison? Did they really deserve that? What had she and Harry done?

It could have been her. If Harry hadn't been there, hadn't intervened, she might be the one facing years behind bars. She wobbled as she carefully placed her glass on the table. 'I think...,' she began.

Harry moved his hand to her neck and stroked it gently.

Rosa felt a sense of calm permeate her as she relaxed under the hypnotic movement of his fingers.

'It's okay,' he whispered so low no one else could hear. 'I'm right here with you. You have nothing to reproach yourself for. It's all out of our hands.'

'Chris didn't give much away,' Jack continued, 'He couldn't talk about this particular case, but he did refer to a similar one a few years ago; that's what happened with it. I'm sorry, Rosa,' he added, belatedly appearing to notice her anguish.

'They don't deserve your compassion. Look at all those times that louse Ken threatened you,' Jenny reminded Rosa. 'They deserve whatever punishment the law metes out to them. You're well rid of the lot of them – the Health Service is, too. And it could have been you facing charges – if they'd had their way. Now forget the bastards and concentrate on getting on with your life.'

'You're right.' Rosa shivered, but it was with exhilaration rather than fear. A smile lit up her face as Harry pulled her back against him. She turned to meet his eyes, eyes filled with love. She had a lot to be thankful for. It had been an eventful year and she was a different person from the one who'd celebrated her birthday alone by the river.

Here she was, surrounded by friends, in love with and loved by this wonderful man who'd...

Alex continued to read from her phone, 'And the Manager of

Capital Works and a few others. Her source is impeccable – the wife of the Chairman of the Board.' She looked up. 'So! It's all happening.'

'Hi Dad!' The gathering was interrupted by the arrival of a pair of young people. 'You said to drop in before we set off. The gang are planning to leave for the North Shore on the seven o'clock ferry, so here we are.' Lucy looked around the group. 'What's up? This is Jaz,' she added, pulling forward her companion who seemed unfazed by her brief introduction.

'We're celebrating,' Harry said, leaving Rosa to fetch a bottle of champagne which had been chilling in an ice bucket. 'I told you Rosa had been completely cleared, exonerated...'

'Yeah, yeah.'

'And that I'd had good news from Sydney.'

'Yeah. That too. Mum's finally agreed to let go and get a life. Wish she'd let me loose too.'

'Yes. I...'

'We'll pop down to Sydney to see her after Chrissie.' She drew Jaz to her side, including him in the conversation. 'And we have something to tell her too. I hope you're going to support me in this, Dad.'

Harry frowned, seemingly unsure what was coming next.

'After Sydney we're planning a trip to Thailand. It's a four-week project. We'll be working to support community efforts to help reintegrate elephants into their natural habitat. They've been in tourist camps,' she added, clearly seeing blank looks. 'Doesn't that sound great,' she enthused. 'Jaz found the program and it's just perfect.'

'Just perfect,' Harry repeated gloomily. 'And I suppose you want me to clear it with your mother?'

'Would you?' Lucy waltzed over to give him a hug, then turned to Rosa. 'Glad things worked out for you. I knew Dad could do it, if anyone could. Sandy said...'

Rosa felt her cheeks warming. So Lucy had been talking about her too? Was nothing secret? But it really didn't matter. Nothing mattered, except those good friends and Harry – the man who'd managed to effect the miracle. And nothing could remove the smile from her face, the bubble of joy which welled up when she looked at the man standing beside her.

'That sounds exciting, Lucy,' she said, smiling at the young girl. 'It's a worthwhile project. Won't your mum...?'

'No way,' Lucy laughed and accepted a glass of champagne from her father. 'But maybe you and Dad... and Jaz has a persuasive way with him when he tries.' She stuck her tongue out at her companion. 'Anyway it's all booked. We should go soon.' She emptied her glass in a couple of gulps. 'See you at the weekend.'

Harry shook his head as the two left as quickly as they'd arrived.

Harry filled everyone's glasses, then threw an arm around Rosa's shoulder again.

'Are you planning a celebration?' Alex asked.

Rosa felt Harry's hand squeeze her shoulder to preclude her replying. 'Apart from this? I don't think so,' she said.' I want to forget it ever happened. My sister will be arriving soon with her family and we plan celebrate Christmas together. It'll be the first time for years that we've all been together. Mum will be able to be there too. And...'

'My divorce will be through by then too, and we...' He beamed at Rosa who was glowing with happiness. She held out her hand to show off the ring Harry had given her that very morning which she'd managed to keep hidden till then.

Alex whooped with delight, while Jenny moved over to hug Rosa. 'I'm so happy for you. I told you it would work out.'

'And you were right.'

'And your daughter?' Jenny asked Harry who was making no attempt to hide his pleasure.

'She's good with it. More concerned with her own love life, right now.' He looked at Rosa and took her hand in his.

'I'm sorry you guys won't be here for Christmas. We can't persuade you to stay?'

'No.' Jenny shook her head. 'It's time my family met Mike, and we'll be off to Oregon in the early part of the year. But we'll be back up here before then. And Rosa has found someone to help with the bookshop.'

All eyes turned towards Rosa.

'Lucy's offered to step in on a part-time basis,' she said. 'She's decided to base herself with her dad while studying at Beachhead Uni and it'll put some cash in her pocket. He loves the shop, too.' Her smile widened and she grasped Harry's hand tightly, delighted at how Lucy had welcomed her relationship with her dad.

Harry turned to Alex and Jack. 'Rosa and I would like you to join us by the river on Christmas morning.'

As they were vociferous in their agreement, Rosa added, 'We want to make it a special day. We'll grab a table, put up some balloons and tinsel. Mum will be there, along with my sister and her family, and Lucy – probably Jaz too. You can go your own ways afterwards, but first we'll have champagne for breakfast.

THE END

From the Author

Dear Reader,

First, I'd like to thank you for choosing to read Champagne for Breakfast. I hope you enjoyed Rosa's journey and, if you've already read my Oregon Coast books, I hope you enjoyed meeting old friends again.

If you did enjoy it, I'd love it if you could write a review. It doesn't need to be long, just a few words, but it is the best way for me to help new readers discover my books.

If you'd like to stay up to date with my new releases and special offers you can sign up to my mailing list at my website, http://maggiechristensenauthor.com/ and you'll also get a FREE book. I'll never share your email address, and you can unsubscribe at any time.

You can also contact me via Facebook Twitter or by email. I love hearing from my readers and will always reply.

Thanks again.

Maggie Christensen

Acknowledgements

As always, this book could not have been written without the help and advice of a number of people.

Firstly, my husband Jim for listening to my plotlines without complaint, for his patience and insights as I discuss my characters and storyline with him and for being there when I need him.

John Hudspith, editor extraordinaire for his ideas, suggestions, encouragement and attention to detail.

Jane Dixon-Smith for her patience and for working her magic on my beautiful cover and interior.

The Inkstained Groupies and The Noosa Writers who saw early drafts of this novel for their support and encouragement, my critique partner, Karen, for her eagle eye and continuing patience and my beta readers, Louise, Helen and Toni for their willingness to read the final draft of this novel.

Annie of *Annie's books at Peregian* for her ongoing support and advice.

And all of my readers. Your support and comments make it all worthwhile.

About the Author

After a career in education, Maggie Christensen began writing contemporary women's fiction portraying mature women facing life-changing situations. Her travels inspire her writing, be it her frequent visits to family in Oregon, USA or her home on Queensland's beautiful Sunshine Coast. Maggie writes of mature heroines coming to terms with changes in their lives and the heroes worthy of them.

From her native Glasgow, Scotland, Maggie was lured by the call 'Come and teach in the sun' to Australia, where she worked as a primary school teacher, university lecturer and in educational management. Now living with her husband of thirty years on Queensland's Sunshine Coast, she loves walking on the deserted beach in the early mornings and having coffee by the river on weekends. Her days are spent surrounded by books, either reading or writing them – her idea of heaven!

She continues her love of books as a volunteer with her local library where she selects and delivers books to the housebound.

A member of Queensland Writer's Centre, RWA, ALLIA, and a local critique group, Maggie enjoys meeting her readers at book signings and library talks. In 2014 she self-published *Band of Gold* and *The Sand Dollar, Book One of the Oregon Coast Series*, in 2015 *The Dreamcatcher, Book Two of the Oregon Coast Series* and *Broken Threads* and in 2016 *book Three of the Oregon Coast Series, Madeline House*.

Champagne for Breakfast while a stand-alone novel, follows the story of Rosa who readers first met in *The Sand Dollar*, and reunites readers with old friends Jenny and Mike from the *Oregon Coast Series*.

Also by Maggie Christensen

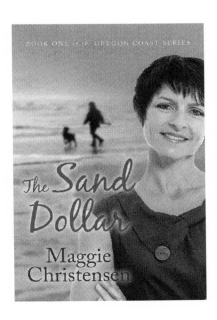

A well-kept secret and a magical sand dollar. Can Jenny unravel the puzzle of her past?

What if you discover everything you believed to be true about yourself has been a lie?

Stunned by news of an impending redundancy, and impelled by the magic of a long-forgotten sand dollar, Jenny retreats to her godmother in Oregon to consider her future.

What she doesn't bargain for is to uncover the secret of her adoption at birth and her Native American heritage. This revelation sees her embark on a journey of self-discovery such as she'd never envisaged.

Moving between Australia's Sunshine Coast and the Oregon Coast, *The Sand Dollar* is a story of new beginnings, of a woman whose life is suddenly turned upside down, and the reclusive man who helps her solve the puzzle of her past.

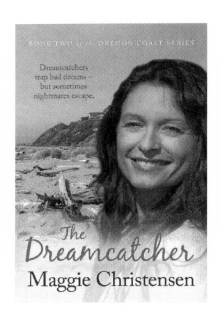

Dreamcatchers trap bad dreams – but sometimes nightmares escape.

Ellen Williams, a Native American with a gift for foretelling the future, is at a loss to explain her terrifying nightmares and the portentous feeling of dread that seems to hang over her like a shroud.

When Travis Petersen – an old friend of her brother's – appears in her bookshop *The Reading Nook*, Ellen can't shake the idea there's a strange connection between her nightmares and Travis' arrival.

Suffering from guilt of the car accident which took the lives of his wife and son, Travis is struggling to salvage his life, and believes he has nothing to offer a woman. But Ellen's nightmares come true when developers announce a fancy new build, which means pulling down *The Reading Nook* – and she needs Travis' help.

Can Ellen and Travis uncover the link between them and save her bookshop? And will it lead to happiness?

A tale of dreams, romance, and of doing the right thing, set on the beautiful Oregon coast.

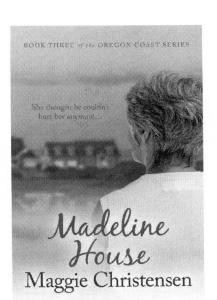

BOOK THREE *of the* OREGON COAST SERIES

She thought he couldn't
hurt her anymore...

Madeline
House
Maggie Christensen

She thought he couldn't hurt her anymore — she was wrong.

When Beth Carson flees her controlling husband, a Sydney surgeon, and travels to Florence, Oregon, she is unsure what her future holds. Although her only knowledge of Florence comes from a few postcards found in her late mother's effects, she immediately feels at home there and begins to put down roots.

But Beth's past returns to haunt her in ways she could never have imagined. Distraught over alarming reports from Australia and bewildered by revelations from the past, Beth turns to new friends to help her.

Tom Harrison, a local lawyer, has spent the past five years coming to terms with his wife's death, and building a solitary existence which he has come to enjoy. Adept at ignoring the overtures of local women and fending off his meddling daughter, he is intrigued by this feisty Australian and, almost against his will, finds himself drawn to her when she seeks his legal advice.

What forces are at work to bring the two together, and can Beth overcome her past and find a way forward?

Set on the beautiful Oregon Coast this is a tale of a woman who seeks to rise above the challenges life has thrown at her and establish a new life for herself.

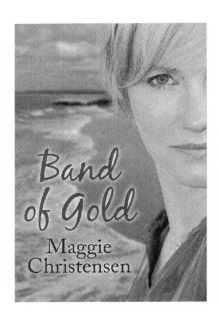

A relationship after a failed marriage. Can Anna love again? Does she dare?

Anna Hollis believes she has a happy marriage. A schoolteacher in Sydney, Anna juggles her busy life with a daughter in the throes of first love and increasingly demanding aging parents.

When Anna's husband of twenty-five years leaves her, on Christmas morning, without warning or explanation, her safe and secure world collapses.

Marcus King returns to Australia from the USA, leaving behind a broken marriage and a young son.

When he takes up the position of Headmaster at Anna's school, they form a fragile friendship through their mutual hurt and loneliness.

Can Anna leave the past behind and make a new life for herself, and does Marcus have a part to play in her future?

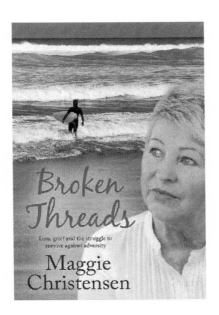

A story of loss, grief and the struggle to survive against adversity.

Jan Turnbull's life takes a sharp turn towards chaos the instant her eldest son, Simon takes a tumble in the surf and loses his life.

Blame competes with grief and Jan's husband turns against her. She finds herself ousted from the family home and separated from their remaining son, Andy.

As Jan tries to cope with her grief and prepares to build a new life, it soon becomes known that Simon has left behind a bombshell, and her younger son seeks ways of compensating for his loss, leading to further issues for her to deal with.

Can Jan hold it all together and save her marriage and her family?

Made in the USA
Middletown, DE
13 February 2022

61054033R00161